Savor the praise for Joanne Fluke's Dangerously Delicious Hannah Swensen Mysteries!

PEACH COBBLER MURDER

"Her tastiest yet."
—*Kirkus Reviews*

SUGAR COOKIE MURDER

"A clever and delicious treat for Christmas."
—*Mystery Lovers Bookshop News*

FUDGE CUPCAKE MURDER

"This fifth installment of the Hannah Swensen mysteries is Fluke's best offering to date."
—*Times Recorded News* (Wichita Falls, TX)

"Scrumptious."
—*Publishers Weekly*

"A calorie-laden delight, this book is comfort food for the reader's soul."
—*Romantic Times*

LEMON MERINGUE PIE MURDER

"A wonderful mystery . . . This book is as warm and cozy as a dozen Cinnamon Crisps! This series may remind some of another well-known series that includes recipes, but it's better!"
—*Cozies, Capers and Crimes*

BLUEBERRY MUFFIN MURDER
(A BOOK SENSE 76 TOP TEN MYSTERY PICK)

"A delightful confection."
—*Library Journal*

STRAWBERRY SHORTCAKE MURDER

"Tasty enough to serve mystery readers."
—*Booklist*

"A comfortable, cozy read, with a few recipes thrown in for later enjoyment. For fans of culinary mysteries."
—*Library Journal*

CHOCOLATE CHIP COOKIE MURDER

"An entertaining debut with some delectable recipes as a bonus."
—*Kirkus Reviews*

"Keeps the reader in suspense from beginning to end. Hard to put down."
—*Northern Herald* (North Central Minnesota)

Books by Joanne Fluke

Hannah Swensen Mysteries

CHOCOLATE CHIP COOKIE MURDER
STRAWBERRY SHORTCAKE MURDER
BLUEBERRY MUFFIN MURDER
LEMON MERINGUE PIE MURDER
FUDGE CUPCAKE MURDER
SUGAR COOKIE MURDER
PEACH COBBLER MURDER
CHERRY CHEESECAKE MURDER
KEY LIME PIE MURDER
CANDY CANE MURDER
CARROT CAKE MURDER
CREAM PUFF MURDER
PLUM PUDDING MURDER
APPLE TURNOVER MURDER
DEVIL'S FOOD CAKE MURDER
GINGERBREAD COOKIE MURDER
CINNAMON ROLL MURDER
RED VELVET CUPCAKE MURDER
BLACKBERRY PIE MURDER
DOUBLE FUDGE BROWNIE MURDER
WEDDING CAKE MURDER
CHRISTMAS CARAMEL MURDER
BANANA CREAM PIE MURDER
RASPBERRY DANISH MURDER
JOANNE FLUKE'S LAKE EDEN COOKBOOK

Suspense Novels

VIDEO KILL
WINTER CHILL
DEAD GIVEAWAY
THE OTHER CHILD
COLD JUDGMENT
FATAL IDENTITY
FINAL APPEAL
VENGEANCE IS MINE
EYES
WICKED
DEADLY MEMORIES
THE STEPCHILD

Published by Kensington Publishing Corporation

JOANNE FLUKE

Fudge Cupcake Murder

KENSINGTON BOOKS
www.kensingtonbooks.com

KENSINGTON BOOKS are published by

Kensington Publishing Corp.
119 West 40th Street
New York, NY 10018

First Kensington Hardcover Edition: March 2004

ISBN-13: 978-1-4967-1403-9
ISBN-10: 1-4967-1403-2
First Kensington Trade Paperback Printing: November 2005

eISBN-13: 978-1-61773-128-0
eISBN-10: 1-61773-128-5

10 9 8 7 6 5 4 3

Printed in the United States of America

This book is for Walter

ACKNOWLEDGMENTS

Thank you to Ruel, who's always willing to "talk story," even in the wee small hours of the night. And thanks to our kids, who aren't shy about asking for seconds or thirds. Thank you to our friends and neighbors: Mel & Kurt, Lyn & Bill, Gina & Brian, Jay, Bob M., Amanda, John B., Dr. Bob & Sue, and everyone who reached for a cookie, took a bite, looked blissful, and said, "Mmmm!"

Thank you to my talented editor, John Scognamiglio, for his constant support. *(You ARE the best!)* And thanks to all the good folks at Kensington, who keep Hannah Swensen sleuthing and baking to her heart's content. Thank you to Hiro Kimura, my cover artist, for his incredible Fudge Cupcake. *(I really wish my grocery store stocked those sprinkles!)* Big hugs to Terry Sommers and her family for critiquing my recipes. Thanks to Jamie Wallace for shepherding my Web site, MurderSheBaked.com. And a big hug to all my e-mail and regular mail friends who share their love for Hannah and the crew at The Cookie Jar with me.

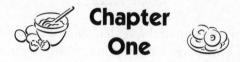

Chapter One

Hannah Swensen moved to the front of the rectangular box and braced herself. Although she had no specialized training, she felt like a member of a bomb squad who was preparing to disarm an explosive device. Taking a deep breath for courage, Hannah reached forward and released the catch that held the grate in place, jumping back to what she hoped would be a safe distance.

"Good heavens!" Hannah gasped as Moishe shot out of the veterinarian-approved small dog carrier and barreled into the kitchen. She'd had no idea her feline roommate could move that fast. He resembled an orange and white blur with multiple feet, all of them moving at warp speed.

Hannah picked up the carrier and stashed it in the laundry room cupboard. The one time she'd forgotten to put it away, Moishe made inroads on the plastic, and it now looked as if a miniature plow had been digging furrows in the top. At least the plastic carrier had held up better than the cardboard one she used the first time she took Moishe to the vet. By the time she arrived, the cardboard was in shreds and Moishe was out and prowling around in the back of her truck, yowling in outrage.

Pausing in the doorway, Hannah was relieved to hear a loud crunching noise coming from the depths of the kitchen.

The early morning trip to the vet had been traumatic for both of them and Moishe was attempting to forget the ordeal by eating. It was a good thing she'd topped off his food bowl before they left the condo.

Hannah grabbed the bag of "senior" kitty crunchies her vet had recommended and carried them to the kitchen. Doctor Bob warned her that some cats rejected new food and he'd handed her a handout of helpful tips that were supposed to transform all cats into eager eaters of senior fare.

Moishe raised his head from his bowl to glare at Hannah balefully. It was the same look one might give to a traitor or an unfaithful spouse, and Hannah immediately felt guilty.

"Okay, I'm sorry. I know you hate to go to the vet," Hannah did her best to explain to a cat who'd never looked more unforgiving. "You were due for your shots and I'm only trying to keep you healthy."

Moishe stared at her for another long moment and then turned back to his food bowl again. Hannah took advantage of this temporary truce to pour a cup of coffee from the thermos she'd filled before they'd left. "I'll be right back," Hannah said to the ears that stuck up over the rim of the food bowl. The rest of Moishe's face was buried in its depths. "I have to change clothes. You shed all over my new sweater."

Moishe didn't deign to reply and Hannah headed off toward the bedroom. Her resident feline always shed when he was unhappy. It wasn't Doctor Bob. Moishe liked him as well as a cat could like the man who gave him his shots and prodded him in undignified places. He just hated the process of traveling there.

Once Hannah had changed into clothing less hairy, she came back to the kitchen to find Moishe sitting beside an empty food bowl. Since there was no time like the present to try out his new cuisine, Hannah dumped in the senior food and crossed her fingers for luck. Leaving Moishe sniffing the new food suspiciously, she slipped into the old bomber jacket she'd found at Helping Hands, Lake Eden's thrift shop, and headed for the door. But before Hannah could grab the battle-scarred shoulder bag purse that contained everything she might need for the day and then some, the phone rang.

"Mother," Hannah muttered in the same tone she reserved for the expletives she tried not to use around her five-year-old niece, Tracey. It had to be her mother. Delores Swensen was a genius at calling at precisely the moment that Hannah intended to step out the door. Sorely tempted to let the answering machine bail her out, Hannah thought better of it. Her mother would only call again at an even more inconvenient time. Giving a deep sigh, she retraced her steps and grabbed the wall phone above the kitchen table.

"Hello, Mother," Hannah said, sinking down in a chair. Conversations with Delores were seldom brief. But the voice that answered her wasn't her mother's.

"I called the shop, but Lisa said you were coming in late because you had to take Moishe to the vet."

"That's right," Hannah said, getting up to pour the last of the coffee into her cup. It was her sister and conversations with Andrea weren't exactly short either.

"There's nothing wrong, is there?" Andrea asked.

"Only with my ears. Moishe yowled all the way there and all the way back. He's fine, Andrea. I just took him in for his shots and his yearly checkup."

"That's good," Andrea said, sounding relieved. "I know how crazy you are about him. Did you take one of Bill's posters to the vet's office?"

"Yes. Sue was just putting it up in the window when I left."

"Oh, good. Every poster helps. Have you read the paper yet?"

Hannah glanced down at her purse. The *Lake Eden Journal,* still in its heat-sealed plastic sleeve, was stuck in the side pocket. "I'm bringing it to work with me. I thought I'd read it when I take my break."

"Look at it now, Hannah. Turn to page three."

"Okay," Hannah agreed, proceeding to do just that. But page three was the editorial section, where she didn't see anything that would account for Andrea's excitement.

"Do you see it?" Andrea asked, an I-know-something-you-don't-know note in her voice.

"No."

"It's the election poll!"

Hannah bent over the paper for a closer look at the small box Rod Metcalf had been running in the paper for the past month. Then she let out a whoop of excitement. "Bill's running neck and neck with Sheriff Grant!"

"That's right! I told him we could do it! Of course the election's still two weeks away and anything can happen, but wouldn't it be wonderful if Bill actually *won?*"

"Absolutely! You've done a wonderful job running his campaign, Andrea."

"Thanks. I've got some other news, too."

"What's that?"

"Doc Knight moved up my due date to the third week in November."

Hannah frowned. "Can he do that?"

"Sure. It's all guesswork, anyway. Everybody thinks they can tell, but they can't. Bill's mother says she's sure the baby will be born on election night, but I think she just wants to take my place at Bill's victory party. Mother's holding out for early December. She says I'm not as big as I was with Tracey and it'll be a while yet. Then there's Bill. He thinks I'll have the baby early, like before Halloween."

"When do *you* think it'll be?"

"On Thanksgiving Day, just as we're sitting down to dessert."

"How can you tell?" Hannah asked. "Is there some sort of sixth sense that expectant mothers have?"

"No, it's just that your pecan pie is my favorite part of

Thanksgiving dinner. And I'm looking forward to it so much, I just know I'm going to miss it."

"You won't miss it. If you have to go to the hospital, I'll bake another pie and bring it to you."

"That's so sweet! Thanks, Hannah. I'd better run . . . or maybe I should say *waddle*. My balance is off today. I'll check in with you later."

Hannah said goodbye and hung up the phone. She refilled Moishe's water and told him what a good boy he was. And since he appeared to be eating his senior fare without a problem, she crumpled up the tip sheet Doctor Bob had given her and tossed it in the trash. Then she pulled on her gloves and headed out the door.

An icy wind greeted Hannah as she stepped outside, and she shivered as she descended the stairs to the ground floor. It was only the middle of October, but it was time to think about resurrecting her winter parka. Once she'd gone down another flight of stairs to the underground garage, Hannah headed straight for her candy apple red Suburban, the vehicle all the Lake Eden children called the "cookie truck," climbed in behind the wheel, started it up, and headed up the ramp toward the exit.

Hannah drove through her condo complex, turned left on Old Lake Road, and took the scenic route to town. Its circuitous course wound around Eden Lake and although it was longer than the interstate by several miles, Hannah preferred it. There was something soothing about driving past Minnesota family farms and groves of maple trees sporting colorful fall leaves. She preferred the scent of cool water and aromatic pine to the exhaust from whatever car she happened to be following on the interstate.

As Hannah waited for the stoplight at the intersection of Old Lake Road and Dairy Avenue, she spotted a perfect telephone pole. Since there was no one behind her, she pulled over at the side of the road and retrieved one of

Bill's posters from the back of her truck. It only took a moment to tack it up on the pole and Hannah grinned as she stepped back and faced the larger than life-size picture of her brother-in-law's smiling face. The poster bore the legend "Bill Todd for Sheriff" in large block letters and Hannah had promised Andrea that she'd put up at least six posters every day.

Ten minutes later, Hannah pulled into the alley and turned in at the small white building that housed her bakery and cookie shop. Once she'd parked in her spot and gone in the back door, she washed her hands and went through the swinging restaurant-style door into the coffee shop, prepared to relieve her young partner, Lisa Herman. She found Lisa on a tall stool behind the counter, surrounded by a crowd of morning cookie buyers.

"Here she is now!" Lisa called out, looking very relieved to see Hannah. "You can ask her yourself."

The crowd swiveled toward Hannah and she noticed that Bertie Straub had stationed herself in front as the point man. Bertie was still wearing her bright purple smock from the Cut 'n Curl and the scowl on her face inversely mirrored the gold happy face on the bib of the smock.

"Well, it's about time!" Bertie said, glancing pointedly at her watch. "We saw that Bill's ahead in the polls. Do you honestly think he's going to win?"

"Of course Bill's going to win!" It was her mother's voice. Hannah turned toward the doorway to see Delores standing there, resplendent in a fashionable royal blue pantsuit and sporting a "Bill Todd for Sheriff" button on her collar. "And if you don't vote for him, Bertie Straub, you'll have to deal with me!"

Bertie gave an audible gulp. "I'm going to vote for him, Delores."

"I should hope so!" Delores walked over to take Hannah's arm. "I need to see you in the kitchen, dear."

Moments later, Hannah's mother was settled at the workstation with a cup of coffee and two Peanut Butter Melts. Hannah sat down on an adjoining stool and waited patiently while Delores ate one cookie in dainty bites.

"Delicious!" her mother declared, wiping her hands on a napkin. "Have you heard from Norman?"

"Not yet," Hannah said, hoping this wasn't going to turn into a lecture about her reluctance to commit to one particular man. Hannah liked Norman Rhodes and dated him whenever the opportunity presented itself, but her mother believed that any female who wasn't married by the time she renewed her TV Guide subscription for the second time was doomed. Now that Delores had gone into the antique business with Norman's mother, Carrie, both of them were nudging for nuptials.

"Carrie says he's all tied up with the convention," Delores went on. "He's heading up a panel on cosmetic dentistry, you know. It's quite a coup for a practitioner of Norman's age."

"I know, Mother. Norman told me all about it before he left for Seattle."

"Maybe not all," Delores looked a bit smug. "Did he tell you that Beverly is on his panel?"

"Beverly who?" Hannah asked, even though asking wasn't really necessary since Delores was all primed to tell her.

"Doctor Beverly Thorndike."

"Oh," Hannah said, deciding a one-word response was wisest since she had no idea who Doctor Thorndike was.

"Carrie told me they were planning to be married, but Beverly decided she was too young to make that sort of commitment. At least she gave back the ring. But you must know all this so I won't go into it again."

Hannah nodded, even though she knew nothing about Norman's failed engagement to Beverly Thorndike, female dentist.

"That's not the reason I came in," Delores said, reaching

into her purse to pull out a recipe card. "I'm sorry I'm late, but here's my recipe for Hawaiian Pot Roast."

Hannah did her best not to sigh as she reached out and took the handwritten card. Hawaiian Pot Roast was her mother's favorite recipe and Hannah had eaten enough of it to last her a lifetime.

"I was in a rush when I copied it. You can read it, can't you?"

Hannah glanced down at the recipe and nodded.

"It's not too late to get it in the Lake Eden cookbook, is it, dear?"

Hannah wavered. Saying it was too late would be a handy excuse and it was theoretically true, since the deadline Hannah had given to the other contributors had come and gone. But if she said it was too late to her mother, Delores would never let her hear the end of it. In the interest of family peace, Hannah was obliged to include it.

"It's not too late," Hannah said, earning a smile from her mother.

"Thank you, dear. I know I should have turned it in sooner, but I've been so busy lately with Bill's campaign and the store. And now I'd better run. We're expecting a shipment of Chippewa artifacts and Jon Walker promised he'd stop by to see if he could tell if they're authentic."

Delores gave a little wave and ducked out the back door. Granny's Attic was the next building over and she could dash across the parking lot. Hannah waited until the door had closed behind her mother and then she glanced down at the recipe. "*Four* cups of sugar?"

Lisa came into the kitchen just in time to hear Hannah's comment. "Is that Rose's coconut cake recipe?"

"No, it's Mother's Hawaiian Pot Roast."

"And it's that sweet?"

"Enough to make your teeth ache. Mother wrote it out for me and she wants it in the cookbook. Do you think that I should . . ."

"No," Lisa interrupted, shaking her head. "She'll never forgive you if you don't include it."

"You're right. I'll reduce the sugar, but I can't make too many changes. If Mother doesn't recognize her own recipe, I'm going to be on her kill-now-and-bury-later list for the rest of my life."

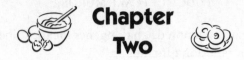

Chapter Two

The last of the customers had left, the front door of The Cookie Jar was locked, and Hannah and Lisa were in the kitchen, mixing up the cookie dough for the following day. Lisa tore off a strip of plastic wrap to cover a batch of Chocolate-Covered Cherry cookies and glanced up at the clock. "Hannah?"

"Hmm?" Hannah retrieved the chocolate she'd melted for her batch of Black and Whites and added it to her mixing bowl.

"It's getting late and you've got class tonight. Why don't you go home now?"

Hannah glanced over at her petite partner and smiled. "You're still a teenager and you're trying to mother *me?*"

"I'm not trying to mother you. And I won't be a teenager much longer. I'm turning twenty next month." Lisa drew herself up to her full five feet, two inches, but her stern effect was spoiled by the fact that one bouncing brown curl had escaped from her health department mandated hairnet.

Hannah gave her bowl a final stir and reached for the plastic wrap. "Maybe I will. But if I do, I'll come in early tomorrow and do all the baking before you get here."

"Deal!" Lisa held out her hand and Hannah shook it. "Do you want me to help you with your class tonight? Herb's tied up until nine, but Marge said to call her anytime and she'll come over to sit with Dad."

"That's okay, Lisa. I can handle it." Hannah knew that Lisa liked to stay at home with her father whenever she could. Jack Herman had Alzheimer's and Lisa had turned down a college scholarship to stay home and be with him. Things were a bit easier now that Lisa was engaged to Herb Beeseman, Lake Eden's security and parking enforcement officer. Herb's widowed mother, Marge, had dated Lisa's father in high school and she seemed to enjoy spending time with Jack so that "the children" could go out.

Hannah had just finished stashing her bowl in the walk-in cooler when there was a knock on the back door. She walked over to answer it and found Beatrice Koester standing there, shivering in the cold. "Hi, Beatrice. Come in."

"Hi, Hannah. Lisa." Beatrice stepped into the warm kitchen and smiled. "I can only stay a minute. Ted's waiting for me in his truck."

Hannah took a moment to wave to Ted, owner and operator of Lake Eden's salvage yard. Ted waved back, but he looked disgruntled. He probably wanted to get back to work. Hannah shut the door and turned back to Beatrice. "Technically we're closed, but if you want some cookies we can get them for you."

"Thanks anyway, Hannah. I just came to bring you a recipe. I know it's late, but I was going through some of Ted's mother's things and I just found it."

"For the Lake Eden cookbook?" Lisa asked.

"Yes. It's for her Fudge Cupcakes. Ted just loves them and they're really good. I asked Mother Koester for the recipe more times than I can count, but she kept forgetting to give it to me."

"I'm glad you finally got it." Hannah said with a sympathetic smile. "Some people really hate to share recipes and I'll bet Ted's mother was one of them."

"That's what I thought, but Ted said I was wrong, that his

mother really forgot to bring it all those times she came to visit. Of course, Ted's mother could do no wrong."

Hannah bit back a smile. She hadn't known Ted's mother, but it sounded as if she could have been the inspiration for quite a few bad mother-in-law jokes.

"Is it too late to put in the cookbook? Now that Ted's mother is gone, he thinks it would be a fitting memorial to her."

Hannah reached out and took the recipe. There was no way she could refuse Beatrice when she looked so worried. "It's not too late. I'll see it goes in."

"Oh, thank you, Hannah! But there might be a little problem."

"With the recipe?" Hannah glanced down at the handwritten card.

"Yes. Just look at the list of ingredients."

Hannah read the list of ingredients aloud. "Unsweetened chocolate, sugar, butter, flour, milk, and . . . uh-oh."

"What is it?" Lisa asked.

"It says, *Add one-half cup* secret ingredient."

"I love recipes like that!" Lisa clapped her hands. "It's always something nobody can guess. What is it this time?"

Hannah shrugged and so did Beatrice. Lisa glanced from one to the other and then she caught on. "It doesn't say?"

"You got it." Hannah turned to Beatrice. "Did you ever taste the cupcakes?"

"Yes, and they were wonderful! Alma made them for Ted every year on his birthday, but she wouldn't let me watch her."

"What did they taste like? Describe them to us."

"Well . . ." Beatrice drew a deep breath and closed her eyes. "They were really good dark chocolate, and they were heavy, not like one of those light cake mixes. They didn't rise much like those pretty rounded cupcakes you see in magazines, but that was okay because Alma mounded up the fudge frosting on top and you got even more that way. She said they were supposed to have dimples for the frosting."

Hannah laughed. She couldn't help it. That was a great way to explain a cake that hadn't risen as far as you'd expected, and most people, Hannah included, wouldn't mind a bit as long as the frosting was good. "Can you describe the frosting?"

"Yes, I can. It was fudgy and just a little chewy and it melted in your mouth. I always thought that if you heated it, it would make a perfect fudge sauce for ice cream."

"Sounds good. Think back to the cupcakes. Was there any kind of hidden or subtle flavor that you can remember?"

"Not really, but . . ." Beatrice stopped speaking and frowned slightly.

"But what?" Lisa urged her.

"They had a . . . a sort of German flavor."

"A German flavor?" Hannah thought about all the chocolate cakes she'd eaten. "Was it like German Chocolate Cake?"

Beatrice shook her head. "No, nothing like that."

"Do you think it had sauerkraut in it?" Lisa asked. "My mother used to make a chocolate cake with sauerkraut."

"I know it wasn't sauerkraut. I make that cake myself." Beatrice gave a little sigh. "It was sweet and tangy at the same time, like one of those good German tortes. You know the kind I'm talking about. They're really rich and even if you're full to bursting, you just want to keep on eating until they're gone."

"No wonder you wanted the recipe!" Hannah smiled to set Beatrice at ease. "What do you think, Lisa? Can we figure out Alma's secret ingredient?"

"We can try. They sound different than the fudge cupcakes that my mother used to make, but I've got some ideas already."

"Great." Hannah turned back to Beatrice. "Was the cupcake smooth? Or did it have chunks of things inside?"

"No chunks. It was smooth and it tasted almost like eating a chocolate bar."

"That helps," Lisa said, nodding quickly. "It eliminates most of the solid things you might add to the batter like nuts, coconut, and chopped fruit."

"True, but it *doesn't* eliminate anything that's finely ground, pureed, or melted," Hannah argued.

Beatrice looked very distressed. "I'm sorry I brought this whole thing up. If Ted wasn't so all-fired set on having his mother's recipe in the cookbook, I'd tell you to just forget it."

"No way!" Both Hannah and Lisa spoke at once. There was a very brief moment of silence and then all three women burst into laughter.

When they'd stopped laughing, Lisa spoke up. "We'll figure it out, Beatrice. Hannah and I love a good mystery and at least this one doesn't involve a dead body."

"Only my mother-in-law," Beatrice quipped. And then she looked slightly shocked at her own humor. "I'm really glad Ted wasn't here to hear that!"

Hannah gave her hair a final brush and glanced in the mirror one last time. From the neck down, she looked very "teacherly" in her navy blue pantsuit and white blouse. From the neck up, it was another story. The humidity had been high today and her hair was a riot of unruly red curls. Hannah pulled it back, secured it all in the silver clasp her youngest sister, Michelle, had bought from one of her artist friends at Macalester College, and flicked off the light in her bedroom.

"I won't be late," Hannah promised, reaching down to pet Moishe as he followed her down the hall. "I'm just going to the school to be what I was going to be before I became what I am now."

Moishe gave a little yowl and stared up at her. Maybe it was her imagination, but he looked simply stupefied by the explanation she'd just uttered and Hannah burst into laughter. "Sorry. That was confusing. I'll be teaching an adult cooking class at the school and then I'm going out to dinner with Mike. Don't worry. I'll leave you with plenty of food."

Hannah was still chuckling over her sentence structure as she hurried down the stairs. She was looking forward to her date tonight with Lake Eden's most popular unmarried man. Mike Kingston had moved to Lake Eden just over a year ago, recruited from the Minneapolis Police Department by Sheriff Grant to head up the Winnetka County Detective Division. Since Mike was Bill's partner, both Andrea and Bill favored him for the position of brother-in-law. Delores liked Mike, but she'd teamed up with Carrie to push Norman, and Michelle, Hannah's youngest sister, liked both of them. So did Hannah and that was why she couldn't choose one over the other. Perhaps it was just as well that neither man had proposed. Sharing her life with someone who didn't use a litter box might be nice, but Hannah didn't really want to give up any of her independence.

Twenty minutes later, Hannah drove into the school parking lot. She was early and it was deserted. She pulled up as close to the home economics classroom as she could, grabbed her box of supplies, and headed for the delivery entrance. When Jordan High had been designed, the architect had put in an outside door for ease in delivering kitchen equipment and supplies. The regular teacher, Pam Baxter, had given Hannah a key when she'd agreed to take over the night cooking class. Instead of learning cake decoration, as Pam had originally planned, Hannah's class would be testing all the recipes that had been submitted for the Lake Eden cookbook.

Hannah stepped inside and flicked on the lights, blinking like an owl caught in the beam of a searchlight. The multiple overhead lighting fixtures were bright enough to turn night into day. When her eyes adjusted, Hannah set her box on a counter. Pam Baxter's pantry contained all the staples, but she'd brought the special ingredients her class would need for the recipes they were testing tonight. One of the ingredients was a package of sweetened dried cranberries for the cookies Hannah had just created. Since they were made from cranberries and cranberries grew in a bog, she planned to call them Boggles.

Five minutes later, Hannah was ready to teach. Her name was written on the blackboard in the unlikely event there were students who didn't know her, stacks of recipes were ready to be dispersed to the five groups that would bake at the five kitchen workstations, and the sign-in sheet was displayed on a clipboard at a desk in the front row. The only thing missing was Hannah's class and she had over an hour before her students would arrive.

Hannah sat down at the desk, but it didn't feel right. Perhaps she'd been wise to change her career plans. She was a lot happier in front of an oven than she was behind a desk. She got up and walked to one of the workstations. She'd put the extra time to good use by mixing up a batch of Alma Koester's Fudge Cupcakes without the secret ingredient. Once she'd tasted them, Beatrice might be able to tell what was missing.

Boggles

Preheat oven to 350 degrees F.,
rack in the middle position

2 cups melted butter *(4 sticks)*
2 cups brown sugar
2 cups white sugar
1 teaspoon baking powder
1 teaspoon baking soda
1 teaspoon salt
4 eggs—beaten
2 teaspoons vanilla
½ teaspoon cinnamon
¼ teaspoon nutmeg
4 cups flour
3 cups sweetened dried cranberries *(Craisins or
    another brand)****
3 cups rolled oats *(uncooked oatmeal)*

*** *If you can't find the cranberries where you live
you can substitute any chopped dried fruit such as
dates, apricots, peaches, etc.*

Preheat oven to 350 degrees F. Melt butter in large
microwave-safe bowl. Add sugars and let cool a bit. Add
eggs, baking powder, baking soda, salt, and vanilla. Add

flour and mix. Then add the cranberries and oats and mix everything up. The dough will be quite stiff.

Drop by teaspoon onto a greased cookie sheet, 12 to a sheet.

Bake at 350 degrees F. for 12-15 minutes. Cool on cookie sheet for 2 minutes. Remove to rack until cool.

Yield: 10 to 12 dozen, depending on cookie size.

These freeze well if you roll them in foil and put them in a freezer bag.

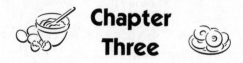

Chapter Three

Hannah had just finished frosting the cupcakes when she heard someone approach in the hallway outside her classroom door. Perhaps it was Mike and he was early.

"Is my nose wrong, or do I smell chocolate?"

Hannah sighed as she recognized the voice. Then she put a friendly smile on her face and turned toward the doorway. Sheriff Grant had never been one of her favorite people, but he was a good customer at The Cookie Jar and it was wise to be friendly to the man who was Bill and Mike's boss. "Your nose is right. I'm trying out a recipe for the Lake Eden cookbook."

"It sure smells good." Sheriff Grant moved closer to the counter and Hannah noticed that he was listing toward the cupcakes at approximately a forty-five degree angle.

"Would you like to taste one?" Hannah offered. "I think they're cool enough."

"That'd be great! I haven't had anything to eat since lunch and I need to stick around until Kingston gets here. Got some paperwork for him to pass out."

Hannah packaged up four of the cupcakes. She knew Mike was teaching a self-defense class in the room next door. "Do you want to leave the paperwork with me? I can make sure he gets it."

"No, that's okay. I'll just wait in the parking lot and catch him when he drives in." Sheriff Grant accepted the package Hannah gave him with a smile. "Thanks, Hannah. This is really nice of you."

"Maybe not," Hannah replied with a grin.

"What do you mean?"

"These cupcakes are an experiment and I haven't even tasted them yet."

"Do you want a report on how I like them?"

"That would be great," Hannah said with a smile. "You're a brave man, Sheriff Grant."

"Why's that?"

"For all you know, they might be poisoned. After all, my brother-in-law is running against you in the election."

When Hannah's students arrived, she divided them into five groups, one group for each workstation in Jordan High's home economics room. Then she set them to work testing pastry recipes. One group had the cookie recipe she'd developed, another was baking a pie, the third group was in the process of making a cobbler, the fourth group had a tea bread recipe, and group five was baking a coffee cake.

"What is it, Hannah?" Beatrice came rushing over when Hannah motioned to her.

"I baked a batch of cupcakes before class. I need you to taste one and tell me what you think."

Beatrice took a cupcake from the plate Hannah offered. She chewed thoughtfully for a moment and then she shook her head. "I'm sorry, Hannah. These aren't like the ones I remember."

"I know. I made them plain, without the secret ingredient. I thought you might be able to tell what's missing."

Beatrice took another bite and chewed slowly. Then she shook her head again. "I just can't tell. I know it's something. These are really good, but the ones Mother Koester made had a wonderful aftertaste and they weren't quite as dry. You got the frosting just right though. It's exactly the same as she used to make."

"Thanks, Beatrice. You've been a big help."

"I have? All I did was tell you that you don't have it right."

"I know, but you also gave me a clue. If these are drier cupcakes, the secret ingredient must be something that makes them moist. Now all I have to do is figure out what it is."

"I'm glad I helped. What makes cupcakes moist besides water, or milk?"

"Several different things. Pudding in the batter could do it. So could more eggs, more butter, more oil, or adding some kind of moist ingredient. Even baking them in a slower oven or for less time might do it."

Beatrice looked amused. "That doesn't narrow it down much."

"No, it doesn't. But we have more information than we did this afternoon and I'm going to jot down some things to try. If you think of anything else to tell me about the cupcakes, just give me a holler."

Hannah's class crowded seven students at each of the five workstations, in a classroom designed for less than thirty students. The only thing that saved the situation from becoming total chaos was the fact that these were women who were used to cooking together in community or family kitchens. Hannah gave each group seven tasks to be performed during the baking and the tasks were assigned by drawing names. First there was a leader, the person responsible for the group. Then there were two fetchers. They foraged in the pantry to gather the ingredients. One group member was the designated measurer. She measured the various ingredients and assembled them in appropriate bowls and cups. Another group member was in charge of mixing the ingredients, and the last two group members were in charge of preheating the oven and preparing the baking pans. Once the batter or the dough had been mixed, the leader was the one who put it into the baking pans and placed it in the oven.

"Hannah?" Edna Ferguson, the head cook at Jordan High and leader of one of Hannah's groups, waved frantically at her across the room.

"What is it, Edna?"

"It's this tea bread dough. It's not right. Come over here and stir it and you'll see what I mean."

Hannah hurried to the workstation and gave the bowl a stir. The dough was as thin as crepe batter.

"See what I mean?"

"I see. Are you sure you followed the recipe exactly?"

"I'm positive," Edna said, nodding so vigorously her tight gray curls bounced.

"I'm positive, too," Linda Gradin spoke up. "I did the measuring and I watched while Donna mixed it all up."

Donna Lempke nodded. "We even talked about the flour. It just didn't seem like it would be enough and we had Edna double check the recipe. That's what it says, Hannah. A cup and a half."

"Let's see." Hannah took the recipe that Edna handed to her and frowned as she read it. There was definitely a discrepancy between the amount of liquid and dry ingredients.

"Should I add more flour?" Edna asked. "It'll never turn out right this way. I think another cup'll be just right."

"No, you'd just be guessing at the amount. This is Helen Barthel's recipe. Let's call her and check."

"I'll do it," Charlotte Roscoe volunteered.

"Thanks, Charlotte," Hannah said, smiling at the school secretary. "We'll just wait while you run up to your office."

Charlotte drew a cell phone from her pocket. "This is faster. Does anybody know Helen's number off the top of their head?"

One student was reciting the number when Hannah heard

Gail Hansen call out from the group at the next workstation. "Could you come here for a minute, Hannah? We don't know if these cookies are big enough."

Hannah walked over to look. Gail's group was testing the Boggles she'd developed. "They look just perfect, Gail."

"Good!" Gail slipped the cookies into the oven and motioned for Irma York to start the timer. "I'm a little worried about one thing in the recipe, though."

"What's that?"

"You say to form the dough into walnut-sized balls. That just won't *fadge* in some parts of the state."

"Won't what?"

"Won't *fadge*." Gail gave an embarrassed laugh. "Sorry, Hannah. I went to a Regency club meeting this afternoon and I'm still talking that way. I just mean it won't work, that it might confuse a lot of people. I'll bet there are plenty of folks in the big cities who'll think you mean a shelled walnut."

"Really? I never thought of that, but you could be right. I'd better reword it."

"I just talked to Helen," Charlotte called out. "She checked her recipe book and it's two and a half cups, not one and a half cups. Edna was right when she wanted to add another cup."

Hannah gave Edna a thumbs-up for guessing the amount of flour correctly. Of course that wasn't all that surprising. Edna had been baking almost every day for the past forty-plus years.

Hannah had just turned to group three to see how their pie was coming when she heard a bloodcurdling scream.

"What was *that?*" Hannah gasped, her eyes darting around the room to make sure that none of her students was hurt.

"I don't know!" Edna sounded thoroughly shocked. "Should we call the police? I'm almost sure it came from the classroom next door."

Hannah laughed, her fears put to rest. "If it came from next door, it *is* the police. Mike Kingston's in there with his self-defense class. He's probably teaching his students to scream if someone tries to mug them."

The words had just left Hannah's mouth when more screaming ensued from the classroom next door. This was followed by blasts on whistles and instructions to back off. It was definitely Mike's class making all that noise. Hannah and her students shared another laugh and then they went back to their baking.

It wasn't easy to concentrate on testing recipes when the class next door was so noisy, but Hannah's students managed to do it. By the time nine o'clock rolled around and the class officially ended, they had divided up the baked goods so that everyone could have some to take home, cleaned the workstations, and decided which recipes they wanted to test in their own kitchens as homework. Five minutes later, Hannah's classroom was deserted and she was just doing a final check of the pantry when Mike knocked on the open door.

"Hi, Hannah. Are you ready for that steak?"

"I've been dreaming about it all day." Hannah turned to look at him and her breath caught in her throat. Steak wasn't the only thing she'd been dreaming of. Tall, rugged, and handsome, it was no wonder that every single woman in town, and some that weren't so single, were staying awake nights trying to think of ways to attract Mike's attention. If the Winnetka County Sheriff's Department wanted to put out one of the beefcake calendars that so many other groups were doing to raise money, all they'd have to do was put Mike on the cover and they'd have a bestseller. "Did Sheriff Grant catch you on your way in? He stopped by here and he said he had some handouts for you."

"He was waiting for me when I pulled into the parking lot. I told him I wouldn't pass out the flyers."

"Why not?"

"They were Grant for Sheriff flyers."

"They were?" Hannah started to chuckle. "No wonder he didn't want to leave them with me! And isn't there some kind of rule about passing out political flyers in school?"

"There's a rule. When I mentioned it to him, he decided he'd just hand them to people when they drove in."

"I take it you're not voting for Sheriff Grant?" Hannah teased.

"Of course not. I'm voting for Bill. He's my partner and my best friend. You should know that, Hannah."

"I do," Hannah said with a sigh. There were times when Mike was far too serious to be teased and it seemed that this was one of them. "I wonder if Sheriff Grant's still around. I gave him some cupcakes to test for me and he promised to let me know how he liked them."

"If he's gone, I'll ask him for you tomorrow." Mike picked up Hannah's jacket and held it for her. "Let's go. I skipped lunch and I'm hungry."

Hannah slipped into her jacket and was about to pick up her shoulder bag purse when she remembered the garbage. "Just let me run out with the trash. I want to make sure that backdoor's locked anyway."

"Need some help?"

"I can handle it. There's just the one bag. You can double check the ovens and stovetops to make sure they're all turned off."

Hannah grabbed the garbage bag and headed out the delivery door, blinking in the light of the high-wattage security light that came on as she passed by the sensor. She headed for the Dumpster, opened the lid, and lifted the bag. But before she dropped it inside, Hannah happened to glance down into the depths of the Dumpster.

For one shocked moment, Hannah froze, the bag of garbage suspended over the Dumpster and her mouth forming a perfectly round "o" of surprise. Then she pulled the bag back, set it down on the asphalt, and told herself that she must be imagining things, that there really hadn't been something in the bottom of the Dumpster that had resembled a human arm.

Looks are deceiving, Hannah repeated one of her grandmother Elsa's favorite sayings several times in her mind, and then she stepped back for a second look. It was an arm all right. And the arm was attached to a body.

"Uh-oh," Hannah groaned, swallowing hard, and at that exact moment, the security light cycled off. The sudden absence of the megawatt glare made the darkness seem even more intense and Hannah had all she could do not to scream. She reminded herself that she had two choices. She could stand here wondering if she'd really seen what she thought she'd seen, or she could run back inside and get Mike.

The delivery door opened with a creak and Hannah almost jumped out of her skin. Then she heard a voice. "Hannah? Is there a problem?"

It was Mike's voice. Hannah swallowed hard. It seemed she had a third choice. She could say that there was a problem and ask Mike to get over here on the double. That would be the wisest choice, if only she could find her voice.

"Hannah?"

"Over here," Hannah gulped out the words.

"What is it? You sound funny."

Hannah took a deep breath. And then she said, as clearly as she could. "There's a body in this Dumpster."

Mike wasted no time in joining Hannah. He pulled out his flashlight, trained the beam inside, and groaned. "It's Sheriff Grant."

"Dead?" Hannah asked, watching Mike as he leaned forward into the Dumpster to feel for a pulse.

"Yes."

Hannah gulped, trying to accept the fact that someone she'd spoken to less than three hours ago was inside a school Dumpster, dead.

"Looks like someone hit him on the back of the head. There may be another wound, too. There's a big smear of dried blood on the front of his uniform."

Despite her revulsion, Hannah looked at the area Mike indicated with his flashlight. He was right. There was a smear of something dark on Sheriff Grant's uniform shirt. She cleared her throat and forced herself to speak. "That's not blood."

"It's not?"

Hannah shook her head. "It's fudge frosting. Sheriff Grant died eating one of my cupcakes!"

Chapter
Four

Hannah had no sooner stepped inside her condo than the phone rang. She knew exactly who it was and she headed straight for the kitchen to answer it. "Hello, Mother."

"Hello, *Mother*? How did you know it was me?"

"Who else would it be? Andrea probably called you right after Bill called to tell her."

"Well . . . actually, that's right." Delores sounded a bit perturbed that Hannah had guessed her gossip source. "I just can't believe that you found another body!"

"It's true, but you shouldn't be jealous. I let you find the last one." Hannah glanced down at Moishe, who was rubbing against her ankle so hard he was very close to knocking her off balance. His bowl was empty and he didn't seem to mind the switch in his diet at all. "Hold on for a second, Mother. Just let me feed Moishe and then we can talk."

Hannah set the phone on the table and walked over to the broom closet where she kept Moishe's food. She unlocked the padlock, opened the door and poured Moishe a bowlful of his new food. It might have seemed strange to guard cat food with a padlock, but it kept the bag safe from the feline who wasn't shy about getting his own breakfast, lunch, or dinner. Moishe had defeated every other attempt Hannah had made to keep him out of the broom closet, but he hadn't figured out the padlock yet. He had made progress on the wooden door, though. There was a series of bite and claw marks near the bottom and Hannah suspected it was only a matter of time before her four-footed roommate triumphed once again.

"Okay, Mother. I'm back," Hannah said, grabbing the phone and sitting down at the table in one fluid motion. "What did *you* hear?"

"Not much. All Bill told Andrea was that you found Sheriff Grant inside the school Dumpster."

"That's what happened all right."

"I feel so sorry for poor Nettie Grant!"

"Me, too," Hannah said. Sheriff Grant's wife had practically gone into seclusion three years ago when the Grants had lost their only child in a car crash.

"This is going to be so difficult for her," Delores went on. "She was just getting over Jamie's death, and now her husband is gone, too! Do you think they're related, Hannah?"

"Who?" Hannah asked, thoroughly confused by her mother's question.

"Not who . . . *what!* I'm talking about Jamie's death and Sheriff Grant's death."

"I don't see how they could be related, Mother."

"Use your head, Hannah. We know that Nettie was totally grief-stricken when Jamie was killed and it took her almost a whole year to come out of her depression. It must have hit Sheriff Grant just as hard. I wouldn't be a bit surprised to find out that his grief had gotten the best of him and he'd decided that he just couldn't go on any longer."

"You mean . . . suicide?"

"Of course I mean suicide. Do you think that's what happened?"

"No."

"Why not? It makes sense to me."

Hannah sighed deeply. She hadn't intended to give her

mother any of the gruesome details, but she couldn't let Delores run around town expounding her suicide theory.

"It wasn't suicide, Mother."

"How do *you* know?"

"I think it's unlikely that Sheriff Grant ate one of my cupcakes, bashed himself in the back of the head so hard that he cracked it open, and then dragged himself to the school Dumpster and crawled in to die. I'll admit my cupcakes weren't perfect, but they weren't *that* bad."

"This is not the time to be flippant, Hannah!"

"Right," Hannah said and then she was perfectly silent. Her mother was a bright woman. It might take her a moment or two, but Delores would pick up on the obvious.

"Wait a minute!" Delores was so excited her voice shook. "Did you say that Sheriff Grant was killed by a blow to the back of his head?"

"That's right."

"But that's impossible, unless . . ." Delores drew out her last word so long it came out of Hannah's receiver as a hiss. "He was murdered! Why didn't you tell me before?!"

"You didn't ask."

"Well, I'm asking now. And a good daughter would have told me before I *had* to ask! Sit down if you're not sitting already, and tell me everything that happened. And don't you dare leave anything out!"

Ten minutes later, Hannah hung up the phone. Her neck was sore from cradling the phone between her head and her shoulder while she talked and foraged for something to eat, but her hunt through the refrigerator and the pantry had been successful. It was a far cry from a steak, but she managed to open a can of tuna, mix it with a little mayonnaise, and spread it on a piece of dark pumpernickel. She spread a second piece of pumpernickel with cream cheese softened in the microwave and topped it off with wafer thin slices of sweet onion that Lisa had grown in her greenhouse. Once the two halves of the sandwich were stacked together and cut into quarters, Hannah poured herself a glass of what she called Chateau Screwtop, the white jug wine currently on sale at CostMart.

"You've got your own yummy food," Hannah said, glancing down at Moishe. He was pressing against her ankle again and a twenty-three pound cat could press hard.

Moishe yowled and Hannah realized that she was being ridiculous. Who was she trying to kid? The most expensive cat food in the world couldn't compare to one of her tuna sandwiches.

Once she'd managed to seat herself on the sofa despite Moishe's efforts to trip her, Hannah flicked on the television with the remote control and bit into her sandwich. Delicious! Lisa's onion was excellent. She'd have to remember to mention it tomorrow morning when Lisa came in to work. In the meantime, there was a whole sandwich to eat and Hannah applied herself to that task with true dedication.

Once the sandwich was gone and Moishe had been pacified with several morsels of tuna that she'd set aside for him, Hannah settled down to watch television with her glass of wine.

Cable programming was nothing to write home about on this particular Monday night and Hannah flicked through the channels, wondering how anyone could be content to stay home and watch television. There was only one program that interested her, a study of holiday fruitcakes and how they had evolved over the years.

Hannah watched with interest. Most of the fruitcakes they showed were beautiful when they were sliced, the candied fruit resembling brightly colored jewels under the lights. She'd always thought that in a perfect world, fruitcake would taste as good as it looked. Unfortunately, as far as Hannah was concerned, it didn't. There was only one fruitcake that Hannah liked and it was her own recipe. She created it for her father and it didn't have a single speck of citron or candied fruit. It was called Dad's Chocolate Fruitcake and she planned to put it in the Lake Eden cookbook.

The program was almost over when Hannah caught a glimpse of an orange and white blur out of the corner of her eye. It was Moishe, heading off to the laundry room, even though he'd just come from there a few minutes ago. Now that she thought about it, Hannah was almost sure she'd seen him take the same route several times.

"Are you okay, Moishe?" Hannah asked, getting up on her feet. Moishe never went into the laundry room unless he needed to use his litter box. If his new senior food was upsetting his stomach, she'd call the vet in the morning.

When Hannah stepped into the laundry room, she found Moishe standing by his litter box. But instead of getting in, as she expected him to, he just leaned over the side, dropped something in, and reached out with a paw to cover it.

"That's strange," Hannah commented, watching as her cat headed back to the kitchen again. Several months ago, Moishe had buried the back half of a mouse in his litter box. Perhaps he'd caught something and was giving it the feline version of a decent burial.

Hannah grabbed the scoop and exhumed the item that Moishe had buried. It wasn't a mouse, or a part of a mouse. It wasn't even a cricket, or a moth. It was a pristine nugget of his new senior cat food. Suddenly suspicious, she dug around a bit in the litter box, uncovering more evidence of Moishe's distaste. By his choice of burial spot, her cat was making a graphic comment about the palatability of his dinner.

"Okay," Hannah sighed, accepting the inevitable. Nothing was ever as easy as it seemed.

As she stepped into the kitchen, Hannah glanced over at Moishe. He was standing by his food bowl, watching her every move. His yellow eyes seemed to brighten as she headed for the broom closet and his stash of old kitty crunchies. When she took out the bag, his eyes fairly gleamed with an eager light.

"You win, Moishe," Hannah said, rinsing out his bowl and filling it with his regular chow. She knew she was surrendering in the war between feline wits and human wits, but there was no way she wanted to listen to hungry yowls all night.

The next day, The Cookie Jar was crowded. It seemed that almost everyone in town had heard about Sheriff Grant's murder, and Hannah suspected that her own mother had spread the word to at least half the population of Lake Eden all by herself.

"Absolutely not," Hannah said, pouring more coffee as she responded to Bertie Staub's question. It was the same answer she'd been giving all morning. Everyone who came in for cookies and coffee wanted to know if she'd be investigating.

"But don't you want to help?" Bertie asked, turning to smile at Andrea, who'd just come in the front door.

"I'll help in any way I can, but only as a private citizen."

"But what if they ask you to help? Would you do it then?"

"They won't." Hannah slid over to make room as Andrea ducked behind the counter. "One of their own has been killed and they'll want to run their own investigation. I wouldn't dream of interfering and I'm not involved in any way."

"Yes, you are," Andrea hissed, just loud enough for Hannah to hear it. Her lips were perfectly stationary and fixed in a smile, and Hannah was impressed. She hadn't known that Andrea had ventriloquism skills.

"Kitchen," Andrea said under her breath and around the fixed smile she still wore. "I need to talk to you."

Hannah motioned for Lisa to take over the counter and led Andrea back through the swinging door to the kitchen workstation. Her sister settled on a stool and Hannah sat down beside her. "What is it? You look rattled."

Andrea paled at that observation. "Oh, no! Do you think anyone noticed?"

"You mean out there?" Hannah gestured toward the coffee shop.

"Yes."

"No one except me. And that's only because I know you so well. What's wrong?"

"Everything! My world is spinning and there's nothing I can do to stop it!"

Hannah decided not to remind Andrea that spinning is what the world did, and without the pull of gravity, they'd all fall off. "I think you need some orange juice. You look a little pale."

"Coffee," Andrea corrected her. "I didn't have my one cup this morning. I was too upset to make it."

As Hannah went to the kitchen coffee pot to pour Andrea a cup, she wondered how anyone could be so upset, they couldn't make coffee. This was especially puzzling in Andrea's case, since all she did was put a spoonful of instant coffee in a mug, fill it with water, and microwave it until it was hot enough to drink.

"Thanks, Hannah." Andrea accepted the mug and curled her hands around it. Then she took a long sip and sighed gratefully. "That's *so* good! I feel much more in control now."

"Good. Why did you feel out of control in the first place? And what did you mean by what you said back there?"

"What did I say?"

"I was telling Bertie that I wasn't going to interfere in Sheriff Grant's murder investigation and you said, *Yes, you are.* And you said it without moving your lips."

"Oh, that. I learned how to talk that way in seventh grade. Mr. Becker used to give us demerits if he caught us talking in class, so we learned to talk without moving our lips. He never caught on and we did it all year long."

"Not *that!* I'm talking about when you said I was going to interfere in Sheriff Grant's murder investigation."

"You are. You have to do it, Hannah. Bill needs you."

"Are you sure about that?"

"I'm positive."

Hannah gave Andrea a long level look. "Are you telling me that Bill asked you to ask me to investigate Sheriff Grant's murder?"

"Not exactly."

"How, exactly?"

"It's Mike." Andrea took another sip of her coffee and her eyes began to flash fire. "He's a first-class jerk! I still can't believe that I invited him into my home and fed him sandwiches and everything, and then he turned on us like a rat in the grass!"

"Snake," Hannah corrected her automatically.

"What?"

"It's snake in the grass, not rat in the grass. What did Mike do?"

"He betrayed our trust, that's what he did! If you ever speak to him again, I'll . . . I'll disown you!"

Since Andrea only used that threat when she was upset, Hannah decided not to mention the fact that sisters couldn't disown sisters. If looks weren't deceiving, Andrea was working herself up into a full-scale snit. Her cheeks were red and her eyes were flashing fire. Hannah hadn't seen her this angry since high school, when someone had spilled grape soda on her favorite pink cashmere sweater.

"Mike is . . . just awful! He's a . . . a . . . ." Andrea stopped and covered her tummy with her hands. "I'd better not say what I'm thinking. I just read an article that said babies hear sounds before they're born and I don't want little Billy to hear how mad I am."

"Just take it easy and tell me what Mike's done to get you so riled up."

"Mike . . ." Andrea stopped and took another deep breath, letting it out with a whoosh. "Mike thinks Bill murdered Sheriff Grant!"

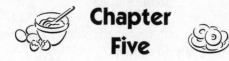

Chapter
Five

Hannah felt as if she'd been punched in the stomach. She was about to ask Andrea what she meant when she noticed the color of her sister's face and rushed to the counter to get her a medicinal dose of chocolate.

"Here, Andrea." Hannah shoved two Black and White cookies into her hand. "You need chocolate."

"What I need is for Mike to drop dead!"

"Understandable, considering the circumstances." Hannah gestured toward the cookies. "Eat. Now."

"All right, all right," Andrea sounded peeved, but she took a big bite of the first cookie. Then she took another bite, and another, finishing it in a gulp. The second cookie was gone just as quickly as the first and Hannah was relieved to see that a little color was beginning to come back to Andrea's cheeks.

"You look better," Hannah told her, feeling a lot better herself. Andrea had turned so pale she'd wondered if she ought to call Doc Knight.

"I feel better. But I'm still mad at Mike."

"Can't blame you for that," Hannah said leaning over to pat Andrea's hand.

"It's just awful, Hannah! I'm so mad I'm speechless."

"No, you're not," Hannah said, regretting the words the moment they'd left her mouth. Now was not the time to argue semantics. "Just tell me exactly what happened. Maybe there's something I can do to help."

Andrea shook her head once to clear it and then she took a deep breath. "It all started this morning at work. Mike said he had to suspend Bill because Bill was home alone last night and he didn't have an alibi for the time when Sheriff Grant was killed."

"Hold on a second. Mike suspended Bill? How did he have the authority to do that?"

"He's acting sheriff, now that Sheriff Grant's dead. It's right in the rulebook. The highest ranking deputy assumes the sheriff's position until a new sheriff is elected."

"Oh." Hannah grabbed her shoulder bag purse and pulled out one of her ever-present stenographer's notebooks, the kind she used for important notes. "You said Bill didn't have an alibi for the time that Sheriff Grant was killed. What time was that?"

"I don't think Bill knows. Mike hustled him out before he could find out anything about the investigation."

"Okay. You also said that Bill was home alone. Where were you?"

"I took Tracey and two of her friends to a movie at the mall. Now I wish I hadn't. The movie was awful, one of those horrible cartoony things where the people don't even look real and the ..."

"Okay," Hannah interrupted what she figured would be a tirade about the quality of children's movies. "Let's get back to Bill's suspension. Is this just a procedural thing? Or does Mike really think that Bill killed Sheriff Grant?"

"I don't know for sure. But Bill told me that Mike really sounded serious when he suspended him. I'm still reeling in shock. I thought Mike was Bill's best friend and I just can't believe that he'd betray him this way."

"It's hard to believe, all right." Hannah agreed, since she was having trouble digesting it herself. But unless Mike's evil twin had come to town and was keeping the real Mike hog-tied in a closet, that was exactly what he'd done.

"Bill didn't do it, Hannah. My husband's no killer."

"Of course he's not," Hannah said in her most comforting tone. It was true. Bill wouldn't hurt a fly, unless he wanted to use it for fishing. "Let's approach this systematically, Andrea. Exactly what did Bill do last night while you were gone?"

"He watched football on cable. And he told Mike that. He even gave Mike the highlights of the game, but Mike said that wasn't good enough, that Bill could have seen all that on the sports news."

Hannah reached out to pat her sister's hand again. "We've got to prove that Bill stayed at home last night. Maybe one of your neighbors saw him. All it takes is one person who passed by the house and spotted him inside at the critical time."

"I know. I already thought of that. I called everyone on the block this morning, but no one saw Bill."

Hannah watched as Andrea twisted a paper napkin into a rope. Was she imagining that it was made of hemp and it was tightening around Mike's neck? Mike had been a friend, a confidant, and practically a member of the family. Hannah could understand why her sister felt betrayed.

"Will you help, Hannah?"

"Of course I will. Don't worry, Andrea."

"I can't help it! The future looked so rosy yesterday. The new poll was out and Bill had a really good chance of beating Sheriff Grant in the election. But now that Sheriff Grant's been murdered, everything's changed for the worse. Now, by the time Little Billy is born, Bill might not have a job. And if Mike gets his way, he could be in jail for murder!"

Hannah shook her head. "That'll never happen. I promise it won't."

"But how do you know?"

"I won't let it happen. Go home, Andrea. Bill's got to be

feeling pretty rotten and none of this is his fault. That means he's going to need some tender loving care. I'll come over right after my catering job and we'll work out a game plan to clear him."

"Okay." Andrea looked relieved that Hannah had given her something constructive to do. "What time is your catering?"

"At noon. I should be at your house by one-thirty at the latest."

"Perfect." Andrea levered herself to her feet. "I'll make us lunch. We'll have toasted peanut butter and jelly sandwiches."

"Sounds good to me," Hannah said. Andrea was the world's worst cook, but making toasted peanut butter and jelly sandwiches didn't require a high level of culinary expertise.

The rest of the morning was busy and space in the coffee shop was limited to standing room only. It took both Hannah and Lisa to wait on the crowd until the predictable lull came at shortly past eleven, when most Lake Eden residents decided it was too late for a morning cookie and too early for a lunch cookie. The moment the last patron had gone out the door, Hannah motioned Lisa over to their favorite booth in the back and told her about Bill's suspension.

"You're kidding!" Lisa gasped, her eyes wide with surprise. "Mike actually suspects Bill?"

"That's what Andrea says. And it must be true because he put Bill on suspension."

"But that's . . . that's . . . that's ridiculous!" Lisa sputtered.

"Of course it is. I can't help hoping this is all a huge misunderstanding. But if it isn't . . ."

"You're going to solve the case and clear Bill," Lisa interrupted. "Of course you will. What else can you do? You'll save him, Hannah."

Hannah laughed. "You make me sound like Superwoman."

"I guess," Lisa gave a slightly sheepish grin, "but you're

good at investigating murders, Hannah. Everybody says so. And I don't want you to give a second thought to business. I'll take care of The Cookie Jar."

Hannah reached out to pat her partner on the back. "I know you will. Sometimes you're just too good to be true, Lisa. Nobody can be that nice. I keep wondering if you don't have some kind of perfectly dreadful secret vice."

"Like what?" Lisa looked intrigued.

"I don't know. Give me a little time and I'll come up with something. In the meantime, see if you can figure out what Beatrice Koester's missing ingredient is. She called me again his morning, all worried that Alma's recipe won't go in the cookbook."

"I'll work on it," Lisa promised. "I tried marshmallow cream last night, but that turned out to be a big gooey mess. Do you want me to help you load up?"

"Load up?"

"For the catering," Lisa explained. "You're due there in less than an hour."

Hannah thunked her forehead with the heel of her hand. "Right. For a second there, I forgot all about it."

"That's not surprising. You have a lot on your mind."

"True," Hannah gave Lisa a smile. "I guess it's a really good thing that I live in a small town."

"Why's that?"

"Because even when I don't know what I'm doing, somebody else always does."

Hannah had just stashed the last box of cookies inside her truck when Mike pulled up next to her and got out of his cruiser. He looked so handsome she had all she could do not to rush into his arms. But as much as she might like him to put his arms around her and kiss her, and she'd like that a whole lot, she had to remember that this was the man who had suspended Bill and practically accused him of murder.

Mike took one look at her expression. "What's the matter? You look like someone just took away your favorite toy."

"That figures," Hannah muttered under her breath. She still wanted Mike. Nothing could change that. But family loyalty came first. "How dare you suspend Bill! It's preposterous!"

"You heard?"

"You bet I heard!"

"I didn't want to suspend him, Hannah, but I had to. Try to look at it from my point of view. Bill had a motive. Sheriff Grant was his opponent in the election and several people heard them arguing before Bill left the station last night. You know Barbara Donnelly, don't you? Sheriff Grant's secretary?"

"I know her." Hannah had known Barbara Donnelly for years and Barbara didn't pull any punches. If she'd told Mike that Bill had argued with Sheriff Grant, then he had.

"Barbara was sitting at her desk when Bill stormed out of Sheriff Grant's office and she heard Sheriff Grant shout, "You'll win over my dead body."

Hannah gave an exasperated sigh. "That was just a figure of speech. I'm really surprised that Barbara took it seriously."

"She didn't take it seriously. But she did say that both Bill and Sheriff Grant were pretty steamed up. If they met up later, tempers could have flared. Somebody was mad enough to bash in Sheriff Grant's head. And since Bill doesn't have an alibi for the time of the murder, I had no choice but to remove him from the investigation."

Hannah had to admit that Mike had a point, but she wasn't about to tell him that. "You said that Bill had no alibi for the time of the murder. What time was Sheriff Grant killed?"

"Between eight and nine-thirty."

Hannah made a mental note of that and then she turned to face Mike squarely. "I'm really surprised at you, Mike. I thought partners always stuck together. Don't you have any loyalty to Bill?"

"Of course I do!" Mike looked outraged at the question. "Bill's my best friend. You know that. But I have to put my personal feelings aside in a murder investigation. It's *because* Bill is my partner and my friend that I have to bend over backwards not to give him any preferential treatment. It's really important that I follow the rulebook on this one. And since I'm working it alone, it's not going to be easy."

"You're working it alone?" Hannah was surprised. "Why didn't you pick one of the other deputies to help you?"

"Because I can't trust anyone at the station except Lonnie Murphy and he won't be back for almost two weeks."

Hannah was confused. "But why would you trust Lonnie and not any of the other deputies?"

"Because Lonnie's the newest hire and Sheriff Grant always treated the new deputies well for the first six months. After that, the honeymoon was over."

"What do you mean?"

"At the end of six months, he started criticizing them. Sheriff Grant could be a real bear about protocol and almost everyone on the force had plenty of reasons to hate him."

"Like what?"

"Delayed promotions, denials of personal time off with pay, and ridiculously picky reprimands that kept them from getting their merit increases." Mike ticked them off on his fingers. "You must have heard this before, Hannah. Bill knew all about it. Sheriff Grant nailed him last year."

"I remember," Hannah said. "Andrea told me that Bill got a reprimand for having his tie on crooked after an all-night stakeout."

"That's exactly the sort of thing I'm talking about. I'm going through the files right now to check out those reprimands and most of them are bogus."

"And you think someone might have killed Sheriff Grant over an unfair reprimand?"

"Not really. I can't believe that any deputy would be mad enough to actually kill him, but it's my duty to check everyone out."

Hannah's ears perked up. "You mean an internal investigation?"

"That's right. And I could really use Bill's help. Cut me a little slack here, Hannah. Suspending Bill hurt me just as much as it hurt him."

Hannah didn't dignify that statement with a response. Instead she just stared at Mike until he dropped his eyes.

"Well . . ." Mike said, shifting from foot to foot. "I'd better run. I'll see you later."

Not if I see you first! Hannah thought, not voicing the reply she would surely have given in junior high. She kept her lips zipped, waited until Mike had driven off, climbed into her cookie truck, and headed off to her catering job.

Chapter
Six

It was after one in the afternoon when Hannah climbed back into her cookie truck. The catering had gone well and the event had been a success. Marge Beeseman signed up the volunteers she needed for her book drive, the ladies of the Friends of the Lake Eden Community Library loved the Cherry Winks, and Hannah managed to dodge a bullet with her mother. It was obvious that Delores didn't know about her son-in-law's suspension. And since Andrea hadn't yet broken the news, Hannah had decided that it wouldn't be nice to tell her and usurp her sister's position.

Hannah took a deep breath as she pulled up in Andrea and Bill's driveway. This would take all her tact, and tact wasn't her long suit. Bill would be upset over his suspension and Andrea would be upset if Hannah offered one word of criticism about the lunch she'd prepared.

Since Andrea's Volvo was in the driveway, Hannah parked her truck behind it and got out to press the front doorbell. She could hear the chimes ringing inside and she grinned. Andrea and Bill had one of the new musical doorbells and it was playing the first four bars of the Viking's fight song. Viking supporters were nothing if not loyal.

When Andrea pulled open the door, she looked apologetic. "Sorry it took me so long. I was just finishing the toast."

"Oh," Hannah said, stepping inside and sniffing the air.

Carbon. Andrea had burned the toast. "Anything new I should know about?"

"Nothing. Come on in, Hannah. Bill's in the kitchen waiting for you."

Hannah followed her sister down the hallway and into the bright, sunny kitchen. When Andrea and Bill purchased this house, the kitchen had been a prime selling point. It was called a "gourmet kitchen" and Hannah envied the built-in double ovens, island stovetop with a barbecue grill in the center and padded benches around it on three sides for entertaining. It would be great fun to grill shish kabob appetizers while your guests watched. Even main courses would be more fun. There was a rotisserie attachment that allowed you to cook roasts or a whole chicken while your guests watched their entrée turn slowly over the grill.

Andrea's kitchen was truly ideal. To start with, it was huge, the size of most dining rooms and kitchens combined. There was an alcove for the round oak kitchen table and a rustic brick fireplace that made the huge room cheery. There was a fire in the fireplace now, and Hannah was almost positive that Bill had built it. Andrea didn't like to bother with a fire, because she seldom spent much time in the kitchen.

Hannah spotted Bill at the window seat in front of the bay window that overlooked the tree-lined back yard. As she walked over to greet him, she thought again of what an attractive couple her brother-in-law and sister made. Andrea was gorgeous with her long blonde hair, china blue eyes, and petite figure. She even looked good now, when she was eight months pregnant. Bill was Andrea's exact opposite with dark brown hair, brown eyes, and a football quarterback's physique. Last year he had started to put on a little weight around the middle, but since he had been working out with Mike every morning, his spare tire had completely disappeared. "How are you doing, Bill?"

"Okay, considering. Andrea said you've got some ideas."

Hannah glanced over at her sister, but Andrea was busy

assembling sandwiches at the counter. "Um . . . sure, I do. We'll figure something out, Bill. Don't worry."

"Here's lunch!" Andrea announced, carrying a tray to the kitchen table. "We can talk about it after we eat."

"Thanks, honey."

Bill gave Andrea a smile as he walked to the table and sat down in a chair. Hannah followed suit, but her smile slipped alarmingly as she caught sight of the sandwiches piled on the platter. She knew they were toasted peanut butter and jelly sandwiches, but she wouldn't have guessed it if Andrea hadn't told her what she was planning to make. The toast was just this side of incinerated and the filling that leaked out between the slices of toast was tan and bright green!

"What kind of jelly is that?" Hannah asked, staring at the plate of sandwiches.

"Mint. I thought I had a full jar of grape in the pantry, but all I could find was the mint. Help yourself, Hannah. They're better when the toast is still hot."

Hannah sighed, hoping she sounded disappointed. "Thanks, Andrea. The sandwiches look delicious, but I'm going to have to pass."

"But why?"

"I did a stupid thing. I filled up on cookies while I was catering."

"Oh, Hannah!" Andrea's lips tightened. "I made these just for you."

"I'm sorry," Hannah said, and she was. But she was pretty sure she wasn't as sorry as she would be if she ate one of Andrea's peanut butter and mint jelly sandwiches.

"But you knew I was making lunch. I told you."

"I know you did. It's just that Mother came over to talk to me and . . ."

"Say no more," Andrea waved away any further explanations. "I always eat when Mother's around, too. It's comforting. I think it's a throwback to childhood when she was always criticizing us."

"*Was?*" Hannah's brows shot up at her sister's use of past tense.

"Yes, at least as far as I'm concerned. I did what she wanted. I got married, I gave her a granddaughter, and pretty soon she'll have a grandson to spoil. I don't get criticized anymore. Mother saves it all up for you."

"It's true," Hannah said with a sigh. "Mother doesn't seem to realize that what's right for you isn't necessarily what's right for me."

"Of course it's right for you. You just haven't found the right man yet. And it's certainly *not* the man we thought it might be! That rat! I still can't believe that he could . . ."

"Great sandwiches, honey!" Bill interrupted, heading Andrea off at the pass. "The mint jelly's really different. I like it."

"Really?" Andrea gave Bill a radiant smile.

"Absolutely." Bill turned to Hannah. "Since you're not eating, talk to me, Hannah. Do you have any great ideas for proving my innocence?"

"Maybe. At least I got some information. I know that Sheriff Grant was killed between eight and nine-thirty last night. And I know that you had a fight with Sheriff Grant before you left the station."

"We did exchange words," Bill admitted, "but that's all we exchanged. Sheriff Grant offered me a raise if I backed off on the campaign. I told him I wouldn't."

"And that's when he shouted that you'd only win over his dead body?"

"That's when. Of course he didn't mean it. He said that a lot. Ask anyone at the station."

"I believe you," Hannah said, meeting Bill's eyes. "How about calling in some markers at the station? I'm sure you have friends who could tell you what's going on in the investigation."

"I do. And they would. But I can't ask them, Hannah. A

suspended detective can't interfere in any way with an ongoing investigation. It's in the rulebook."

"Forget the rulebook. If you *don't* interfere, you could get charged with a murder you didn't commit! You're not going to just sit here twiddling your thumbs and waiting for Mike to catch the killer, are you?"

"Of course not. I promised Mike I'd stay right here and keep a low profile, but there's nothing in the rulebook about a suspended detective's *family* interfering in the case."

Hannah started to grin. "You mean, like a certain sister-in-law?"

"You got it. I can't actively follow any leads, but I can advise you. All you have to do is come to me with any clues you find and we'll put our heads together."

"Deal! Now let's concentrate on finding you an alibi. Did you get any phone calls between eight and nine-thirty last night?"

"Only two and they won't do any good. They were both sales calls."

Hannah held up her hand. "Hold on a second. Those sales calls *could* do some good. I worked for a telemarketing firm for about a week while I was on summer break at college."

"About a week?" Andrea looked confused. "Did you get fired?"

"No, I quit. It scared me that I was beginning to get good at it. I really didn't want to sell carpet cleaning for the rest of my life. But I remember that all of our calls were logged in automatically. The supervisor could get a printout of what time we called a certain number and how long we talked."

Andrea gave Hannah a thumbs-up before she turned to Bill. "Do you remember what the telemarketers were selling, honey?"

"I remember the first one. It was a timesharing thing. You know the type. They start out by telling you you've won a free weekend at a resort and then, when you get there, they try to sell you a timeshare. It was something about vacations in the tropics. I didn't listen to the whole sales pitch. I just told the girl that we weren't interested and hung up."

Hannah exchanged glances with Andrea. "What time did the call come in?"

"I'm not sure. I didn't look at the clock. But I don't think it was very long after Andrea left."

"Okay. How about the second call?"

"It was from a roofing company, but I don't remember the name. They said they were working in the area. Of course they always say that."

"Maybe they were telling the truth this time," Hannah pointed out. "At least it's worth a shot. Just keep your eyes open for anyone who's getting a new roof."

"I can do that," Andrea said. "After I pick up Tracey at school, we'll drive around a little and see if we can spot someone getting a new roof. But how do we track down the timeshare?"

"Gus York," Hannah said.

"Gus York bought a timeshare?"

"Not that I know of, but Irma came to my class last night and she mentioned that Gus was staying home to take sales calls. She said he got a real kick out of bugging the telemarketers by listening to their whole sales pitch, asking a whole bunch of questions, and then saying he guessed he wasn't interested after all."

"Sounds like Gus has way too much time on his hands," Bill commented.

"You're right, but he might remember the name of the vacation timeshare company." Andrea reached for a notepad that said *Groceries* in big green letters at the top and jotted a note. Then she jotted a second note, and as Hannah watched, she jotted a third, a fourth, and a fifth.

"You filled up half a page reminding yourself to call Gus York?"

Andrea shook her head. "Don't be silly."

"Then what else did you write?"

"My grocery list. I just remembered that we needed grape jelly, peanut butter, apple juice, instant coffee, and bread."

Cherry Winks

Preheat oven to 375 degrees F.,
rack in the middle position

1 cup melted butter *(2 sticks)*
1 cup white sugar
2 beaten eggs *(just whip them up with a fork)*
1 teaspoon vanilla
3 Tablespoons maraschino cherry juice
1 teaspoon baking powder
½ teaspoon baking soda
½ teaspoon salt
1 ½ cups chopped pecans
2 cups flour *(not sifted)*

approximately 2 cups corn flakes, crushed *(measure before crushing)*
1 small jar of maraschino cherries for garnish

Melt the butter and add the white sugar. Then add the eggs. Stir it all up with the vanilla, cherry juice, baking powder, baking soda, and salt. Add the chopped pecans and the flour, and mix well.

Crush the corn flakes and put them in a small bowl.

(I put them in a plastic bag, seal it, and then crush them with my fingers.)

Roll dough balls with your hands about the size of unshelled walnuts. *(If the dough is too sticky, chill it for a half hour or so and then try it again.)* Roll the dough balls in the crushed corn flakes and place them on a greased cookie sheet, 12 to a standard sheet. Smush them down a bit so they won't roll off.

Cut the cherries into quarters and place one on the top of each cookie. Press the cherry down with the tip of your finger.

Bake at 375 degrees F. for 10 to 12 minutes, or until nicely browned. Cool on the cookie sheet for 2 minutes, then transfer to wire rack to finish cooling.

Yield: 6 to 7 dozen, depending on cookie size.

These are very pretty cookies. They're really popular at The Cookie Jar on Valentine's Day. I also make them at Christmas using red cherries to decorate some and green cherries to decorate the others.

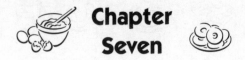

Chapter Seven

"I'm home, Moishe," Hannah called out, opening the door to the condo and holding out her arms. True to form, her orange and white, furry medicine ball made a running jump into her arms, purring madly. Who needed a husband? Moishe's greetings were quite enthusiastic enough.

"Are you hungry? Or did you miss me?" Hannah asked, knowing that both answers were yes. She kicked the door shut behind her, placed Moishe on top of the back of the couch, and shed her coat on the seat of the chair by the front door.

Moishe yowled and bounded for the kitchen. Hannah followed, knowing exactly what he wanted. She gave him fresh water and then she opened the broom closet to get his regular crunchies. As she set the bowls down on the mat, she said, "I didn't have time to stop by Doctor Bob's office and pick up another tip sheet. That means you get a reprieve tonight, but . . ."

Hannah stopped speaking abruptly as the phone rang. She toyed with the idea of letting her answering machine get it, but she was in the mood to do battle with a salesman.

"Oh, Hannah! I'm so glad you're home!"

"Andrea?" Hannah flopped down in one of the aluminum tube chairs that had come with her second-hand kitchen table. "You don't sound good. What's the matter?"

"You've got to help me, Hannah!"

"Is the baby com . . ."

"No!" Andrea interrupted. "This doesn't have anything to do with the baby."

Hannah did her best to remain calm. Her sister sounded on the edge of a nervous breakdown. "Just tell me what's wrong and I'll fix it."

"You have to do something to clear Bill right away!" Andrea gasped, breathing hard.

"I'm trying, Andrea. What's got you so upset? You were fine when I was there."

"Deer stew."

"Excuse me?"

"Deer stew! While I was driving around with Tracey, looking for roofers, Bill's father came in from the farm. He brought some packages of meat from their freezer and a whole bunch of vegetables. Bill thawed some meat and he's making deer stew!"

"That's nice."

"No, it's not! Don't you understand, Hannah?"

Hannah took a deep breath and shrugged, even though she knew her sister couldn't see it. "No, I don't. What's wrong with deer . . . uh . . . venison stew?"

"It's a matter of principle. That's important, Hannah. There's just no way I'm going to eat Bambi!"

"You won't be eating Bambi. Bambi survived, right along with Thumper and Flower. It was Bambi's mother that got turned into stew."

"That's even worse! I'm just glad Tracey's not home."

Hannah breathed a sigh of relief as a new subject was introduced. "Where's Tracey?"

"It's Karen Dunwright's birthday and they're having a sleepover at the farm. She invited all the girls in her class. Now about this stew, Hannah . . . what am I going to do?"

"Eat the vegetables and leave the meat. It's too bad you don't have a dog. Then you could . . ."

"I get it," Andrea interrupted her, "but we don't have a dog."

"Okay. All you have to do is wear an apron and line the inside of the pocket with plastic wrap. Drop the meat in the pocket when Bill's not looking and get rid of it when you clear the table."

"That should work," Andrea said, sounding very relieved. "I still need to get out of here, though. I don't dare stick around after dinner."

"Why not?"

"Since Bill's home all day now, he's decided to help me with the housework."

"That's nice," Hannah said, wishing that she had a man to help her with her housework.

"No, it's not. Bill cleaned the kitchen."

"What's wrong with that?"

"Tracey's science project was sitting in a dish on the windowsill. She was supposed to let a potato sprout and then plant it."

"Uh-oh," Hannah said with a groan, guessing the rest. "Bill threw it out?"

"That's right. I dug it out of the garbage, but the sprout broke off and now Tracey has to start all over again. She's not going to be happy when she comes home tomorrow."

"No, I guess she won't be. But it was a mistake that anyone could have made. I throw out potatoes with sprouts all the time."

"Even if they're on the windowsill in a little dish?"

"No."

"That's what I thought. Can you think of some reason to come and get me right after dinner? I'm ready to kill him."

"I understand," Hannah interrupted. "Maybe there's someone we can interview tonight. Just give me a second to check my notes and I'll see."

Hannah grabbed her notebook and flipped through the pages. She hadn't interviewed the family of the victim yet and she had no idea if Nettie had an alibi for the time of her husband's death. Tonight could be the perfect time to find out.

"Here's something," Hannah said, earning a relieved sigh from Andrea, "and there's no way Bill can object. Tell him I'm picking you up right after dinner and we're going to pay a condolence call on Nettie Grant."

"Are we going to console? Or sleuth?"

"A little of both."

"Good! I'll be ready, Hannah. Just pull in the driveway and honk the horn. I'll come right out."

The curtains were open and Hannah glanced in at Andrea's living room as she pulled into the driveway. Things weren't all coming up roses at the Todd household. The couch Bill's parents had given them for a wedding present was no longer up against the far wall and the big-screen television had been moved. It seemed that in addition to arming himself with mop and vacuum, Bill had repositioned the living room furniture. Hannah still remembered the diagrams Andrea had shown her of the living room and how she'd agonized over exactly where to place each piece of carefully chosen furniture. No wonder her sister had exhibited such an urgent desire to leave home!

Hannah gave a polite beep on the horn and Andrea came rushing out. She pulled open the door, jumped in the truck, and banged it shut again. "Let's go. Quick. Before Bill tries to give me a warmer coat or tells me I forgot my gloves or something."

"That bad?" Hannah put the truck into gear and backed toward the street.

"Even worse. I sneezed during dinner and he was sure I was getting the world's worst cold."

"Are you?"

"No. I just got a piece of dust up my nose, that's all."

"So, how was dinner?" Hannah reached the end of the drive-way, backed out, and then drove forward down the street.

"Gruesome. The vegetables were still crunchy and Bill didn't bother to pare the carrots or peel the potatoes before he put them in. He's really an awful cook, Hannah."

Hannah bit her tongue and didn't say a word about the pot calling the kettle black.

"Your trick with the apron worked fine, though. And that reminds me . . . stop at the first dog you see."

"What?"

"Just stop when you see a dog. I've got all that deer meat in my coat pocket and I'll give it to him."

"Okay, but I thought you were going to throw it away."

"I was until I remembered that Bill takes out the garbage. If he saw it, it would hurt his feelings."

Hannah glanced at Andrea, but her sister wasn't being sarcastic. Andrea really did seem to be worried about hurting Bill's feelings. Maybe that's what marriage was, a lot of give and take. This time Andrea was on the giving side, but next time she could be the one who was taking. "I admire you, Andrea. If someone came into The Cookie Jar while I was gone and rearranged all the tables and chairs without asking me, I'd slap him silly."

"I'd never do that," Andrea said with a smile. "I just keep telling myself that the minute Bill goes back to work, I can break a couple legs off that hideous couch his parents gave us and say he must have cracked them when he moved it. And then I can go out furniture shopping and replace it with something I like."

Twenty minutes later, after stopping to make Gil and Bonnie Surma's German shepherd extremely happy, Hannah pulled up in front of Nettie's duplex and cut the lights. "Grab that bag of Cashew Crisps in back of your seat, will you?"

"Sure." Andrea reached back to get the cookies. "Are you taking them to Nettie?"

"I'd feel strange coming here without bringing something."

"I feel strange coming here period. I really shouldn't be paying a condolence call, not when Bill's a suspect in her husband's murder."

"Nonsense." Hannah grabbed Andrea's hand and pulled her forward. "Nettie knows that Bill's no killer. Besides, she's all alone and she could probably use some company."

"How do you know that?"

Hannah gestured behind her. "No cars on the street. They were probably double-parked here this afternoon."

"What if Nettie's tired and wants to rest?"

"Then we'll make our excuses and leave. But I'm willing to bet she'll be happy to see us, especially since you didn't eat much for dinner and neither did I."

Andrea turned to look at her sister in consternation. "What does that have to do with anything?"

"You can bet every one of Nettie's friends has been here with food today. Her refrigerator is probably packed and she'll be glad to see two people with appetites."

"You could be right. People always bring their best dishes when there's a death in the family. They did when Dad died."

"I remember. The sheer number of casseroles, Jell-O molds, and cakes was staggering. It would have been just like a big potluck dinner if anyone had cracked a smile."

Cashew Crisps

Preheat oven to 350 degrees F.,
rack in the middle position

1 ½ cups melted butter *(3 sticks)*
2 cups white sugar
2 teaspoons vanilla
1/8 cup molasses *(2 Tablespoons)*
1 ½ teaspoons baking soda
1 teaspoon baking powder
½ teaspoon salt
1 ½ cups finely ground salted cashews *(grind them up in your food processor with the steel blade—measure AFTER grinding)*
2 beaten eggs *(just whip them up with a fork)*
3 cups flour *(no need to sift)*

Microwave the butter in your mixing bowl to melt it. Add the sugar, the vanilla, and the molasses. Stir until blended, then add the baking soda, baking powder, and salt. Mix well.

Grind up the cashews in your food processor. Measure AFTER grinding. Add them to the bowl and mix. Pour in the beaten eggs and stir. Then add the flour and mix until all the ingredients are thoroughly blended.

Let the dough sit for a few minutes to firm up. Then form dough into small walnut-sized balls and arrange them on a greased cookie sheet, 12 to a standard sheet. *(These dough balls spread out so make them fairly small. If the dough is too sticky to form into balls, chill it for a few minutes and try again.)*

Flatten the balls slightly with a spatula or the palm of your impeccably clean hand, just enough so they won't roll off when you put them in the oven.

Bake at 350 degrees F. for 10 to 12 minutes, or until the edges turn golden brown. Cool on the cookie sheet for 2 minutes, then remove to a wire rack to finish cooling.

Yield: Approximately 10 dozen, depending on cookie size.

(Mother thinks I should put a small nugget of milk chocolate in the center of the balls, but she ALWAYS thinks I should add chocolate to my recipes.)

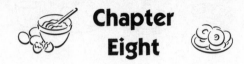

When the door opened in response to Hannah's knock, she almost stepped back in shock. Nettie was dressed in jeans and a bright pink sweatshirt. To Hannah's knowledge, Nettie had never worn casual clothes before. She'd always dressed in designer clothing. But there was an even bigger change and Hannah just stood there and blinked. Nettie's brown hair, which had always been impeccably curled and coiffed, was now in a casual and slightly untidy ponytail.

"Nettie?" Andrea asked, and Hannah could tell her sister was also wondering if the grieving widow had a relative who resembled her in every aspect but dress and grooming.

"It's me." Nettie gave a little smile and gestured for them to come in. "You both look shocked. I guess I must look different."

"You do," Hannah said, recovering first. "Do you want us to come back another time?"

"Come in and visit for a while. Everyone else left an hour ago and you caught me indulging a whim."

"The jeans?" Hannah guessed, following Nettie into the living room.

"That's right. Jim hated it when I wore them. He said it wasn't the right image for a sheriff's wife. The last time I put them on has got to be at least twenty years ago. I was afraid they wouldn't fit, but they do. Of course I was never really slim like you, Andrea. Not even when Jim and I met."

"I'm not slim now. Doc Knight weighed me yesterday and I've gained twenty pounds in the past two months." Andrea walked over and took a seat on the sofa.

"You'll lose that in a hurry when you have the baby." Nettie turned to Hannah. "Would you girls like something to eat? The ladies left me enough food for months."

"Well, maybe just a bite . . . or a dozen bites," Hannah said.

"Just help yourself," Nettie said with a smile. "The baked goods are on the counter in the kitchen and they put the Jell-O and meats in the refrigerator. Did your mother tell you she dropped by this afternoon?"

Both Andrea and Hannah shook their heads.

"The whole Regency Romance Club was here. Your mother pointed out that in Regency England widows had to stay in full mourning for at least a year and then they could be in half-mourning. That meant they were allowed to dress in gray or lavender."

"How long did half-mourning last?" Andrea leaned forward as she asked the question. She appeared intrigued and that didn't really surprise Hannah. Her sister was always interested in fashion.

"According to your mother, half-mourning usually lasted a year or two, but there were quite a few women who never wore bright colors again. And then there were others, like Queen Victoria, who remained in full mourning for the rest of her life." Nettie glanced down at her bright pink sweatshirt and shrugged. "Thank goodness the customs are a lot different now! Of course, I'm not out in public, either."

Hannah stood up, preparing to head to the kitchen. "I'm going to see what the ladies left in the way of food. How about you, Nettie? Can I bring you something?"

"A ham sandwich would be nice. I was just so happy to see that ham when Carrie Rhodes carried it in. It's that spiral-cut kind from CostMart and it's absolutely delicious. I adore ham, but Jim didn't care for it. We never had it in the house unless he was gone overnight."

"How about you, Andrea?" Hannah turned to her sister.

Andrea looked uncomfortable and Hannah could tell that she was nervous about being alone with Nettie. "A ham sandwich sounds wonderful, but I'll go with you. Then I can help carry things."

"Hannah can manage for a minute alone." Nettie reached out and put her hand on Andrea's arm. "I need to talk to you, Andrea."

Nettie's dining room area was part of the living room and the kitchen was at one end. Since the rooms flowed together without walls and the shutters that could be used to cordon off the kitchen were open, Hannah could keep an eye on Andrea and Nettie while she made the sandwiches.

"Look, Andrea," Hannah heard Nettie say. "I know all about Bill."

"You do?" Hannah could see Andrea's panicked expression from where she stood at the kitchen counter.

"I just wanted you to know I think it's pure hogwash."

"Then you don't think that Bill . . ."

"Of course not!" Nettie interrupted, reaching out to pat Andrea's hand. "And that's exactly what I told Mike when he was here."

Hannah watched as her sister visibly relaxed. Andrea even ventured a small smile. "I really felt strange about coming over here, Nettie. I wanted to offer my condolences, but I just wasn't sure how you felt. I mean . . . it could have been awkward."

"Mustard, Nettie?" Hannah called out from her spot at the kitchen counter.

"Yes, thank you."

"Andrea?"

"Yes. Doc Knight told me I should watch it with the spices, but I've been really good today."

Hannah added the mustard, put a piece of lettuce on top of the ham, slapped on the top slices of bread, and cut each sandwich into fourths on the cutting board. Then, since the sandwiches were all the same, she arranged them on a platter around a small dish of pickles she'd found in the refrigerator.

"Soup's on," Hannah called out, carrying the platter into the living room. "Can I get anyone something to drink? There's a whole cooler of soft drinks on the counter."

"I'll take a Diet Coke, if it's there," Andrea made her choice. "And if it's not, I'll have a diet anything."

"The same for me," Nettie said, smiling at Hannah. "Unless you'd rather have wine. Your mother brought me a nice bottle of Bordeaux."

Hannah shook her head. "Thanks anyway, but I'm driving and Andrea can't drink."

"Just because we can't doesn't mean you can't," Andrea jumped in quickly, turning to give Hannah a wink. "I think you should have some, Nettie. It's been a rough day and you need to relax. Hannah? Why don't you pour a glass of wine for Nettie?"

For a brief moment, Hannah was confused by the wink, but then she caught on. Andrea believed that Nettie would be more forthcoming if she drank some wine. Hannah spotted it on the bar at the end of the living room, went over to open it and pour a glass, and carried it back to their hostess.

"Thank you, Hannah." Nettie put down her sandwich and took a sip of wine. "There's dessert if you want some later. I stuck four cakes in the freezer, but there's at least five still out on the counter."

Hannah remembered the dessert she'd brought and she reached for the bag and handed it to Nettie. "I almost forgot . . . these cookies are for you. I guess it's a little like bringing coals to Newcastle."

"No, it's not." Nettie shook her head. "No one else brought cookies, and I like cookies better than cakes, anyway. What kind are they?"

"Cashew Crisps. I hope you like them."

"I adore these cookies." Nettie drew one out of the bag and bit into it. "Mmm. These are absolutely scrumptious. I tasted one when you first started baking them and I told Jim they were the best cookies I'd ever had."

"I'm surprised he never brought any home for you. He used to come in a couple times a week to pick up orders."

"Oh, he took most of those to the office. And he wouldn't have bought cashew cookies home, anyway. Jim didn't like cashews."

Andrea exchanged a glance with Hannah. "But you do?"

"Cashews are my favorite nut. That's why I love these cookies so much."

Hannah took another bite of her sandwich and chewed thoughtfully. It seemed that Nettie's likes and dislikes hadn't mattered much to her husband. Sheriff Grant didn't liked ham, so he'd refused to have it in the house. And even though Hannah had been baking Nettie's favorite cookies for over a year now, Sheriff Grant never bothered to take them home to her.

"I know what you're thinking," Nettie said, staring hard at Hannah.

"You do?"

"I believe so. You're thinking that my husband was a selfish man. And you're right. Jim thought he was the center of the universe and other people just floated in orbits around him. Sometimes they were useful and he liked them. Other times they weren't, and he didn't."

A tear rolled down Nettie's cheek and Hannah leaned forward. "Are you all right?"

"Yes. It's just that you can't be married to a man for twenty-six years without feeling abandoned when he's gone." Nettie took a deep breath and faced both Hannah and Andrea squarely. "Can I be frank?"

"Of course," Hannah said.

"You've probably guessed that life with Jim wasn't any

picnic. There were big problems in our marriage that we just couldn't resolve. You probably know that I almost had a breakdown when Jamie died."

"It must have been awful."

"It was. It took a whole year of counseling before I learned to cope . But I *did* learn to cope. Jim never did. That's one of the reasons I spoke with Howie Levine on the Saturday before Jim died. I went in to ask his advice about a divorce."

Andrea's mouth dropped open and Hannah had to work to keep hers closed. She hadn't heard a word about the Grants breaking up.

"No one knows except you two. My meeting with Howie was confidential, but someone will find out about it, sooner or later. And since I don't have an alibi, that'll make me the number one suspect in my husband's murder."

Hannah's ears perked up. "You don't have an alibi?"

"No. I was working alone in the sewing room, finishing an appliqué wall hanging for a client."

"Where's your sewing room?" Hannah asked, intending to check out the location of windows. It was always possible that one of Nettie's neighbors had spotted her working on the night the sheriff had been killed.

Andrea and Hannah followed Nettie up the stairs and down the hallway. She stopped at the second door to open it and ushered them in. "This is my sewing room. It's where I was working the night Jim was killed."

Hannah looked around the small, crowded sewing room in surprise. She'd thought that Nettie's workroom would be much more spacious. For years, she had been quite well-known, locally, for making appliqué wall hangings to order. Her work had been featured in several craft magazines and she always won a blue ribbon at the Minnesota State Fair. Just last year, a big name decorator had ordered several of Nettie's wall hangings to use in a celebrity's home. There had been a tour of the home on national television with an interview with the celebrity in front of a large wall hanging Nettie

had designed. Since then, Nettie had been deluged with orders from people who were willing to pay large amounts of
money to have an original Nettie Grant hanging on their
wall.

"I love it, Nettie!" Andrea crowed, having somehow made
her way between the sewing machine and the cutting table
strewn with bolts of cloth to stand in front of the wall hanging Nettie had just completed. "The cows look so real, I almost expect them to moo. Who gets it?"

"The Minnesota Dairy Council commissioned it for their
headquarters."

Hannah turned to look at the wall hanging, but she didn't
try to get any closer. The room was so small she couldn't
have managed it without knocking Andrea off her feet. "I
like it a lot, Nettie. The cows look like they're all enjoying
some huge joke at our expense."

"That's exactly what I wanted, but I doubt that anyone
else will catch it." Nettie turned to smile at Hannah. "Their
big concern was that I have every breed of cow in Minnesota
represented."

Hannah sidled past the ironing board, steadying the iron
as she went, and made her way to the single window. The
drapes were heavy and no one passing outside could have
seen any shadows from within. "Did you have the drapes
open that night?"

"Yes. I see what you're driving at, Hannah, but it won't do
any good. The Maschlers live on that side and they were
gone."

"You asked them?"

"Mike did. He called right after I brought him up here to
show him what I was doing when Jim was killed. Jerry
dropped Kate off at the school and then he went bowling
with a couple of friends. And Richie was out with his
friends."

"So you didn't see or hear anything from next door?"

"I heard the television. They must have left it on as a burglar deterrent and I wish they'd switched it to another channel. It was some kind of kung fu movie and the yelling and grunting almost drove me crazy."

Andrea looked surprised. "It was really inconsiderate of Kate to leave the television on so loud."

"Oh, it wasn't that loud. I wouldn't have heard it at all if I'd had the window closed. But I had to open it because I was cutting material. If I don't, the fibers and dust make me sneeze. This is a really small room and it's impossible to keep to keep it dust free."

"It certainly is tiny," Hannah commented, glancing around her again.

"It's the smallest bedroom. When Jamie died, I thought I'd move my things to his room. It's a lot larger. But Jim didn't want me to touch anything in there. He was so insistent about it, I didn't."

"You mean . . . everything is still just the way it was when Jamie was alive?"

"That's right. I tried to talk him into giving some of Jamie's things to charity, but he just couldn't bear to get rid of anything, not even the clothes in the closet."

Hannah looked over at her sister. Andrea looked a little sick and that was understandable. Leaving a dead boy's room intact for three years was a peculiarity that had crossed over the line into obsession.

"He wouldn't even let me clean in there," Nettie went on. "He said he'd take care of it. And he kept it locked so that I couldn't go in there when he wasn't home."

"Did he go in there sometimes?" Andrea pulled herself together enough to ask.

"Almost every night. He used it as a sort of home office. He said it made him feel close to Jamie to be surrounded by his things."

Hannah was thoughtful as she followed Nettie and Andrea back down the stairs. When you saw a person almost every day and you lived in the same small town, you thought you knew them. But it turned out that Hannah hadn't really known much about Sheriff Grant at all.

A few minutes later, the three women were back in the living room, eating slices of Rose MacDermott's famous coconut cake. Hannah had cut the slices double the size that Rose served at the café, working under the theory that larger was better.

"Did Rose give you the recipe for the Lake Eden cookbook?" Nettie asked, finishing her last forkful.

"Not yet," Hannah answered with a grin. "She keeps promising, but I don't think she's quite ready to give it up."

Andrea looked thoughtful. "Maybe she's afraid that if people know how to make it, it'll hurt her sales at the café."

"That wouldn't happen." Nettie seemed convinced. "Most people don't have time to bake. I never did. Now I almost wish I had. What Jim really wanted was a movie wife."

"A what?" Andrea asked.

"A movie wife. You know the type. She's a great mother, she cooks like a dream, she wears makeup and dresses up even when she's cleaning out the cupboards, and she always puts her husband first. I tried to be the wife Jim wanted, and I think I succeeded when Jamie was alive. But after our son died, it started to feel more and more like a farce." Several tears rolled down Nettie's cheeks and she brushed them away with the side of her hand. "So when are you going to start grilling me?"

Andrea gulped. "Grilling you?"

"You and Hannah are investigating my husband's murder, aren't you?"

"Yes, but . . ."

"You girls will have to put me down as a suspect. You won't be doing a good job if you don't. I'm strong enough to have hit Jim over the head and dragged him to that dumpster. And Kate Maschler, bless her nosy little soul, saw me arguing with Jim on the day he was killed."

"What about?" the question was out of Hannah's mouth before she could rephrase it politely.

"I really don't want to go into that, Hannah. It's personal and it can't possibly have any bearing on Jim's murder."

"Okay," Hannah said. She recognized a stubborn look when she saw it and she knew Nettie wouldn't say another word about the argument she'd had with her husband.

"Unless you girls can come up with a more likely candidate, I'm the prime suspect."

Andrea shot Hannah a look of pure desperation, and Hannah knew that the response would be up to her. She'd heard Delores say that Nettie could be candid, but she hadn't expected her to be quite that outspoken. "You're a suspect, but we don't think you did it."

"Why not?"

"Why follow your husband to the school and take the chance that someone might see you kill him? A wife can find a more secluded place."

Nettie thought about that for a moment. "I can see your reasoning on that. But if I didn't kill him, who did?"

"That's what we were hoping you could tell us," Andrea chimed in. "Did Sheriff Grant have any enemies?"

Nettie just stared at her for a moment and then she started to laugh, an incongruous reaction from a woman whose cheeks were wet with tears. She laughed until tears of mirth mingled with her tears of grief and then she stopped with a quivering sigh. "Yes," she said. "And we'll be here all night if I name all of them."

Hannah was in the middle of serving coffee and cookies to the St. Jude Society the following day, when Andrea came rushing into the basement of St. Peter's Catholic Church, almost mowing down Father Coultas in the process. She arrived at Hannah's side breathless, but there was a huge smile on her face. After a few gasps of air and a gulp of the water that Hannah handed her, Andrea was calm enough to speak. "Gus York found some notes he took on that time-sharing call. He scribbled them on the back of his gas bill. The name of the company is 'Fun in the Sun' and they're based out of Fort Lauderdale, Florida."

"And you checked with them to see if they called your house?" Hannah asked, pouring a cup of coffee and handing it to Bridget Murphy.

"Yes," Andrea answered, moving behind the catering table to pour tea for Immelda Giese, the housekeeper who had been with Father Coultas since the day he'd arrived in Lake Eden. "These cookies look great. What are they?"

"Hannah's Bananas," Immelda told her. "Hannah made them just for me. Have one, dear. Bananas have potassium and they're good for you, especially when you're p.g."

Andrea looked confused and Hannah nudged her. "Pregnant."

"Oh. Right." Andrea reached out and took a cookie. "And Hannah made these just for you?"

"That's right, dear. Father just loves my banana bread. I usually bake it for him every week, but we're waiting for a new oven in the parish house. When Hannah said she'd make banana cookies, we were thrilled."

Andrea bit into the cookie and started to smile. "These are wonderful, Hannah."

"They're almost as good as Immelda's banana bread," Hannah said diplomatically, and she noticed that the housekeeper looked pleased as she left the line to find a seat.

The next few minutes were taken up with serving coffee and cookies, but soon the members of the St. Jude Society were content and Hannah and Andrea could talk.

"So what did the people at Fun in the Sun tell you about calling Bill?" Hannah asked.

"They're going to get back to me. The supervisor had to request the records and that might take overnight, but she should have them by tomorrow afternoon at the latest. She promised to call me on my cell phone the minute they came in."

"Good work," Hannah said, smiling at her sister. If anyone else had told Hannah that a telephone solicitor would call with information, she wouldn't have believed it. But Andrea had a way of making people do whatever she wanted them to do. It wasn't simple manipulation, because everyone felt good about helping Andrea in the process.

"These cookies are really good, Hannah." Andrea helped herself to a second cookie from the tray that Hannah had placed on the long table. "Are you baking them for Halloween?"

"No, I want to come up with something a little more festive."

"You did chocolate cookies with orange icing last year, didn't you?"

Hannah nodded. "I'll do them again this year if I can't come up with anything else."

"Speaking of Halloween," Andrea paused to grab another cookie, "Tracey wants to know if you're going to the Haunted Basement and the Halloween party at the community center."

"Of course I'm going. I go every year."

"Good. Tracey's all excited about her costume and she wanted to make sure you'll see it."

"What is she going to be this year?" Hannah asked, knowing that her five-year-old niece would be cute in whatever costume she chose to wear.

"She's still wavering between a fairy princess and a pirate."

Hannah laughed. "What a difference! I'll bet she chooses the fairy princess."

"Maybe, but she loves the parrot that goes with the pirate's costume. It sits on your shoulder and there's a little switch you can press to make it talk. All the fairy princess has is a wand and it doesn't even light up or anything."

"The talking parrot is definitely a selling point," Hannah said gravely, filling the coffee carafe she used to make the rounds of the tables.

"You go first with the coffee. I'll follow you with the hot water and tea bags. Then we can split up and pass the cookies."

"Thanks, Andrea." Hannah was grateful. Catering was always easier with two people. "What does the parrot say?"

"You know . . . *Shiver my timbers!* and, *Yo ho ho and a bottle of rum!* Piratey things like that. I think there's one about dead men on a chest or something like that."

"Fifteen men on a dead man's chest."

"That's right. And then it's, *A drink for the devil and none for the rest!*"

"What was that about giving the devil a drink?" Father

Coultas asked, coming up to the catering table just in time to hear Andrea's last comment.

Andrea blushed slightly. "Sorry, Father Coultas. I was just telling Hannah about the talking parrot that comes with Tracey's pirate costume."

"I've met that parrot," Father Coultas said. "Immelda's grandson rented that costume last year and the bird got stuck on *ho*. It just said *ho, ho, ho* over and over like some kind of deranged Santa Claus. It was driving poor Immelda crazy until I took the batteries out."

When Hannah stepped into her kitchen with the cookies left over from her catering job, Lisa came barreling through the swinging door. "Thank goodness you're back, Hannah!"

"What's wrong?" Hannah asked, noticing the high spots of color in Lisa's cheeks.

"Nothing's wrong. I just overheard something you should know, that's all. Hold on a second. Herb's here and I'll ask him to mind the counter."

Hannah poured herself a cup of coffee from the kitchen pot and sat down at the workstation. A moment later, Lisa rushed back in and sat down on an adjoining stool.

"You said you overheard something?" Hannah prompted.

"That's right. I kept my ears open, just the way you asked me to do, and I found out that Sheriff Grant and his wife had a big argument when he came home for lunch on Monday."

Hannah's eyes widened. This could be the fight that Nettie had refused to discuss. "Andrea and I saw Nettie last night. She told us she'd fought with Sheriff Grant, but she wouldn't say what the fight was about. Who told you, Lisa?"

"Kate Maschler, but she didn't exactly tell me. She told Becky Summers."

"You were doing the invisible waitress trick?"

"That's right. I was at the table next to theirs refilling coffee cups and they didn't even notice me. Kate told Becky that

Nettie Grant followed the sheriff out to his car and she looked madder than Kate had ever seen her before. Kate opened her window in time to hear Nettie say that she was going to rent to them and she had a perfect right to do it since she'd inherited the duplex before they were married."

"Sounds serious," Hannah commented. "What did Sheriff Grant say to that?"

"He said he was sick of hearing about it and Nettie should drop it, that there was no way he'd have them under his roof."

"Who's *them?*"

"I don't know. That's when Kate and Becky pushed back their chairs and left. Do you think it's important, Hannah?"

"It could be," Hannah said, thinking about it. If Nettie had promised to rent half of the duplex to someone and Sheriff Grant went to tell the people they couldn't move in, it might have resulted in a fight that escalated to murder.

"I think you should run next door, Hannah. When they were leaving, I heard Becky say she had to find the right dress to wear to her nephew's wedding. They probably went straight to Claire's shop."

Hannah headed for the door. Visiting Mother and Carrie's shop was one thing, but she didn't need any urging to visit her neighbor on the other side. Claire Rodgers was a good friend and she wanted an update on Claire's romance with Reverend Knudson, the Lutheran minister.

A chill wind was blowing as Hannah dashed across her parking lot and knocked at the rear door of Beau Monde Fashions. She heard the far-off sound of geese honking as they migrated south for the winter and she glanced up at the battleship-gray sky. A ragged vee was just disappearing over the tops of the pines that lined both sides of Third Street. The songbirds had already left and now the geese were bailing for the winter. Soon only the winter birds would be left, bright blue Jays, vivid red Cardinals, and glowing green and yellow

Nuthatches sitting high in the pines like jewels amidst the branches.

"Hannah?" Claire looked both pleased and surprised as she opened her back door. "Come in. It's cold out there."

"I know. Do you have customers?"

"Not a soul. It's been a slow afternoon."

"I'm sorry to hear that," Hannah commiserated. The financial life of a small business owner was often touch and go.

"Oh, it's all right. The morning was very good and Becky Summers was just in. She bought three dresses."

"How's Reverend Knudson?"

"He's just fine, Hannah." Claire's smile was positively beatific. "He's also very persuasive. He's going to announce our engagement the Sunday before Christmas."

"You said yes!" Hannah grinned at her friend. With one failed romance behind her, Claire had finally found a man she could love and trust.

"You'll be there for the announcement, won't you, Hannah?"

"I wouldn't miss it for the world," Hannah promised. She knew Claire was nervous about the congregation's reaction to the engagement. Although no one except Hannah, Andrea, and Norman knew for sure, everyone in town suspected that Claire had at one time been Mayor Bascomb's mistress. "If anyone gives you a rough time about it, just let me know and I'll cut them off from cookies for life."

Claire laughed, but she sobered quickly. "You know? I believe you would. You're a good friend, Hannah."

"I'm a good friend who wants to pump you for information," Hannah amended it. "You've heard about Bill, haven't you?"

"Of course, and the whole thing is absurd. You're trying to clear him?"

"Yes. Did Kate and Becky mention the fight that Sheriff Grant had with his wife?"

"They mentioned it."

"Did they happen to drop the name of the renters Nettie wanted for the duplex?"

Claire shook her head. "I don't think they knew. They were speculating about it while Becky was trying on dresses. Kate said it had to be someone with a child."

"Really?" Hannah's ears perked up. This was grist for the sleuthing mill. "Why did Kate think that?"

"Because right before Sheriff Grant drove off, he rolled down his window and shouted out that he wouldn't have that child under his roof. Except he didn't say *child*."

"What did he say?"

"I don't know, but it must have been bad because Kate said she wouldn't repeat it."

"How about you, Claire? Do you have any idea who the disputed renters could be?"

"They could be Nettie's relatives. Last year, she asked my advice on finding a Christmas present for a little girl. I told her about The Pink Giraffe in Anoka, but I warned her that their things were expensive. She said that didn't matter, that it was for family and she wanted to buy something special."

Hannah was impressed. Claire had put two facts together and come up with a very good clue. "Do you happen to know what she bought?"

"Yes, I do. She told me all about it the next time she came in. She said she found a child's chair that looked like a seated plush bear and The Pink Giraffe had shipped it free the week before Christmas."

Hannah thanked Claire for her help and headed out the back door, racing across the parking lot and into her own warm kitchen. Once she'd washed her hands and put on the apron she used to serve customers, she pushed through the door to the coffee shop and hurried to the counter to relieve Lisa.

"Oh, Hannah! Thank goodness you're back!"

Hannah noticed the distressed expression on Lisa's face. "What's wrong?"

"It's your mother. She's called six times in the past twenty minutes."

"Uh-oh," Hannah sighed. No wonder Lisa looked distraught. "Take a break, Lisa. I'll man the counter for a while."

Lisa shook her head. "I don't need a break. I just need you to run to Granny's Attic and talk to your mother before she calls here again. She sounded really suspicious the last time she called. I swear she thinks I'm hiding you in the pantry."

"Okay. I'm going." Hannah hung up her apron and dashed out the front door, ducking into the next storefront. The bell tinkled as she pushed open the door and Delores looked up from her position behind the antique counter.

"Hannah! Well, it's about time! Come with me."

Before Hannah had time to do more than blink, Delores came around the counter, took her hand, and dragged her up the stairs to the room they used for coffee breaks.

"Sit down, Hannah. I want an explanation!"

"Of what?" Hannah was thoroughly confused.

"Why didn't you tell me yesterday, when we met at the library? A mother shouldn't be the last one in town to know!"

Hannah thought fast. It was obvious that her mother had found out about Bill's suspension. "I would have told you yesterday, but it wasn't my place. I knew Andrea wanted to be the one to break the news to you."

"Oh. That's different." The hard expression in Delores's eyes softened. "I do wish Andrea had told me sooner, but I suppose the poor dear was probably trying to spare my feelings."

"I'm sure that's it, Mother," Hannah managed to choke out the words.

"Poor Bill!" Delores sighed and shook her head. "Poor Andrea! And in her condition, too! Can't you talk some sense into Mike? Surely he doesn't actually believe that Bill killed anyone!"

"I tried, Mother. I talked to Mike about it yesterday, but he wouldn't budge an inch. He's as stubborn as an ox."

"Well . . . I'm glad you found that out now. Just think how terrible this would be if you were married to him."

"I don't think there's any danger of that, at least not right now," Hannah said under her breath.

"What was that, dear?"

"Nothing, Mother. Just thinking out loud."

"At least you've been warned about Mike's true nature. That's certainly worth something."

"True."

"Andrea said that you're going to investigate. I want to help you, dear. What would you like me to do?"

Hannah was about to say she'd have to think about it when she realized that she did have something Delores could do. She needed to find out who'd received that stuffed bear chair from the Pink Giraffe and her mother was the perfect person to find out for her.

"What is it, dear? You thought of something, didn't you?"

"Yes, and here's the situation," Hannah said. And then she proceeded to tell her mother all about the fight Nettie'd had with Sheriff Grant on the day of his death and the fact that Nettie had wanted to rent to a family with a little girl. She explained about the Christmas present Nettie had ordered from the Pink Giraffe and then she asked the important question. "Do you think you can find out who got that present?"

"Why of course I can!" Delores sounded pleased at being asked. "But why don't you just ask Nettie?"

"I don't think it'll do any good. I already asked her about the fight. She said it was personal and she didn't want to talk about it."

Delores shrugged. "You struck out, dear. If Nettie says she doesn't want to talk about something, wild horses couldn't drag it out of her. But finding out about the present should be no problem. They know me at the Pink Giraffe. It's where I get most of Tracey's gifts."

"Could you call right now and ask?"

"I could, but it would be better for me to go there in person. It's much more difficult to say no face-to-face."

"You're right. Could you take a couple hours off this afternoon and drive there?"

Delores shook her head. "I could, but it won't do any good. They're closed during the day on Wednesdays. They open at seven this evening, but I can't go there tonight."

"Why not?"

"Because I have . . . plans."

"Oh?" Hannah waited a moment, but her mother didn't elaborate. "What kind of plans, Mother?"

"Personal plans."

Hannah digested that answer and when no more elaboration was forthcoming, she began to worry. "Is there something wrong, Mother?"

"Like what, dear?"

"Like . . . your personal plans don't include a visit to Doc Knight, do they?"

"Of course not!" Delores gave a little laugh. "If I get sick, you'll be the first to know about it. This is just something . . . personal. And I don't want to discuss it."

Hannah took one look at her mother's set face and knew she'd get nowhere by further probing. Delores could rival Nettie in the wild-horses-couldn't-drag-it-out-of-her department. Rather than annoy her mother with more questions, Hannah switched gears. "Will you be able to drive to The Pink Giraffe tomorrow?"

"Yes. I'll pick up Tracey after morning kindergarten and take her with me."

Hannah started to grin. "That might not be a good idea, Mother. It could be dangerous."

"What do you mean? How could going to a children's store be dangerous?"

"Oh, it won't be dangerous for you or Tracey personally,"

Hannah said, her smile growing wider. "But taking Tracey inside could put your credit cards in jeopardy."

Delores laughed. "You're right, dear. But Granny's Attic is doing very well and I can afford to indulge my only grand-daughter a bit. Did Claire tell you what Nettie bought?"

"Yes, a child's chair shaped like a seated plush bear and she had it delivered in time for Christmas."

"I'm sure I can . . ." There was a crash outside the door and Delores stopped in mid-sentence. "What was *that?*"

"I don't know. It sounded like someone dropped some-thing heavy that rolled . . ."

"Sorry." Luanne Hanks, Delores and Carrie's assistant, stuck her head in the doorway. "I was carrying a brass um-brella stand and I tripped. Don't worry. It's not damaged. I checked."

Delores walked over to put her arm around Luanne's shoulders. "I don't care about the umbrella stand. I'm much more concerned about you. You're shaking, Luanne. And you're as pale as a ghost. Are you hurt?"

"No, I'm fine. I was just worried that I'd damaged the um-brella stand."

"Nonsense! You know it's not worth more than twenty dollars. And that's on a good day."

Hannah glanced down at the floor. She didn't see anything that Luanne could have tripped over.

"Oh, there's nothing there," Luanne said, correctly inter-preting the direction of Hannah's gaze. "I just tripped over my own feet, that's all."

"Well, I'm glad you're all right," Hannah said, waving goodbye to her mother and Luanne, and heading down the stairs. If she remembered correctly, Luanne had been on the girls' gymnastic team before she'd dropped out of high school. She was normally as surefooted as a mountain goat and it was doubtful that she'd trip over her own feet. Something was wrong. Luanne had looked absolutely terrified when she'd poked her head in the doorway and Hannah was sure it had nothing to do with worrying about whether she'd damaged the umbrella stand. Why was Luanne so frightened? And did her fright have anything to do with Sheriff Grant's murder?

Hannah's Bananas

Do not preheat oven—this dough
must chill before baking

1 ½ cups melted butter *(3 sticks)*
2 cups white granulated sugar
¾ cup mashed very ripe banana *(2 medium or 3 small)*
4 teaspoons baking soda
1 teaspoon salt
2 beaten eggs *(just whip them up with a fork)*
4 cups flour *(no need to sift)*
2 cups finely chopped walnuts or pecans *(measure AFTER chopping)*
½ cup white granulated sugar for later

Melt butter in a large microwavable bowl. Stir in the sugar, beaten eggs, baking soda, and salt. Choose bananas that have black freckles on the skin so they're almost overripe. Mash them until they're smooth (*you can do this in a food processor or by hand*). Add the banana puree and mix thoroughly. Mix in the flour and then the nuts. Cover your bowl and refrigerate it for 4 hours (*overnight is fine, too*).

When you're ready to bake, preheat the oven to 350 degrees F., rack in the middle position.

Roll the chilled dough into walnut-sized balls with your hands. (*This dough is quite sticky—you can wear plastic gloves if you like, or wet your hands slightly so the dough won't stick to them.*) Put ½ cup white sugar in a small bowl and roll the balls in it. Place the dough balls on a greased cookie sheet, 12 to a sheet. Press them down just a little so they won't roll off on the floor when you put them in the oven. Then return your bowl to the refrigerator and let it chill until it's time to roll more.

Bake for 10-12 minutes at 350 degrees F., or until they're lightly golden in color. They'll flatten out, all by themselves. Let them cool for 2 minutes on the cookie sheet and then move them to a wire rack to finish cooling.

These cookies freeze well. Roll them up in foil, place the rolls in a freezer bag, and they'll be fine for 3 months or so, *if* they last that long.

Yield: Approximately 10 dozen, depending on cookie size.

Lisa's cousin Beth says these are great when they're dunked in hot chocolate.

Carrie Rhodes also loves these cookies. She says that middle-aged women should eat bananas every day because they need extra potassium. (*I bit my tongue when she said "middle-aged"—Carrie's at least fifty-five and people don't usually live to be a hundred and ten!*)

Chapter
Ten

Hannah was still thinking about Moishe when she pulled into her parking spot at The Cookie Jar on Thursday morning. When she picked up a replacement tip sheet this morning, Sue assured her that one of the ten suggestions was bound to work and that Moishe couldn't hold out forever. But Hannah knew Moishe much better than that. If her cat decided that he didn't want to eat his senior food, he could be even more stubborn than the other Lake Eden male who had once been part of her life, Mike Kingston.

"Hi, Lisa," Hannah called out as she came in the back door. "Sorry I'm late."

"That's okay. I thought you'd be even later." Lisa's voice floated out of the coffee shop and a moment later she pushed through the door, carrying a steaming mug of coffee. "Did you get your problem solved with Moishe?"

"No. I got a tip sheet for switching him to the new food, but whoever wrote it doesn't know Moishe."

"True. How about sprinkling a little fresh catnip on his new food?"

"That's tip number seven." Hannah held out the sheet. "And number eight is drizzling some tuna juice over the top of his bowl. I don't have high hopes for any of them."

Lisa looked thoughtful. "Maybe Moishe's just too smart

to be fooled by tricks. Have you had a heart-to-heart with
him and told him why his new food is good for him?"

"Of course. I felt a little stupid getting down on the floor
with him, but I did it anyway. I think he understood me, Lisa.
He really paid attention to everything I said. But after I finished and I was getting up off the floor, he stomped over to
his food bowl and tipped it over with his paw."

"Uh-oh. You've got a real problem on your . . ." Lisa
stopped talking as the back door opened and Andrea stood
there. "Hi, Andrea. Come in."

"Thanks. It's nice and warm in here." Andrea walked over
to one of the stools at the workstation and sat down.

"How about some coffee?" Hannah asked.

"Yes! I've been saving up my coffee allotment, Hannah.
Yours is a lot better than my instant."

Hannah headed for the coffee pot. Everyone knew that instant couldn't hold a candle to real coffee brewed from
scratch.

"Here you go." Hannah set the mug in front of her sister.
"What brings you out so early?"

"I got a phone call from the supervisor. She checked the
records for me."

"Fun in the Sun?" Hannah asked, reaching for her notebook.

"That's right. One of their representatives called Bill at
eight-twenty and the call lasted one minute."

"Good. Just let me jot that down."

"The only thing is, I don't think it helps Bill any. I drove
from our house to the school and timed the trip. It took me
twenty minutes. Not that he did it, of course, but Bill could
have killed Sheriff Grant at eight and gotten home in time to
take the Fun in the Sun sales call."

"Wrong," Hannah said, flipping through the notebook
until she found the right page. "I was standing right there in
the parking lot while Mike looked for bloodstains. He found

they were heaviest right next to Sheriff Grant's car and Mike said that's where it happened. Since the car was at least ten yards away from the Dumpster, it must have taken the killer at least a couple of minutes to drag Sheriff Grant's body there and put it inside."

"And if Bill had done that, he would have missed the Fun in the Sun call by a couple of minutes?"

"Absolutely."

"Thanks, Hannah." A relieved smile spread over Andrea's face. "Could the other call, the one from the roofing company, clear Bill completely if it came in at the right time?"

"Maybe. Didn't you tell me that you got home from the movie with Tracey at nine forty-five?"

"That's right. I looked at my watch when we got out of the car. I was feeling a little guilty because I'd kept Tracey up so late on a school night. I told her to go in the house, kiss her dad, and go straight to bed."

Hannah turned to a clean page in her notebook and crunched the numbers. "The second call could clear Bill if it came in at approximately ten minutes after nine. The time frame's tight, but that would do it."

"Great! I'm going to drive around and look at more roofs, Hannah. I've got to find out who made that second call."

"Take your coffee with you," Hannah urged, dumping the contents of Andrea's mug into a disposable cup.

"Thanks. I'll be back if I find anything."

Lisa waited until Andrea had left and then she turned to Hannah. "What's this about roofs?"

It took Hannah a moment or two, but Lisa caught on right away when she explained about the time frame and how the second telemarketing call could provide an alibi for Bill.

"I'll call Herb right away," Lisa promised.

"Are you going to ask him if he got the same telemarketing call?"

"That wouldn't do any good. Herb always hangs up the

minute they say, *And how are you this evening?* I just thought that since he makes his rounds every hour, he could keep his eye out for roofing trucks."

Hannah had just finished baking an extra batch of Pecan Chews for a special order when the phone rang. Since Lisa didn't pick up right away, Hannah assumed that she was waiting on a customer and grabbed the wall phone in the kitchen. "The Cookie Jar. Hannah speaking."

"I'm glad you answered, Hannah."

"Hi, Mother," Hannah said quickly. Delores sounded a trifle breathless. "Where are you?"

"I'm at a pay phone on the street outside The Pink Giraffe. Guess who got that bear chair for Christmas!"

Hannah rolled her eyes heavenward. "Sheriff Grant is dead, Bill's the prime suspect, Norman's in Seattle and he could be playing spin the dental drill with his ex-fiancé, and I'm on the outs with Mike. My life is pretty grim right now . . . and you want me to play guessing games?"

"I'm sorry, dear. Let me rephrase that," Delores sounded only slightly apologetic. "It's just that I'm so surprised. My friend at The Pink Giraffe said that they shipped the bear chair to Suzie Hanks!"

"Luanne's daughter?"

"Yes. What do you think that means?"

Hannah blinked. And then she blinked again. "I'm not sure, but I'll find out. Don't say anything to anybody until you hear from me, all right?"

"But . . . but . . . but . . ."

Delores was sputtering like a badly tuned motor and Hannah interrupted. "Calm down, Mother. It might mean nothing at all."

"But how could *that* be?"

Hannah thought fast. "Nettie's active in quite a few charities, isn't she?"

"You know she is."

"Let's say one of her charities decided to give a really nice Christmas gift to a needy child. Suzie Hanks would certainly fit the bill."

"That's true," Delores sounded thoughtful. "But why would Nettie tell Claire that she was looking for a present for a relative?"

"Maybe there were other people in Claire's shop and Nettie was protecting the child's identity. You know how touchy Luanne is about accepting charity."

There was a long silence. Hannah knew that her mother was thinking it over. The silence stretched out with only the faint crackles on the line, the earmarks of a long distance call. Finally Delores cleared her throat and spoke again. "You have a point, Hannah. And Nettie's smart enough to realize that Luanne would have packed up that chair and sent it right back if she'd known it was charity. But do you think that's really what happened? It seems pretty far-fetched to me!"

"I know it does, but it's possible." Hannah tried to sound as if she believed her own story. "You just keep mum until you hear from me. I'll run right over to Granny's Attic and find out from Luanne personally."

"Luanne's out at the Ferguson family farm auction. They're selling a wonderful treadle sewing machine, and there's an oak butter churn that I have my heart set on buying. There's some milk glass, too, and you know how popular that is. Promise me you won't disturb her when she's bidding, Hannah. She has to concentrate."

"I won't disturb her, but I need to get to the bottom of this. And just as soon as I do, I'll tell you."

Delores made a little sound of distress. "You have no idea how difficult it's going to be not to tell a few of my closest friends and get their opinion on . . ."

"Don't you dare!" Hannah interrupted with a warning.

"All right, I won't. My lips are sealed until I hear from you. But I'd better hear from you soon!"

* * *

Once Hannah had explained things to Lisa, she headed out to the Ferguson farm. It was only a mile from the site of Norman's new house and since his contractor and crew weren't there, Hannah pulled into the driveway to see how the house was progressing.

"How about that? It's beginning to look like a house," Hannah said to the purple grackle that was pecking at something in the yard. The foundation had been poured, the framing was complete, and the workmen had almost finished the sheer walls. Once the roof was on and the doors and windows were secure, it would be snug for the winter.

Even though Norman had invited her to come out to see the progress several times in the past, Hannah felt a bit like an intruder as she opened the front door. Actually, opening the door was a bit silly. The tall windows that would go on either side of the door were still missing and she could have simply stepped through the framing. All the same, there was something wonderfully ceremonial about turning the knob and opening the front door of the house they'd designed together for the dream house contest.

"Nice," Hannah said, stepping into the foyer and gazing up at the staircase that led to the second floor balcony. Then she climbed the stairs and headed down the hallway to the children's bedrooms. They looked like empty boxes now, but Hannah could imagine a boy's room with model airplanes hanging from the ceiling, and a girl's room with a window seat where she could sit and dream. There was another room for an office or hobby room . . . and then there was the master bedroom.

Hannah held her breath as she entered the master bedroom. It was exactly as she had imagined, with an outside balcony where the happy couple could have coffee in the morning and look out over the lake. There was also a river rock fireplace that would keep the room toasty in the winter and provide a romantic touch.

Hannah sighed past the lump in her throat. She suspected that all it would take was a little more encouragement and Norman would propose. Then this house would be hers, this wonderful house she'd designed with a man she firmly believed would make a near-perfect husband. The only thing stopping her from giving Norman the encouragement he'd need to make the whole thing official was the curse of indecision. How could she accept a proposal she'd engineered from Norman when she wasn't sure that she was willing to give up her relationship with Mike?

And what relationship was that? Hannah thought with a frown, the altercation they'd had about Bill foremost in her mind. But even though she was at odds with Mike for not trusting and supporting her brother-in-law, there was still an attraction between them she couldn't deny. As much as she loved the idea of living in the dream house she'd helped to design, she knew she wasn't ready to make that choice.

She glanced around her one more time and headed for the stairs. She'd dealt with enough for one day and there was still the meeting with Luanne to consider. The front door banged as she shut it behind her and Hannah tried not to think of how final it sounded as she hurried to her cookie truck. Her love life, or lack of it, was becoming a problem, but she didn't have the time to deal with it now. Norman could wait. Mike could wait. The important thing now was clearing Bill by solving Sheriff Grant's murder.

Chapter Eleven

The Ferguson family farm was large, with land stretching out as far as the eye could see from the two-story farmhouse that sat smack dab in the middle of the acreage. Hannah drove up to the house and parked, then followed the cardboard signs to the pole barn where the auction was being held. As she approached, she could hear Chuck Ganz, the auctioneer, rattling off numbers and patter so fast that it almost sounded as if he spoke in a foreign language. Chuck had once told Hannah that it took three things to be an auctioneer: a good memory for numbers, a quicksilver tongue to spit them out as fast as the ear could hear, and the courage of a grizzly to get up in front of all those people and risk making a fool of yourself.

It sounded like the bidding was just winding up, and Hannah stopped inside the open door to listen for a moment. Chuck stood on a platform at the opposite end of the shed, gesturing expansively and talking nonstop. Dressed in unremitting black from head to toe, he sported a wide yellow tie that he claimed was his personal beam of sunshine on a cloudy day. It was something he said at the start of every auction and not really very funny, but people liked Chuck and they always laughed because he expected them to.

"Sold for eighty-three dollars to the gentleman in the tan

hunting jacket," Chuck called out, banging his gavel on the podium. "Pay the banker on your way out."

Hannah spotted Luanne sitting next to an empty chair near the middle of the crowd. Several people had gotten up to stretch and Chuck was fortifying himself with another mug of coffee from the big thermos he kept in back of the podium. Hannah headed down the center aisle between the folding chairs and squeezed past knees to get to the vacant chair next to Luanne.

"Hi, Hannah." Luanne looked surprised to see her when Hannah slid into the chair. "Are you here to bid on something?"

Hannah reached down to rub her shin. A man wearing pointy-toed cowboy boots had moved just as she was trying to inch past him. "No, I came out here to talk to you."

"Just a second." Luanne glanced down at her auction book. "I need to bid on something in this next lot."

The bidding started and Hannah watched as Luanne raised her auction paddle. Almost simultaneously, Chuck pointed to her and rattled off a musical string of numbers. Luanne raised her paddle again, but this time Chuck acknowledged her with a nod and swiveled to repeat several other bids. Hannah turned to survey the room. Paddles were popping up all over. Luanne must be bidding on a very popular item. The bidding slowed once, faltered, picked up again, and then slowed a second time. If Hannah had judged the competition correctly, there was only one person bidding against Luanne, an older man with snowy white hair who was wearing a gray suit. Hannah studied him surreptitiously, but she didn't think she'd ever seen him before. Perhaps he was one of the "auction junkies" that Chuck had told her about, the crowd of men and women who made the circuit of the farm actions, hoping to pick up antiques at low prices that they could turn around and sell for a tidy profit.

Chuck was on "going twice" before Luanne raised her

paddle again. She had a bored expression on her face, and she gave a little shrug to the man in the gray suit as if to say, "I'm not sure I really want this, but I'll give it one last bid." The man in the gray suit frowned slightly and gave his own shrug, lowering his paddle and nodding toward her.

"Sold! To the pretty little lady in the green sweater," Chuck called out, pointing to Luanne.

"Great!" Luanne said, giving Hannah a smile of triumph. "Your mother's going to love the antique spinning wheel I just bought."

Hannah smiled back. Luanne was right. Delores loved spinning wheels. But discussing antiques wasn't why she'd come out to the auction to see Luanne. "I really need to talk to you, Luanne."

"Okay. Just let me listen to what's coming up next."

Hannah watched Chuck take his place behind the podium again. He banged his gavel to get everyone's attention and waited until the crowd was silent.

"Lot number two-six-nine, ladies and gentlemen. We call this one our sporting package. Six hand-painted duck decoys, a stuffed moose head in A-one condition, two bowling balls, a rod and reel that's seen better days, and a tackle box full of fishing lures."

Luanne turned to Hannah. "We can talk now. I'm not bidding on anything until they get to the upstairs furniture. Carrie's interested in a sleigh bed that belonged to Mrs. Ferguson's mother-in-law, and there's a dresser set from the fifties that your mother wants for a decorator who's doing her client's bedroom in retro."

"I don't like retro. It's so yesterday."

"But it's very popular with . . ." Luanne stopped speaking when she noticed Hannah's grin. "I get it. Retro. Yesterday. Really, Hannah!"

"Sorry. I couldn't resist." Hannah took a deep breath. This wasn't a venue that invited confidences, but no one was paying any attention to them and she had to broach the subject of the bear chair with Luanne.

Luanne seemed to catch Hannah's mood, because she began to frown. "What is it, Hannah? You look upset."

"I am. I need to know why Nettie Grant bought that bear chair for Suzie last Christmas."

"Oh!" Luanne was so startled, her hands flew up to her face. Unfortunately, the paddle was still in her right hand and Chuck interpreted that as a bid and announced it. Both Luanne and Hannah listened with frowns on their faces as Chuck trolled the room for other bids, but no one else seemed to be buying. After several more minutes of patter, Chuck pointed to Luanne and announced that she'd won.

"I'm sorry, Luanne," Hannah said, the soul of contrition. She hadn't meant to make Luanne bid on something she didn't want.

"That's okay. It was only ten dollars over the minimum bid."

"How much is that?" Hannah asked, already planning to reimburse Luanne for her loss.

"Forty dollars. The moose head is worth three times that and we can get ten dollars or more apiece for the decoys."

"So you came out all right?" Luanne nodded and Hannah breathed a big sigh of relief. "Okay. Let's get out of here before I make you bid on something else."

After a chorus of *pardon me*'s, Hannah and Luanne finally exited the pole barn and picked their way down the rutted road to the house. It was deserted, but Hannah made her way unerringly toward the kitchen.

"No chairs?" she asked, gazing around at the empty room.

"They sold them with the kitchen table." Luanne said, taking up a position to the right of the kitchen sink. "I know. I bought them."

"Well . . . there's always the counters," Hannah said, hoisting herself up on a kitchen counter and waiting until Luanne had done the same on the other side of the sink.

"Nettie bought Suzie that chair because she's her grandmother," Luanne blurted out, her eyes meeting Hannah's in an unwavering gaze. "Jamie Grant was Suzie's father."

"I didn't know."

"No one knew, not even my mother." Luanne gave a deep sigh. "She doesn't know to this day. But now that you've tracked it down this far, I guess there's no point in keeping secrets."

Hannah winced, feeling as guilty as sin. "I'm sorry, Luanne. I know it's your private business, but . . ."

"You have to know," Luanne finished the sentence for her. "It's okay, Hannah. I'm sure you won't tell anyone you don't have to tell. Besides . . . the reason I couldn't tell anyone before is . . . uh . . . there's no polite way to way this, but . . . my reason is dead."

"Sheriff Grant?"

"Yes. He threatened to cause all sorts of trouble if I told."

Hannah listened as Luanne filled in the blanks. The summer before she started her senior year at Jordan High, Luanne went with her mother to clean the sheriff's station. That's where she met Jamie, who was home from college. As Hannah nodded sympathetically, Luanne told her about the hot summer evenings when she'd walk out to meet Jamie at the end of Old Bailey Road. If they felt like going somewhere, they'd take in a movie at the mall, or go out to Eden Lake for a late night swim. Other times, when they wanted to be alone, Jamie would bring along a six-pack and they'd park on the old logging road that overlooked the lake. Luanne was thrilled to be dating a college guy and she saw Jamie almost every night for the two weeks before he left to go back to college.

"I know I was foolish," Luanne admitted with a sigh.

"A lot of girls are at sixteen," Hannah said, remembering

how thrilled her high school friends had been when a Jordan High graduate who was now a "college man" had come home for vacation and asked one of them out on a date. "When did you discover that you were pregnant?"

"Not until Jamie was gone. I wrote him a letter to tell him and I said I wanted to keep the baby. I really believe he cared about me and he would have done the right thing. Maybe we wouldn't have gotten married, but I know that he would have helped me with the baby. But the day after I mailed the letter, Jamie got killed in that car wreck. He never even got the chance to read it."

"What happened to your letter?"

"Someone from the dorm boxed up all of Jamie's things, including the unopened letter from me, and mailed the box to the Grants."

"Did they open your letter?"

"Yes, and both of them read it. Sheriff Grant made Nettie promise that she'd keep quiet about it and stay away from the baby."

"But why?" Hannah was shocked.

"Because I'm trash . . . at least that's what Sheriff Grant called me." Luanne took a deep breath and sat up a little straighter. "He said I got pregnant on purpose to trick Jamie into marriage. He even accused me of seducing Jamie."

Hannah gave a little snort. "Number one, you know you're not trash. And number two, it takes two to tango."

"I know that. And so did Sheriff Grant, but he wouldn't admit it. He came out to the house to see me and he said that if I ever told anyone that I was carrying Jamie's baby, he'd make my life miserable."

"That's pretty harsh," Hannah commented, her frown deepening.

"I know. He was a harsh man. He told me that his son's name and memory were unblemished and he was going to make sure they stayed that way. He also said that if I was smart and I kept my mouth shut, he wouldn't have to change any personnel out at the sheriff's station."

Hannah was puzzled. "What did he mean by *that?*"

"My mother had a contract to clean out there three times a week. It was our main source of income."

Hannah felt sick. "So he coerced you into silence by threatening to fire your mother?"

"He didn't exactly threaten, at least not in so many words, but I knew he'd fire my mother in a heartbeat if I didn't cooperate."

"So that's why you kept silent about Suzie's father?"

"That's one reason. The other reason is that it was nobody's business but Jamie's and mine. And Jamie was dead."

"So is Sheriff Grant," Hannah said, her eyes narrowing slightly. "It must be a relief now that he can't threaten you any longer."

Luanne swallowed hard. "Not really. Remember when I dropped that umbrella stand? It was because I'm so scared. I'm in big trouble, Hannah, and the whole thing's bound to come out."

"About Suzie's father?"

"That's just part of it. Once people find out that Sheriff Grant was threatening me, they'll think I killed him."

"Did you?" the question popped out before Hannah had time to squelch it.

"No! Of course I didn't kill him!"

"Then stop worrying about it."

"I can't. I'm going to be a suspect the minute somebody finds out about the fight I had with Sheriff Grant."

"Fight?" Hannah's ears perked up. "When? Where? What did you fight about?"

Luanne took a deep breath. "The *when* was Monday night, and the *where* was the school parking lot. The *what* is that Nettie called me and offered me the other half of their duplex. Sheriff Grant found out about it and he was waiting for me when I pulled in the lot."

"Okay," Hannah said, remembering the altercation that Kate Maschler had overheard between Nettie and Sheriff Grant. "Did you accept Nettie's offer?"

"No. I wanted to, but I was worried about how Sheriff Grant would react. I told Nettie that we'd love to move in, but only if the sheriff said that it was okay."

Hannah already knew that Sheriff Grant had objected vehemently and that he'd fought with Nettie about it. "Tell me everything that happened that night in the parking lot," she instructed.

"I wanted to go to your class that night, but a customer came in right before I was ready to lock up. I took care of him as fast as I could and then I drove straight over to the school. Sheriff Grant was there in the parking lot and he motioned me over to his car. He looked really mad."

"How could you tell that by just looking?"

"Well . . . his face was all red and he was moving in that impatient way he has. You know . . . jerky. I didn't really want to talk to him, but I figured I couldn't walk right past him and ignore him."

"I understand," Hannah said. "Go on."

"I walked over to his car. He was eating something . . . I think it was a cupcake . . . and he put it in a bag on the seat. He said he knew that Nettie had offered me the duplex."

"What did you say?"

"I tried to explain that I hadn't accepted, but he yelled at me and accused me of taking advantage of Nettie because she missed Jamie so much. And then he said that for all they knew, Jamie wasn't even the father and Suzie was somebody else's baby. And then he called Suzie a . . . a . . ."

"Never mind," Hannah interrupted quickly. "I can imagine what he said. How did you react to that?"

"I couldn't say anything. I was too choked up. He was just so horrible and he said such awful things to me. I knew I was going to cry, so I just ran back to my car and drove off as fast as I could."

"Where did you go?"

"I drove back to Granny's Attic and just sat there for a while. I didn't want to face anybody until I calmed down. When I was through crying and I'd washed my face, I drove home."

"What time did you get there?"

"A little before nine. I looked at the kitchen clock when I came in."

"And Sheriff Grant was still alive when you drove out of the school parking lot?"

"Oh, yes," Luanne said, shivering slightly. "I saw him in my rearview mirror, standing next to his car and shaking his fist at me."

"What time was that?"

"I'm not sure. I know I drove into the lot at five minutes after eight. I remember looking at my watch when I got out of the car to see how late I was going to be for your class. I don't think I talked to Sheriff Grant for more than a couple of minutes, so it must have been about ten after eight."

"Close enough," Hannah said, making a mental note to add Luanne's information to her notebook. "Did anyone else see you with Sheriff Grant?"

Luanne frowned and shook her head. "I don't think so. If they had, they would have said something by now. There were lots of cars in the lot, but as far as I know, everyone else was inside the school."

"That's all I need for now, Luanne." Hannah slid down from her perch on the counter. "Thanks for being so honest with me."

"Do you . . . uh . . . have to tell anybody else about Suzie's father?"

"No, but I'm pretty sure Mother's figured it out."

"That's what I was afraid of." Luanne looked sick. "I knew she was going to the Pink Giraffe and your mother could get information from a rock if she wanted to. The rock wouldn't even know it had talked."

"True," Hannah agreed with a grin. Delores could get information effortlessly. Andrea had inherited that same ability, and Hannah wished that she had, too.

"Do you think she'll tell anyone?"

"Mother?" Hannah didn't say anything else. She just stared at Luanne in disbelief.

"Never mind." Luanne looked a bit embarrassed. "I know better than to ask that. If your mother hasn't told anyone yet, it's only a matter of time."

"I told her not to say anything until she heard from me and that should hold her for a couple of hours. If I were you, I'd call Mother and Carrie and tell them yourself. Maybe none of this will have to get out, but it couldn't hurt to get them on your side, just in case."

"You're right. That would be the smart thing to do. Do you think they'll fire me when they find out who Suzie's father is?"

Hannah stared at Luanne in amazement. "They hired you without knowing who Suzie's father was. Why would knowing make a difference?"

"Then you don't think they'll care?"

"Oh, they'll care. They'll probably bend your ear right off, trying to convince you to move in with Nettie."

"Because she's all alone now?" Luanne looked a little sad at that thought.

"No, because if you live right here in town, they can get you to work longer hours."

Chapter Twelve

Hannah woke up the next morning to the sound of contented feline purring. It grew louder and when she opened her eyes in the early morning gloom, she saw a pair of yellow eyes staring down at her expectantly.

"Okay, I'm getting up," Hannah said, sitting up with a groan and reaching out to flick off the alarm, which was due to go off any second. Moishe often woke her up right before the alarm sounded and she didn't really mind. Waking up to a purr was much more pleasant than startling awake to eardrum-piercing electronic beeping.

Hannah slipped her feet into the fur-lined moccasins she kept near the bed and padded down the hall to the kitchen. "Come on, Moishe. I'm too tired to fight with you this morning. I'll just give you what you want for breakfast."

Even though she knew she shouldn't have, Hannah'd given in last night and filled Moishe's bowl with his regular kitty crunchies. Tip number six on her vet's list of ways to convince him to eat senior fare hadn't worked any better than tips one through five. Last night's attempt involved drizzling the juice from a can of tuna over the bowl and, for a moment, Hannah thought it might actually be successful. Moishe headed straight for his food bowl and licked the senior pellets with gusto. Unfortunately, that's all he did. When Hannah examined his food more closely, she discovered that

Moishe had licked off every bit of the tuna-flavored juice and left the senior nuggets, pristine and untouched, in his bowl.

The coffee was ready and Hannah poured a cup. She took one bracing sip, then went to the broom closet where she kept Moishe's regular food. When he had been fed and watered, Hannah slugged down a mug of coffee and hurried off to shower and dress.

Hannah often boasted that she could get ready for work on automatic pilot, without completely opening her eyes. This morning was no exception and fifteen minutes later, Hannah walked into the kitchen again. Her eyes were now wide open, her hair was dry, and she was appropriately dressed for her workday in jeans and a long-sleeved top that bore the legend, *Take Life with a Grain of Chocolate.*

Moishe's bowl was empty and Hannah refilled it before settling down at her kitchen table with a fresh cup of coffee and what she'd come to think of as her crime book, the green-lined steno pad she carried with her constantly. This steno pad was no different than the dozen or so steno pads placed in every room of her condo. She'd also taken them to The Cookie Jar and put them in the kitchen, storage room, pantry, and coffee shop. Perhaps it was all those years of attending college lectures and taking notes, but Hannah tended to regard being caught without pen and paper as a sin even worse than substituting margarine for butter in one of her cookie recipes.

What did she know about Sheriff Grant's murder? Hannah paged through her notes. According to the autopsy report, the sheriff died between eight and nine-thirty and the cause of death was a blow to the head with a blunt instrument. Sheriff Grant had been standing a few feet from his car when he was assaulted. The killer then dragged the sheriff's body at least ten yards to the school Dumpster and toppled him inside.

Hannah stopped and stared at her notes. Perhaps it wasn't all that important, but she should find out if Sheriff Grant had been dead, or alive when the killer dragged him to the Dumpster. Andrea could get that information for her. All her sister had to do was call Doc Knight, ask him some trumped up pregnancy question, and get him to talk about the autopsy.

Once Hannah had written *Dumpster—dead or alive?* on her to-do list, she snapped the notebook shut and reached for her jacket. But before she had her arm in the sleeve, the phone rang.

"Mother," Hannah muttered, earning a mini-growl from Moishe. Delores Swensen's name did not appear on his list of favorite people, or even of those people he could tolerate. Hannah dropped her jacket and reached for the phone. "Hello, Mother."

"It's not Mother. It's me," Andrea's voice came over the line. "But I'm calling you about Mother. Do you know what's wrong with her?"

"Many things, but she's our mother and we love her anyway," Hannah shot back with a grin.

"Don't joke, Hannah! I really think there's something wrong. Mother's just not herself and . . . and . . . I couldn't sleep at all last night thinking about it. That's why I'm calling so early."

"Calm down, Andrea. Getting upset isn't good for the baby. What do you mean, Mother's *just not herself?*"

"Well, you know how she feels about Tracey. Mother adores her, right?"

"Absolutely."

"And she loves to spend time with Tracey."

"That's true, she does."

"Well, I called her last night and asked her if she wanted to come to the library with us next Saturday. They're having a special program for kids and their grandparents."

"That's right up Mother's alley. She loves things like that."

"That's what I thought," Andrea said with a sigh, "but Mother didn't seem all that eager. And then, when I suggested that she take Tracey after the program and keep her overnight, she said she'd have to let me know, that she might have other plans."

Hannah frowned. That wasn't like their mother at all. Delores loved to keep Tracey overnight and her granddaughter always came first. "What other plans did Mother have? Did you ask?"

"Of course I did, but she told me it was none of my business. And then she said I should remember that she had a life of her own."

Hannah's mouth dropped open. "Mother has a *life?*"

"That's what she said. Do you think it's a man?"

"Mother?! Not a chance."

"But you'll find out for sure, won't you? You're so good at investigating, Hannah."

"I'll try," Hannah said reluctantly, mentally adding it to her list of things to do, right behind solving the murder and clearing Bill, and just ahead of trying to run a business and get her stubborn cat to eat his new food. "I'll let you know as soon as I find out anything."

"Good. Is there anything I can do to help?"

Hannah bit back the urge to say, *Stop giving me things to do,* and glanced down at her steno pad. "You can help with the murder investigation. Think of some excuse for calling Doc Knight and see if you can get him to tell you whether Sheriff Grant was dead when the killer put him in the Dumpster."

"Yuck!"

"I know, but I don't want to ask Mike for any favors and Bill can't find out this time."

Andrea sighed. "You're right. I'll do it today. I'm not quite as queasy as I was yesterday. I'll get all the results of the autopsy while I'm at it."

"Do you think Doc'll tell you?"

"Of course. I'm a real estate agent. We're trained to get information."

Hannah thanked her sister and hung up the phone. She'd just finished filling Moishe's food and water bowls and was stuffing her steno pad into her purse when the phone rang again. She grabbed it and sat down in the chair again, pulling out her notebook. "That was fast! What did Doc say?"

"What was fast?"

Hannah groaned as she recognized her mother's voice. "Sorry, Mother. I thought it was Andrea. She promised to get back to me."

"Is there something wrong with the new baby?"

"Not that I know of. Why?"

"You mentioned Doc."

"Right," Hannah began to smile. Perhaps she could use her mother's worry about Andrea to her advantage. "Andrea called a couple of minutes ago."

"But it's not even six-thirty yet!"

"I know. She was having trouble sleeping. I told her to call Doc and maybe he could give her something."

"That was a good idea. The poor dear is probably worried sick about Bill."

"Actually, no." Hannah took a deep breath and prepared to drive in the nail. "Andrea's worried about you."

"About me? Why would she worry about *me?*"

"She said you didn't jump at the chance to keep Tracey next Saturday night. And when she asked you why, you told her that you had a life."

"Oh." Delores was silent for a long moment. "Well . . . I suppose I could change my plans and keep Tracey if it's that important to her."

"What plans are those, Mother?"

"None of your business, dear. I may be your mother, but I'm entitled to some privacy when it comes to my personal life."

Hannah gave it up as a bad job. Her mother was almost as stubborn as Moishe. When Delores decided to keep a secret, no one could pry it out of her. "Okay, Mother. We won't discuss it any further."

"Good. You're the daughter with the most sense, Hannah. Except when it comes to men, that is. How you could date that awful Mike Kingston is beyond me!"

Hannah didn't rise to the bait. It was just too early in the morning to fight. "I've got to get to work, Mother. Is there anything specific you wanted?"

"Yes. Thank you for reminding me, dear. I called to tell you that Sheriff Grant's funeral is on Sunday at Jordan High at two o'clock."

"It's at the *school?*"

"Yes, in the auditorium. It's the only place that's large enough. He was very well liked and they expect a huge turnout. You're going, aren't you?"

Hannah sighed. She hated funerals. "I don't know, Mother."

"Well, you have to go. The killer always shows up at the graveside."

"*What?*"

"That's the way it happens in the movies. By the way, all the businesses in town are closing at noon on Saturday as a sign of respect."

"They are?" Hannah was surprised. This was the first she'd heard about it.

"They will when they read the notice in the paper. Carrie and I wrote it up and Rod promised to publish it today."

"Okay, Mother," Hannah said. With Delores and Carrie spearheading the effort, any business in Lake Eden that didn't close at noon on Saturday would be roundly criticized.

"Andrea should go the funeral," Delores went on. "It's right for Bill to stay away since he's a suspect, but the family should be represented."

"So Andrea's going with you?" Hannah asked, glancing up at her apple-shaped clock. The hands were moving inexorably forward and if she wanted to finish most of the baking before Lisa came in, she'd have to leave in less than five minutes.

"She can't go with me dear. The Regency Romance Club is

doing something special. We're all arriving together and we're going to sit behind Nettie in a show of support."

"That's nice, Mother." Hannah said warily. She had the feeling she knew what was coming next.

"That's why I want you to take Andrea. Call her the minute you get to work and tell her you think she should go with you."

Hannah was about to say she still wasn't sure she'd be attending Sheriff Grant's funeral, but before she could even open her mouth, Delores said goodbye and hung up.

"She did it again," Hannah said to Moishe, who was staring at the phone with his ears back. He always seemed to know when his least favorite person called. Delores liked to be the one who ended the conversation and hung up first, and she usually succeeded. It was par for the course for the woman who always wanted the last word.

Chapter
Thirteen

By the time Sunday morning rolled around, Hannah was frustrated beyond belief. She tried the rest of the tips on the list and Moishe hadn't even sampled his new food. She planned to call Doctor Bob in the morning to see if he had any new suggestions, but for the present, she was stumped. And since she didn't feel like fighting with her stubborn four-footed roommate this morning, she caved in again.

Moishe gave a sound that was half purr, half grateful mew as Hannah filled his bowl with his regular crunchies. But instead of gobbling them up as he usually did, he came over to rub against her ankles.

"You're welcome," Hannah said, pouring her second cup of coffee. "You can go ahead and eat. I'll just sit at the kitchen table and wake up."

As Moishe crunched happily, Hannah's thoughts turned to Sheriff Grant's murder. For the most part she was getting nowhere fast, but one of her questions had been answered. Although Doc Knight had refused to give Andrea a copy of the autopsy report, he answered her question off-the-record. The blow Sheriff Grant suffered to the back of his skull killed him almost instantly.

Hannah's suspect list was growing, although she doubted that any of them had murdered Sheriff Grant. There was Nettie, who had no alibi, and Luanne, who didn't have one either. Then there was Bill, but Hannah refused to add him to her suspect list. It would have been great if they'd been able to track down Bill's second call, but Hannah called every roofing company in the county and found that none of them used telemarketers. Andrea and Tracey drove all over to look for anyone either getting a new roof or having their old roof repaired, and Herb had kept a sharp eye out for roofing trucks on his rounds. They all did their best, but the roofer who may or may not have been working in the Lake Eden area was still anonymous.

After another bracing sip of coffee, Hannah stood up and stretched. It was time to start the day. The Cookie Jar wasn't open on Sundays, but she decided to go in anyway to take inventory of their supplies. Since it was a relatively clean job that shouldn't take more than a couple of hours, she dressed in something appropriate for a funeral, and wore an apron over it just in case.

"You might know it!" Hannah muttered from the top of the stepstool, as the phone in the kitchen of The Cookie Jar began to ring. She waited through three rings, juggling a canister of cocoa in one hand and a bag of flaked coconut in the other, then set them back on the shelf and climbed down. It was almost impossible for her to ignore a ringing phone. It could be an emergency, something she needed to respond to right away. It could be Bill, saying that Andrea had gone to the hospital to have the new baby. It could be Norman, calling from the dental convention, trying the shop because he'd been unable to reach her at her condo. It could be Mike, saying that he'd caught the murderer and Bill was free to come back to work. And it could be a salesman, which was much more likely, even on a Sunday.

Hannah hurried across the floor and grabbed the phone. "The Cookie Jar. Hannah speaking."

"Oh, Hannah! I'm so glad I caught you!"

Hannah gripped the phone a little tighter. It was Andrea and she sounded frazzled. "What's wrong, Andrea?"

"Uh-oh! Just hang on a second, okay?"

Hannah listened to the sound of the open line. She heard soft footsteps and then a bang and a click as a door closed and locked. "Andrea?"

"It's okay. I'm here now." Andrea's voice was not much more than a whisper.

"Where's here?"

"In the bathroom."

"Why are you whispering?"

"Because Bill just came back to the bedroom and I don't want him to hear what I'm saying. Hold on again, Hannah. He's knocking on the door."

Hannah held on. What else could she do? She heard Andrea say something to Bill, but her words were muffled. Then she heard what sounded like running water. "Andrea?"

"I'm still here. I just told Bill you called me and I had to take the phone in here, because I had to . . . you know. Can you come over early, Hannah? Please?"

Hannah glanced toward the open pantry. She'd just started the inventory and if she stopped now, she'd have to come in early tomorrow morning to finish. On the other hand, she could bring Andrea here and her sister could write things down as Hannah counted them. "I could come early. But why?"

"Bill's cleaning out my closet. I'm trying to be understanding, but he keeps asking me why I'm keeping certain things and I just want to kill him!" There was a whoosh as Andrea took a deep breath and let out again. "It's terrible, Hannah. He actually said I should throw away that wonderful pair of red clogs I bought at the mall last summer."

Hannah remembered the clogs. Andrea had taken advantage of a giant shoe sale and paid only five dollars for them. "But you told me that they hurt your feet when you wore them. You said they practically crippled you."

"I know, but it's just a matter of getting used to them, that's all."

"You mean you have to break them in?"

"Not exactly. Clogs are wood. They don't break in. But my feet will adapt."

Hannah wanted to say that feet shouldn't have to adapt to shoes; shoes should adapt to feet. Andrea was crazy if she thought otherwise, but Hannah resisted the urge to tell her so. It wasn't a warm, supporting comment to make to a sister who was beginning to resemble the Goodyear blimp.

"So can you pick me up early, Hannah? I just don't know how much more of this closet cleaning I can handle."

"Sure," Hannah said, not wanting to deny Andrea anything at this stage of her pregnancy. "Can you be ready in fifteen minutes?"

"I can be ready in less time than that. Just hurry, Hannah. He's driving me nuts and I'm afraid I'll say something I'll regret later. I do love him, you know."

"I know."

Hannah hung up to the sound of a toilet flushing. Andrea was obviously pulling out all the stops to convince Bill that she'd had to take the phone in the bathroom.

"There's Mother," Andrea said, nudging Hannah as they walked into the lobby of the Jordan High auditorium. Even though they arrived a half-hour early, the Lake Eden Regency Romance Club was already there in full force.

Hannah glanced in the direction of Andrea's gaze and caught her mother's gesture. "Uh-oh. She wants us to come over."

"We might as well do it," Andrea said with a sigh, taking a step in her mother's direction. "She probably wants to criticize your outfit."

"What's wrong with my outfit?" Hannah looked down at her navy blue dress and shoes.

"Nothing, but Mother'll find something. Do you want me to head her off at the pass?"

"That would be great. Do you think you can?"

"Of course. Just watch."

Hannah watched as Andrea sailed up to their mother and whispered something in her ear. Delores looked surprised for a moment and then she smiled from ear to ear, an unusual expression at a funeral. There was another volley of whispered conversation and then the two parted, and Andrea came back to Hannah's side.

"It's so crowded, I thought I was going to get bowled over before I got back here. Mother says hi. Let's go talk to some other people before she remembers what she wanted to talk to us about in the first place."

Hannah glanced out over the crowd and spotted Beatrice Koester. "There's Beatrice and Ted. I want to ask him about his mother's cupcakes."

"The ones with the secret ingredient?"

"Right. Just stick behind me and I'll run interference." Hannah led the way across the crowded lobby, clearing a path for her sister. Beatrice looked as she always did, neat as a pin in a charcoal gray dress with a white collar. Ted, however, was tugging at the sleeves of his suit and Hannah was sure he'd rather be wearing his coveralls and towing a car on his flatbed.

"I'm glad you're here, Ted," Hannah said, once she'd greeted Beatrice and made sure that Andrea had engaged her in conversation.

"Why's that?" Ted frowned slightly and his heavy eyebrows almost touched.

"I've been trying to figure out that recipe for your mother's cupcakes."

"Beatrice has been working on it at home and I've never had so many bad cupcakes shoved down my throat. I finally had to tell her to knock it off."

"Oh," Hannah said, biting back a smile at the mental image Ted's words had created. Beatrice was a small woman, barely five feet tall, while Ted topped six feet and looked as if could eat a whole cow for breakfast. "I thought it might help if you could describe your mother's cupcakes for me."

"Chocolate. And when you bit in, it wasn't all air. You know what I mean?"

"I think so. They were heavy?"

"I'll say!" Ted gave a little grin, exposing one silver-capped tooth. Hannah remembered Norman saying he'd like to recap it in something that looked like real tooth enamel. "A tin of her cupcakes probably weighed as much as an air filter."

Hannah had the insane urge to laugh, but she asked another question instead. "What else do you remember about them?"

"The frosting. Best fudge frosting I ever ate. My mother was some cook!"

"I'll bet she was," Hannah said, wondering if she'd ever have a child who'd say that about her. "Was there anything really unusual about the cupcakes? Something you haven't mentioned?"

Ted thought for a moment and then he nodded. "Yeah. The paper cups were gold foil and she had them sent from a place in Chicago."

Before Hannah could even think about asking another question, the doors to the auditorium opened and people began filing inside. The Koesters got in line with the other mourners, but Andrea grabbed Hannah's hand and tugged her around to the side door so that they could avoid the crowd.

Someone, undoubtedly Digger Gibson, Lake Eden's funeral director, had arranged for soft organ music to play over the auditorium speaker system. Hannah recognized "Largo." Digger had played the same piece at her father's funeral and it brought back depressing memories. "I hate funerals," she sighed.

"Me, too," Andrea echoed the sentiment and motioned Hannah into the back row of seats on the left side of the auditorium. "You take the second seat and I'll take the aisle. That way we'll have this row to ourselves."

Hannah moved sideways to take the second seat. "Only until someone asks us to stand up so they can squeeze past us."

"That won't happen." Andrea sat down in the aisle seat and pointed to the seatback, which was only an inch shy of touching her stomach. "Since I'm so big, no one can squeeze past me. And there's no way they'll have the nerve to ask me to get up and move out into the aisle."

Hannah bit back a grin as she put her purse down on the empty seat next to her. It seemed that pregnancy had some perks. She was about to say that when Sean and Don, the twins who ran the gas station and convenience store out on the highway, came in the side door and took the seats directly in front of them.

"Hi, Andrea. Hannah," either Sean or Don greeted them. Hannah couldn't tell them apart since they were wearing suits instead of their Quick Stop shirts with the names embroidered over the pockets.

"Hi, Sean," Hannah said, deciding that guessing was worth it since she had a fifty percent change of getting it right.

"I'm Don. He's Sean."

"You win some and you lose some," Hannah muttered under her breath. "Sorry, guys. You know I can't tell you apart. Who's minding the store?"

"We're closed," the other twin said, the one whose name, Hannah now knew, was Sean. "We figured we should come to the service to prove we weren't mad at Sheriff Grant."

"Mad?" Hannah's ears perked up.

Don nodded. "He told us we couldn't sell those little cordial chocolates anymore. Sean explained that we never sold them to kids, but Sheriff Grant said it didn't matter, that if they had one drop of alcohol in them, we needed a liquor license.

"And they were our best selling candy," Sean complained.

"I don't think we would have minded so much," Don went on, "but he walked over the shelf, loaded them all up in a box, and confiscated them."

"And we could have returned them for credit," Sean added.

"Is that legal?" Hannah asked, glancing over at Andrea.

"I don't know." Andrea gave a little shrug and then her eyes narrowed. "I bet you guys were really mad."

"We were steaming," Don admitted, evidently not realized he'd just given them a motive for murder.

"Yes, we were." Sean looked a little sheepish. "I wanted to go out to the station and demand them back, but Don stopped me."

"I told him it wasn't smart to make a county sheriff mad. And then, when we found out Sheriff Grant had been murdered, I was really glad I'd stopped Sean from going out there."

"I was glad too," Sean added, standing up to let some people into their aisle.

While the twins were busy making small talk with their new seatmates, Andrea nudged Hannah. "Did you get that?"

"I did and it's a motive . . . sort of. I wonder which twin was working on Monday night? And I wonder what the other twin was doing?"

"I'll ask around," Andrea promised. "I know a couple people who can tell them apart."

"Good. So what did you say to Mother to make her forget about criticizing me?"

"Oh, that." Andrea gave a nonchalant shrug. "I just told her that if the baby was a girl we were going to use her name."

Hannah's eyes widened. "But I thought you told Bill's mother that if you had a girl, you'd use *her* name."

"I did."

"But . . ." Hannah stopped speaking and sighed. "Okay. I

know you think it's a boy, but what happens if it's a girl? You can't use both names. Mother and Regina would be all upset over which one you put first."

Andrea shook her head. "Relax, Hannah. I *know* it's a boy. I had the test. Just don't tell anyone, okay? Bill's old-fashioned and he wants to be surprised."

The service was long and Hannah shifted uncomfortably in her seat. It seemed everyone who had known Sheriff Grant wanted to give some sort of eulogy. Hannah felt sorry for Nettie Grant, who had to sit through it all and be gracious. Why did people feel they had to *share* so much? Hannah could care less that Sheriff Grant had once helped Lydia Gradin get her car out of the ditch in the middle of a snowstorm.

"I'm glad the casket's closed," Andrea leaned over to whisper to Hannah. "Otherwise it looks like dead people are just sleeping and they might get up any minute."

Hannah didn't want to mention why an open casket would have been impossible. She'd seen Sheriff Grant right after his demise and there was no way that Digger could work a miracle of that magnitude with putty and makeup.

It seemed as if the line of people who were waiting to sing Sheriff Grant's praises in life would never end. Hannah glanced at her watch and saw that over an hour and a half had passed. She was almost ready to nudge Andrea and ask her to pretend that she'd gone into labor so that they could leave, when Digger went to the podium.

"We all loved Sheriff Grant and I know some of you have been waiting for quite a while to give your remembrances of him, but out of courtesy to his widow, I'll ask you to be seated so that we can conclude the service."

Hannah breathed a big sigh of relief when a final tribute had been uttered and the service ended. After a reminder that there would be a brief ceremony at graveside, Hannah and Andrea slipped out of the row and headed for the parking lot.

"Are you okay?" Hannah asked, unlocking the passenger door so that Andrea could get into the cookie truck.

"I'm fine. I just don't want to go to graveside, that's all. That always depresses me and I just read an article that said a mother's emotions can affect her unborn baby."

"Okay," Hannah put her truck in gear. "I'll have to hurry and take you home then. I need to go out to the cemetery."

"But why?"

"I need to check the crowd. The killer might be there."

"You think?" Andrea looked surprised.

"It's Mother's idea. She saw it in a movie."

Andrea shrugged. "It's worth a try. Go ahead, Hannah. I'll wait in your truck and watch for anyone who drives in and lurks around."

"Thanks, Andrea." Hannah put the truck in gear and drove out of the parking lot. "I can always use another pair of eyes."

"I know, and it's going to cost you."

"I figured that," Hannah said, gesturing toward the rear of the truck. "I've got a couple of dozen cookies back there."

"What kind are they?"

"Surprise cookies. They were Lisa's idea and they're leftovers from the meeting I catered last night."

"What's the surprise?"

"If I told you, it wouldn't be a surprise." Hannah reached back to get one of the bags and handed it to Andrea. "Taste one and tell me if you like them."

Andrea bit into the cookie and smiled. "This is good, Hannah, and I love the chewy part in the middle. Is it a chocolate-covered nut?"

"It could be. Try another one. Lisa put at least a half-dozen different surprises in the middles."

"Mmm," Andrea bit into another cookie. "This one tastes like some kind of nougat. I like these, Hannah. They're fun because you don't know what you're going to get. How do you make them?"

"Bridge mix."

"What?"

"Bridge mix. You've had it before, Andrea. It's mixed kinds of chocolate candy in a bag. They've got it down at the Red Owl."

"I know exactly which candy you mean."

"Lisa says if they're out of bridge mix, you can use those miniature candy bars they have for Halloween. All you have to do is cut them up into pieces."

"Good idea," Andrea said, taking another cookie. "Did you decide on your cookies yet, Hannah?"

"What cookies?" Hannah pulled up to the gates of Brookside Cemetery and parked outside the wrought iron fence. She could see Sheriff Grant's grave in the distance, but no one was there yet. The mourners were probably still at the school, paying their respects to Nettie.

"The cookies you're going to bring to the Halloween party."

"Not yet," Hannah said, mentally adding the Halloween cookies to her list of things to do. "Are you sure you want to stay here by yourself?"

"I'm sure." Andrea clutched the bag of cookies a little tighter. "I should be able to see the back of the crowd from here. Make sure you stand on the other side of the grave and then we'll have it covered."

"Good idea. Anything else?"

"Yes. Do you think you can duck out before they say the final prayer? I don't want to be here when they lower the casket. I just hate that part."

"Me, too," Hannah said, knowing that Andrea was thinking about their father and reaching out to give her a hug.

Surprise Cookies

Do NOT preheat the oven—dough
must chill before baking

1 cup melted butter *(2 sticks)*
1 cup white sugar
½ cup brown sugar
2 beaten eggs *(just whip them up with a fork)*
1 teaspoon baking soda
½ teaspoon salt
1 teaspoon vanilla
2 Tablespoons water *(or coffee, if you have some left over from breakfast)*
3 cups flour *(no need to sift)*
1 package bridge mix or assorted chocolate candies ***
4 to 5 dozen walnut halves *(or pecan halves)*

*** If I can't find bridge mix, I like to use chocolate wafers or Hershey's assorted miniature candy bars cut into four pieces. You can even use full size chocolate candy bars if you cut them up into small pieces.

Melt the butter and mix in the sugars. Add the beaten eggs, baking soda, salt, vanilla, and water (or coffee).

Add the flour and mix thoroughly. Then chill the dough for at least an hour (*overnight is fine, too*).

Preheat oven to 375 degrees F., rack in the middle position.

Scoop out a tablespoon of dough and form it around a chocolate wafer (*or a piece of cut up candy bar*). Place a walnut half (or pecan half) on top and place it on a greased baking sheet, 12 cookies to a standard sheet.

Bake at 375 degrees F. for 10 to 12 minutes, or until nicely browned. Cool on cookie sheet for two minutes and then transfer the cookies to a wire rack.

Yield: 8 to 10 dozen, depending on cookie size.

(When I use Hershey's miniatures, Mother always tries to guess which cookies have the Krackles bars inside. If she gets one with a piece of Mr. Goodbar, she passes it to me.)

Chapter Fourteen

There was no one suspicious at graveside, unless Hannah wanted to count Bertie Straub, who stared at the casket throughout the short service without blinking. But Hannah knew that Bertie was probably trying to figure out what Nettie had spent on the funeral. Andrea didn't see anyone that struck a sour note either, and Hannah had kicked herself all the way home for even considering taking a tip from her mother.

"Hi, Moishe," Hannah called out, opening the door to her condo and bracing herself to receive the flying ball of orange and white fur that hurtled itself in her arms. She carried him in the kitchen, set him down by his food bowl, and filled it with the food he liked. Then she headed off to her bedroom to put on her usual Sunday attire.

Five minutes later, dressed in jeans and an old pullover sweater, Hannah settled down on the couch to vegetate. She was a bit hungry, but that could wait. She wanted the mindless oblivion of a documentary on something of absolutely no interest to her. Then she could curl up and doze and perhaps catch up on some of the sleep she'd lost since Sheriff Grant had been killed.

Hannah woke up to a ringing phone and an announcer's nasal voice describing the mating habits of the dung beetle.

She reached out for the phone and said hello before she realized that she could have let the answering machine get it.

"Oh, Hannah! I'm so glad you're home!"

It was Andrea's voice and Hannah almost groaned out loud. She wasn't sure she had the patience to sympathize with another domestic crisis tonight. But sisterly concern took precedence over things like sleep, and food, and personal time at home. "What's the matter, Andrea?"

"Bill cleaned out the refrigerator while we were at Sheriff Grant's funeral and he threw out all my nail polish!"

Hannah wondered if she should have her hearing checked. Or perhaps she was still asleep and this was one of those strange dreams that didn't make any sense. She could have sworn that Andrea had said *nail polish*. "Bill threw out your what?"

"My nail polish."

Hannah was relieved to know that her hearing was fine, and she must be awake if she'd heard Andrea correctly. But asleep or awake, she was still confused by her sister's answer. "Why do you keep nail polish in the refrigerator?"

"It lasts longer that way. You know how after you use about half a bottle, the rest gets all gunky and thick?"

"No."

Andrea sighed so loudly that Hannah could hear it over the line. "You'd know it if you wore nail polish. And you should, Hannah. Your nails are a disgrace. Mother and I were just talking about . . ."

"Forget it, Andrea," Hannah interrupted. "In my line of work, nail polish would last about five seconds before I ruined it."

"You're right, I suppose. Anyway . . . if you keep nail polish in the refrigerator, it doesn't dry out. I read that in a beauty tip column and it really works. I keep mine in those little round cups on the door."

"The egg keepers?"

"So that's what they're for! Anyway, I used to keep the bottles in the meat drawer, but they rolled around in there. I moved them to the egg keepers and they fit really nice."

"And Bill threw out all the bottles?"

"Well . . . he didn't actually throw them out, but he might just as well have. He took them out and put them in a box for safekeeping. And now he can't remember where he put the box. I just know that by the time we find it, the polish will be all gunky. That's why I need to get out of here, Hannah. I'm really mad at him and I have to cool off. And there's another reason, too."

"What's that?" Hannah asked, settling back on the sofa. This could take a while.

"Bill said that since Tracey's gone, he's going to clean out the attic tonight."

"Where's Tracey?"

"At Mother's. She called and asked if Tracey could stay overnight. I think she felt guilty because she turned me down the other day."

Hannah snorted. "Guilty? Mother?"

"You're right. That can't be it. But Bill's going to want me to go up to the attic with him and I just know we're going to have a big fight over which things to toss and which things to keep."

"And if you're busy and you can't help him, he might forget the attic and do something innocuous like watch sports on television?"

"Exactly. So what time can you pick me up?"

Hannah shook her head to clear it and glanced at her watch. It was already eight-fifteen. "Forty-five minutes?"

"Perfect. I'll think of some excuse for Bill. Just honk the horn when you get here and I'll come right out."

"I brought the list of suspects Nettie gave us," Andrea said, as Hannah backed out the driveway. "I thought we could go over it together and try to remember if we spotted any of them at the funeral."

"That's good. Where are we going?"

"Let's go to Bertanelli's. I'm in the mood for one of their pizzas."

"You didn't have dinner?"

"Of course I did, but I didn't eat very much. Bill made chicken and it wasn't very good. You drive and I'll call a couple of names on the way there."

Hannah glanced at her watch. It was already nine-fifteen. "It's a little late to call now, isn't it?"

"For here it is, but I haven't checked out Ivan Hill yet. He lives in California and it's only seven-fifteen out there."

Hannah took the road out of town. If Andrea wanted a pizza, that's what they'd get. "Who's Ivan Hill?"

"The father of the other boy in the car when Jamie was killed."

"Right," Hannah said and turned onto the highway. If what Nettie told them was accurate, Ivan Hill could be their killer. Sheriff Grant had been harassing Mr. Hill, calling him on the phone and trying to dig up evidence that his son had been drinking and driving, even when the initial accident report clearly stated that Jamie was behind the wheel. Sheriff Grant couldn't bring himself to blame his son, not even when the lab reports confirmed that Jamie's blood-alcohol level had been three times the legal limit. Nettie had said it was possible that the long-suffering Mr. Hill finally snapped and decided to end her husband's harassment.

Hannah kept her eyes on the road, but she listened as Andrea placed the call and got Ivan's wife on the line. Once Andrea had explained that Sheriff Grant was dead, the rest of the conversation was one-sided and there was little Hannah could learn from phrases like "Oh, that's too bad," and "I'm so sorry."

"Well, that was a waste," Andrea said, disconnecting the

call and tossing her phone back in her purse. "Ivan Hill had a heart attack the night before Sheriff Grant was murdered."

"He's dead?"

"No, he's going to make it. But his wife said they had to do a triple bypass and he's still hooked up to all kinds of monitors. He's in the clear, Hannah. There's no way he flew to Minnesota less than a day after open-heart surgery and bashed in Sheriff Grant's head."

"I guess not," Hannah said, turning in at their favorite pizza place. Bertram and Ellie Kuehn owned the pizzeria and between the two of them, they couldn't come up with a single drop of Italian blood. But when they ran their first names together, it sounded Italian and that's why they'd named their place Bertanelli's.

"I can hardly wait," Andrea said, unbuckling her seat belt and getting out of the truck. "I'll make more calls while we're waiting for our order. I want an Ellie's special with everything on it. How about you?"

"That's fine with me. How about the anchovies?" Hannah raced a little to keep up. Even though Andrea complained she was having trouble with her balance, she could certainly move fast when there was food involved.

"Hold on. Let me check." Andrea stopped in mid-waddle and looked down at her ankles. Even in the dim glow of the neon sign that beckoned them to the best pizza in Winnetka County, Hannah could see that they were swollen.

"You'd better not," Hannah advised. "Your ankles look like sausages."

"I know. I probably shouldn't eat pizza either, but I really want it."

"Let's compromise," Hannah suggested. "We'll get a medium pizza instead of a large and then you won't eat as much."

Andrea gave her a saucy grin as she pushed open the door and the aroma of freshly baked pizza embraced them. "Wanna bet?"

Five minutes later, they'd placed their order and were waiting at a table in the back with large diet cokes and a tray con-
taining glass shakers of Parmesan cheese and crushed red
peppers, and a basket of moist towelettes in individual foil
packages.

"I love this place," Andrea said, looking around her with
pure adoration. "Their pizza's the best and they always . . ."

"What is it?" Hannah asked, when Andrea stopped speaking abruptly.

Andrea took a deep breath and when she replied, her voice
was shaking. "It's him!"

"Who's *him?*" Hannah asked, wondering if there was a
more grammatically correct way to ask the question.

"Mike." Andrea said his name with pure distaste. "He's
sitting in a booth in near the front with someone I don't
know. She's wearing a sheriff's department jacket, so maybe
Mike hired her to . . ." Andrea stopped and swallowed hard,
". . . replace Bill."

Hannah sat up straighter for a better view and her stomach slammed all the way down to her toes as she caught sight
of Mike. He was so handsome and she was so ready for this
whole fight to be over. Here he was, a mere twenty feet away,
and she couldn't even smile at him the way the new deputy
was doing, or reach out and take his hand the way the new
deputy was doing, or . . . Hannah gasped as the new deputy
turned to look toward their booth.

"What's the matter?" This time it was Andrea's turn to
ask. "Your face just turned a really funny color."

"That would be green."

"What?"

"Never mind. The woman with Mike isn't a new deputy."

"Well, that's a relief! Who is she then?"

Hannah decided to answer, even though it wasn't a relief
at all. "Her name is Shawna Lee Quinn."

"What a name! She sounds like an actress, or a singer."

Or an exotic dancer, Hannah thought, but she didn't say

it. "She's the newest civilian employee at the station. Sheriff Grant hired her when one of the secretaries retired."

"How do you know that?"

"The last time I was out at the station, when I was still speaking to him, Mike introduced me to her."

"Oh. Well, what is she doing with Mike?"

Hannah sighed. "Probably everything."

"What?"

"Never mind. Maybe Mike promised her dinner if she stayed late. He's the acting sheriff and he could do that."

"She's certainly attractive," Andrea commented, watching as Shawna Lee slipped out of the jacket, "and she knows how to dress. That's a really expensive sweater."

Yeah, too bad they didn't have it in her size! Hannah bit back the old taunt from high school.

"Oh, good. Here comes our pizza." Andrea was all smiles as the waitress approached their table. "Half for you and half for me?"

"Right," Hannah said, even though any appetite she'd managed to drum up had disappeared right along with the jacket that Shawna Lee had removed to show off her incredible figure. Hannah remembered thinking that the secretary was pretty when Mike had introduced them, but she hadn't been jealous. Of course that had been a work situation and she hadn't seen Shawna Lee in action. Tonight was different. Tonight she acted as if she were out on a date with Mike, looking up at him under her lashes and reaching out to touch his arm. Maybe she *was* on a date with Mike. It certainly wasn't impossible. After all, Hannah had made it clear that she didn't want anything to do with him.

"Have some pizza, Hannah." Andrea looked concerned as she noticed the direction of Hannah's gaze. "You don't want him. He's a jerk and he wasn't fair to Bill."

"Right."

"Not only that, they deserve each other. I saw her batting

her eyes at the man in the next booth while Mike was reading the menu. She's probably about as loyal as Mike is."

"Right."

"So have some pizza and forget about Mike. You're better off without him. You wouldn't want to be seen with the kind of man who . . ." Andrea stopped speaking as her phone rang. She dived into her purse with her hand to retrieve it. "Hello?"

Hannah spared Mike one more glance and then reached out for the pizza. She'd be darned if she'd let him spoil a perfectly good pizza for her!

"Hi, Doc. I didn't think doctors worked on Sundays."

Hannah bit into the pizza and chewed thoughtfully. It must be Doc Knight, getting back to Andrea about some question she'd asked.

"I've got a couple of minutes if you don't mind me chewing and talking at the same time. Hannah and I just ordered a pizza."

Hannah took another bite of her pizza and frowned slightly. It wasn't quite as good as it had been in the past. Of course, the last pizza she'd eaten in Bertanelli's had been with Mike. And they'd been seated in the very same booth where he now sat with Shawna Lee.

"Oh, no!" Andrea groaned, snapping Hannah out of her unhappy thoughts. "You know me, Doc. I've never been anemic in my life. You're kidding, right?"

Hannah's full attention shifted to her sister. Andrea had sounded positively panic stricken.

"All right, I will," Andrea said with a deep sigh, "but I hope you know what you're doing. You have no idea how awful this is going to be for me."

Hannah's frown was a full-scale glower by the time Andrea said goodbye and turned off the phone. "What did Doc say? You're going to be all right, aren't you?"

"I'll be fine as long as I follow his advice."

"Which is?" Hannah asked, leaning back and waiting.

"I'm anemic and I'm retaining water. Those two things aren't good for the baby. I'm supposed to up my prenatal vitamins to two a day, I have to get at least nine hours sleep, and I can't have any salt in my diet."

"Uh-oh," Hannah groaned, looking at the pizza.

"You take it home with you. I can't have any more." Andrea looked extremely depressed.

"I can understand why you're upset," Hannah said, waving at the waitress and gesturing for a carry-out container.

"No, you can't. I haven't told you the worst part yet. Doc wanted to stick me in the hospital until the baby was born, but he said he wouldn't as long as I agreed to a restriction."

"What restriction?"

"I can't be on my feet for more than four hours a day!"

"Uh-oh," Hannah said with a wince. For a person like Andrea, who was usually on the go for most of her waking hours, Doc's restriction would be a real hardship. "Try to look on the bright side, Andrea. It's only for a couple more weeks."

Andrea opened her mouth. Hannah had the uncomfortable feeling that she was about to get blasted with a megadose of her sister's ire when Andrea's cell phone rang again. "Saved by the bell," she murmured, as Andrea answered the phone.

"Hi, honey," Andrea chirped, in a real effort to be cheerful. That told Hannah that her caller was either Tracey or Bill. "Harry Wilcox? Of course I remember him! He's okay, isn't he?"

Hannah listened as she scooped the pizza into the carryout box the waitress had brought, but she didn't learn much of interest by hearing Andrea say *yes* five times in a row.

"Let's go, Hannah." Andrea dropped her phone in her purse and stood up. "Bill just got a call from Harry Wilcox and he wants us to come back to the house right away."

Hannah met Harry Wilcox, a veteran Winnetka County

Deputy, during Bill's first year on the force. Harry had been Bill's mentor and also his first partner. "Harry and his wife are okay, aren't they?"

"They're fine. It's just that Harry heard about Sheriff Grant's murder and he called Bill to talk about it. Bill says Harry had an idea about why the sheriff might have been killed."

"Okay. I'm ready." Hannah grabbed the takeout box and was about to leave the booth when Andrea grabbed her arm.

"Let's walk past Mike's booth on the way out. When he says hello to us, we can cut him dead."

"Really, Andrea!" Hannah did her best to sound shocked. "Don't you think that's a little childish?"

Andrea thought about it for a moment and then she dipped her head in a nod. "I guess it is a little childish. I don't blame you for not wanting to do it."

"Did I say *that?*" Hannah countered with a grin. "We'll walk on by and let him see what he's missing."

The two Swensen sisters linked arms and set off in tandem toward Mike's booth. They arranged fixed smiles on their faces and they kept their eyes straight ahead. Hannah sneaked a glance at Mike's booth and her smile slipped alarmingly. He was paying so much attention to Shawna Lee he didn't even notice them.

Hannah marched straight past the booth without a second glance. As she opened the door and ushered her sister out, she vowed that Mike would pay for not even glancing their way. She wasn't sure how, but she'd exact a price one way or another.

Chapter Fifteen

Andrea gave an exasperated sigh as Hannah approached her house. "Bill did it again!"

"Did what?"

"He put the trash cans in front of the driveway again. Do you want me to move them so you can drive in?"

"Don't bother. I can park right here behind Bill's car. There's plenty of room."

Once Hannah had parked, Andrea led the way to the front door and fumbled in her purse for her keys. "I hope Harry called at the right time."

"What time is that?"

"Before Bill finished cleaning the attic. If I'm lucky, he didn't get to that big box by the chimney and I won't have to answer a bunch of questions about why I saved all those back issues of fashion magazines."

"Hi, honey!" Bill called out as they walked into the house. "Bring Hannah back here to the kitchen. I made coffee for her."

Hannah followed Andrea into the kitchen and they sat down at the kitchen table. Once Hannah cupped her hands around the mug of coffee that Bill had brewed, and inhaled the fragrance, she smiled. "This is real coffee!"

"It's French roast. I ground the beans myself," Bill told her, and then he turned to Andrea. "Doc Knight called here and I gave him your cell phone number. There's nothing wrong, is there?"

Andrea sighed. "Nothing that a little rest won't cure. I'm anemic and I'm retaining water."

"I was afraid it would be something like that. It's a good thing I'm home, because now I can take care of you. Doc gave you instructions, didn't he?"

"Yes, he did." Andrea rolled her eyes behind Bill's back, and Hannah did all she could do to not laugh. "We can talk about that later. Tell us what Harry had to say. Hannah's got to get home soon."

"I'll tell you just as soon as you get on the couch and put your feet up. Your ankles are swelling again. Come on, Hannah. Bring your coffee and come into the living room."

Once Andrea was settled on the couch, Bill told them the gist of his conversation with Harry. "He said Sheriff Grant gave him a choice between early retirement with full benefits or a demotion in rank. It was all because of a case he was working."

"What case was that?" Andrea wanted to know.

"The Dew Drop Inn case."

"Oh, that!" Andrea exclaimed and sat up a little straighter. "Do you remember it, Hannah?"

"No. But I know the building that Sean and Ron turned into The Quick Stop used to be the Dew Drop Inn."

"You must have been away at college at the time," Andrea said. "It was in all the papers. Sheriff Grant closed it down in a big raid for illegal gambling and selling liquor after hours."

"It happened right before the last election," Bill explained. "It was all over the papers and it's probably the reason Sheriff Grant won by a landslide."

"That's what everybody said at the time," Andrea recalled. "But I don't remember reading anything about Harry Wilcox in any of the papers."

"That's because his name wasn't there. Sheriff Grant took over the case on the day of the raid and claimed credit for everything Harry did. And when Harry complained, Sheriff Grant accused him of insubordination and forced him into early retirement."

Andrea's mouth dropped open. "That's horrible! I just can't believe Sheriff Grant had the gall to take Harry's case right out from under his nose like that!"

"Well, he did. And Harry said that if we dug back into the records, we might find a pattern. He figured that if Sheriff Grant stole his case, he might have stolen other cases to win the other elections."

"Makes sense. And it's motive," Hannah said, pulling out her notebook and writing it down.

Andrea frowned slightly. "What do you mean?"

"Harry was pretty mad about being taken off the Dew Drop Inn case, wasn't he, Bill?"

"He sure was! It was the biggest case of his career and Sheriff Grant stole all the glory. But he told me that there was nothing he could do about it. He needed that retirement money and Sheriff Grant didn't give him any options."

"The biggest case of his career," Hannah murmured. "That's got to hurt when it happens. Even now when it's years later, it still has to rankle. I can see where someone might want to even the score."

"Harry?" Bill sounded shocked. "That's crazy, Hannah. There's no way Harry flew back here from Arizona and killed Sheriff Grant!"

Hannah took another sip of her coffee. It really was very good. "I didn't mean Harry . . . necessarily. What if the lead man on one of those other cases decided to put a permanent stop to Sheriff Grant's stolen glory?"

"You mean kill Sheriff Grant before he could do it again?" Andrea asked, looking a little sick.

"That's right. Who would know about all those old cases?"

Bill shrugged. "They'd be in the old files, but it would take months to dig through them all."

"We don't have to do that," Andrea said, looking very pleased with herself.

"We don't?" Hannah asked.

"Of course not. We'll just get it from the horse's mouth."

"But Sheriff Grant's dead," Hannah pointed out.

"I meant the other horse, Secretariat," Andrea said. When they just stared at her, she started to laugh. "I made a joke! Barbara Donnelly's been Sheriff Grant's *secretary* for years and she knows everything that goes on at the station. That's why I said *Secretariat*, get it?"

"Brilliant," Hannah said with a grin. Andrea's joke was good considering that it came from a hugely pregnant wife whose husband was suspected of murder. "Barbara should be able to tell us about past elections, but she might not know what Sheriff Grant was intending for this year. We have to find out if any deputy was working on a big case, one that Sheriff Grant could have planned to use to win the race against Bill."

Bill sighed so deeply it came out as a groan. "This suspension is just about killing me! If I could just go to the station and talk to the other guys, I could find out in two seconds flat. But that's not allowed."

"It's okay, honey," Andrea spoke softly, reacting to the tone of frustration in her husband's voice. "You're doing a lot to help."

"Maybe. I just wish I could do more. At least I'm here to make sure you get your proper rest and nutrition. And I'm getting some things done around the house. That reminds me . . . I threw out a whole box of old fashion magazines I found in the attic. You must have stuck them up there and forgotten about them. That's one job that's done."

"You finished cleaning out the attic?" Andrea's voice shook slightly and Hannah wondered what else her sister had squirreled away up there.

"I sure did. It wasn't hard once I carried down all those bags of old clothes."

Andrea gasped. "But I was saving those for Tracey to play dress up!"

"She never could have used that many. There must have been dozens of them. I called my dad and he came to get them. Mom's going to use them for quilts."

Andrea tipped her head up and looked toward the ceiling, and Hannah suspected she was asking for divine intervention to keep her from killing Bill. Perhaps this would be a good time to leave. "I'd better be going," Hannah said, getting to her feet. "I've got to get up early tomorrow."

"Me, too." Bill also rose to his feet. "I'm going to repaint this room tomorrow."

"Oh?" Hannah asked, since Andrea seemed incapable of speech.

"Dad promised to run down to the hardware store to pick up the paint for me. I thought I'd get a really bright yellow to lighten the place up a little. Enamel would be good. That way we can just wash the walls when they get dirty."

Hannah glanced at Andrea, who still looked as if she was contemplating homicide with husbandly intent, and took charge. "You can't paint this week."

"Why not?"

"The KCOW weatherman said it might rain and everyone knows that enamel never dries completely if you use it when the humidity's high."

"Really?" Bill frowned slightly. "I never heard that."

"Well, it's true. If you don't believe me, just come down to The Cookie Jar and touch the windowsill in my kitchen. I painted it right before a thunderstorm two years ago and it still feels tacky."

Andrea shot Hannah a grateful glance and then she turned to Bill. "Will you get your jacket and walk Hannah out to her truck? With a killer on the loose, I don't think she should take any chances."

The moment Bill had left to get his jacket, Andrea motioned Hannah closer. "Thanks, Hannah. That bit with the enamel was brilliant."

"Thanks. It was also true."

"Whatever. All I know is we've got to clear Bill, and fast. Being home with my feet up is bad enough, but with Bill here doing pet projects around the house and babying me, it's murder."

Hannah knew what she had to do and she took Andrea's warning seriously. It might not be murder yet, but if Bill spent many more hours as a househusband, it would be.

Hannah spent a few more moments talking to Bill and then she climbed into her truck. She started the engine, flicked on the lights, and noticed something she hadn't seen when she drove up.

"Bill?" Hannah called out, after she'd lowered her window.

"Yeah, Hannah."

"When did you break your taillight?"

"Oh, that," Bill said, shrugging it off as inconsequential. "It must have happened on Monday night. It was broken Tuesday morning when I went to work. I had to drive through the vehicle checkpoint at the station and they wrote me a repair ticket."

Hannah was surprised. "They have a vehicle checkpoint at the sheriff's station?"

"Sure. We're training civilian volunteers to run all the vehicle checkpoints. It'll free sworn officers up for other duty. For practice, we set up a checkpoint at the station and the volunteers stop all cars coming and going from the parking lot."

Hannah nodded, waiting for Bill to catch on. She wasn't disappointed.

"Hold on a second!" Bill sounded very excited. "The checkpoint was operating on Monday night when I left the sheriff's station. The taillight wasn't broken then. That means it happened after six on Monday night, because they ticketed me at seven the next morning."

"That's right," Hannah said, smiling like a proud parent. Bill was getting the hang of logical thinking.

"Andrea told me about the math you did on the telemarketing calls. If I can find the person who hit my car and it happened at the right time, it could be my alibi!"

"You're right. It could be." Hannah got out of her truck to examine the taillight. "Where was your car parked on Monday night?"

"Really close to where it is right now. I left room for one car to park behind me without blocking the driveway."

"You were expecting company?"

"Not really, but Andrea was going out with Tracey and I thought maybe I could talk Dad into coming over to watch the game with me."

"I wish that had happened," Hannah said. If Bill's dad had been with him, they wouldn't be in this fix.

"Me, too. But Mom invited the neighbors for dinner and he had to stay home."

One of the living room windows opened and Andrea stuck her head out. "Is something wrong?"

"No, something may be *right*," Hannah said, exchanging a smile with Bill. "Someone hit Bill's car on Monday night. If we can find out when it happened and who did it, he might have his alibi."

"What color car hit Bill's car? Can you tell?"

Hannah bent over to look at the lens of the taillight. It was cracked and hanging by the edge, but there was a smear of dark yellow paint on the red gel. "There's some paint here. It's kind of a gold color but not sparkly."

"I saw that car on Monday night," Andrea hollered out. "Come back inside and I'll tell you about it. I'm freezing with the window open."

Hannah grinned as Andrea shut the window with a bang.

It was a still night and it wasn't that cold, but it was clear Andrea wanted them to come to her so that she could be part of the team.

It only took a few moments for Andrea to give her information. Just as Hannah had thought, the little that Andrea knew could have been conveyed through the open window, but her sister enjoyed being in on the action. She told them that when she'd come home from the mall with Tracey, the cars on the street were bumper to bumper and she'd had to squeeze past a Harvest Gold Mercedes to get into their driveway.

"You're sure it was Harvest Gold?" Bill asked.

"I'm sure. I remember thinking that if I bought a brand new Mercedes, I wouldn't want it to be the same color as an old refrigerator."

Hannah laughed. Her sister had the color pegged. In addition to white, there had been three colors for kitchen appliances in the late sixties and early seventies; harvest gold, avocado, and bronze. The thought of any one of those shades on a new car was enough to give a sane person pause. "So who owns this Mercedes? Do you have any idea?"

"No, but Lorna Kusak should know. She was giving a Firelight Candle party and that's why there were so many cars on our street. I'm really sorry I was busy and I couldn't go. Firelight has a new scent, raspberry frappe, and I'd like a candle for the bathroom. It would exactly match the towels, and . . ."

"Are you absolutely sure the Mercedes was new?" Hannah interrupted her sister in the middle of what would undoubtedly be a discussion of bathroom decor.

"I'm positive it was new. It still had those paper dealer plates. And you know what *that* means."

Bill started to grin. "I know. Wait here, honey. Hannah and I will run over to Lorna's and find out."

"Right," Hannah followed Bill to the door. When someone in a town the size of Lake Eden got a new car, it entitled the owner to bragging rights. Lorna was bound to know who owned it. "We'll come back and tell you, I promise. And if Lorna has any of those raspberry frappe candles left, I'll buy one for you."

Five minutes later, Bill was on the phone with Betty Jackson. He put his call on speakerphone so that Andrea and Hannah could hear. Hannah was sipping a reheated cup of coffee while Andrea sniffed her new candle.

"I'm sorry I'm calling so late, Betty, but it's really important."

"That's okay, Bill." Betty's voice was warm and friendly. "I've got the day off tomorrow and I'm staying up late to channel surf. My new microwave dish is unbelievable, over four hundred channels and I'm trying them all out."

"Sports?" Bill asked, and he looked envious.

"Twenty-five channels devoted to every sport known to man." Betty gave a little laugh. "They even have curling from the rink in Bemidgi. Can you imagine?"

"Wow!" Bill gave an impressed sigh and Andrea nudged him with her foot. He looked startled for a moment and then remembered why he'd called Betty in the first place.

"Did you hear about my new promotion?" Betty asked, before Bill could open the subject of his car and hers. "Now I'm an executive assistant to Max's cousin at the dairy. Cozy Cow is doing so well, I just hired two new secretaries to fill my old job. But I'm sure that's not what you called about. You probably want my insurance information. I forgot to write it on the note I left under your windshield wiper when I bumped into your car on Monday night."

Hannah high-fived her sister and Andrea high-fived back, but they weren't out of the woods yet. They sat back and waited for Bill to obtain the critical information that would clear him.

"Your note must have blown away, Betty. There was nothing under my windshield wiper."

"Really? Then how did you know to call ..." Betty paused and gave an embarrassed little laugh. "Never mind. You're a detective, after all. Of course you found out it was me. I'm really mortified about it, Bill. I still can't believe I misjudged the distance. It's just that the Mercedes is a lot bigger than my old VW."

"That's okay, Betty. I understand."

"Thank goodness for that!" Betty sounded very relieved. "Hold on a second and I'll get you my insurance information so you can file a claim."

"There's no need for that," Bill answered quickly, before Betty could leave the line.

"But I have good insurance. I know they'll take care of everything. All you have to do is file a claim and they'll replace ..."

"I don't need it, Betty," Bill interrupted her. "I'll just pick up another taillight at Ted Koester's junk yard and put it in myself."

"Are you sure?"

"I'm sure. If I file a claim, it could raise your insurance rates and it's just not necessary."

"Okay, Bill. I'm sure you know best. I'll pay for the taillight. Just let me know how much it is."

"I'll do that. Do you remember what time you hit my car, Betty? It could be really important."

"I remember," Betty said, and she sounded very confident. "It was ten after nine. I left Lorna's house at five after, because I wanted to get home in time to feed my cats, put in a load of laundry, and watch the ten o'clock news."

"And you're sure about the time?"

"I'm positive. I looked at my watch when I climbed into the car. Are you sure you don't want to file an insurance claim, Bill? I'm clearly in the wrong here."

"No need, Betty. And the next time you see me, remind me to give you a big hug."

"For hitting your car?" Betty sounded confused.

"Not exactly. It's *when* you hit my car that counts. That was the luckiest accident I ever had."

There was a moment of silence and when she spoke again, Betty sounded even more puzzled. "Okay. If you say so."

"Do you mind if Mike Kingston calls you tonight to verify what you told me?"

"No . . ." Betty sounded a bit dubious. "You're not going to . . . uh . . . charge me with anything, are you?"

"No way I'd do that. I just need you to tell him what time you hit my car, so he knows it was parked outside my house at the time."

"Oh. Well, sure. I can do that." Betty sounded like she wanted to ask more questions, but she didn't. "I'm going to watch a movie in twenty minutes. Could you have him call before then?"

Bill agreed, and right after he'd disconnected the call, he punched in Mike's cell phone number. Once Mike had Betty's number and had promised to call right away, Bill hung up the phone and hugged both Andrea and Hannah. "Thanks for all your help. It's going to be good to get back to work again!"

"I'm sure it will," Andrea said, and Hannah noticed that her sister looked absolutely delighted that Bill's suspension was about to be over.

"Mike's going to buy us breakfast to celebrate," Bill announced, turning to Hannah. "I'm going in at six to go over what he's done on the case so far, and we'll meet you at The Corner Tavern at seven-thirty."

Andrea's face lit up with a smile. "Oh, good! I love their pancakes."

"Not you, honey," Bill told her. "You have to stay here with your feet up. Hannah will bring you takeout, right Hannah?"

Hannah said she would, knowing that her sister was disappointed. But Bill would be working and at least Andrea wouldn't have to watch him do any more househusband chores. Perhaps it was time to remind Andrea of her blessings. "Look on the bright side, Andrea. Now that Bill's going back to work, you can sleep in."

"Right," Andrea said, and she looked much more cheerful. "I'll set the alarm for eight-thirty, Hannah. Then I'll be up when you bring me breakfast. Can I give you my order now?"

"Sure." Hannah grabbed her notebook and flipped it to a blank page.

"I'll have pancakes, and blueberry syrup, and a couple of eggs over easy, and bacon and . . ."

"No salt," Hannah interrupted her.

"Right. No bacon then. I'll have home fries, whole wheat toast with no butter and lots of those little packets of jelly, and something else on the side instead of meat, like tomatoes sprinkled with sugar."

Hannah made a face. Both Andrea and Michelle had adopted Delores's habit of sprinkling tomato slices with sugar. Hannah, on the other hand, took after their father and liked hers sprinkled with salt.

"Okay. What to drink?"

"A chocolate shake. There's no salt in that."

"That's really strange," Bill said, frowning slightly.

"You mean a chocolate shake for breakfast?"

"Huh?" Bill looked totally confused and Hannah knew he hadn't been listening while Andrea gave her breakfast order.

"What's strange, Bill?" Hannah asked, reaching for her jacket. It was already past eleven and if she didn't head for home soon, there would be little point in going to bed.

"There was music playing when Mike answered his cell phone and I know his stereo's broken."

Hannah gave Andrea a look and Andrea gave it right back

to her. After seeing Mike at Bertanelli's with Shawna Lee, it didn't take a rocket scientist to figure out that Mike might have gone home with her. And if he had, that meant he hadn't been exactly pining away for the eldest Swensen sister while he'd been on her persona non grata list.

Chapter Sixteen

Monday morning came earlier than Hannah anticipated. It arrived at four-thirty in the morning when she rolled over on what felt like small boulders in her bed and discovered the Moishe had brought her the contents of his food bowl during the night.

"All right, I give up," Hannah sighed, sitting up to switch on the lamp by her bed and jam her feet into her slippers. Moishe wanted his regular food back. That much was clear. And perhaps he'd done her a favor by waking her up this early. If she could manage to get ambulatory and awake enough to drive by five, she could get to work early and finish the baking before she left to have breakfast with Mike and Bill.

Hannah fed Moishe his regular fare and downed a second cup of the strong coffee her grandmother had called Swedish Plasma, then walked back to the bedroom to excavate her sheets from beneath the senior cat food rubble. Rather than try to save the nuggets, Hannah opened the bedroom window, brought the corners of the sheet together to make a bundle, and shook it out as an offering to passing cats that were not as discriminating as Moishe.

"What would you like, Hannah?" Mike said, smiling at her across the table.

An explanation of what's going on with you and Shawna Lee, Hannah thought, but she said, "Pancakes, maple syrup, and eggs sunny side up."

"Coffee?" the waitress asked, favoring Hannah with a smile.

"Yes, please. And lots of it. I didn't get much sleep last night."

"Me, neither," Mike said, and Hannah clamped her lips shut. No way she was going to ask why!

"I slept like a baby," Bill volunteered. "I think it was because the pressure was off. It was awful not being able to prove I didn't do it."

"Just be glad you're not in France." Mike reached out to pour a cup of coffee for Hannah from the carafe. "Their system is guilty until proven innocent, not the other way around like us."

Hannah clamped her lips shut. It seemed to her that the Winnetka County Sheriff's Department had adopted the French system. Bill had been suspended until he could prove his innocence.

Twenty minutes later, their food had been served and they'd done a good job of cleaning their plates. Bill went up to the counter to order Andrea's takeout breakfast while Mike stayed behind in the booth with Hannah.

Mike gave her a big smile and reached out to touch her hand. "I've really missed you the past couple of days, Hannah."

It's been seven days, and that's more than a couple, Hannah thought, keeping her expression as neutral as possible. She could have argued with the verb in Mike's sentiment as well. How could sharing a booth at Bertanelli's with Shawna Lee Quinn possibly be construed as missing her?

"I sure could have used your help last night," Mike went on.

"Oh, really?" Hannah's eyebrows shot up. From where

she'd been sitting it hadn't looked as if Mike had needed help from anyone! "With what?"

"Remember the secretary I introduced you to the last time you came out to the station?"

Hannah looked thoughtful, pretending to make an effort to remember. "You mean the new one? Sharon Lee, or something like that?"

"Shawna Lee. She was with the Minneapolis Police Department. I used to work with her."

Hannah did her best to look innocently interested. "I think you might have mentioned that."

"She's only been here for a month and she doesn't know anyone in town. She could really use a friend."

How about an enemy? I could manage that, Hannah thought, but she didn't say it. Jealousy was an ugly emotion and it was better to keep it close to the vest. "I'm sure she'll find one. People are friendly around here."

"That's true. I didn't really expect you to take her on as your pet project, but I thought maybe you could introduce her to somebody that . . ."

"Ronni," Hannah interrupted him.

"What?"

"Ronni Ward," Hannah named Lake Eden's three-time bikini contest winner and the biggest flirt in Winnetka County. "Does she still teach that step aerobics class out at the station?"

"Yes, she does. It's really popular with the deputies."

"I'm sure it is. Maybe Shawna Lee should enroll. I think she'd have a lot in common with Ronni and they're about the same age."

"Thanks, Hannah." Mike gave her a smile that sent Hannah's blood pressure soaring. "I knew you'd come up with something. You're the nicest person I know and you're a real problem solver."

Hannah was just wondering if putting two flirts together

would neutralize them, like subtracting a number from itself, when she looked up to see Bill approaching the booth. It was amazing what a difference an alibi made. Now that he was back on the job, Bill was standing up straighter, walking with more confidence, and smiling a whole lot more.

"They said Andrea's takeout will be ready in ten minutes and the waitress will bring it over to you. Mike and I should leave. We've got a lot to do today."

"I'm really glad I'm not in the doghouse with you any-more, Hannah." Mike scooted over to Hannah's side of the booth and kissed her on the cheek. Hannah had the urge to turn her head so that his lips connected with hers, but since Bill was watching, she didn't. "I bet you're really relieved," Mike said with a grin.

Hannah wasn't at all sure what he meant. "Why would I be relieved?"

"Because now that Bill's back on the case with me, you can drop your murder investigation."

"That's right," Bill said, smiling at Hannah. "We're really grateful for everything you've done so far, but it's time for you to step aside and let the professionals take over."

Hannah's mouth fell open and she clacked it shut again, hoping that no one had noticed. "You . . . um . . . want me to step aside?"

"Yes." Bill zipped up his jacket. "Don't worry, Hannah. Now that we're both on the case, we'll have two trained ob-servers to assess the situation."

And this from the trained observer who was ready to paint Andrea's light blue living room with bright yellow enamel! Hannah thought.

Mike began to frown and Hannah knew that he, at least, had noticed her lack of enthusiasm. "I really hope you're not going to interfere in our investigation. You *are* planning to drop it, aren't you?"

Hannah just stared at Mike for a moment. Who did he think he was kidding? Dropping her investigation now would be like jerking a cake from the oven before it had time to rise. But both Mike and Bill seemed very serious and Hannah knew it wouldn't be prudent to tell them that it was simply not in her nature to leave a job half-finished.

"Of course I'll drop it," Hannah said.

"I really thought they were smarter than that," Andrea said digging into her stack or pancakes. "They actually expect us to drop it?"

"That's what they said. And I told them I would."

"You *did?*" Andrea's fork dropped from her fingers with a clatter. "But you were lying, weren't you?"

"I wasn't exactly lying. I prefer to think of it as a half-truth. I promised them I'd drop the investigation, but I didn't say *when* I'd drop it."

"That's different." Andrea gave a relieved smile. "So what do we do next?"

"Since you can't be on your feet, you can run our office from here."

"We have an office?" Andrea looked amused.

"We do now."

"Okay, I'll run the office. Do you want me to call the rest of the names on that list Nettie gave us and see if they have alibis?"

"That would be great. You're really good on the phone."

"Of course I am. I'm a real estate agent. What are you going to do?"

"I'll run out to the sheriff's station and pump Barbara Donnelly for information about those old cases Sheriff Grant may have stolen. And while I'm there, I'll ask her about his work schedule. If we can figure out what he was doing and who he saw the day he was killed, that might help."

"A timeline," Andrea said, nodding wisely. "That's what they do in all the detective movies, but it hasn't really helped us yet."

"I know." Hannah sighed deeply. Establishing a timeline

for the day of Sheriff Grant's death would probably work about as well as standing at graveside, attempting to spot anyone suspicious.

"Well, there's always a first time." Andrea, ever the optimist, grabbed the maple bar Hannah had brought her for dessert and took a big bite.

"Okay, I'm out of here," Hannah said, plumping Andrea's pillows, moving the phone closer so that it was at hand, and fetching a second pen just in case the first ran out of ink. Then she waved goodbye and went back out to her cookie truck. She'd stop in to say hello to Lisa, ask her to tell Herb to call off the search for roofing trucks, stop at the vet's office to ask for more advice about Moishe and their on-going battle with the senior food, and deliver cookie orders on her way to the sheriff's station. And if she just happened to run into Shawna Lee Quinn while she was walking down the ugly green corridors of the sheriff's station, she planned to nicely, very nicely, put a little crimp in her plans to snare Mike.

"Hannah? Is that you?" Shawna Lee's mouth curved up in a smile as Hannah walked into the sheriff's outer office. "Mike told me all about you and how nice you were. I know I only met you once before, but I feel as if we're friends already!"

Hannah forced a pleasant expression. There was a limit to how much bubbling enthusiasm she could take in any one day. One more comment from Shawna Lee and she'd be on overload. "Hi, Shawna Lee. Is Barbara on a break?"

"No." Shawna Lee put on a tragic face. "It's just so sad, Hannah. Barbara took a leave of absence . . . you know, one of those compassionate things? I'm afraid it's of indefinite duration."

"What does *that* mean?"

"It means we don't know how long she'll be gone," Shawna Lee answered Hannah's question literally. "Barbara worked with Sheriff Grant for years, you know. And she said she just wasn't sure she could come back to work without him. They were like partners. You know what I mean?"

"Sure," Hannah said. "So you're filling in for Barbara until she comes back?"

Shawna Lee nodded and her ash blond curls bounced. Then she leaned a little closer and said, "Just between you and me, I don't think Barbara will be back. She really lost it when she heard that Sheriff Grant had been killed. She even misfiled a bunch of daily reports."

"She did?" Hannah was surprised. Everyone said that Barbara was a great secretary and it would be out of character for her to misfile reports. "Do you remember what was in those reports?"

"Not really. I didn't pay that much attention. I just looked for the ones that were misfiled and put them back in the proper places. It took me hours and I found all but one. Just as soon as I get some extra time, I'm going to go through the folders paper by paper until I find it."

"I'm curious," Hannah said, giving Shawna Lee a smile that she hoped would invite confidences. "How do you know there's still one report missing?"

"I can tell by the file folder."

"What file folder?"

"There's a hanging file folder with nothing in it."

"Oh. And you don't think Barbara was in the habit of storing her hanging folders that way?"

Shawna Lee shook her head. "I know she wasn't. There weren't any other empty folders in the cabinet and there's half a box of them in her supply drawer. There's a report missing. I'm sure of it."

"Well, good luck in finding it," Hannah said, turning to go. That missing report could be important and Shawna Lee had already told her everything she knew. Now Hannah needed to talk to Barbara Donnelly.

"I'm really glad you dropped by, Hannah."

"You are?" Hannah turned back.

"Yes. I wanted to find out how your sister was. I bet she's really relieved that her husband is back at work. She's about ready to have those twins, isn't she?"

"She's not having twins."

"Really?" Shawna Lee looked surprised. "But the last time I saw her out here at the station, she was so big and awkward. Of course that's understandable. It must be terribly difficult to look attractive when you're that pregnant."

"Andrea manages," Hannah said, bristling. Shawna Lee had no right to criticize her sister.

"She does have some very cute maternity outfits. Still, I'm sure she'll be glad to get her shape back. Bill will probably be glad, too."

"Why's that?" Hannah asked, just waiting for Shawna to say something catty and seal her fate.

"It can't be any fun for a guy to get close and personal when his wife looks like a balloon." Shawna Lee gave a little laugh and she didn't seem to notice that Hannah hadn't joined in. "I really hope you'll put in a good word for me with your sister and Bill. I'm a good secretary and I'd love to get this job and work for Bill, especially since he's bound to win the election now."

Hannah smiled and it wasn't a nice smile. "You're wrong, Shawna Lee. Bill might not be the next sheriff."

"But why not? He's the only one running now that Sheriff Grant is dead."

"True. But Sheriff Grant could still win. The ballots are already printed and his name is on them."

Shawna Lee's mouth formed a perfect round circle for an instant. Then she recovered and started to frown. "You mean that the people could elect a dead man?"

"It's been known to happen," Hannah said, taking a certain glee in informing Shawna Lee of that fact. "If it does, Mike will keep the job of Acting Sheriff until the Winnetka County Board of Supervisors can schedule another election."

Shawna Lee cocked her head to the side and stared at

Hannah for a moment. Then she smiled. "Well, that'd be great, too. Mike's my boss right now and I just adore him. Just between you and me, he was the one who talked me into moving up here from The Cities and applying for this job in the first place."

"She actually said I looked like a balloon?" Andrea's eyes started to blaze. "That does it. She'll work for Bill over my dead body!"

"That's what I figured," Hannah said.

"And right now she's working for Mike?"

"That's what she said."

Andrea's eyebrows shot up at the tone in her sister's voice. "Okay. You can relax, Hannah. I'll take care of her."

"What are you going to do?"

"It's what we're both going to do."

"What's that?"

"I'll call Barbara Donnelly and set up a meeting. You convince her to come back to work so that little Miss Quinn has to go back to the typing pool."

"That'll get her away from the top office, but she'll still be out there at the station."

"Not for long," Andrea said, giving a knowing little smile. "She's not going to like being demoted. I can practically guarantee that. And she might be so unhappy, she'll leave."

"What if she doesn't?"

Andrea shrugged. "Maybe I'll help to find her another job. You know how it is when you're a real estate professional. You hear about all sorts of interesting career opportunities."

Fifteen minutes later, Hannah walked out of the Lake Eden Veterinarian Clinic clutching a small white bag. The contents of the bag had cost her more than Mike paid for the four breakfasts at The Corner Tavern this morning, but if it worked, the expense was worth it. Doctor Bob had prescribed a bottle of vitamins to aid in the health of the senior cat. If Hannah could manage to dose Moishe every night, she could throw away the senior chow and continue to feed him the regular kitty crunchies he preferred.

Hannah climbed behind the wheel and put the white bag in the glove compartment. She doubted that any senior cats would attempt to break into her cookie truck to steal it, but she wasn't taking any chances. Then she drove straight to The Cookie Jar to check in with Lisa.

"Your sister called," Lisa greeted Hannah as she came into the kitchen. "Barbara's going to be at Danielle Watson's dance studio at three today. She'll be watching her granddaughter's dance practice."

"Thanks, Lisa. Do you want a break? I can take over the counter for a while."

"No, I'm fine. It's been slow today, except for a couple of girls who were skipping science class. They wanted me to turn on MTV while they were eating their cookies and they were really disappointed when I told them that we didn't have cable. The cable was out last Monday night and they told me that there was some big concert on MTV. The station was rerunning it at ten this morning and the girls weren't happy about missing it again."

Hannah was about to reply when what Lisa had said hit her. "Are you sure the cable was out on Monday night?"

"I'm positive. Dad wanted to see a movie and I had to run out to the video store so he'd have something to watch."

"Do you think the cable was out all over town?"

"Their recorded message said it was. *Lake Eden and surrounding areas,* was how they put it. I'm going to subtract a day from our cable bill."

"Good idea." Hannah pulled her notebook from her purse and started paging through it. "Thanks for telling me, Lisa. There's something here that doesn't make sense."

"What?"

"Here," Hannah said, joining Lisa behind the counter. She

glanced at the few tables that were filled, but no one was paying any attention to them. "Nettie doesn't have an alibi. She was working alone in her sewing room and she had the window open. When I asked her if any of the Maschlers might have seen her through the window or heard her sewing machine, she said no, they were out for the evening. But she also said the television was on really loud and Kate had left it tuned to a kung fu movie."

"What time was that?"

"Between seven and nine."

Lisa shook her head. "Impossible. You can only get four channels without cable and none of them were showing movies. Believe me, I know. I flipped through before I went out to the video store for Dad."

"So . . . it must have been a tape," Hannah said, frowning slightly. "But Kate wouldn't have put on a tape and then left the house."

"Of course not. But she has a teenage son, doesn't she?"

"Richie. Kate told Mike that he was out that night with friends."

"Wrong. Richie was *in* that night with friends. And he probably didn't tell his parents. They watched a tape, the movie that Nettie heard, and then they cleared out before Kate and Jerry got home."

"And they lied about it because they probably drank some beer while they were watching the movie?"

"It's good to know you're not *that* old." Lisa gave Hannah a pat on the back. "If it wasn't beer, it was probably a girl. And in that case, they might not have been all that interested in the movie."

"Right. So I should talk to Richie?"

"Sure. Unless you want someone younger and more in touch with the teenage mentality to do that research for you."

Hannah grinned. "And that would be you?"

"It would be me. And it just so happens that one of the girls who was here this morning left her class notebook. I'll call the school to tell them it's here and when she comes to pick it up, I'll ask her which girl is dating Richie Maschler. And then I'll talk to his girlfriend and find out what really happened on Monday night."

Chapter Seventeen

Hannah opened the street door at the side of the Red Owl Grocery and climbed the long stairway leading up to the second floor. The stairs had been newly carpeted and Hannah admired the way that Danielle had decorated the walls with dance diagrams, each set of footprints in a different color.

As she climbed, Hannah heard faint strains of music that became louder with each step she took. And when she opened the heavy door at the top of the stairs, the music rolled out to greet her, something upbeat and jazzy that she didn't recognize.

Hannah stood there staring for a moment. Danielle's dance studio was impressive. With the exception of a wall that sectioned off rooms at the rear and an area of red deep pile carpeting in front of it that contained padded theater seats, the rest of the space gleamed with a highly polished wooden floor and mirrored walls. The only wall that wasn't mirrored was the one facing the street and it contained the high narrow windows that Danielle had loved when Andrea first showed her the loft.

Looking up, Hannah noticed tracks on the ceiling. She was puzzled for a moment. Then she spotted the red velvet curtains that were stored in alcoves in the walls and realized that the curtains could be pulled to cordon off a large area for the stage.

"Clever," Hannah murmured, looking back up at the tracks again. She'd seen tracks like that on the ceilings of hospital rooms so that an individual patient in a double or triple room could have privacy.

Danielle rushed over the moment she noticed Hannah standing by the door. "How wonderful to see you, Hannah! Tracey's doing very well in her dance class."

"That's good to hear," Hannah said, giving her a warm smile. Danielle looked really good. The anxious, scared-rabbit expression she'd worn in the past had gone the way of the theatrical makeup she'd been forced to use to cover up the signs of her husband's abuse. "How's business, Danielle?"

"I'm doing better than I ever thought I would. And to think that Boyd pooh-poohed the idea of my opening a dance studio! He said it would never go in a town the size of Lake Eden."

"Looks like Boyd was wrong," Hannah said, adding an addendum to that sentence in her mind, *about a lot of things!*

"All my classes are filled and I'm looking for an assistant teacher in the evenings so I can offer more sessions. Do you know anyone?"

Hannah was sorely tempted to suggest Shawna Lee Quinn. If she worked two jobs, she'd be too busy to go out with Mike. But because Danielle was a friend and friends didn't try to pull the wool over each other's eyes, Hannah ditched that idea. "I'll call you if I think of anyone," she said.

"Great. I'd really like to start another ballroom dancing class. I have enough names on the waiting list."

Hannah was surprised. "I wouldn't think the kids would be interested in ballroom dancing."

"Quite a few of them are, but I was talking about my seniors class. I just love working with them, Hannah. Most of them know the basics already. It's just a matter of brushing up and getting back in practice. And the cheerleaders are really a lot of fun. They're doing a dance routine at the Halloween party and Mr. Purvis lets them out of study hall to practice. You'll stay and watch, won't you?"

"I'd planned on it. I'm meeting Barbara Donnelly. I need to talk to her."

"Of course you do. Your mother mentioned that you were investigating and secretaries always know a lot about their bosses. Barbara's in the dressing room helping the girls with their hair, but that's her coat and purse on that seat at the end of the first row. You can sit next to her."

Once Danielle rushed off to see if her cheerleaders were ready to perform, Hannah took the seat next to Barbara's. It was padded in all the right places and it cradled her like a pillow. It was so comfortable that Hannah almost nodded off. Between getting home late last night and rolling over on the contents of Moishe's food bowl early this morning, she'd had a grand total of four hours sleep. That wasn't enough. All she had to do was look into the mirror at the dark circles under her eyes to know that.

The music that Danielle played over the loudspeakers was pleasant. Hannah leaned against the cushioned seatback and closed her eyes to appreciate it better. It would be fun to dance to this music, and she had two men to dance with her. Norman had even taken dance lessons and he'd improved so much, she no longer had the desire to lead. And Mike . . . well . . . dancing with Mike was like . . . she really shouldn't think of that now.

There was a warm hand on her arm and Hannah smiled. Here was Mike now, asking her to dance. He was a bit late. The music had been playing for quite some time now, but perhaps he'd been busy. He was patting her arm now, saying her name, and she did her best to open her eyes. She'd just nodded off a bit sitting here and listening to the music while he'd been . . . been . . .

"Hannah? Wake up."

No, it wasn't Mike. It was a woman's voice. Her college roommate? No, college was over so that couldn't be right.

"Hannah? Come on, Hannah."

"Huh?" Hannah's eyes popped open and she sat up with a start. She looked over at Barbara Donnelly and blinked. What was Barbara doing in her bedroom?

"Sorry, but you were starting to snore," Barbara said with a grin. "I'm surprised you could sleep with that music so loud."

Hannah shook her head. "I wasn't sleeping. I was just resting my eyes."

"Sure. And checking the inside of your eyelids for holes."

Hannah took stock. Her eyes felt scratchy, her arm had little pinpricks of sensation where she'd jammed it up against the adjoining seat, and her teeth seemed to have knitted sweaters. There was no sense denying it. She'd been asleep. "You win. I admit I was sleeping. But I don't snore."

"Of course you don't. No one ever does." Barbara sat down in her chair. She looked like an aging prima ballerina herself, with her tall, elegant body and dark hair pulled back into a twist at the nape of her neck. "You wanted to talk to me about Sheriff Grant?"

"That's right."

"And the boys don't know you're here?"

Hannah grinned. Barbara was no slouch. "Bill's alibi was confirmed last night and he went back to work this morning. Mike took us to breakfast to celebrate and he told me I should be relieved that I don't have to investigate any longer."

"For a smart cop, Mike can be a pretty dumb guy when it comes to women," Barbara commented, exchanging smiles with Hannah. "Of course Sheriff Grant was no prize, either."

"That's what I heard. You don't think that Nettie . . . ?" Hannah threw the suggestion out there and let it hang, waiting for Barbara to pick it up.

"Never," Barbara said, shaking her head. She sounded very definite. "It wasn't a marriage made in heaven, but Nettie loved him. She might have divorced him, but she'd never have killed him."

"That's what I thought. Any guesses as to who did?"

Barbara thought about it for a moment and then she sighed. "Not really. There were plenty of people that didn't like him, but I don't think any of them would actually kill him."

Just then the curtains began to move and both Hannah and Barbara stared up at the ceiling. Within thirty seconds, a stage was cordoned off and behind the drawn curtains, they could hear the girls coming in from the dressing room and taking their places.

"Here we go," Barbara said, turning to smile at Hannah. "I must have seen this thirty times in the past two weeks, but it never gets old for me. Krista's really good, Hannah. You're going to love it."

"I'm sure I will," Hannah said, feeling a pang of loss. Barbara was wearing the very same smile Hannah's grandmother had worn when she'd come to Washington Elementary to see Hannah as a pilgrim in her first grade Thanksgiving pageant. It hadn't seemed to matter in the slightest that Grandma Ingrid had helped her memorize the lines and she'd known everything that Hannah was supposed to say and do. She'd still been practically bursting with pride when Hannah and the rest of her class had taken their curtain call.

The music swelled to a crescendo and segued into Tchaikovsky's *Swan Lake*. It was a perfect choice for Halloween since it had been used in several big-name horror movies. After a few bars played, the curtains opened and Hannah almost laughed out loud as she saw the costumes the cheerleaders were wearing.

"Aren't they darling?" Barbara whispered.

Darling wasn't the word Hannah would have used to describe the costumes. This was obviously a darker version of

Swan Lake since the girls were wearing black leotards and leggings with huge black bat wings attached to their arms.

As they watched, one girl moved to the center of the stage and began to dance a solo, dipping and swooping almost as if she were flying. Something about the girl was very familiar and the moment Hannah realized what it was, she turned to whisper to Barbara. "When did Krista grow up?"

"It happened when I wasn't looking. It seems like just last week I was reading her *Winnie the Pooh*. That's Leah Koester next to her."

"Beatrice's granddaughter?"

"That's right. I'm surprised Beatrice isn't here today. The only other practice she missed was the one last Monday night."

"She came to my cooking class," Hannah said.

"I know. When both of us realized that we were going to miss that practice, we made arrangements for Ted to pick the girls up when they were through and take them to a classmate's birthday party. We're certainly not going to do *that* again!"

"Why not?"

"Ted must have been rushed or something, because he didn't change clothes or stop off at the school to switch to Beatrice's car like he was supposed to do. The girls had to ride in Ted's work truck, and Krista got a rust stain on the skirt of her new party dress."

"That's too bad," Hannah commiserated.

"I still can't believe my daughter-in-law's attitude. She didn't even try to get the stain out. She just told Krista it was ruined and they'd go shopping at the mall for a new dress!"

"That does seem a little hasty," Hannah said, knowing that she was treading on eggshells.

"It's a good thing Krista inherited some sense from my side of the family! She took the dress to Marguerite and Clara Hollenbeck."

Hannah caught on immediately. Since Marguerite and Clara did the church linens and always got them spotless, Krista must have gone to them for advice. "Did they tell her how to remove the stain?"

"They were just leaving town when Krista caught them, but they're coming back this weekend. They offered to keep the dress and take a look at it then."

Once all the girls had taken turns in the center spotlight, the dance concluded and the curtains were drawn. The parents and grandparents who had come to watch the rehearsal applauded, and so did Hannah.

"You liked it?" Barbara asked.

"It was wonderful and I'm sure it'll be a big hit with the kids on Halloween. Do you have a few minutes, Beatrice? I've got some questions."

"I've got as long as it takes. The girls have a ride back to school and all I have to do is run downstairs and go grocery shopping."

Hannah grabbed her notebook and pen and asked about Sheriff Grant's work schedule the week before he was killed. She took notes on everything Barbara told her, but nothing seemed out of the ordinary. "Was there anything odd you can think of? Any strange phone calls, or visits?"

"No," Barbara said, shaking her head. "I've thought about that ever since I took compassionate leave. There was absolutely nothing unusual."

"You said he spent a lot of time out of the office?"

"That's right. But that wasn't unusual, either. Sheriff Grant was a good politician and he always worked on something really big right before an election."

"Like what?" Hannah asked, even though she knew exactly what sort of thing Barbara was talking about.

"Like a high profile case that would prove what a good sheriff he was and get him reelected."

"And he did this before every election?"

"Before you ask, I don't know what it was this time. I don't even have a clue. Sheriff Grant never let anyone, me included, know what he had before he broke it to the media."

"Okay. Let's talk about the past cases. Do you think any of the original detectives would be mad enough to kill Sheriff Grant for stealing their cases?"

Barbara looked startled for a moment and then she smiled. "You *are* a good detective! But how did you find out about that?"

"Harry Wilcox. He called Bill and suggested that it might be a motive for murder."

"He was right, in a way. It could have been a motive, but it wasn't. Before I left the station, I checked out the detectives who lost their cases and none of them could have killed Sheriff Grant."

"Why not?" Hannah asked.

"One died in an accident last year, another was in Europe with his wife, and a third was in Chicago for the birth of his granddaughter."

"Did you check on Harry?"

"Of course. I called and chatted with his wife. She mentioned that they went to a dinner party that night."

"Thanks, Barbara," Hannah said, jotting down all the pertinent information. Barbara had done her work for her and it was time to move on. "I went out to the sheriff's station and spoke to Shawna Lee. She's taking your place while you're on leave."

Barbara stared at Hannah in surprise. "She is?"

"That's right. You don't approve?"

Barbara looked very uncomfortable. "It's not that Shawna Lee's incompetent. She's actually a very good secretary. But her people skills are . . . well . . . let's just say that I wouldn't have chosen her. What was she doing when you saw her?"

"She said she'd found some reports that were misfiled and she was putting them back in the proper place."

Barbara began to frown. "I certainly hope she didn't mention it to anybody, especially since she probably thought I'd done it."

"I don't know about that, but she did think you'd done it. She was very understanding about it, though. She said she knew you'd worked for Sheriff Grant for years and you were bound to be shocked and upset over his murder."

"That's true," Barbara said, "but I didn't misfile those reports. Sheriff Grant's the one who couldn't put a file back in its jacket. He was always pulling reports and taking them home with him. And he insisted on putting them back in the file drawer himself so I wouldn't know which ones he'd taken."

"He was that secretive?"

"Oh, yes. He didn't want anyone to know his business, not even me. I used to call him James Bond."

Hannah grinned at the comparison between the handsome, debonair James Bond and short, stocky Sheriff Grant. "I'll bet you didn't say it to his face."

"Yes, I did. He took it as a huge compliment. He was really into James Bond things. I think he fancied himself as some sort of super spy." Barbara chuckled a bit over the memory. "He really thought he was putting one over on me with those reports."

"But he wasn't?"

"Heavens, no! I knew exactly which reports he'd taken. They were the ones that I found misfiled."

Hannah laughed, but she sobered quickly as something occurred to her. "Do you think the misfiled reports could have something to do with the big case he was working on to win the election?"

"Oh, I don't think so. If Sheriff Grant took them as part of his investigation, he would have kept them."

Hannah drew in her breath sharply as she remembered a comment Shawna Lee had made. "Shawna Lee told me she thought one report was missing."

"Why did she think that?"

"Because there was one hanging file folder with nothing in it."

"She's right. I never put a hanging file folder in the cabinet unless there's a report in it."

"If you went out there and looked, is there any way you could tell which report was missing?"

Barbara shook her head. "Sorry, Hannah. The hanging file folders weren't labeled. I really wouldn't have the slightest idea."

Hannah sat there thinking for a moment. She had the sneaking suspicion that the missing report was an important clue to Sheriff Grant's murder, but she had no idea how to find it. "It's a lot easier in the movies."

"It sure is! And it's a lot more exciting and romantic, too."

"I'm not that sure about the romance," Hannah said, remembering the smoldering looks Shawna Lee had given Mike at Bertanelli's. "I heard you were thinking about quitting. You're not going to do it, are you?"

"Well . . . I've been there a long time and the pay's not that good. I was doing some thinking about taking early retirement."

"Please don't," Hannah said with a frown.

"Why not?"

"Two words. *Shawna* and *Lee*. If Bill wins the election for sheriff, she might end up as his secretary. Andrea's really upset about that and she asked me to plead with you to go back to work."

"I see. How about if Bill doesn't win?"

"Then Mike will keep the job of acting sheriff until the board elects a new one. And Shawna Lee will be his secretary."

"So then *you* want me to go back to work, too."

"Right. How about it, Barbara? You're not going to let us down, are you?"

"Well . . ." Barbara gave a little sigh. "I guess I could go back for a while, at least until the new sheriff gets off to a good start."

Hannah started to grin. "Thanks, Barbara. We were hoping you'd stay at least for a month or so. That'll give Andrea a chance to explore other career options for Shawna Lee."

"Other career options?" Barbara looked puzzled.

"That's right. Preferably something in a foreign country, or perhaps outer space."

Chapter Eighteen

"I thought I heard you come in." Lisa opened the swinging door to the kitchen and stuck her head in.

"It sounds busy up front," Hannah remarked, hearing the sound of a multitude of voices from the coffee shop.

"It's packed. I just wanted to tell you I've got news on the Maschler front."

"You do?" Hannah hung her jacket on the hook by the back door and looked at Lisa inquiringly.

"Come up front when you're ready and I'll tell you. They're all gossiping about Mike anyway and once you answer their questions, they won't pay any attention to us."

"What about Mike? What questions?" Hannah asked in quick succession, freezing in the act of washing her hands.

"Babs Dubinski saw a blonde in Mike's Jeep last night and he was turning off the highway into his apartment complex. She told all the ladies when she came in to have her hair done, and they all came over here."

"Why?" Hannah asked, even though she already knew the answer.

"To find out if you know about it. And if you don't, they want to be the first to tell you."

"Give me strength," Hannah murmured with a sigh. "Just say you told me and now I know about it."

Lisa shook her head. "That's no good. I'll have to give them some kind of scoop, or they'll never leave."

"Okay." Hannah thought for a moment. "Tell them I don't know for sure, but I think the blonde was Mike's temporary secretary, Shawna Lee Quinn. And I have no idea why she was in Mike's Jeep when he drove into his apartment complex."

"That should work. As long as they have her name, they'll go back to the Cut 'n Curl and see what they can dig up about her. I'll come back and give you the all-clear when they leave."

"Thanks, Lisa," Hannah said, keeping her expression carefully neutral until Lisa had gone back into the coffee shop. Then she began to wash her hands again, scrubbing them much harder than necessary. She had to find out what was going on between Mike and Shawna Lee. And if Mike wasn't forthcoming the next time she saw him, she'd just have to run up the street to the Cut 'n Curl and sic Bertie and her customers on him!

Getting the all-clear took a while and Hannah had time to mix up a batch of Molasses Crackles for the next day. She'd just stashed the bowl in the cooler when Lisa poked her head in the door.

"They're gone. You can come up front now."

Hannah wasted no time pushing through the swinging door and stepping into the coffee shop. She'd felt like a coward hiding out in the kitchen. She took one look at the glass serving jars behind the counter and gasped. "What happened to all the cookies?"

"Bertie and her customers had four apiece."

"I guess there's nothing like a little gossip to fire up the appetite." Hannah poured a cup of coffee for herself and sat down next to Lisa on one of the tall stools behind the counter. The coffee shop was almost deserted with the exception of four ladies at a table in the back and they were engrossed in their own conversation. "I'll fill the serving jars after you tell me about Richie Maschler."

"That sounds like a bribe to me," Lisa said, giving Hannah an impish smile.

"It is. You said you talked to Richie?"

"No, I talked to Cheryl Coombs."

Hannah's brows came together in a puzzled frown. "What does Cheryl Coombs have to do with it?"

"Nothing directly, but her daughter Amber is dating Richie."

"I see," Hannah said. "And you asked Cheryl where Amber was last Monday night?"

"Exactly. It turns out that Amber was supposed to be home studying for an algebra test. Cheryl had to work that night and Amber wasn't supposed to leave the house."

"But she did and Cheryl caught her?"

"Red-handed. Cheryl's boss told her to take off work early and when she got home, Amber wasn't there."

"Uh-oh," Hannah said. "What time did Amber get in?"

"Not until a quarter to ten, fifteen minutes before Cheryl was supposed to come home from work."

"And Amber admitted that she was with Richie?"

"She told Cheryl that she was at Richie's house and they watched a kung-fu movie. She tried to argue the case that they weren't really alone, that Nettie was right next door with her sewing room window open, but Cheryl didn't buy it and took away Amber's cell phone."

"That's a punishment?" Hannah was surprised. Having a cell phone seemed more of a punishment than a perk to her. If she carried one, Delores could call her any time of the day or night!

"Losing cell phone privileges is even worse than being grounded," Lisa told her, a smile hovering around the corners of her mouth. "You know how girls love to talk for hours on the phone."

"Not just girls," Hannah said with a sigh, thinking of her

mother, who was the queen of long-winded telephone talkers. "Thanks, Lisa. I'll take those serving jars and fill them."

"Okay. I'll hold down the fort out here. What do you want me to do if Mike comes in?"

Hannah's eyebrows shot up. "What makes you think he might come in?"

"The gossip hotline. Somebody's bound to say something to him soon."

Hannah thought about that for a moment. Bertie and her ladies must have called several people by now and Delores would have been high on their list. When Mother heard, she'd call Andrea, and Andrea would call Bill, and Bill would say something to Mike, and . . . "You're right," Hannah said interrupting her own train of thought. "Mike could come in. If he does, delay him."

"How am I supposed to do that?"

Hannah shrugged. "I don't know. Tell him I'm busy. That'll be true."

"It might be true, but he'll want to know why he can't see you."

"Right." Hannah thought for a moment and then she threw up her hands in defeat. "I don't know what you can tell him. You were class valedictorian. *You* think of something."

The Cookie Jar was usually crowded the hour before closing with people who stopped by to have a last cookie, and others who wanted to take a dozen home to the family. Hannah manned the counter while Lisa bagged takeout cookies until the rush was over and only three tables were still filled.

"I'll go back to the kitchen and start mixing up tomorrow's cookie dough," Hannah told Lisa.

"I can do it, Hannah. You've got cooking class tonight."

"That won't be a problem. I'll pick up some fast food on

the way and eat it in the truck. And all I have to do when I get home is change clothes, feed Moishe, and give him his vitamin supplement."

"Vitamin supplement?" Lisa looked concerned. "Is it a pill? It's really hard to give a cat a pill. They just spit it right out again when you're not looking."

"This is a liquid with a dropper. All I have to do is open his mouth and squirt it in. That should be really easy."

"I hope you're right," Lisa said, and she looked as if she wanted to say more, but the front door opened and Beatrice Koester came in. She placed a cardboard box on the counter and Lisa looked puzzled when she peered inside. "What's all this, Beatrice?"

"It's my homework from Hannah's class. I've got three bottles of dressing, a bag of lettuce pieces, and a stack of paper bowls. I thought you might want to try them out on your customers to see which one they like best."

"Good idea," Hannah said, turning to Lisa. "Why don't you see if our customers are willing to do a taste test. Then we can tally the results and we'll put the most popular one in the Lake Eden cookbook."

"What are they?" Lisa asked, picking up the bottles one by one and shaking them.

"Russian, blue cheese, and French. Ted and I like the French best, but that's just us."

"I really like the bottles," Lisa said. "They're just the right size for salad dressing. Where did you get them?"

"Ted's mother had three shelves of them in her basement. Ted thought I was crazy for packing them up and moving them all back here, but they come in handy for all sorts of things."

"Thanks, Beatrice." Hannah gave her a warm smile. "Are you coming to class tonight?"

"I'll be there. I made more dressing so everyone there can sample it, too."

"Good. I'll try to get there early to make another stab at

those cupcakes. Have you thought of anything else about them that I should know?"

"Not really," Beatrice said and she began to frown. "I called a couple of Alma's old friends last night, but they didn't know either. One lady even asked Alma about it when she was so sick. She really wanted that recipe and she tried to convince Alma that it should live on. But Alma told her that the recipe for those cupcakes was her secret and she planned to take it to her grave."

Hannah shivered slightly, wondering how many secrets Sheriff Grant had taken to his grave. It was a good guess that one of those secrets was the cause of his death.

"What's the matter, Hannah?" Beatrice looked concerned. "You look like a goose just walked over your grave."

"Maybe one did," Hannah said, wondering about the origin of the old expression.

"Do you want me to help Lisa with the salad test?" Beatrice asked.

"That would be fine, if you've got the time."

"I do. I don't have to go out to the yard until six-thirty. Ted's working late tonight and I'm going to bring him dinner."

"I thought he closed early on Monday nights," Hannah said, remembering the sign she'd seen the last time she'd passed the salvage yard.

"He does, usually. But he knows I've got class and he figured he might as well work. There's really a lot of money in auto salvage."

"That's good to hear," Hannah said.

"We're doing so well, we bought a new crusher. It's a lot faster than the old one and it's really something to watch a whole car go in and a cube of metal come out."

"I'll bet it is," Hannah said, attempting to think of a polite way to make her escape. Beatrice was unusually talkative today.

"You've really got to see it to believe it. Why don't you

drive out and take a look when you've got a little extra time?"

"I'll have to do that," Hannah said, realizing that Beatrice had just provided a way for her to excuse herself and get out to the kitchen. "And speaking of time, I'm running out, especially if I want to get to class early. See you tonight, Beatrice."

Hannah was about to back out of her parking spot when Mike pulled up to block her. Hannah watched in the mirror on her door as Mike got out of the cruiser and approached her truck. The legend on her mirror read, *Objects in mirror are closer than they appear,* but it should have read, *Objects in mirror are angrier than they appear.* Mike looked ready to spit nails as he opened the passenger door and got into the truck with her.

"Why did you tell everyone in town that I ditched you for a blond?" Mike asked, his eyes flashing fire.

"I didn't."

"You didn't?"

"Not me. Babs Dubinski spotted you taking a blond into your apartment complex last night."

"That was Shawna Lee. I was just taking her home."

"Shawna Lee lives with *you?*"

"Of course not! She lives in the same apartment complex, that's all. Her car wouldn't start and she needed groceries so I took her to the Red Owl."

"Oh," Hannah said, maintaining her pleasant expression. She wanted to ask Mike why that shopping trip had ended up at Bertanelli's Pizza, but she didn't.

"She invited me over to her place for dinner as a thank

you, but she's a lousy cook and I took her out for pizza instead."

Hannah's suspicious heart did a little jump and skip as
Mike smiled at her. She reminded herself that there was only
one way Mike could *know* that Shawna Lee was a lousy
cook, and her heart slowed to a regular rhythm again.

"You're probably wondering how I know she's a lousy
cook," Mike said, appearing to read Hannah's mind.

"Actually . . . I was," Hannah admitted.

"We had a potluck lunch out at the station and she
brought tuna hotdish. It was awful."

"Oh, really?" The hackles on the back of Hannah's neck
subsided and she felt better immediately. At least the woman
Mike claimed wasn't her competition was a lousy cook.

"There's only one exception and that's her baking. She
makes great brownies."

"That's nice," Hannah said, making a mental note never
to bake brownies for Mike.

"I've always been crazy about brownies," Mike went on,
not realizing that he was digging a deeper hole. "And with
Shawna Lee's brownies, you never know what kind of good
things you're going to get. Last Thursday, she put in miniature marshmallows and pecans. It was almost like eating
rocky road ice cream. Maybe you should try something like
that, Hannah. They'd probably go over great in your shop."

Mike's grin was engaging, the kind of grin that conjured
up thoughts in Hannah's mind of walking in the summer twi-
light holding hands, or ducking under a tall pine in the winter to share a kiss that chased away the cold. Then she
reminded herself that Mike had just suggested she bake
Shawna Lee's brownies to sell in her shop and she began to
bristle. The more she thought about it, the angrier she got,
and she had the urge to kick Mike in the shins. It was only
through supreme effort of will that she managed to keep
both feet firmly on the floor mat.

"So are we all okay now?"

"Okay about what?" Hannah asked, rousing herself from contemplating how many years she might get for assault and battery on an acting sheriff.

"About me taking Shawna Lee out to the grocery store and then to Bertanelli's for pizza."

"Sure." What else could she say?

"And I guess I'd better tell you the rest before somebody else does it for me. After the pizza I went over to Shawna Lee's apartment to help her hook up her surround sound."

"That's neighborly," Hannah said, inwardly fuming.

"I think she'd give you her brownie recipe if I asked her. Do you want it?"

Hannah blinked away the red she saw before her eyes. "No, thanks. I'm sure I can come up with something on my own."

"When you do, I'll taste them for you. I can tell you if they're as good as hers."

"Right," Hannah said, and then she clamped her lips together before she could say any more and verbally abuse an acting sheriff.

"Bill's waiting for me. I've got to run."

Mike reached out for her and pulled her into his arms before Hannah could come up with the strength to resist. His lips came down on hers and even though Hannah knew she was being a slave to her own desires, she didn't pull back. Kissing Mike was like flirting with fire, passing the flame close enough to heat, but not burn.

"I really missed you, Hannah," Mike breathed, pulling her closer. And even though Hannah was in an awkward position with one foot wedged under the brake pedal, his embrace was still thrilling.

Long moments passed in pure bliss before Mike finally released her. Hannah could feel that her breathing was ragged and she took a deep breath and let it out again in a shuddering sigh.

"How about some night this week?" Mike asked, opening the passenger door.

"What?"

"Will you have dinner with me some night this week? I'll call you when I can get free and set up the time."

"Sure," Hannah said and then the manners Delores had taught her kicked in. "That would be really nice, Mike. Thank you for asking."

Mike reached over to touch her cheek and then he was gone. Hannah blinked as the door closed behind him and drew another deep breath. What would a more sophisticated woman do with a man like Mike? It didn't seem to matter how angry she was with him. He still made her knees turn weak, her pulse race, and her stomach bounce all the way down to her toes.

Hannah buckled her seatbelt, started her engine, and checked her rearview mirror to make sure that Mike and Bill had driven away. But all she saw was gray. Her windows were steamed up. She was a bit old at thirty, but she'd finally joined the ranks of teenage couples that kissed in parked cars in cold weather and steamed up the windows.

"Come on, Moishe. Doctor Bob said you'd like it. It tastes really good." Hannah held Moishe with one hand and nudged the tip of the dropper against his mouth with the other. "It'll be all over in a second if you just open up."

Moishe glared at her balefully and his mouth remained tightly closed. For a cat who normally mewed and yowled on his prowls around the condo, Moishe had gone perfectly mute the moment he'd spotted the dropper in her hand.

"Don't make me late," Hannah warned, nudging a little harder with the dropper. "It's down the hatch with the vitamins and then you can have the food you really like."

Moishe gave a growl deep in his throat, but his mouth remained tightly closed. Hannah could tell he wasn't buying it. The growl gained in volume as she continued to poke at his mouth with the dropper and suddenly, as quick as lightning, Moishe backed out from under her hand, did a flip in midair, landed with a thud on the carpet, and streaked off toward the bedroom.

"Uh-oh," Hannah groaned, fearing the worst as she followed him. Just as she expected, Moishe had taken up a highly defensible position under her bed, where he knew she couldn't reach him.

"You know I can't pull you out when you go under there," Hannah complained, dropping to her knees to peer under the bedspread. "Come on out and take your medicine, Moishe. The other kitties like it."

A keening yowl emanated from the dark recesses where the head of the bed met the far wall. Hannah stretched out on her stomach and reached under the bed as far as she could, but the only things she encountered were a crumpled tissue, an old sock with a hole in the toe, and a ball point pen.

More yowls ensued as she pulled her hand back, and Hannah sighed as she got to her feet. "Right. Sure. You wouldn't do it when I had the dropper ready, but *now* you open your mouth!"

Once Hannah's five groups were involved in their baking, she motioned for Beatrice to join her by the rack of cupcakes she'd baked. "Try one of these. I didn't frost them this time, but you can probably tell if I'm on the right track."

"I think I can," Beatrice said, taking one of the cupcakes and peeling off the paper liner. She took a bite, chewed and swallowed, and then she shook her head. "Sorry, Hannah. These aren't right. Alma's were heavy, but not this heavy. Is that peanut butter I taste?"

"Yes. Whatever Alma used, it wasn't that thick. I knew it wasn't going to work, but since I'd mixed them up already, I figured I might as well bake them."

"They're not Alma's, but they're good," Beatrice said, reaching out for a second one. "Maybe you've got a new recipe here, Hannah."

"That's how I develop some of my cookie recipes. I start

with an idea of how it should taste and a basic no-frills cookie recipe. Then I add and subtract ingredients until what I bake matches what I've imagined. Sometimes I stop short of the mark if I stumble on a really good variation. I remember when I was trying to make . . ."

"Hannah? We've got a problem."

Hannah stopped in mid-sentence and turned to see Winnie Henderson waving at her. Winnie looked distressed and there wasn't much in this world that rattled Winnie. She never gave her exact age, but Hannah knew that she was old enough to have outlived four husbands, given birth to two children by each, and have almost three-dozen grandchildren and great-grandchildren that loved to come and stay with "Grannie," who'd played on an all-female baseball team during the Second World War and could still hit a ball out of the park.

"I'll tell you more later," Hannah told Beatrice, and then she hurried over to Winnie's kitchen workstation. "What's wrong, Winnie?"

Winnie gestured toward her mixing bowl and gave the contents a stir. "It's this banana bread. It smells great, but it's going to come out as heavy as a rock. Stir it yourself if you don't think I'm right."

"No need for that," Hannah said, shaking her head when Winnie offered her the spoon. "I can see you're right. The batter's much too stiff and it probably won't rise at all. Are you sure you measured everything correctly?"

Geraldine Goetz, who was the measurer in the group, nodded quickly. "I know we did. Luanne stood next to me and we double-checked everything."

"How about the flour. Did you sift it?"

"No," it was Lolly Kramer's turn to answer. "It called for unsifted flour. I scooped it out and leveled it off with a knife just the way you told us to."

Hannah smiled. "You did that exactly right, Lolly. And if

you measured correctly and used all the right ingredients, the fault has to be with the recipe. Whose is it?"

"Regina Todd's," Winnie handed her copy of the recipe to Hannah. "Do you think we should call her to see if she left out something?"

"Don't bother. If this is Regina's recipe, I know what's wrong. Show me the eggs you used, Patsy."

Patsy Beringer opened the refrigerator, took out a carton of eggs, and handed them to Hannah. "I used these. They're okay, aren't they?"

"They would be if this weren't Regina's recipe." Hannah breathed a sigh of relief now that she'd arrived at the answer to the problem. There would have been big fireworks between the two families if Hannah had failed to put Andrea's mother-in-law's recipe in the Lake Eden Cookbook.

"Why is Regina's recipe different?" Winnie asked, and Hannah realized that she hadn't explained her cryptic comment.

"Regina raises laying hens and the eggs she gets are at least double the size of the large eggs you can buy at the Red Owl. When she said three eggs, she meant three of *her* eggs, not three ordinary eggs."

Understanding dawned in Winnie's eyes. "I get it. More eggs would be more liquid. But how much more liquid can an egg add?"

"You'd be surprised. If a recipe doesn't specify the size, always use medium to large eggs. Each medium to large egg should yield a quarter of a cup."

"Then three eggs is three-fourths of a cup?" Winnie sounded surprised.

"It's supposed to be." Hannah handed the carton of eggs to Lolly Kramer. "Let's test it out. I think doubling the eggs ought to fix up that banana bread batter. Break three into a measuring cup, Lolly, and whisk them up with a fork. Then we'll see how much we get. We have to mix them up anyway, since we're trying to incorporate them after the fact."

Lolly broke three eggs into a measuring cup and whisked them until they were a uniform color. Then she set the cup down on the counter so the contents could settle and she could read the measurement.

"Three-quarters of a cup," she announced stepping back so that the others in her group could move closer and see for themselves. "Do you always measure your eggs this way, Hannah?"

Hannah shook her head. "I don't measure mine unless they seem unusually small or unusually large. And I always mix them up before I measure them. That way I can pour out some if I have too much, or add another egg if I don't have enough."

Winnie, who was a lot stronger than her small size would indicate, dumped the extra eggs into the bowl and mixed them into the batter. It took a few minutes, but soon they were incorporated.

"This feels about right," Winnie said, giving the mixture another stir and then handing the spoon to Hannah. "You try it."

Hannah stirred the batter. "It should work now. Pour it into the pans and let's bake it. If it turns out all right, we'll revise the recipe by doubling the eggs."

Several other groups asked for Hannah's opinion on various aspects of baking and soon the Jordan High Home Economics room was filled with delicious smells. There was an apple pie, a pan of pecan bars, a lemon poppy seed cake, Hannah's own recipe for German Chocolate Cake Cookies, and Andrea's mother-in-law's banana bread. All these different sweets baking at once had everyone's mouth watering.

Hannah walked from group to group, making sure she made contact with each of her students. She answered the occasional question, gave advice where it was needed, and offered her expert opinion when Donna Lempke couldn't decide if her group's lemon poppy seed cake was ready to take out of the oven. Then, when everything was cooling including the ovens, Hannah sat down at the teacher's desk and assembled recipes for her students to take home and test.

It was quiet in the huge room, even though the members of her class were chattering among themselves. Hannah was puzzled for a moment and then she realized that she was comparing the noise level this week with the noise level last week. Mike was no longer teaching the class next door and there were no more yells and whistles. Rick Murphy had taken over as the self-defense instructor and he'd told Hannah, before his class had started, that he planned to take his students outside during the second half of the period so that they could practice approaching a parked car and walking in a dark parking lot.

Once Hannah's class received their homework and divided up the goodies from the night's baking, everyone except Hannah headed for home. When the last of her students had left, Hannah checked the workstations to make sure everything was shipshape. That done, the only chore that remained was taking out the garbage.

Hannah picked up the garbage bag and headed for the outside door. She opened it, took one step toward the Dumpster, and stopped in her tracks. She knew she was being silly, but it seemed like tempting fate to approach the same Dumpster where she'd found Sheriff Grant.

"Hannah?"

A voice called out behind her and Hannah almost spilled the garbage. She whirled, then gave a sigh of relief as she saw Rick Murphy. "You scared me, Rick!"

"Sorry. I meant to get here earlier, but one of my students wanted some advice on home security. Just hand me that bag and I'll carry the garbage out for you."

"You will?" Hannah was puzzled. "But I can do it, Rick. It's not like my arm's broken or anything."

"I know, but Mike asked me to stop by after class and do

it. And then I'm supposed to walk you out to your car. Mike said that since he couldn't be here, he wanted me to make sure you weren't alone."

Five minutes later, Hannah was in her cookie truck, driving home, and there was smile on her face that had enough wattage to light up Eden Lake's official Christmas Tree. Mike had been concerned and he'd asked Rick to look out for her. That was really very sweet of him, almost sweet enough to make Hannah forget all about Shawna Lee's perfect figure and her fantastic brownies . . . almost, but not quite.

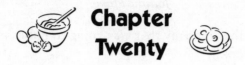

Chapter Twenty

Hannah stood at the sink at The Cookie Jar, pulling on gloves to protect the deep scratch Moishe had given her this morning when she'd held him down and tried to give him his vitamins. Lisa poked her head in from the coffee shop. "Telephone for you. It's Kurt Howe."

"Okay, tell him I'll be right with him," Hannah said with a sigh, heading for the phone. If the morning was any indication, Tuesday was not going to be a good day. It had started with a bang at five in the morning when Moishe decided to go fishing in the toilet. He'd only done that once before and it was shortly after she'd taken him in. Moishe was a bright cat. The moment he'd realized that his actions hadn't pleased her, he'd left all standing water, with the exception of his water bowl, untouched. As Hannah climbed out of bed to wipe up the surprisingly large amount of water that he'd splashed out on the bathroom floor, the thought crossed her mind that Moishe might have done it on purpose to get even for the vitamins she'd attempted to squirt down his throat. After several cups of life-giving coffee, she dismissed that notion as paranoid and gave the vitamins another try, which resulted in the deep scratch she was currently protecting.

"Hello, Kurt." Hannah greeted him, wincing a bit as the scratch began to throb under the tight latex glove. Kurt worked for the company that was going to publish the Lake Eden cookbook.

"Hi, Hannah. I called to see how the cookbook's coming along."

"Just fine. I'm teaching a night class at the school and we're testing all the recipes. Then we're going to have a big potluck dinner for the whole town and let everyone vote on which recipes should be included."

"When's the potluck?"

That question surprised Hannah. Kurt hadn't been that interested in their schedule before. Perhaps he wanted to come to Lake Eden to taste the recipes and vote? "We haven't set a firm date yet, but I want to do it right after Thanksgiving. We'd love to have you come, if you can."

"I'll try to make it. Just call and give my secretary the date. I've got some really big news, Hannah. I convinced my publisher to release your cookbook early. We thought it would be a perfect gift for the holiday season."

"You mean Christmas?"

"Christmas, Hanukah, Kwanzaa, whatever. It's going to be mostly buffet recipes, right?"

"Well . . . I guess you could call them buffet recipes. In Lake Eden we just say potluck."

"I like that better, personally. Potluck is much more ethnic. But my publisher wants to use the words *holiday* and *buffet* in the title. Do you think you could live with that?"

"Well . . ."

"He's sure it would sell better in upscale places like New York and Los Angeles."

Hannah's eyebrows headed for the ceiling. When Kurt first mentioned the cookbook, she'd envisioned something that would be sold locally, or perhaps statewide. She'd never even considered the possibility that it would be sold all over the country.

"Hannah? I know people voted and you decided on *Green Jell-O, A Lake Eden Potluck Cookbook* as a title, but my publisher doesn't think that'll do well nationally. He'd rather have *Holiday Buffet.* If you absolutely hate it, I can go back to him with alternatives."

"No," Hannah managed to croak out. "No, he probably knows best. After all, *buffet* is just a fancier name for *potluck.* But these are pretty simple recipes. Is that all right?"

"Give me an example."

"Well . . . there's Edna's Make Ahead Mashed Potatoes. She brings them to every potlu . . . uh . . . buffet we have. And then there's my mother's Hawaiian Pot Roast, and a couple of variations of Minnesota Hotdish."

"That all sounds great. You're making me hungry, Hannah."

"I know what you mean," Hannah said, feeling a bit hungry herself. "But since your publisher wants a fancier title, doesn't he want fancier names for the recipes?"

"Like what?"

"Like . . . Minnesota Hotdish could be Minnesota Cassoulet."

"No, *hotdish* is good. It'll make people think about sitting around the dinner table with family and friends. Just leave the recipe names the way they are, Hannah. If we have problems with any of them, we'll get together and change them."

"And our deadline is still the same?"

Kurt gave a little laugh. "I'm afraid not. That's the reason I called. Hold onto your hat, Hannah."

"Why?" Hannah sucked in her breath and held it. She had the feeling she wasn't going to like Kurt's answer.

"We're going to need everything in three weeks."

"Three weeks?!" Hannah was so shocked she almost dropped the phone. "But it wasn't supposed to be for three *months!*"

"I know. This is a fabulous opportunity, Hannah. My publisher's going to pull out all the stops to make your cookbook a success. I know the deadline is tight and it'll be a lot of work, but think about how proud everyone will be to see their favorite recipes in print."

"I'm thinking, I'm thinking," Hannah said. And she was. Perhaps she could do it if she had help.

"So shall I tell my publisher it's a go?"

Hannah took a deep breath and let it out again. And then she said the words that would add several big helpings to her already overflowing plate. "Yes, Kurt. Tell him it's a go."

An hour later, Hannah walked up to the counter at Lake Eden Neighborhood Pharmacy. Lisa had insisted that she talk to Jon Walker to get some kind of antibiotic cream for her hand. The cat scratch Moishe had given her this morning was puffing up and it was painful to touch.

"Hello, Hannah. What's wrong with your hand?" Jon greeted her.

"Cat scratch." Hannah held it out so that he could see. "Lisa sent me down for some antibiotic cream."

"Good for her. Cat scratches can be dangerous. Haven't you ever heard of cat scratch fever?"

"Only on an old rock and roll record my father used to play in the garage. There was one about poison ivy, too."

"A full-blown case of cat scratch fever and you'd wind up in the hospital. But don't worry, Hannah. We caught this in plenty of time. You should take some oral antibiotics to clear up the infection, and I'll get you some over the counter cream. Filling your prescription might take a while. I'll drop it off on my afternoon break if you'll treat me to a cookie."

"You're welcome to a cookie, but I don't have a prescription."

"You will just as soon as I put in a call to Doc Knight. Here's your cream. Use it morning, noon, and night and keep water away from that scratch."

Five minutes later, when Hannah walked in the front door of The Cookie Jar, Lisa was on the phone. She motioned to Hannah and Hannah slipped behind the counter to join her.

"It's Andrea," Lisa said, "and you should take it in the

kitchen. She says she's got news for you about you-know-what. I'll stay on until you pick up."

Hannah took enough time to slather on some of the antibiotic cream and then she picked up the phone. "I'm on now, Lisa."

"And I'm off," Lisa replied, hanging up with a click.

"Hi, Hannah," Andrea greeted her. "I called to tell you that Sean and Don have an airtight alibi for last Monday night. A bus came in a little before eight and it had a flat tire. Sean and the driver changed it while Don waited on all the passengers."

"Okay. I'll put it in the book."

"And I contacted all the names on Nettie's list. Every single one has an alibi."

Hannah was so astounded she gulped. "Every name? But there were so many!"

"No, there weren't, not when I weeded out all the sheriff's department personnel that Bill and Mike are checking."

"You're right," Hannah said, giving her sister a thumbs-up she couldn't see over the phone. "There's no sense in duplicating our efforts. So you wrote down the alibis and now you want me to verify them?"

"No, I already did that."

"You did? But how did you find the time?"

"It's a trade secret I learned in real estate school. Do you remember that old perfume ad, *Promise her anything, but give her Arpege?*"

"Not really."

"Well, you would if you ever wore perfume. It's a little like that . . . only different."

"Okay," Hannah said, dropping the discussion, since Andrea's explanation had raised more questions than it had answered.

"So what's next? I'm chained to this couch, I've already done everything I can think of, and I'm going to go crazy just sitting here."

"I don't really have any . . ." Hannah stopped in mid-sentence as the perfection solution to her sister's boredom occurred to her. Andrea could type a lot faster than Hannah could. And ever since Hannah had agreed to meet Kurt Howe's new, shortened deadline, she'd been wondering how she'd ever find the extra hours to get all those recipes typed up.

"What?" Andrea asked. "You thought of something I could do, didn't you?"

"Yes. Is your laptop handy?"

"I've got it right here. What do you need?"

"How about doing some typing for me? It's really important."

"What kind of typing?"

"Recipes for the Lake Eden Cookbook, except it's not called the Lake Eden cookbook anymore. Now it's called something with *Holiday* and *Buffet* in the title, but we don't have to change the names of any recipes."

There was a long silence and when Andrea spoke again, she sounded worried. "I think you'd better start from the beginning, Hannah. For a logical person, you're not making much sense."

It took a few minutes, but at last Andrea had the full story of Kurt Howe's call and how the deadline had been moved up. "And it's actually going to be published in time for the holidays?" she asked.

"That's what Kurt said."

"Then of course I'll type your recipes. Bring them over and I'll get started."

Hannah glanced at the clock. "I'll leave here at eleven and I'll bring you lunch. What do you want?"

"Pizza, but I can't have it. Too much salt."

"What *can* you have?"

"I've got a list right here." Hannah heard paper crinkling and then Andrea came back on the line. "I'm looking at my diet sheet now. It looks like I can eat almost anything that doesn't taste good."

Hannah laughed. She couldn't help it. Sometimes Andrea was funny without even realizing it. "How about a chef's salad with dressing on the side. I can stop by the café."

"That sounds good, but how about dessert? Will you bring me some cookies?"

"Sure. What kind do you want?"

"Something with chocolate and pecans. I'm dying for some chocolate and pecans are my favorite nuts. But you don't have time to make cookies just for me, do you?"

"I've got time," Hannah said, already planning out which ingredients to use to make some special cookies for her sister.

Andrea's Pecan Divines

Preheat oven to 350 degrees F., rack in the middle position

2 cups melted butter *(4 sticks, one pound)*
3 cups white sugar
1 ½ cups brown sugar
4 teaspoons vanilla
4 teaspoons baking soda
2 teaspoons salt
4 beaten eggs
5 cups flour *(no need to sift)*
3 cups chocolate chips
4 cups chopped pecans

Melt the butter. (*Nuke it for 3 minutes on high in a microwave-safe container, or melt it in a pan on the stove.*) Mix in the white sugar and the brown sugar. Add the vanilla and the baking soda and mix. Add the eggs and stir it all up. Add half the flour, the chocolate chips, and the chopped pecans. Stir well to incorporate. Add the rest of the flour and mix thoroughly.

Drop by teaspoons onto greased cookie sheets, 12 cookies to a standard-size sheet. If the dough is too sticky to handle, chill it slightly and try again. Bake at 350 degrees F. for 10 to 12 minutes or until nicely browned.

Let cool two minutes, then remove cookies from the baking sheet and transfer to a wire rack to finish cooling.

Yield: Approximately 10 dozen.

Andrea says these are the best cookies she's ever tasted and I saved her life by baking them.

Chapter
Twenty-One

Hannah felt good as she sat on the high stool behind the cash register at The Cookie Jar and surveyed her world. Every table was filled and all of her customers had been coffeed, teaed, and cookied. Now they were busy talking to each other as they munched and sipped, enjoying themselves. The glass serving jars had been replenished, the counter couldn't have been wiped down any better, and all the sugar, creamer, and artificial sweetener containers had been filled to the brim. She'd already delivered the recipes to Andrea, along with one of Rose's best chef salads, and there was nothing else she needed to do until Lisa came back from lunch.

"Hi, Hannah!" Jon Walker stepped into the coffee shop and took a seat at the counter. "Here's your prescription. Doc says you should take two right away and one more tonight before bed. From then on it'll be one pill, three times a day."

"Thanks, Jon." Hannah took the white bag, stashed it behind the counter, and grabbed three of Jon's favorite Oatmeal Raisin Crisps. She placed them on a napkin and served them with a mug of hot, black coffee. "It's on the house. And thanks for the personal service."

"No problem. The antibiotic Doc prescribed is expensive, but it should do the trick. I gave you a discount because I know your health insurance doesn't cover drugs."

"How expensive was it?" Hannah asked, holding her breath. She wasn't exactly broke this month, but there wasn't all that much left over in the budget, either. Moishe's shots and vet visit hadn't come cheap and his vitamins had been much more expensive than the human equivalent.

"I put the invoice in the bag."

Hannah took it out and gulped as she read the total. The little bottle of pills that Jon just delivered cost over eighty dollars!

"Sticker shock," Jon commented, looking sympathetic. "Ted Koester had that same look on his face."

"Ted is taking these, too?"

"That's right. And when he picked up the prescription he told everybody in the drugstore about it so I'm not breaking any confidences. He gashed his arm on a piece of metal at work last week. It probably would have been okay if he'd washed it out right after it happened, but he didn't and it got infected."

"Poor Ted. Hold on a second, Jon. I'll get my purse and write you a check."

A minute or two later, their business finished, Hannah perched on her stool while Jon sipped his coffee. "Are you decorating the drugstore for Halloween again?" she asked.

"I've got the girls working on it right now. If I don't pop up behind the counter as the mad chemist stirring something that looks like slime in a beaker, the kids will be really disappointed."

"They really get a kick out of seeing the business owners in costume. Lisa's carving pumpkins to put in our window."

"What are you wearing for a costume?"

"Lisa's going to be a black cat. She showed me the costume last week."

"She's bound to look cute in something like that, but I asked about you."

Hannah shook her head. "I'll stick to the kitchen. That way I won't have to come up with a costume. And if I have to come up front for any reason, I'll put on the same old sheet I used last year and be the Ghost of Cookies Past."

"You're going to the community center for the party, aren't you?"

"I wouldn't miss it. I'm going to take Tracey since Andrea has to stay home with her feet up."

"The baby?"

"Doc Knight's orders."

"Are you bringing cookies for the party?"

"Of course. Twenty dozen, just like always. The only problem is, I haven't decided which cookies to bring. I'd like to do something special for Halloween."

"How about corn cookies? My mother made those for Halloween when we lived on the reservation."

"Corn cookies?" Hannah was puzzled. She'd never heard of corn cookies, but she knew that corn was a basic ingredient in Native American cooking. Perhaps it was a tribal custom to bake cookies with corn in them for Halloween, but that seemed odd. Hannah was fairly sure that Halloween had no celebratory significance in American Indian culture.

"What's the matter, Hannah? Haven't you ever heard of corn cookies?"

"No, I haven't," Hannah said, wondering how to word the second half of her response. "Are they . . . uh . . . an old Indian recipe?"

Jon threw back his head and laughed long and hard. Several people seated at the tables turned to stare at him, but he just laughed harder. When he had calmed down enough to speak again, he asked, "An old Indian recipe? I guess you're right, in a way. My mother's an old Indian."

"I didn't mean *that!*" Hannah retorted, chuckling along with Jon. "But I really would like to know more about them. Are corn cookies ethnic, or tribal, or whatever's politically correct to say now?"

Jon shrugged. "I really doubt it. As far as I know, my mother was the only woman on the reservation who baked them."

"Did she use corn meal? Or canned corn?" Hannah asked. She was about to add cornflakes to her list of possibilities, but Jon was laughing so hard he wouldn't have heard her anyway.

"None of the above. I'm not talking about real corn, Hannah. My mother made pumpkin cookies and decorated the tops with candy corn."

Hannah climbed the stairs to her condo with resolve. She was determined to give Moishe his vitamin supplement. Several of her patrons had offered advice on medicating cats and a couple of techniques sounded as if they might work. First of all, she had to put on a heavy, long-sleeved shirt. Everyone agreed that this was important. She also had to wear gloves to guard against scratches and bites. Trudi Schmann thought that Hannah should tie Moishe up so that she could use both hands to medicate him. She'd even suggested duct-taping his feet together. That unhelpful hint had gone in one of Hannah's ears and out the other. Everyone knew that Trudi didn't like cats.

Vern Kleinschmidt suggested tranquilizing Moishe so that giving him the vitamins would be easier. But the moment the suggestion left his mouth, he realized that there was no way to tranquilize Moishe without giving him a pill. And if Hannah had to hold him and give him a pill, she might as well give him the vitamins.

Lisa came up with the best feline offensive, the one Hannah intended to use. She was going to wrap Moishe tightly in a large bath towel so he couldn't scratch, set him on her lap facing her, and hold him in place with her legs. Then she'd have both hands free and could use one to block his nose. Moishe would be forced to breathe through his mouth, and when he opened it, she'd squirt in the vitamins.

"I'm home," Hannah called out as she unlocked the door to her condo, but no orange and white blur hurtled itself into her arms. Moishe must be keeping a low profile, perhaps because he felt guilty for scratching her this morning. "Moishe? Where are you, boy?"

Hannah tossed her shoulder bag purse and her jacket on the chair by the door and started the search for her missing cat. With the exception of tipping the couch on end so that she could see beneath it, she explored every feline hiding place in the living room and came up with nothing.

Hannah flicked on the kitchen light and checked the narrow space by the side of the refrigerator, the seats of the chairs that were pushed under the formica table, and the area behind the kitchen wastebasket. She even looked on top of the refrigerator, although he hadn't jumped up there in a while. Moishe wasn't in the kitchen.

He wasn't in the laundry room, either. Or the guest bedroom. Hannah stepped into her bedroom and called out again. Moishe had to be here. There was no way he could have gotten out.

She was about to go through the rooms again when she heard a pathetic mew. Then Moishe appeared, pulling himself out from under the bed. Hannah's heart plummeted to her toes when she saw him. Something was terribly wrong. Her poor kitty was trembling so hard he could barely move and he was crawling along on his belly.

"Come here, sweetheart," Hannah crooned, reaching out to carefully gather him into her arms. She held him gingerly, fearing he might be injured, and set him on his favorite goose down pillow.

Moishe looked up at her as she sat down on the bed beside him and Hannah could swear he blinked away a tear. Then he pulled himself closer to her and licked her hand.

"Poor baby," Hannah murmured, leaning down to nuzzle him on the top of his head. "Did something scare you?"

Moishe mewed again and pushed his head up against her hand, soliciting more gentle pets from his mistress. Hannah obliged and felt for injury. Nothing seemed to be broken, and there were no wounds that she could see or feel.

After several long minutes of scratching and soothing, Moishe was calm again. Hannah made sure that he was bribed into complacency by a handful of his favorite salmon-flavored kitty treats, and then she headed off to see if she could spot what had disturbed him.

The windows were secure and the door had been locked when she came in. Finding nothing amiss in any of the other rooms, Hannah headed into the bathroom. And that was when she found the telltale piece of evidence that told her exactly what had happened. The liquid vitamin supplement she'd left on the kitchen counter was now in the bottom of her toilet bowl.

"Uh-oh," Hannah groaned. No wonder Moishe had been trembling when he'd come out from under the bed! He knew he'd done wrong.

Should she punish him? Hannah considered it for a split second and quickly discarded that notion. Moishe had been kicked around and abused during his former life on the streets. This was a safe haven for him and there was no way Hannah was going to jeopardize the trust they'd built up in one another. Everyone said that unless you caught your pets in the act, punishment after the fact would only confuse them. And the way that Moishe had trembled, mewed pitifully, and crawled to her on his belly when she'd come home certainly indicated contrition.

Hannah fished out the bottle of vitamin supplement and put it in the cabinet under the sink. She couldn't bear to throw away something that had been that expensive, but she didn't intend to use it again. It was simply too traumatic for both of them. There had to be something else she could do that wouldn't upset either one of them. Tonight she'd feed Moishe his regular kitty crunchies. They'd both been through enough for one day. And tomorrow morning she'd stop by the vet's office and ask Doctor Bob's advice.

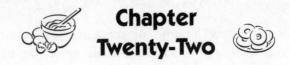

Chapter
Twenty-Two

"Is that a new cookie recipe?" Lisa asked the next morning, bringing Hannah a fresh cup of coffee from the urn. They'd finished the baking and now they were relaxing at their favorite table in the back until it was time to open.

"It's a new recipe, but it's not for cookies. I stopped by the vet's office this morning and Sue gave me a recipe for making Moishe's senior cat food from scratch."

"Uh-oh," Lisa said with a frown. "My brilliant plan to give Moishe his vitamins wasn't so brilliant after all?"

"It could have been brilliant, I just don't know. I never got the chance to test it out. When I got home last night, Moishe was hiding under the bed and his vitamin bottle was at the bottom of the toilet bowl."

"I guess that tells you what he thinks of food supplements."

"It certainly does," Hannah said with a grin. "Anyway, I decided to try something that both of us could live with. Cooking his food doesn't seem to be that difficult."

"Let me see." Lisa peered over Hannah's shoulder at the typewritten recipe. "You're going to boil liver for him every morning and every evening?"

"It's worth it as long as I don't have to give him those vitamins."

"How about the rest of this stuff? You have to cook that,

too." Lisa read the list of additional ingredients and shuddered. "This sounds really horrible, especially for breakfast."

"It's not that bad, Lisa. It's almost like an omelet, if you think about it."

"I don't want to think about it, especially first thing in the morning. What is this last ingredient, calcium carbonate?"

"It's what's in eggshells. Sue said I could just crush the shells really fine and add the powder to Moishe's food. The whole thing'll be like a crunchy liver omelet with a side of rice."

"Yuck. Just thinking about it is making me sick. I don't know what's worse, the liver or the eggshells. Do you think he'll eat it?"

"I think so, especially when I finish seasoning it. I can't bear the thought of making an omelet without salt and pepper and maybe a little dash of garlic powder."

"But animals aren't supposed to have seasoning."

"Says who? I bet that comes from people who never had to taste pet food. If I were a cat or a dog, I'd want my dinner spiced up with a little seasoning. I might even douse it with ketchup if I could figure out how to get the cap off the bottle."

When Lisa came back from lunch, she handed Hannah a bag from the Red Owl. "Here, Hannah. I picked up a sack of candy corn. Where do you want it?"

"In the kitchen, on the counter by the sink."

Hannah made the rounds with the coffee carafe while Lisa took the bag to the kitchen and washed her hands. When she came back out, she was wearing her hair net and one of the pretty serving aprons that a local seamstress had made for them.

"You should see the community center," Lisa said. "The seniors are helping to decorate it for Halloween and it looks really good."

"How's the Haunted Basement coming along?"

"It's almost done. They were just moving in the furniture while I was there. Edna was in the kitchen, filling the bags of treats for the kids, and she had an idea for Alma's cupcakes."

"What's that?" Hannah asked. Edna had been baking for almost half a century and she knew what she was doing.

"She said she thought it had to be some kind of thickened liquid."

"I agree," Hannah said. "Did she have any suggestions?"

"Only one, but she said it couldn't be right."

"What was it?" Hannah wanted to know. Even if Edna's suggestion wouldn't work for the secret ingredient, it might give them some ideas.

"Sweetened condensed milk."

"But that could be it! The recipe could use more sugar and it's just about the right consistency. Why didn't Edna think it would work?"

"Because Alma was known for pinching her pennies."

"You mean sweetened condensed milk would be too expensive for her to use in a recipe?"

"Not exactly. Edna said Alma would use it, but she sure wouldn't throw any away."

"I get it," Hannah began to smile. "The recipe calls for half a cup and there's more than that in the can. But maybe Alma doubled the recipe."

Lisa shook her head. "Edna thought of that. Even if she doubled the recipe, she'd still have a quarter cup left in the can. Edna said Alma never would have stood still for that."

"Edna's probably right," Hannah said, refilling her coffee cup. "When you get a second, Mayor Bascomb needs another Molasses Crackle and Mrs. Jessup wants a dozen Peanut Butter Melts to take home with her. Call me if it gets really busy. I'm going to mix up a batch of Corn Cookies for us to test."

* * *

Hannah had just finished decorating her first pans of Corn Cookies when there was a knock at the back door. She slid the pans on shelves in the bakers' rack and hurried to the door.

"Sorry to bother you, Hannah." Barbara Donnelly stood there, shivering in the bitter wind that blew down the alley, "but I just thought of something you should know."

Hannah glanced up at the iron-gray sky. The KCOW weatherman hadn't predicted snow, but he could be wrong . . . again. "Come in and warm up, Barbara."

"Do you think it's going to snow?" Barbara asked, stepping into the warm kitchen and sniffing appreciatively.

"Maybe. Sit down at the workstation and I'll get you a cup of coffee. You can be my taste tester for the test batch of Corn Cookies I just baked."

"That's a job I can sink my teeth into," Barbara quipped, accepting the cookies that Hannah brought her. "These must be for Halloween. They're cute, Hannah. I like the candy corn on top."

Hannah waited until Barbara took a bite, then asked the important question. "Are they good?"

"Very good. They'll be perfect for the party." Barbara took another bite. "I think he had it with him, Hannah."

"Who had what where?" Hannah asked, missing only the *when* and the *why*. According to her college journalism professor, the five w's were the basis of all good reporting.

"Sheriff Grant. I've been thinking about that missing report and I'm almost positive that he took it. There were only two keys to the file cabinet. I had one and Sheriff Grant had the other."

"But wouldn't you have noticed it was missing?" Hannah asked, fetching her steno pad and flipping it open to take notes.

"Not unless I'd had a reason to look for it. I didn't go through the files every day."

"So you have no idea when Sheriff Grant took it?"

"None at all," Barbara shook her head, "but I might know where it is."

Hannah's head snapped back from her notes as if a puppeteer standing above her had pulled a string. "Where do you think it is?"

"In his briefcase. He always put the important papers in there."

"But . . . wouldn't Mike have found it?"

Barbara shook her head again. "Not unless he knew how to open the secret compartment. And I'm almost positive that Sheriff Grant didn't tell anyone about *that.*"

"What secret compartment?"

"The one in the James Bond briefcase I gave him for Christmas last year. I always bought him James Bond things for gifts. I ordered it from a catalogue."

"And it had a secret compartment." Hannah jotted down a note. "What did it look like, Barbara?"

"The secret compartment?"

"No, the briefcase."

"It was just an ordinary brown leather briefcase. That's what was so great about it. You could never tell it had a secret compartment just by looking at it."

"So Mike could have found it, searched it, and not realized that something was hidden inside?"

"That's certainly possible. The secret compartment is tricky to open and you'd never see the catches if you didn't know they were there. You have to release them in a certain order."

"Do you know how to do it?"

"Of course I do. I had to help Sheriff Grant figure it out. You just . . ."

"I don't have to know, Barbara," Hannah said, interrupting her description of the procedure. "If I come across the briefcase, I'll bring it to you to open. Any ideas on where I might find it?"

Barbara thought about that for a moment. "If it's not in his squad car, it has to be in his home office."

"Couldn't it be in his office at the sheriff's station?"

"No. I already called there to check." Barbara held up a hand to cut off Hannah's question. "Don't worry. Shawna Lee doesn't know why I wanted to know. I just told her that she might find some extra keys in Sheriff Grant's briefcase and she ought to take them out and give them to Mike."

Hannah thought about what Barbara had told her. "If the briefcase was in the squad car, Mike must have it. But if it's in Sheriff Grant's home office, he probably doesn't. I'd better go over to Nettie's and check."

"You can't do that."

"Why not?"

"Sheriff Grant's home office is still taped off. Nettie told me that before she left town."

"Nettie's gone?"

"She left yesterday morning for Wisconsin. Jim's youngest sister took it really hard and Nettie went to help her with the kids. She told me she'd be gone at least a week, maybe two."

After Barbara left, Hannah baked the rest of the cookies. And while she baked, she thought about how she could get into Nettie's house to search Sheriff Grant's home office. By the time she was finished with the baking, she hadn't come up with a single possibility, and she sighed as she picked up the platter of cookies to carry them out for Lisa and their customers to taste.

The phone rang just as Hannah was heading for the swinging door and she put the platter down on the counter again to answer it. "The Cookie Jar. This is Hannah speaking."

"Oh, I'm so glad I caught you, dear!"

Hannah came close to groaning. It was Delores and she wasn't really in the mood to talk to her mother. Still, Delores *was* her mother and that entitled her to preferential treatment. "Hi, Mother. What can I do for you?"

"That's a presumptuous question, Hannah. You're assuming that I want something from you. What if I don't want anything at all?"

"Then I apologize," Hannah said quickly.

"That's better," Delores said, and her voice sounded much friendlier. "But as it turns out, you were right. I did call to ask you a favor."

"Then what can I do for you, Mother?"

Hannah burst out laughing and so did Delores. It was a rare moment when mother and daughter were on the same wavelength, appreciating each other's sense of humor.

"I was wondering if you'd have time to pick up Tracey from Kiddie Korner at five and take her out to The Pumpkin Patch to pick up her costume. I promised Andrea I'd do it, but something came up."

"I can do it," Hannah said, jotting a note so she wouldn't forget. "Which costume is she getting?"

"The pirate. Andrea called and put it on reserve for her. And while you're there, you might want to pick up a costume for yourself, since you're taking Tracey around on Halloween."

"I might just do that," Hannah said, knowing that saying this would please her mother. She had no intention of renting a costume, not when she had a perfect good sheet with holes cut out for ghostly eyes.

"Thank you, Hannah. I really appreciate you doing this for me. It would have been a terrible time crunch if I'd tried to get out there and back before six. And I never would have had time to dress!"

"Dress for what?" Hannah was curious. As far as she knew, her mother didn't have any club meetings on Wednesday nights.

"Ballroom dancing with Winthrop."

"Winthrop?" Hannah's voice was not entirely steady as she echoed the name. "Who's Winthrop?"

"Oh, the most marvelous, sophisticated man! He reminds me of Kenneth Branagh. And he's such a talented dancer."

"Winthrop?"

"Yes, dear. I've never danced with Kenneth Branagh."

"But you've danced with Winthop?"

"Of course. We waltzed last Wednesday night."

"Where?" Hannah asked.

"At the Red Owl."

That stopped Hannah in her tracks for a moment, then she drew a deep breath. "Let me get this straight, Mother. You went dancing at the Red Owl?"

"That's right, dear. Winthrop is simply a master at the waltz. I don't know when I've had so much fun!"

"Okay . . ." Hannah paused, trying to think of a reasonable response. When one didn't occur to her, she decided to wing it and tell her mother exactly what she was thinking. "I know they play music for shoppers over the loudspeakers, but I really can't believe you actually waltzed up and down the aisles with another customer. I'm surprised you didn't knock down that pyramid of soup cans they put up as a display in the middle of the store!"

There was silence for a moment. Then Delores started to laugh. She laughed so hard she didn't seem to notice that Hannah wasn't joining in.

"I didn't dance in the grocery store, Hannah," Delores said, when she had calmed down a bit. "I danced *above* the grocery store in Danielle's studio. That's just so funny, dear. I can hardly wait to tell Winthrop."

Hannah felt like a first-class fool. She'd completely forgotten that Danielle had named her studio the Red Owl Dance Studio. No doubt Delores would have a laugh fest with Winthrop about Hannah's misconception, but her embarrassment wasn't the issue here. "You still haven't told me who Winthrop is, Mother."

"He's another student, dear. Carrie and I signed up for Danielle's ballroom dancing class and our first lesson was last Wednesday. Poor Carrie got stuck with Earl Flensburg, but I got Winthrop for a partner. Isn't that just wonderfully lucky for me?"

"Lucky," Hannah repeated, suspecting that luck hadn't had anything to do with it; some kind of dirty dealing had to have gone on. If Winthrop really was as handsome and fleet of foot as her mother had described, Delores would have pulled out all the stops to have him as her partner. Hannah wanted to ask how she finagled that feat, but Delores wouldn't tell her anyway, so she sighed and settled for saying, "Okay, Mother. You go have fun dancing the waltz with Winthrop tonight."

"Oh, it's the tango tonight, dear. That's why I need time to get dressed. I bought a darling outfit with slits on both sides of the skirt. I'm going to be the envy of every woman there."

"Mmm," Hannah murmured, settling for the most impartial comment she could make. But after she said goodbye and hung up the phone, she realized that she had the answer to Andrea's question. Their mother was involved with a man, at least in dancing class. As Hannah pushed open the door to the coffee shop and headed in to rejoin Lisa, she couldn't quite shake the vision of her mother dancing a sultry tango with a rose held between her teeth.

CORN COOKIES

Preheat oven to 375 degrees F.,
rack in the middle position

2 cups white sugar
1 cup butter *(2 sticks, 1/2 pound)*
1 egg
1 15-ounce *(by weight)* can mashed pumpkin *(I used Libby's)*
1 cup chopped walnuts
1 cup golden raisins
1 teaspoon cinnamon
½ teaspoon cardamom
1 teaspoon salt
2 teaspoons vanilla
2 teaspoons baking soda
2 teaspoons baking powder
4 cups flour *(no need to sift)*

package of candy corn

Melt the butter. Add the sugar and mix. Let the mixture cool to room temperature and then stir in the egg. Add all of the rest of the ingredients except the flour, mixing after each addition. Add the flour, one cup at a

time, and mix it thoroughly. Let the cookie dough sit for 5 minutes to "rest."

Drop by spoonful on a greased cookie sheet, 12 cookies per standard-size sheet. (*If the dough is too sticky, refrigerate it for a few minutes to firm it up.*) Flatten the cookies with a greased spatula. Bake at 375 degrees F. for 8 to 10 minutes.

When the cookies come out of the oven, leave them on the cookie sheets and immediately press pieces of candy corn on top as a design. Do this right away, so that the candy will stick after the cookies have cooled.***

Let the cookies cool on the sheets for 2 minutes and then transfer them to a wire rack to cool completely.

Yield: 6 to 7 dozen, depending on cookie size.

***If you fail to put on the candy corn when the cookies are still hot from the oven, all is not lost. You can put it on later using a little dab of powdered sugar frosting (*powdered sugar with a tiny bit of milk*) as "glue."

Tracey's friends really loved these cookies and they all offered to help me decorate them next year.

Chapter
Twenty-Three

"She didn't!" Andrea was still sputtering when Hannah came back to the room after hanging Tracey's costume in the closet.

"She did. As I recall her description was, the *most marvelous, sophisticated man*. She even compared him to an older version of Kenneth Branagh. I could be wrong, but she sounded pretty smitten to me."

"Smitten? You mean, like . . . in love?"

"I'm not sure about love, but she was a lot more than just politely interested."

Andrea gave an exasperated sigh. "Just what I need! Honestly, Hannah, I've never felt so helpless in my life. Here I am swelling up like a toad and I'm confined to this you-know-what couch while Mother's running around town with a gigolo!"

"What's a gigolo, Mommy?" Tracey asked, coming into the living room in time to hear Andrea's last comment.

"Tracey! I didn't know you were there. Um . . ." Andrea turned to Hannah with a desperate look in her eyes. "Aunt Hannah will tell you what it is."

"It's an Italian word for a man who is skilled at socializing with other people, especially women."

"Oh," Tracey said and she looked wise beyond her years. "You must be talking about Winthrop."

"You know Winthrop?" Both Andrea and Hannah asked the question, almost in tandem.

"No, but he called the last time I was at Grandma's. He said something funny because Grandma's face turned all red and she giggled."

"Mother *giggled,*" Hannah repeated, giving Andrea a look before she turned back to Tracey. "Do you happen to know Winthrop's last name?"

"Harrington. I can spell it."

"That would be good, honey," Andrea said, glancing at Hannah who was already digging in her shoulder bag purse for her notebook.

Hannah wrote down the name, and then she asked the obvious question. "How did you know how to spell it?"

"It was on the flowers."

"*What* flowers?" Andrea and Hannah asked simultaneously.

"The ones Grandma got. Are you mad? I know I'm not supposed to snoop."

Hannah glanced at Andrea, who was fighting valiantly to keep a straight face. "Your mother's not mad this time, but you really aren't supposed to read things like that. When a man sends a woman flowers, the card is meant to be private."

"I know," Tracey said with a sigh, "but I had to know if Winthrop was after Grandma's money."

Andrea looked shocked. "What made you think that Winthrop might be after her money?"

"I saw it on television, Mommy."

"So you think Winthrop might be a criminal?" Hannah asked.

"I don't know. All I did was read his card. It'd be naughty to tell you what it said."

"Not necessarily," Andrea blurted out. "I mean, if Winthrop is a criminal, Aunt Hannah and I should know so that we can protect Grandma."

Tracey looked confused. "So the rules about snooping change sometimes?"

"Yes," Andrea said, glancing over at Hannah. "Aunt Hannah will explain."

Hannah muttered under her breath. If she were to be absolutely truthful, she'd have to tell Tracey that the rules changed every time her mother and her aunt really wanted to know something. "The rules *do* change. Maybe they shouldn't, but they do. It's very complicated and I don't want to get into that right now."

"It's for later, when I'm older?"

"That's right."

"Okay," Tracey said. "The flower note started with two words I didn't know."

"Really?" Hannah was surprised. Tracey had learned to read last year and she could sound out almost any word.

"They looked like *moon* and *cherries* spelled wrong."

"*Mon Cherie!*" Andrea breathed, exchanging glances with Hannah before she turned back to Tracey. "It's a term of endearment in French. Was the rest of the note in French, too?"

"I don't think so because I could read it. It said, *My arms are empty without you.*"

"Oh, brother!" Hannah muttered, trying not to frown. "Did Grandma actually fall for that line?"

Tracey shrugged. "She had this funny look on her face when she read it, like she was going to cry or something."

"Uh-oh!" It was Andrea's turn to groan. "Was there any more to the note, honey?"

"Just his name, Winthrop Harrington. And right after his name, he wrote an eleven."

"An eleven?" Andrea was clearly puzzled. "I wonder what that means?"

Hannah also looked puzzled for a moment and then she laughed. "I think I know. Was it an eleven with a line above it and a line below it?"

"Yes! How did you know, Aunt Hannah?"

"It's a Roman numeral and it stands for *the second*. It means his father is also named Winthrop Harrington."

"Why would he want Grandma to know that?"

"I'm not sure," Hannah said, but she exchanged meaningful glances with Andrea. Delores would be swept off her feet by Winthrop Harrington's ancestry, especially if it included a crumbling old manor house from the Regency period and a title to go with it.

"Did Grandma use any titles when she spoke to Mr. Harrington on the phone?" Andrea asked.

"Titles?" Tracey looked confused. "You mean like the names of books?"

Hannah shook her head. "No, your mommy's talking about words like earl, and viscount, and duke."

"No . . ." Tracey said with a frown, "but she did say something bad."

"What was that?"

"Grandma swore. And she said it right in front of me."

Hannah was shocked. Delores would rather walk over hot coals than swear in front of Tracey. "What did she say, Tracey?"

"I'm not supposed to say it unless I'm in church."

"In church?" Andrea looked thoroughly mystified.

"Your mother will excuse you, this once," Hannah said, smiling at Tracey, who looked very nervous about the direction this conversation was taking. "It's not a trap, Tracey. We really need to know."

Tracey thought about that for a moment. "Okay. Grandma said *Lord*."

"Uh-oh. That's bad," Hannah said with a groan, but when she saw the panicked expression on Tracey's face she reached out for her niece's hand. "Not you, Tracey. When *Lord* is used like that, it isn't swearing. It's something you call a British subject who has a title."

"Oh." Tracey looked very relieved. "I get it Aunt Hannah. It's like when Anna Crinkles meets Lord Bluenose."

"Um . . ." Hannah shrugged and turned to Andrea for guidance.

"That's right, honey," Andrea said and glancing at Hannah. "It's a library book she's reading. Maybe you'd better go finish it, Tracey. Daddy said he'd take you to the library to check out some new books tonight."

Once Tracey rushed off, Hannah and Andrea just stared at each other for a moment. Hannah was the first to speak. "So Winthop's British, he's got a title, he dances like a dream, and he reminds her of Kenneth Branagh. Let's face it, Andrea. Unless we can send him on an expedition to the North Pole, Mother's a goner."

"No, I haven't eaten yet, Mike," Hannah said, holding the phone with her left hand and dropping chunks of beef liver into boiling water with the right. "I'm just making Moishe's dinner."

As if to prove her statement, Moishe yowled from the vicinity of Hannah's left ankle. Hannah glanced down at him and then she addressed what Mike had said. "Believe me, you don't want to know. It would turn you off food for life."

Working with one hand, Hannah managed to scoop out the liver with a slotted spoon, but she gave a little groan as she did it.

Both Moishe and Mike reacted to her groan. Moishe rubbed a little harder against her ankle in kitty appreciation for what she was doing, and Mike asked her what was wrong.

"Nothing if you're a cat," Hannah told him. "I can be ready in twenty minutes. Just buzz me at the gate and I'll walk out to the road to meet you."

Once she'd hung up the phone, Hannah turned her attention to the liver again. It was a dead-looking gray and it smelled like . . . boiled liver. Since boiled liver wasn't anywhere near her list of favorite scents, she was glad she'd thought to tell Mike she'd meet him outside.

"Coming up, Moishe," Hannah said, pulling out a frying pan and setting it on a burner. She turned on the heat, measured out Moishe's allotment of oil, and tossed in the liver and the white rice she'd cooked earlier. Then she dumped an egg in her food processor, shell and all. She whirled it up until she couldn't hear the shell clatter against the blades any longer and added it to the contents of the frying pan.

"Lovely," Hannah sighed, stirring everything around until it congealed into an unappetizing mass. Some seasoning might have helped, but she checked and found out that Lisa had been right; Moishe couldn't have any. Hannah scraped it into Moishe's food bowl and set it on the floor in front of him, faking a big smile. *"Bon appetit."*

Moishe sniffed at his food bowl and for one long moment, Hannah was afraid that he was going to refuse her home-cooked meal. But then he purred, bent down, and took the first bite.

"Do you like it?" Hannah asked, feeling like a Culinary Institute of America student begging for praise from a C.I.A. chef.

Moishe didn't even bother to glance up. He just dove right in for another bite, and then another. The cat who had only sniffed at his food for the past few days was now all teeth and appetite.

"Thank goodness for that!" Hannah murmured, breathing a big sigh of relief. At last she'd found something that Moishe would eat, something that was actually good for him. Leaving her feline roommate to his gastronomic pleasures, Hannah rinsed the dishes, stuck them in the dishwasher, opened all the windows to air out the place, and plugged in the air freshener Delores gave her on her last visit to the condo. Then she took one look at the clock and raced back to her bedroom to change her clothes for her dinner date with Mike.

"Nobody makes onion rings they way they do here," Mike declared, reaching for another fat, crispy golden ring from the basket at the center of the table.

"True," Hannah agreed, popping the last of hers into her mouth. "Do you want to split another order?"

"Why not? I'm taking the rest of the night off. Bill and I worked until midnight last night and eleven the night before. I figure we need a little time away from the investigation to clear our minds."

Hannah waited until Mike had called the waitress over and placed another order for onion rings. Then she asked the question she'd been waiting to ask ever since he'd mentioned the case. "Do you have any suspects?"

"Yes, and no."

"What does *that* mean?"

"It means we've got suspects, but I don't think any of them did it. Neither does Bill and he's got good instincts for things like that."

From past experience, Hannah knew that Mike wouldn't give her any details unless she asked. Even then, he might not tell her anything important. "Which suspects do you have?"

"Uh-uh," Mike said, grinning at her. "You first."

Hannah did her best to look totally innocent. "Me? What makes you think I have any suspects? You told me I should drop my investigation, remember?"

"That's right. Let me rephrase that question. Which suspects did you have before you dropped your investigation?"

Hannah sighed. She wasn't going to get anything out of Mike until she primed the pump. And priming the pump meant she had to give him something first. "Nettie Grant."

"What?"

"You asked me what suspects I had. I had Nettie Grant, but I cleared her."

"You did?"

From the tone of Mike's voice, Hannah could tell he'd switched on the invisible little tape recorder in his mind that all good cops seemed to possess. Although it seemed impossible, he would remember every word she uttered.

"Give," Mike said, leaning forward to gaze at her intensely. "You owe me."

"For what?"

"For dinner. Why did you suspect Nettie Grant?"

Hannah sighed. She could give him this much, at least. "Because she was going to divorce Sheriff Grant and he would have fought her about the settlement. Killing him made her his widow and entitled to everything."

"Your reasoning's right," Mike said, "but how did you find out about the divorce?"

"Nettie told me. But she also told me she didn't kill her husband and I believed her."

Mike frowned slightly. "I don't think she killed him either, but since she doesn't have an alibi . . ."

"She *does* have an alibi," Hannah interrupted him, grinning widely. "Lisa checked it out for me."

"She did? What is it?"

"I'll tell you right after you tell me something I don't know."

Mike narrowed his eyes. Hannah imagined how fierce he'd look to a suspect who'd just been hauled in for interrogation. Thankfully, the fierce glower didn't work that well on her. She met it with her most stubborn look and they locked eyes for long moments, each perfectly silent and each perfectly determined to come out on top. The tension built higher and higher until Hannah just couldn't stand it anymore.

"Someone next door saw Nettie in her sewing room," Hannah told him. And at the very same instant Mike said, "Doc Knight found traces of someone else's blood on the lid of the dumpster."

"The killer must have scratched himself when he put Sheriff Grant inside," Hannah said. At the same time, Mike protested, "But I interviewed the neighbors and none of them were home."

Mike and Hannah stared at each other for a moment and then they both burst out laughing.

"You first," Hannah said.

"No, you first," Mike countered.

Hannah sighed. They were getting nowhere in a hurry. She desperately wanted to know about the blood on the dumpster and the quickest way to find out about it was to tell Mike about Nettie's alibi. "Richie Maschler told his parents he was going out that night, but he didn't. He invited his girlfriend over to watch a movie instead."

"And you know this for certain?"

"The girlfriend's mother told Lisa."

"Okay, Nettie's off my list. I'm really glad you cleared her, Hannah."

"Me, too. I like Nettie. Now how about that blood on the lid of the dumpster?"

"There was a sharp place on the lid of the dumpster where the killer could have cut himself. If it matches the smear on Sheriff Grant's shirt, it's definitely from our guy."

"Did you send it out for DNA testing?"

"Of course. That'll take a couple of weeks."

"And when the results come back you'll have evidence you can use to convict the killer?"

"Absolutely. But first, we have to catch him."

Hannah frowned slightly. "Will the DNA help with that?"

"I don't think so. We'll crosscheck it with the existing database, of course."

"But you don't think you'll get any matches?" Hannah asked, interpreting the tone she heard in Mike's voice.

"It's hard to believe we'll get that lucky. This doesn't have the earmarks of a professional hit, but I don't think it's random, either. Someone who knew Sheriff Grant hated or feared him enough to confront him up close and personal and kill him."

"So . . . you think it's someone local?"

"That's my guess. In a perfect world, I wouldn't have to guess. I'd just test everyone in the county to see whose DNA matches."

"In a perfect world, there wouldn't be any murder and you'd be out of a job."

"True," Mike said with a grin. "That's what I love about you, Hannah. You always put things in perspective."

Hannah took a deep breath and sealed her lips together. She was afraid to ask if he'd meant love as in *like,* or love as in *love.*

Mike didn't seem to mind her lack of response, because he leaned across the table and took her hand, pressing it warmly between both of his. "Do you want dessert now? Or shall we get something to go and take it back to your place?"

Hannah's heart did a tap dance in her chest. Mike had told her he was taking the night off and now he wanted to finish the evening at her condo. Was he about to propose?

"Hannah?" Mike smiled at her.

Hannah's lips turned up in an answering smile. She was glad she was sitting down. Her legs felt weak and her knees were actually knocking together. "Let's get apple pie," she said. And while he was ordering their dessert and paying the bill, she sat there with her fingers crossed, hoping that her mother's room freshener had worked.

Chapter Twenty-Four

"So you didn't learn anything important about Sheriff Grant's murder?" Mike asked, scooping up the last spoonful of vanilla ice cream Hannah had served with his pie.

"Not really," Hannah answered, crossing the fingers on her left hand, the one that wasn't holding her fork, to negate the lie she was about to tell. Learning that Suzie Hanks was Sheriff Grant's granddaughter was important and so was finding out that the sheriff had fought with Luanne in the school parking lot only minutes before he was murdered, but she wasn't about to tell Mike about that. "I was so busy trying to clear Bill, I didn't have much time to investigate. How about you? Did you find any clues when you went through Sheriff Grant's house and car?"

Mike shook his head. "Not a thing."

"Then you don't know if Sheriff Grant was working on a case when he was killed?"

"No. There's a rumor that he was, but no one at the station seems to know anything about it." Mike's eyes narrowed slightly. "You haven't heard anything, have you?"

"Nothing substantial. The only thing I know is that he always worked on a big case right before an election. Then, when he cracked it, he got enough good publicity to get reelected. I figure that he was working on a case this time, too."

"Where did you get *that* idea?"

"From one of Mother's friends," Hannah said, and this time she didn't bother to cross her fingers. Barbara Donnelly was a member of the Lake Eden Historical Society and so was Delores. No one would call them bosom buddies, but they were friends. "I thought he might have left some notes in his desk, or a briefcase, or something."

Mike shook his head. "There was nothing in his office at the station and nothing at the house except a couple of empty briefcases. If he was working on a case, he must have stashed his notes somewhere else."

"You're probably right," Hannah said. And then she opened her mouth and inserted her foot without even knowing she was going to do it. "I wish I could search his home office. Maybe you missed something."

Mike gave her a look that could curdle sweet milk. "I'm the professional here, not you. And I know how to conduct a search. I didn't miss *anything.*"

"Uh-oh," Hannah muttered inaudibly. She'd really stepped in it this time. Now Mike was on his high horse and she had to jolly him down into a good mood. "Would you like the rest of my pie? It was such a big piece I can't finish it."

"Well . . . okay," Mike said, slightly mollified. But Hannah knew it would take more than a few bites of pie to fully placate him.

"How about watching a movie together? I rented the latest shoot-'em-up cop thriller."

Mike turned to give her the curdling look again, but this time it wasn't as acidic. "What makes you think I'd enjoy a movie like that?"

"I don't know." Hannah shrugged. "It just seemed like your thing, that's all."

"And what's my thing?"

"You know . . . the macho law man who can take on dozens of bad guys who are really bad shots with automatic weapons."

Mike threw back his head and laughed. "You've got those movies pegged. When the bad guys shoot, they never hit the hero. They just end up smashing everything that makes a lot of noise or looks really good on camera."

"I've noticed," Hannah said, also noticing that she'd managed to jolly Mike out of his bad mood. "That's the reason I like those movies. I watch to pick the plots apart and see how many mistakes I can find."

"Me, too. So which movie did you rent?"

Ten minutes later, Mike and Hannah sat on her couch, eating the microwave popcorn she'd made and laughing over the mistakes they caught in the movie. Hannah was cuddled up on one side of Mike, his arm around her shoulder, and Moishe was cuddled up on his other side, purring so loudly that they needed to turn up the volume. Hannah's attention was divided. Part of it was on Mike and how right it felt to be nestled close to his side in this cozy domestic situation. The other part was on the movie and the current scene, where the cop went into his dead daughter's room, unchanged since she'd died, and vowed to catch her killer.

"That's so strange," Hannah murmured, not realizing that she'd spoken aloud until Mike turned to her with a questioning look. "It's odd to keep someone's room just the way it was when they were alive. That's what Sheriff Grant did with Jamie's room."

Mike put the movie on pause and turned to her. "How do you know that?"

"Oh, Nettie mentioned it a while back," Hannah said, not saying that *a while back* had been as recent as a couple of days ago. "She said she wanted to clear out Jamie's room, but Sheriff Grant wouldn't let her give away any of his things."

"I noticed that when I searched the room. There was a three-year-old copy of the school paper sitting on the bed table and all Jamie's clothes were in the closet."

"So don't you think that's a little creepy? I mean, leaving everything just the way it was when his son was alive? If he wanted to use it for a home office, he should have cleared it out."

Mike shrugged. "People have their own time frame about things like that. It's a part of the grieving process. When my wife died, it was a full year before I gave away the clothes on her side of the closet and that was only because I got a bunch of new shirts and ran out of room. And I never did clear out her dresser. I still have it just the way it was."

"You mean here? In Lake Eden?"

"That's right. It looks nice in the guest room and I never have any company anyway. I keep it because I need to hold onto some tangible things from the past to remind me of how good life was back then."

Hannah fought back a quick stab of jealousy. Didn't Mike think that his life was good now? But it wasn't fair of her to be jealous, not when he'd been so completely honest with her. When they'd first started dating, Mike had told her that he was still grieving for his wife and that he wasn't ready for a commitment. And she had professed to understand.

"I can understand hanging onto keepsakes," Hannah said, "but I don't think Nettie grieved any less than Sheriff Grant when she wanted to give away Jamie's things and use his room for another purpose. Life goes on. People have to cope. It's an ongoing process."

"You're much more practical than I am. If I died tomorrow, you'd probably ditch the locket I gave you for Christmas, get rid of that picture we had taken at the county fair, and forget all about me."

"No way," Hannah said, reaching out to touch his cheek. "Even without any tangible reminders, I could never forget about you, Mike."

This led to a kiss, as Hannah had expected it might. And that kiss led to another kiss. Moishe yowled once in protest and then jumped off the couch in search of a more stable resting place. Hannah laughed and so did Mike. He'd just pulled her into his arms again when a series of rhythmic chimes caused him to groan and release her.

"Cell phone," Mike said, reaching for his jacket. "I told them to call if there was an emergency."

Hannah bit back her four-letter answer to Mike's explanation. He was a cop. Off-duty, or not. Involved in something else, or not. A cop had to answer when duty called.

"Hey, Shawna Lee," Mike said, and Hannah's ears perked up. A moment later, they went on full alert when he moved away from her toward the far end of the couch. "You're all finished then?"

Hannah glanced at the clock on top of the television set. It was past nine at night. Was Shawna Lee working this late at the sheriff's station?

"Don't worry about it. I told you to call when you were through. I'll be there in less than fifteen. Watch for me from the lobby."

Hannah didn't bother to smooth out her frown when Mike put the phone in his pocket and turned to her. A few moments ago, she'd been steaming with passion, but now she was just plain steaming.

"Shawna Lee said she'd stay at work until I got back from my date with you. Her car's not working right and I promised to give her a lift home."

"Hold on," Hannah said, trying not to grit her teeth. "You told Shawna Lee you'd take her home *after* your date with me?"

"Sure. I knew it wouldn't be a late night since I have to get to work early tomorrow and so do you. I just told her to call when she was through with her filing and I'd pick her up."

"You're obviously unclear on the concept of dating," Hannah muttered, glaring at Mike.

"What's wrong? I'm just giving her a ride home, that's all."

"Consider this," Hannah said, placing both hands on her hips and turning to confront him squarely. "Not all that long ago, we were in each other's arms right here on the couch. I thought it meant something."

Mike reached out for her hand. "It does mean something, Hannah."

"But you let Shawna Lee interrupt us."

Mike thought about that for a split second and then he gave her one of his killer smiles, the ones that made Hannah feel like she'd just stepped on a roller coaster. "Are you inviting me to stay with you?"

"Not on a bet!" Hannah retorted. "You made a promise to Shawna Lee and you'd better keep it!"

Mike was silent for a moment and then he gave a deep sigh. "What would have happened if I hadn't made that promise?"

"You'll never know." Hannah felt like screaming at him, or slapping him across his handsome face, or beaning him with the heaviest object that was handy, but she did none of those things. She just stood up with all the cool dignity that she could muster and handed him his jacket.

"At least I come first with *you!*" Hannah said, motioning for Moishe to follow her into the living room. She set one of the expensive cut glass dessert dishes Delores had given her for Christmas three years ago on the coffee table and filled it with a generous scoop of yogurt. "Yogurt's health food. It's bound to be good for you."

Once Moishe was lapping happily, Hannah went back to the kitchen to put the yogurt container back in the refrigerator and fetch a glass of white wine for herself. She needed to relax and let her anger at Mike and Shawna Lee fade into something less dangerous than thoughts of double-homicide. She took her customary place on the couch, curling up at the end with her favorite pillow under her arm, sipped her wine, and channel surfed for something to numb her senses.

Hannah had just settled on watching a program about sea otters when there was a knock on the door. If it was Mike, he was playing musical apartments and she wouldn't let him in. There was no way she'd allow him to take her home, take Shawna Lee home, and then come back to her.

"Who's there?" Hannah called out, her hand on the dead-bolt.

"It's me. I'm back. Open the door, Hannah."

The voice sounded a lot like Norman's and Hannah put her eye to the peephole before she remembered that it would-n't do any good. Since the light on the staircase was directly across from the peephole, all she could see was a bulky silhouette.

"Norman?" Hannah asked, throwing open the door. And there stood Norman in all his dependable, huggable glory. Norman was as far from Mike as a woman could get and Hannah was glad. One palm-sweating, breath-catching, heart-thudding encounter was enough for one evening.

"Hi, Hannah," Norman said with a grin and Hannah's heart gave a joyful bound. Norman was just the person she wanted to see.

"Come in, Norman." Hannah held the door open wide.

Norman blocked Moishe with a quick step to the side and stepped into Hannah's living room. Then he scooped up her resident feline, turning him tummy up like a baby in his arms, and tickled him under the chin. "I missed you, big guy."

"How about me?" Hannah couldn't resist saying. "Did you miss me, too?"

"That goes without saying. It's not too late for you, is it?"

"It's never too late," Hannah said, wondering if she should adopt that as her personal motto as she took Norman's jacket and hung it over the back of the chair by the door. "Can I get you something to drink? I've got coffee, wine, soft drinks, whatever."

"A diet anything will be fine. I drank enough coffee on the plane."

Hannah rushed to the kitchen to get Norman's drink and when she came back, he was sitting on the couch with Moishe cuddled in his lap. Her cat definitely had his priorities straight this time around. She set Norman's soft drink on the coffee table and took her usual seat at the opposite end of the couch. "So what are you doing back in Lake Eden so early?"

"Andrea paged me at the convention to tell me about Sheriff Grant's murder. When she mentioned that Doc Knight had confined her to the house, I decided to come back right away in case you needed me."

"I'm glad you did. I *do* need you," Hannah said, smiling widely.

"Great." Norman looked pleased to hear that. "What do you want me to do?"

Hannah took a deep breath and blurted out what she'd been thinking ever since Mike had told her about the empty briefcases in Sheriff Grant's home office. "You know Nettie Grant, don't you?"

"Yes. She had some trouble with an impacted molar last year."

"Well, she went to visit relatives in Wisconsin and I need to break into her duplex to search Sheriff Grant's home office for clues. You'll help me, won't you?"

"That's illegal, isn't it?"

"Yes, but we can't let a little technicality like that stop us, not when we've got a murderer to catch. So, will you help me?"

Norman took a deep breath and let it out again. "I'll have to. There's no way I'm going to let you do it alone. When do you want to break in?"

"The sooner, the better. I'd say tonight, but I think we'd better do it in the daylight. That way we won't have to use flashlights and take the chance that a neighbor might spot us. How about tomorrow morning?"

Norman looked reluctant, but he agreed. "Okay."

"Good. You're just wonderful to come back early, Norman. I hope you didn't miss much of the convention."

"That's okay. It was boring anyway."

"Oh," Hannah said, wondering if that description included Norman's ex-fiancée, the dentist. "How about something to eat? I know plane food's not much to write home about."

"Now that you mention it, I am a little hungry. Do you want to go out for a hamburger?"

Hannah shook her head. "No, thanks. I've already eaten, but I'll make you something here. How about a Hole in One?"

"What's that?"

"Something simple I used to fix for my college roommate when we'd stay up late studying. Basically, it's a fried egg and pan toast."

"That sounds good. Do you need any help?"

"No, it's a one-person job. Find something you want to watch on television and I'll be back with your food in a jiffy."

Hannah was smiling as she went off to the kitchen. It was great to have Norman back again. Suddenly everything seemed easier and the heavy weight she'd been carrying around on her shoulders felt lighter by half. That must be the way wives felt when they shared problems with their husbands. Did that mean she should forget Mike and marry Norman?

Making the Hole in One didn't take long. When Hannah came back into the living room with Norman's food, she found him playing the movie she'd been watching with Mike earlier. "Here's your food, Norman."

"That looks good!" Norman said with a smile, putting the movie on pause.

"It is. I still fix it for myself once in a while. I didn't realize you liked cop movies."

"I don't, not usually," Norman gave her a sheepish grin, "but this one is so bad, it's actually enjoyable."

"Let's watch it then." Hannah settled down on the couch next to him and started the movie again, not bothering to mention that she'd already seen the first half with Mike.

The dialogue was trite, the violence was gratuitous, the plot was nonexistent, and the characters were unlikable, but Hannah found that she was enjoying the movie immensely. Perhaps it was the *déjà vu* of it all, the fact that she'd already seen these badly acted scenes with Mike and could almost repeat the clichéd dialogue word for word. Maybe it was because Norman laughed every time one of the actors said something insipid and he was obviously having a good time. It could have been the fact that Norman moved closer to her once he'd finished his meal and draped a friendly, protective arm around her shoulder. But probably it was because Norman was her best friend and much more.

"The end," Norman said when the movie was over.

"And it's about time!" Hannah said with a sigh. "That was the worst movie I've ever seen."

"It was almost as bad as Seattle without you. Every time I saw something funny and I turned to tell you about it, you weren't there."

"I felt the same way." Hannah wasn't surprised when Norman kissed her, but she was surprised at her enthusiastic response. It felt so good to be in his arms again. Being with Norman made her feel safe, and comforted, and contented.

Moishe gave a pitiful yowl and Norman released her. They both turned to find him sitting on the back of the couch staring at them with unfathomable yellow eyes. "Is he jealous?" Norman asked.

"I don't think so." Hannah decided not to mention the fact he'd been deposed once tonight and was probably afraid it would happen again. "He's probably tired and he's waiting for me to turn down the bedcovers."

"Speaking of tired, that's me," Norman said, glancing at his watch. "I'd better call Mother and tell her I'm back in town. If I don't, she might shoot me as an intruder when I come in."

"But isn't your mother in bed by now?" Hannah asked.

"I don't think so. It's only nine-thirty and she usually doesn't go to bed before ten."

"It's eleven-thirty, Norman." Hannah pointed at the clock on top of the television set. "Your watch must still be on Seattle time."

"You're right. I didn't think to change it. It's definitely too late to call Mother. I guess I'll just have to hope I don't scare her to death when I come in."

"Why take the chance that you'll upset her? Just stay here for the rest of the night and go home in the morning."

Norman turned to her in pleased surprise. "You mean . . . stay here? With *you?*"

"Sure. The bed in the guestroom's all made up."

"Oh," Norman said and he didn't look quite as pleased as he had before. "Thanks anyway, but I'd better go home. I wouldn't want any of your neighbors to see me leaving in the morning. They might get the wrong idea."

After Norman had left, Hannah went through her nightly ritual of locking the door, double-checking the windows, and turning off the lights. As she got dressed for bed, she wondered whether Norman would have stayed if she hadn't made it clear he'd be sleeping in the guestroom. He'd certainly never asked to stay with her, the way Mike had. But just because he hadn't asked didn't mean he didn't want to.

Hannah sighed and climbed into bed alone. She was alone

for about three whole seconds. Then there was a thump that shook the mattress, and a rumbling purr as Moishe curled up on the expensive goose down pillow she'd bought for him so he wouldn't steal hers in the middle of the night.

"You're good company," Hannah told him, reaching out to stroke his fur three times before pulling back her hand. Moishe permitted a limited amount of affection, but any more than three pets and he'd move to the foot of the bed.

Hannah pulled up the covers and snuggled in for the night, thinking about the two men she'd entertained in her living room. Both of them had kissed her and she'd enjoyed it, although their embraces were different. Kissing Norman was like taxiing to a stop at the airport after a turbulent flight. It made her feel comfortable and safe. And kissing Mike was like trying to break the land speed record. It was exciting and thrilling. Did she prefer comfort and safety to excitement and thrills? Hannah sighed and buried her head in her pillow. It was hard to choose when she wanted it all.

HOLE IN ONE

One slice of bread *(any kind)*
One egg
Softened butter
Biscuit cutter or juice glass

Spray a frying pan with non-stick spray and set it aside.

Butter the piece of bread on one side. Put it butter-side-down in the frying pan. Butter the side on top. (*Using a rubber spatula makes this easier.*)

With a biscuit cutter or the rim of a juice glass, stamp a hole in the center of the slice of bread. Put the circle you've cut out next to the slice of bread in the pan.

Put the pan on medium heat and wait until the bread starts to fry. Then crack an egg and drop it into the hole in the bread. (*If you're really hungry, you can use two eggs.*) Add salt and pepper to the egg if you wish. When the egg has cooked on the bottom, flip the whole thing, bread and all, with a pancake turner. Also flip the cutout circle of bread. Fry until the egg is done the way you want it.

Tracey loves these for breakfast. She prefers a runny yolk so that she can dip the fried bread in it. If there was ever any doubt, that would prove she's my niece.

Chapter
Twenty-Five

"Let's save a dozen of these for Norman as a welcome home present," Lisa suggested, pulling the last two pans of Orange Snaps from the oven and sliding them onto the bakers rack.

"That's a good idea. I'm really glad he's back in town."

"So is there anything special we have to do today?"

"Actually . . . yes." Hannah took a deep breath to calm her frazzled nerves. She had yet to tell Lisa about the break-in she planned to accomplish with Norman and that was because she felt slightly guilty at contemplating the commission of a crime. She knew she was being silly. She'd never felt guilty about collecting evidence in not-so-legal ways before. But this time it was different. This time she wasn't rushing into things. She'd had the whole night to think about it and she'd gone over all the things that could go wrong in her mind. Her grandmother used to say that it was wise to think before you acted, but if everyone did that, they'd be so busy thinking over the pros and cons that nothing would ever get done.

"What is it?"

"What is *what*?" Hannah had been thinking so intensely, she'd entirely lost the thread of their conversation

"What's the special thing we have to do today?"

"Oh, that." Hannah took another deep breath and

plunged in. "I need you to hold down the fort for a couple of hours this morning. Norman and I are going over to Nettie's duplex."

"But Nettie's gone."

"I know that. If she didn't leave any windows open, we're going to pick the lock."

"But why do that?"

"Because I need to search Sheriff Grant's home office for clues."

"Not that. I mean, why break in when I've got the key?"

"You've got the *key?!*" Hannah's voice hit a high note that made her wonder if her high school music teacher had been wrong to seat her in the alto section.

"Nettie gave it to me when I offered to water her houseplants."

Hannah just shook her head. Lisa had surprising depths. "It occurred to you that I might want to get into her duplex while she was gone?"

"Yes," Lisa said, grinning widely, "and I didn't want you to have to break in."

"I've said it before and I'll say it again. You're a gem, Lisa."

"A diamond of the first water," Lisa said and then she giggled when Hannah gave her a surprised look. "Bonnie Surma called to order cookies for the next Regency club meeting. She used it to describe their guest speaker and I asked her what it meant."

"What did she say?"

"She told me it meant quality and it usually referred to ladies. If they're diamonds of the first water, their appearance is perfect and so are their manners and their breeding."

Hannah thought that over for a moment. "That makes sense. Diamonds are sorted by water, and the best and heaviest gems fall out with the first washing. A diamond of the first water would be very valuable, just like you, Lisa."

"Thanks." Lisa blushed slightly at the compliment. "I

think you should go in through Nettie's backdoor. Her yard is fenced and once you're inside the gate, nobody can see you."

"Good idea."

"And whatever you do, don't touch the houseplants."

Hannah was confused. "I wasn't really planning to, but why?"

"They'd die for sure, and then Bill and Mike would know you'd been there. You've got the biggest black thumb in town."

"You brought your camera?" Hannah asked, spotting it around Norman's neck when he met her in the alley behind Nettie's duplex.

"I thought I'd take pictures as we go along. It'll help to refresh our memory later."

"Good idea. Where did you park?" Hannah asked, opening the gate and hustling Norman inside the fenced backyard.

"Two blocks over. How about you?"

"I walked. I was afraid my truck would be spotted."

"You mean because it's candy apple red with a license plate that says COOKIES and the name of your store on both sides?"

"That's it," Hannah said with a laugh, appreciating Norman even more today than she had last night. "I'm glad you're back, Norman. I wouldn't want to break into a place with anyone else."

Norman smiled and gave her a little hug, obviously taking what she'd said as a compliment. Then he climbed the steps to Nettie's backdoor and took out a little leather case. "Dental tools," he explained, unzipping it. "I thought they'd come in handy for picking the lock."

"I'm sure they'd be perfect, but we don't need them." Hannah reached in her jacket pocket and pulled out the key ring Lisa had given her. "I've got the key."

"Oh. Okay then," Norman said, sounding a bit disappointed as Hannah unlocked the door.

Hannah stepped in, glanced back at Norman, and saw he was frowning. He had obviously wanted to test his skills as a burglar. "Don't put those tools away. The door to Sheriff Grant's home office is probably locked."

"Right." Norman looked much happier as he followed Hannah up the stairs and down the hallway. The pleased expression remained on his face until they arrived at the office door and he noticed that it was taped off. "That's crime scene tape."

"I know."

"But I thought that Sheriff Grant was killed in the school parking lot."

"He was."

"So this isn't a crime scene?"

"Not technically. When Mike sealed it off, he must not have had the KEEP OUT JUST BECAUSE I SAY SO tape."

"I see," Norman said with a grin. "And if we get caught in here, you'll argue that since it wasn't a crime scene, the tape must have been put up by mistake."

Hannah gave a little nod to show that he was right and grinned right back. Then she reached out to check the doorknob. "It's locked, all right. Do you think you can open it?"

"I don't know why not," Norman said, unzipping his leather case of tools again. "Picking a lock has got to be easier than tightening braces."

It was a simple mechanism and picking the lock didn't take long, especially for a dentist with nimble fingers. In less than a minute, Hannah and Norman had ducked under the crime scene tape and were standing inside Sheriff Grant's home office.

"This looks more like somebody's bedroom than an office," Norman commented.

"That's because it *was* a bedroom. It belonged to Sheriff Grant's son, Jamie and it's just the way he left it when he went away to college. Sheriff Grant wouldn't let Nettie throw away any of Jamie's things after he died."

"How long ago was that?"

"Almost three years. Don't you think that's a little weird?"

Norman shrugged. "Maybe, if it's an obsession. But if the sheriff just wanted to hang onto his son's things a little longer, I can understand that."

Hannah turned to look at Norman in awe. He'd managed to walk the fence brilliantly. When the next political office opened up, she was going to nominate him.

"Let me take a base set of pictures," Norman said, proceeding to do just that. "We'll want to remember what this looked like before we started to search."

When Norman had taken pictures from every angle, Hannah handed him a pair of gloves. "I brought these for you. We don't want to leave fingerprints. You can start in the closet and I'll try Sheriff Grant's desk."

"Okay. What are we looking for?"

"Briefcases. If you find any, give a holler. We're also looking for anything that looks like it doesn't belong in a teenager's room or a home office."

Hannah slipped on her own gloves and went through the desk. All she found were old bills, canceled checks, and household accounting records. It looked as if Sheriff Grant had moved all of Jamie's things into one drawer when he'd commandeered the desk. The lower left-hand drawer contained a college catalogue, several transcripts of Jamie's high school grades, a program from the senior prom, a stack of CliffsNotes with sections highlighted in yellow marker, and the thick, dog-eared book Jamie had used to study for the SATs. There was nothing at all from the sheriff's department and nothing to indicate which case Sheriff Grant had been working on at the time of his death.

"I found a briefcase, Hannah," Norman's voice was muffled and Hannah could tell he was in the depths of the closet.

"Is it brown?"

"Yes."

"Then we'll take it with us. Just set it aside and keep looking."

"Okay. Did you find anything in the desk?"

"Not really, unless you're interested in a stack of CliffsNotes."

"A stack of what?"

"CliffsNotes. You know, the yellow and black pamphlets kids use to cram for tests?"

"Oh, those. I thought they were called CliffNotes, like somebody sat on top of a cliff and wrote them."

"No, it's CliffsNotes, like a guy named Cliff Hillegass formed a company to publish them in nineteen fifty-something."

"Okay, I stand corrected. Did you find anything else?"

"Nothing important." Hannah pushed back the desk chair and went to the dresser to check the drawers. They were filled with Jamie's clothes and Hannah felt a bit like a ghoul as she went through piles of his underwear, socks, and handkerchiefs.

"Ouch!" Norman yelped from the recesses of the closet.

"What's wrong?" Hannah asked, hurrying over to see if she could help.

"I just stubbed my toe on something hard. Hand me a flashlight, will you?"

Hannah passed Norman the flashlight she'd brought from her truck and held Jamie's clothing out of the way so that he could see what he'd encountered.

"Looks like a box of car parts," Norman said, backing out of the closet and dragging the box out after him. "Jamie probably had an old clunker he repaired himself."

"Probably. Most high school kids can't afford to take their cars to mechanics to get them fixed."

Norman glanced into the box and frowned. "That's funny. Here's a starter for a Chevrolet and a fuel injection harness for a Ford."

"You must know a lot about cars if you can tell who made the parts just by looking." Hannah was impressed.

"You bet. It also helps that the manufacturer's name is stamped on the bottom."

Hannah laughed, but she quickly sobered when she remembered what Norman had said. "Do you know if you can put a Chevrolet starter and a Ford fuel injection harness in the same car?"

"Not really, but my guess is no. Most car companies don't want their parts to be interchangeable. Do you know what kind of car Jamie drove?"

"No, but I can find out. Will you take some pictures of the car parts, Norman? They might be important. I have to make a phone call."

In less than five minutes, Hannah was back, looking more puzzled than she had when she left. She'd talked to Luanne Hanks and what she'd found out was disturbing. "Did you take the pictures?"

"I took a whole roll. And I found another briefcase while I was at it. It was in the corner by the wastebasket. What did you find out about the car?"

"That's the strange part. Jamie didn't have a car. He borrowed Nettie's whenever he needed one. The rest of the time, he rode his Harley."

Norman glanced down at the box again. "But these are car parts. I'm sure of it."

"And I'm sure that car parts don't fit motorcycles." Hannah sighed and sat down on the edge of Jamie's bed. She tucked her feet back and her heels encountered something hard. "There's something under this bed."

In no time at all both Hannah and Norman were stretched out on the floor, peering under Jamie's bed. She manned the flashlight while he held up the bedspread.

"It's another box," Norman said, grabbing the edge and

tugging it toward them. "It's heavy enough to be more car parts. But why would Jamie have car parts if he didn't have a car?"

"That," Hannah said, reaching out to help Norman with the box, "is the million dollar question."

It took some muscle, but between the two of them, Hannah and Norman managed to retrieve the four boxes of car parts that were stored under Jamie's bed and take pictures of them. Hannah also recovered a brown briefcase that had been under the bed. Once they'd pushed boxes back where they'd found them, Hannah collected the briefcases and they left, locking the door securely behind them.

"Where to now?" Norman asked, opening the passenger door of his car for Hannah.

"Barbara Donnelly's house. She's expecting us. I called her before we left Nettie's."

"And she's going to tell us which one is the James Bond briefcase and open the secret compartment?"

"That's right." Hannah was glad Norman had listened when she'd explained everything last night. She was so tired, she didn't think she could string enough words together now.

"It's at least ten minutes to Barbara's." Norman looked over at her with a worried expression. "Why don't you lean back and take a quick nap. You look really tired."

"I am," Hannah admitted, closing her eyes. And then, lulled by the motion of Norman's car, her mind floated free and she hovered in that timeless place between consciousness and slumber.

"Hannah? We're here."

Hannah opened her eyes to find Norman's car parked in the driveway at Barbara's house. "How did you get here so fast?" she asked. "I just shut my eyes a second ago."

"It was twenty minutes ago. I took the long way around to let you sleep."

"Oh," Hannah felt a little foolish for conking out in Norman's car. "Well . . . thanks."

"Didn't you get enough sleep last night?"

"I guess not," Hannah said and left it at that. There was no way she was going to tell Norman that she'd been awake for over an hour after he'd left, trying to decide whether she'd preferred Mike's kisses, or his.

Hannah climbed the steps to Barbara's neat little house and opened the front porch door. It was a screen porch to keep out mosquitoes and other bugs, and since it was already nearing the end of October, Barbara had winterized it by tacking up heavy plastic on the outside of the screens to keep out the snow flurries that would be coming soon.

"Indoor-outdoor carpeting?" Norman asked, glancing down at the porch floor.

"Artificial turf," Hannah corrected him. "Barbara's brother works for the company that makes it and she gets it for free. She doesn't have room for a garden in back, so she sets pots of flowers out here in the summer and it looks really nice. It's almost like sitting outside without any bugs."

Norman rang the bell and Barbara pulled the door open so fast Hannah concluded she'd watched them come up the walk. "Come in. I just made fresh coffee."

"You're a lifesaver, Barbara. I was so tired, I fell asleep on the way over here."

"Then it's a good thing I made it strong," Barbara said, leading them to her kitchen and seating them at the table. "How about you, Norman?"

"Yes, thanks. I can always use a cup of coffee."

Barbara poured the coffee, handed Hannah and Norman theirs, and took a cup for herself. She put cream and sugar on the table, and then she motioned to the briefcases. "Let me take a look at those. I'm assuming you don't want me to ask where you got them?"

"That's right," Hannah said with a little sigh of relief. She hadn't wanted to lie to Barbara, but Barbara was an employee of the sheriff's department and she had a duty to report any crime that she encountered. Since Hannah had unlocked Nettie's door with the key, she could argue that they didn't break in. But gaining access to Sheriff Grant's home office by picking the lock with dental tools, whether or not the door had been incorrectly crisscrossed with crime scene tape, was as illegal as all get out.

Barbara shook her head as Norman set the three briefcases on the table. "That's not it, and neither is this. But this one . . ."

Hannah held her breath as Barbara picked up the third briefcase. And then she let it out again when Barbara nodded.

"This is it." Barbara opened the briefcase and glanced inside. "It looks completely empty, doesn't it?" When Norman and Hannah both nodded, Barbara tipped the briefcase so that they could see inside. "Now look at the liner. It's got little squares with letters and numbers in them as a design."

"And the letters and numbers mean something?" Norman guessed.

"That's right. You have to put the briefcase on a flat surface and press them in the right order. You start with zero-zero-seven."

"For James Bond?" Hannah guessed.

"Yes. And when you're finished with that, you have to punch in the code word. It's *Bond.*"

Norman and Hannah watched while Barbara punched in the name that had become almost synonymous with *spy.*

"Now you have to hold the briefcase in place with your left hand and twist the handle really hard to the right. When you pick it up again, this is what happens."

Hannah gasped as the bottom of the briefcase dropped down to reveal a space that was open on one side and about a half an inch thick. "Wow!"

"Wow is right," Norman said, staring in awe at the briefcase. "Is that deep enough for a gun?"

Barbara laughed. "That's exactly what Sheriff Grant asked me when I gave it to him. I told him that there was another one for guns, but since he could wear his right out in the open, I figured he didn't need it. This one's for important papers, like the files he used to carry home with him."

"Is there anything in it now?" Hannah asked the important question.

Barbara reached into the narrow space with her fingertips and pulled out a file folder. "Here's that missing report. Let's see what's in it."

Hannah held her breath as Barbara read it. She had the urge to grab it out of Barbara's hands, and she just barely managed to curb that impulse.

"I'm sorry, Hannah." Barbara said as she passed it over. "It's just an incident report that Lonnie Murphy filled out right before he left on vacation."

"Could it be important?" Hannah asked.

"I don't see how. It's just routine."

Norman looked curious. "If it's just routine, why did Sheriff Grant put it in the secret compartment?"

"I don't know, unless . . ." Barbara glanced down at the report again and she gave a little humorless chuckle. "I think I just figured out why. Lonnie forgot to assign a number to it and Sheriff Grant was a real stickler for office protocol. He probably took it home with him, intending to write Lonnie a reprimand."

"That figures," Hannah said under her breath, remembering how picky the sheriff had been about rules and procedures. If Sheriff Grant hadn't been the unlucky recipient of a violent death, Lonnie would most certainly have had a reprimand in his file when he came back to work.

"Read it if you want," Barbara handed the report to Hannah.

Hannah took the report from Barbara and skimmed it quickly. Lonnie had written it to chronicle spotting a suspicious car, using his on-board computer to ascertain that it was stolen, and apprehending the driver.

"See what I mean?" Barbara said, as Hannah handed the report to Norman.

As far as Hannah could see, this incident report didn't have any bearing on Sheriff Grant's murder. Even if the driver's friends had wanted to get even for his arrest, they would have come after Lonnie, not Sheriff Grant.

"This looks pretty straightforward to me," Norman said, looking up from the document. "Would you like us to drop this off at the station for you, Barbara? Hannah said you were out on leave."

Barbara shook her head and reached out for the file. "That's okay. I'll take care of it when I get back to work."

"But Shawna Lee's spending a lot of time looking for it." Hannah was confused. "And you're planning to stay home for at least another week, aren't you?"

Barbara nodded and an impish grin crossed her face. "I'm going to let Shawna Lee keep right on looking. If she keeps busy enough, she won't have time to flirt and maybe we'll be saved from another homicide."

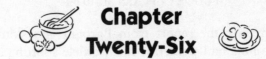

Chapter
Twenty-Six

Hannah's mind was going a million miles an hour as they drove away from Barbara's house. She was so engrossed in her thoughts she only dimly registered the fact that Norman had spoken to her. "Sorry, Norman. What did you say?"

"Do you think Lonnie's stolen car report has anything to do with why Sheriff Grant was killed?"

"I just don't know. Lonnie busted a car thief, and we found car parts in Jamie's room. Cars do seem to be a common denominator here."

"And didn't you say that Jamie was killed in an auto accident?"

"That's right!" Hannah was excited for a moment, but then she went back to being puzzled. "But how does *that* figure in?"

Norman shrugged. "I'm not sure. There's also the fact that Sheriff Grant was killed in a parking lot filled with cars."

"And he was attacked while he was standing by his cruiser," Hannah added with a sigh. "I think we're going overboard on this car thing, Norman."

"Probably. I just thought that if we could find all the pieces, we might be able to figure out how they fit together."

"That makes sense," Hannah said, turning to smile at him. She was about to throw him a mind-bender. "But what if some of the pieces are from another puzzle? Won't they only confuse us?"

Norman thought about that while he waited for the stoplight at the corner of Elm and First to turn green. "Yeah. I guess they might confuse us. How do we get around that?"

"I'm not sure," Hannah replied, feeling helpless in the face of the challenge. "I think the first thing we have to do is gather more facts. That report from Lonnie was pretty sketchy and it was obvious that he wrote it in a hurry. He probably left out things he thought didn't matter. I have to talk to him and find out everything that happened when he pulled over that stolen car."

"That's a good place to start. What do you want me to do while you're doing that?"

"Develop the film. That's a good place to start, too. Maybe we'll spot something important in the pictures that we missed when we were at Nettie's house in person. And do you think you'll have time to do some research on the Internet?"

"Sure." Norman pulled up in back of The Cookie Jar and parked between Lisa's old car and Hannah's cookie truck. "I wasn't supposed to be back from Seattle yet and Doc Bennett's still filling in for me at the clinic. What sort of research do you need?"

"It would really help if you could print out the articles that ran in the *Lake Eden Journal* when Jamie was killed. And do the same thing for the papers in Ann Arbor."

"Why Ann Arbor?"

"Jamie was killed when he was away at the University of Michigan."

"Okay. I'll do a search under his name. Would that be Jamie, or James?"

"Try both. He went by Jamie, but his real name was James just like Sheriff Grant." Hannah remembered what Norman had said and brightened up a bit. "You can do a search just by typing in someone's name?"

"As long as you know where to look."

"And you do?"

"I'm pretty good at it. I can access quite a few public records and that gives me a surprisingly large amount of information."

Hannah thought about it for a long moment. What she wanted to ask Norman to do was an invasion of her mother's privacy, and it would make her feel like a rat. But feeling like a rat might be better than feeling like a dope if her gut-level feelings were right and she failed to take steps to protect Delores from a Romeo swindler.

"What do you need, Hannah?" Norman prompted, when she'd been silent for several moments.

"Winthrop Harrington the Second."

"What?"

"That's his name. I need you to check him out for me."

"Okay. Who is he?"

"That's what I want to know," Hannah said, glancing over at Norman. She knew he could be trusted. If she told him this was a private matter, he'd die before he'd mention it. "I hope I'm wrong, Norman, but he could be a con artist. And the way things are going, he might just become my new stepfather."

Halloween morning came in with a yowl, at least ten minutes before Hannah's alarm clock was due to go off. Moishe was hungry and he wasn't the type to suffer his hunger pangs in silence. Hannah pulled on her slippers and shuffled to the kitchen while she was still half-awake. It was best not to be fully alert when one had to boil liver before daybreak.

Hannah stumbled to the stove and turned the burner on high. She'd set a pot of water at the ready before bed last night. Then she poured a cup of coffee, sipped it until the water boiled, and dropped in the pieces of liver she'd cut up the previous night. When they turned an unappetizing gray color, she scooped them out and put them in a frying pan with oil and the rest of the ingredients.

In less than five minutes, Moishe's omelet was ready and Hannah scraped it into his food bowl. She checked to make sure the stovetop exhaust fan was on its highest setting, poured herself a second cup of coffee, and sat down at her kitchen table, deliberately turning her back on the culinary creation she'd made for her feline. The scent of liver first thing in the morning made her stomach lurch and roil. If the twinges of nausea she felt were anything like the morning sickness Andrea had complained about, she should have been more sympathetic.

It didn't take Moishe long to eat his breakfast, about one-fourth the time it had taken her to prepare it. There was something wrong with this equation. Hannah rinsed out the pan she'd used to boil the liver, the frying pan that had held the omelet, and Moishe's bowl, and stuck them all in the dishwasher. It was already partially loaded with dishes from the previous night. There was the pot she'd used to cook the rice, the bowl and top of the food processor she'd used to whip up the egg and pulverize the shell, and the knife she'd wielded to cut up the liver. Once she'd gathered up the implements she'd used to cook Moishe's breakfast and the containers she'd used to store the egg and the rice in the refrigerator, the dishwasher was almost full. Hannah poured in the soap, set it on wash, and stood there shaking her head. This was crazy. She didn't eat breakfast unless she went out and the only dish she used in the morning was her coffee mug. Yet here she was at five in the morning, washing a full load of dishes she'd dirtied by cooking breakfast for her cat!

The phone rang and Hannah poured another cup of coffee before she walked over to answer it. There was only one person who called her this early. It had to be Delores calling in to give her report. When Hannah hadn't been able to find out where Lonnie was vacationing by asking his family or his friends, she'd tapped her best resource and recruited Delores and Carrie who had promised to research Lonnie's whereabouts on the Lake Eden gossip hotline.

"Hello Mother," Hannah answered. Answering the phone that way had become almost a tradition. Hannah knew her mother would miss these morning squabbles if she simply said hello.

"I wish you wouldn't answer the phone that way, Hannah. What if it wasn't me?"

"Then I'd say, *Sorry, I thought you were my mother.* And they'd say, *That's all right.* And then they'd try to sell me some stock over the phone."

Delores laughed. "Still . . . you shouldn't presume. Think how embarrassed you'd be if it was someone important and you called them *Mother.*"

"You're not someone important?"

"Of course I am. It's just that . . . never mind," Delores said, giving it up with a sigh. "How are you this morning, dear?"

"Not so hot. Do you know the phrase, *Wake up and smell the roses?*"

"Yes, dear. I've heard it."

"Well, this morning it's, *Wake up and smell the liver.*"

"The liver?"

"That's right. Doctor Bob put Moishe on a new diet. I just cooked breakfast for him and it smells awful."

"Well, open the windows, dear. And use some of that air freshener I gave you. It's scented like an English garden."

"Right," Hannah said, wrinkling up her nose. She'd used the air freshener, and if the manufacturer's claim was accurate, she'd be sure to give English gardens a wide berth.

"I always used it when your father made corned beef and cabbage on St. Patrick's Day," Delores said. "He insisted on making it every year and none of us liked it."

Hannah laughed. It was true. More of the corned beef and cabbage had gone down the garbage disposal than into their mouths. But even though Hannah didn't care for the meal, the custom pleased her. It was exactly as her dad used to say; everyone was Irish on St. Patrick's Day.

"Did you find out anything about Lonnie, Mother?"

"Not much." Delores sighed so deeply it came out as a whoosh over the line. "Bridget doesn't even know where he's gone. She told me to check with Rick."

"Did you?"

"Of course I did. Rick doesn't know either, but he thinks Lonnie must be with a girl."

"Did Lonnie tell Rick that?"

"Not exactly, but he refused to say where he was going. And since Lonnie usually tells Rick everything, Rick thinks he was going to meet a girl."

"That makes some kind of sense." Hannah leaned back and took a sip of her coffee. "Any candidates?"

"Only one and that's impossible."

"Which one?"

"Your sister. Rick thought that Lonnie might have gone to the Cities to see Michelle."

"Did he?" Hannah asked, hoping that he hadn't. Delores liked Lonnie well enough, but she wouldn't be pleased if she found out that he was serious enough to visit Michelle at college.

"Of course he didn't. I called Michelle last night and she said she hadn't seen him."

"Did you ask her if she knew where he was?"

"Do I look like a fool, Hannah? Of course I did. Michelle said that she didn't have the slightest idea where Lonnie was, that they were just friends, and Lonnie certainly didn't call to tell her every time he went off on vacation somewhere."

"So she was a little testy because you asked?"

"She was *very* testy. I don't know why. It was just a simple question and I certainly wasn't accusing her of anything."

"Maybe she'd had a rough day at school," Hannah said, voicing the first excuse that came to mind. "Don't worry about it, Mother. I'm sure Michelle feels bad that she was short with you."

"Well, I hope so. There's such a thing as respect for your parents, you know."

"Of course there is and Michelle knows that. She'll probably call you today and apologize."

"No, she won't. She'll just send a card. That's what she always does. If she mails a card, she doesn't have to come out and say that she was wrong."

"Oh, well. A card lasts longer than a phone call." Hannah changed the subject and chatted on for a few more moments. Then she signed off and hung up the phone.

"Methinks the sister doth protest too much," she said to Moishe, who was lapping at his water bowl. "I'm going to call her and see what she says to me."

Hannah poured another cup of coffee, opened her crime notebook to the right page, grabbed the phone, and dialed her sister's number. Delores might be satisfied by Michelle's denial, but Hannah had the sneaking suspicion that Lonnie had been no further away than the length of the phone cord when her baby sister had claimed she hadn't seen him.

Hannah slipped four more pans of cookies into the oven and picked up the phone again. No one was answering at Michelle's rented house and the answering machine wasn't on. She listened to the empty ringing for several more moments and hung up when the back door opened and Lisa came in. "Hi, Lisa. I'm almost through with the Corn Cookies."

"They look great," Lisa said, hanging her parka jacket on a hook and heading for the sink to wash her hands. "Do you want me to start on the regular cookies? Or should I mix up the batch of cupcakes for the sheriff's station? They asked for chocolate with chocolate icing and some kind of design in orange."

"You do them while I bake the cookies." Hannah glanced down at the Fudge Cupcake recipe on the counter. "Why don't you bake some of Alma's cupcakes for the sheriff's station? You can use applesauce as the secret ingredient. I've got some in the cooler. Just set one cupcake aside for Beatrice to taste and decorate the rest."

"Good idea," Lisa said, taking the recipe Hannah handed her and heading for the cooler to get the applesauce.

An hour and a half later, Hannah and Lisa were through with the baking for the day. Everything had gone smoothly. The kitchen at The Cookie Jar wasn't very large, but Hannah and Lisa had been working together for over a year and each anticipated the other's movements. As Hannah carried a mug of coffee over to their favorite booth in the back of the coffee shop, she wondered how she'd ever gotten along without Lisa.

"So what's happening with the murder?" Lisa asked, sitting down across the table from Hannah.

"Not much. I've really hit a snag, Lisa. I think the report we found in Sheriff Grant's briefcase is important, but Lonnie's on vacation and I can't find him to ask him about it."

"Did you check with your sister? Michelle was pretty thick with him the last time she was in town."

"That's who I was trying to call when you came in this morning."

"Well, don't give up. You're bound to catch her sooner or later." Lisa glanced down at her watch. "It's time for me to change into my cat costume. What are you going to wear?"

"My sheet. I'll be a ghost when I'm out here. But most of the time I'll be in the kitchen so I won't have to wear anything at all."

Lisa burst out laughing and Hannah was puzzled until she'd backed up her mental tape and replayed the last sentence she'd uttered. Then she smiled and said, "Don't be so quick to laugh. We'd save a fortune on aprons."

Chapter Twenty-Seven

"Your place looks nice, Hannah," Beatrice Koester said, coming in the front door in answer to Hannah's telephone summons. "I just love the way those orange and black streamers blow in the breeze from the fans. And the pumpkins in the window are just great."

"Lisa did all the decorating."

"She's really good at it. Where's your ghost costume?"

"I spilled melted chocolate on it."

"But how about the kids?" Beatrice glanced around at several pre-school children who were sitting at tables with their mothers.

"I've got another costume right here." Hannah grabbed the box of cornflakes she'd set behind the counter and stabbed it with a plastic knife. "See?"

"See what?"

"I'm a cereal killer."

Beatrice groaned and sat down on a stool at the counter. "That's awful, Hannah. Actually it's awful *and* it's very clever, but nobody in Lake Eden's going to catch on. I bet you had to explain it to everybody."

"You're right. I've been trying to get people to guess for over an hour now and nobody's figured it out. I thought Mayor Bascomb would. You know how he loves puns. But he didn't get it, either."

"This could be a good test."

"A test of what?"

"Compatibility. I've been listening to Doctor Love on the radio and she says spouses should share a similar sense of humor."

Hannah's eyebrows shot up. Was Beatrice listening to the woman who gave romantic advice on KCOW radio because she was having trouble in her own marriage?

"Ted and I don't have the same sense of humor," Beatrice admitted with a frown. "He likes the new sitcoms and I like the old ones like *Three's Company* and *The Golden Girls*.

Hannah wasn't sure how to respond so she kept her lips pressed tightly together.

"The thing is, the couple that laughs together stays together. At least that's what Doctor Love says. So I think that if you find a man who catches on to your cereal killer costume and thinks it's funny, you should marry him."

"Thanks for the advice," Hannah said, reaching under the counter to bring out the cupcake that Lisa had saved for Beatrice. "Sit down and try this. It's the latest attempt."

Beatrice took a bite and smiled in appreciation. "Delicious! Is that applesauce I taste?"

"Yes. Is it Alma's secret ingredient?"

"No, but it's close. Alma's cupcakes were sweeter, but they had a fruity taste under the chocolate. I told you that before, didn't I?"

"Yes. You also said that you couldn't tell which fruit Alma used."

"That's right. The flavor just blended in. It was there, but I couldn't tell what it was. It made the chocolate taste . . . I don't know how to describe it."

"Darker? Richer?"

"That's it. The chocolate tasted darker and richer. And there's one more thing I remember. When raspberries were in season, Alma used to put a nice plump one on top of each cupcake."

"Do you think the fruit Alma used was mashed raspberries?" Hannah asked the logical question.

"I know it wasn't either raspberries or strawberries. Those kinds of seeds always stick between my teeth and that never happened when I ate Alma's cupcakes."

When Beatrice left, taking the rest of the cupcake with her, Hannah refilled her customers' coffee cups. Then she sat down on the stool behind the counter to think. Mashed raspberries would have seeds. There was no way around it. Alma could have juiced them, but that couldn't be right. Edna Ferguson was certain that the secret ingredient was thicker than juice and Hannah had come to the same conclusion.

"Hi, Hannah." Lisa breezed in the door, wearing her cat costume. She had the long, stuffed tail taped in place on her shoulder and it looked very strange. "Don't ever try to drive with a tail."

Hannah laughed. "I'll keep that in mind. What happened?"

"It wrapped itself around the gearshift lever and I had to untangle it every time I backed up. It was a real nuisance."

"So you taped it to your shoulder?"

"Reverend Knudson did it when I delivered the cookies for his meeting. If it didn't look so bad, I'd leave it taped for the rest of the day."

"Leave it for now," Hannah said as an idea popped into her head. "I've got a plan that'll fix it for good. All I have to do is take a quick run to the drugstore."

"Go ahead. I'll take care of everything here. Do you think you could stop off at the Red Owl on the way back? We're running low on pancake syrup and Reverend Knudson ordered a whole batch of Short Stack Cookies for social hour after church services on Sunday."

"No problem," Hannah said, heading off to the drugstore to stock up on the things she needed to fix her partner's problematic tail.

* * *

Hannah came out of Lake Eden Neighborhood Pharmacy smiling. Jon Walker's clerks had done a marvelous job of decorating the drugstore with cutouts of black cats and swooping bats suspended from wires attached to the ceiling. Jon had done his mad chemist act just for her and it had been every bit as good as last year. To make things even better, he gave her a Halloween discount on the items she'd bought for Lisa.

"Hi, Hannah," Florence Evans, the owner of the Red Owl, greeted her as she stepped through the door. One of the checkers must have called in sick, because Florence only worked at the checkout stand when they were shorthanded. "Where's your costume?"

"Back at the shop," Hannah said, not wanting to get into a discussion about costumes or the lack of them with Florence, who held the current record for the lengthiest conversation in Lake Eden.

"So what's new, Hannah?" Florence asked.

"Nothing," Hannah said, knowing that it was wise to give Florence a one-word answer quickly followed by a grocery question. "The pancake syrup's still in aisle three, isn't it, Florence?"

"Yes, and I just got in some wonderful new flavored . . ."

"Thanks, Florence, but all I need is maple," Hannah interrupted what was surely going to be a lengthy description of the new items the Red Owl was stocking. "Lisa's waiting for it back at the shop."

Hannah turned on her heel and headed for aisle three, but Florence had other ideas. Before Hannah could blink, she'd flicked off the light above her register, and stepped out from behind the counter.

"You really should take a look. Those new flavors are really special." Florence linked arms with Hannah and headed toward the rear of the store. "Come along with me and I'll show you."

*   *   *

"There you are!" Lisa looked relieved when Hannah came back into The Cookie Jar. "It's been an hour and I was getting worried."

"Remember the television ad for the Roach Motel?" Hannah asked, setting her bags on the counter.

"I think so. Isn't that the one that said, *Roaches check in . . . but they don't check out?*"

"That's the one. Well, Florence was working the check stand at the Red Owl."

It took Lisa a moment, but then she burst of laughing. "She wouldn't let you check out?"

"That's right. She followed me back to aisle three to show me the new pancake syrups, but what I thought was going to be a real delay turned out to be a lucky break."

"Florence told you something about the murder?" Lisa guessed.

"It wasn't *that* lucky, but she did teach me something about Alma's cupcakes." Hannah opened the grocery bag and pulled out a bottle. She held her hand over the label and asked, "Does this look familiar?"

"That bottle looks just like the ones Beatrice brought in when she was testing salad dressings."

"And where did Beatrice say she got the bottles?"

"From her mother-in-law's basement. And she also said that Alma had lots of them and Ted thought she was crazy for bringing them home."

"Turns out that Beatrice was brilliant for bringing them home. I never would have guessed Alma's secret ingredient if I hadn't seen those bottles."

"You mean you know what it is?" Lisa looked excited when Hannah nodded.

"If I'm right, this is it."

Lisa took the bottle and looked at the label. "Raspberry syrup? That's got to be it, Hannah! And it explains why Alma put a raspberry on top of the cupcakes. You and Edna both thought that it would be a thick liquid and syrup is thick. And Beatrice said they tasted fruity."

"She also said that they tasted German and they're very big on chocolate and raspberry in Europe."

"You've got it, Hannah. I don't think I *ever* would have figured it out."

"You would have if Florence had gotten a hold of you," Hannah said, smiling at her partner. "But let's not crow too much until we test it. Do you want to do it, or shall I?"

"You do it. I'll stay out here since I'm in costume."

"And that reminds me . . ." Hannah grinned as she handed Lisa the white bag from the drugstore. "This ought to fix that tail of yours."

"A sling?" Lisa asked, looking dumbfounded as she drew it out of the bag.

"A sling and a bandage. You know how Moishe's tail is bent at the tip?" Hannah waited until Lisa nodded. "Doctor Bob said it's common for street cats to break the tips of their tails."

"So you want me to break my tail?"

"Yes. Just bend it at the tip and bandage it. Then you can put it in a sling that hangs around your neck and it won't get in your way."

"Those cupcakes smell wonderful!" Lisa sighed in longing as she opened the swinging door between the kitchen and the coffee shop. "You frosted them, too?"

"I thought I should. This has to be a complete test."

"Of course it does. And I really love that fudge frosting. You want me to taste a cupcake, don't you?"

"Help yourself. I'm so sure this is it, I baked a double batch."

Lisa made a beeline for the bakers' rack and grabbed a cupcake. Her mouth headed for the frosting like a child bobbing for an apple and, in keeping with her costume, she practically purred as she tasted it. "This frosting is so good, Hannah."

"I know. I licked out the pan. Do you want me to take a turn up front while you eat your cupcake?"

Lisa shook her head. "There's nobody there. We haven't had a customer for the past thirty minutes."

Hannah considered what Lisa had said. Almost everybody in town was getting ready for Halloween and there wouldn't be many customers for the remainder of the afternoon. It was silly for both of them to stay here, especially when Hannah knew that Lisa was itching to go down to the community center and help her father and the seniors put the finishing touches on the decorations for the Halloween party.

"Here you go, Lisa," Hannah put six cupcakes into a take-out box and handed it to Lisa. "Take off your apron and get out of here."

Lisa caught Hannah's meaning immediately and she began to grin. "You're kicking me out?"

"I am. There's no reason why both of us should be bored, and I have to stay here to make some phone calls anyway."

"Well, if you're sure you don't mind . . ."

"I don't mind," Hannah said. "Go help your dad decorate."

"I will." Lisa looked very pleased as she picked up the cupcake box. "Do you want me to take the Halloween cookies?"

"I'll bring them when I come with Tracey. If you take them, the kids will just get into them early."

"Okay. See you tonight, Hannah. I'll be the cat with the broken tail and Herb's going to be an outhouse."

"An *outhouse?*" Hannah repeated, not sure she'd heard Lisa correctly.

"That's right. He made his costume himself. It's a big box with the bottom cut out and holes in the sides for his arms. The box goes up to the top of his head and he's got a toy rooster he's gluing on the top."

Hannah tried to imagine it, but she couldn't quite do it. "If his head's in the box, how does he see?"

"He made cutouts of a moon and stars and he looks through those. A lot of outhouses have those for ventilation. But that's not the best thing."

Hannah was almost afraid to ask. "What's the best thing?"

"He rigged it so the door opens. And when we dance, I'm going to open the door and step in. Isn't it just great, Hannah? I really think he's going to win the prize."

"Great," Hannah said, and she gave a little wave as Lisa went out the back door. If Herb didn't win the prize for best costume, he certainly should get points for the strangest.

Hannah glanced out the plate glass window and sighed. It was four o'clock in the afternoon and the only customer she'd had was Freddy Sawyer. Doc Knight had placed an order for four-dozen Halloween cookies so that Freddy could dress up in a Superman costume and pass them out to the nurses and patients tonight.

A Siberian husky on a leash trotted past the window and Hannah watched for the owner. It seemed to take a very long time and, for a moment, Hannah thought perhaps someone was playing a Halloween joke. Then Eleanor Cox came into view, holding the handle of a retractable leash. She waved at Hannah, Hannah waved back, and that was Hannah's only excitement for the next fifteen minutes.

Time had never gone so slowly. Hannah decided she should do something more constructive than count the birds that landed in the huge pine across the street, and she reached for the phone. Beatrice hadn't been home the last time she'd called to invite her to taste the cupcakes, but perhaps she'd returned by now.

After ten rings, Hannah disconnected the call and punched in her youngest sister's number. Since she was having no luck reaching Beatrice, she might as well try Michelle again. The phone rang once, twice, and then Michelle answered.

"Michelle?" Hannah asked, hardly daring to believe her good luck. "I'm really glad I caught you."

"Hi, Hannah. What's up?"

"It's Lonnie. I tried everywhere, but I can't find him."

There was a long silence and when she spoke again, Michelle sounded wary. "Why do you need to find Lonnie?"

"I found his incident report in Sheriff Grant's briefcase and I think it might have something to do with the murder."

"*What* murder?!"

Hannah froze for an instant. Was it possible that Michelle hadn't heard? "You know about Sheriff Grant, don't you?"

"What about Sheriff Grant?"

"Somebody killed him last Monday night. They hit him over the head and toppled him into a Dumpster in the Jordan High parking lot. I found him when I carried out the garbage from my cooking class."

Michelle gulped so loudly Hannah could hear it over the phone. "That's just awful! And it happened last Monday night?"

"That's right. And Mike suspended Bill because Bill was a suspect, but we managed to clear him and he's back on the job."

"I really don't believe this, Hannah." Michelle gave a huffy sigh. "I'm less than a hundred miles away, and nobody bothers to tell me anything! Are you sure you didn't leave anything out?"

"Just one thing. Doc Knight ordered Andrea to stay home with her feet up and she's going crazy."

"This is surreal, Hannah. Mother called me last night and she didn't say a word about anything! She just asked me if I knew where Lonnie was and when I said I didn't, she hung up."

"Sorry, Michelle." Hannah began to feel guilty that she'd left her baby sister out of the loop. "I should have called you, but I figured you must know. I can't believe you didn't hear anything about it. You'd think the murder of a county sheriff would make the news."

"Um . . . it might have made the news. It's just that I've been out of touch for a while. I've been really busy . . . uh . . . studying."

"Right," Hannah said, not believing a word of it. Michelle was hiding something and Hannah was pretty sure the thing she was hiding was a who. "Let's cut to the chase, Michelle. Go get Lonnie and put him on the phone. I need to know more about that incident report."

"Lonnie? Um . . . what makes you think that Lonnie is here? When Mother called last night, I told her I hadn't seen him."

Hannah sighed. "That was Mother. This is me. Let me talk to him, Michelle. And stop hedging. I won't tell anybody he was with you."

"He's not exactly *with* me, Hannah. It's a big house and there's plenty of room."

"Right," Hannah said, grinning a little.

"Well, there is. It's not like we're staying in the same room, or anything. I just didn't want Andrea or Mother to know. They'd never understand."

"How about Raj?" Hannah used Roger Allen Jensen's nickname. He was the college boy Michelle had been dating when she came home last July. "Does he understand?"

"Raj is history. We broke up the day after I got back to school. I got really tired of his superior attitude."

"That would do it, all right," Hannah said, remembering how Raj had referred to Michelle's Lake Eden background as colorful and quaint.

"Hold on. I'll get Lonnie. Be careful how you break it to him, Hannah. He's been with me the whole time and he doesn't know anything about Sheriff Grant's murder, either."

Chapter
Twenty-Eight

"Hi, Hannah," Lonnie greeted her. He sounded a bit guilty and Hannah hoped it was the result of going off without telling anyone where he was going, rather than for any other reason. "Shelly says you've got something important to tell me."

Shelly? Hannah's brows headed skyward. Michelle didn't like to be called Shelly. She'd told Hannah that it made her feel like a turtle.

"Um . . . yes, I do have something important to tell you," Hannah said, wondering why Lonnie was permitted to use the nickname Michelle disliked. "I've got some bad news, Lonnie."

"My folks are okay, aren't they?" Lonnie asked, before Hannah could follow up her initial statement.

"They're fine," Hannah reassured him. "Your whole family's fine. Everybody in Lake Eden is fine, except for Sheriff Grant."

The minute the words were out of Hannah's mouth she wished she'd thought of another way to phrase it. She'd never been a master at tact.

"What's wrong with Sheriff Grant?" Lonnie asked, exactly as Hannah had expected he would.

"He's dead," Hannah said, deciding to spit it out now and

deal with the fallout later. "Somebody murdered him last Monday night."

There was a long silence, so long that Hannah wondered if Lonnie had passed out from shock. But then she heard a sigh and Lonnie cleared his throat.

"That's really awful," he said, his voice shaking slightly. "Do Mike and Bill need me to come back home?"

"I don't know, but you can call them if you think you should. Mike's the acting sheriff now. You could say that you were out of touch and you just heard about it."

"Good idea." Lonnie sounded more in control when he spoke again. "Do they have any suspects?"

"I don't know. If they do, they're not telling me."

"I guess they wouldn't. So are you mad?"

"I'm not exactly dancing up and down the streets in de-light," Hannah said with a shrug, even though she knew Lonnie couldn't see it. "Sure, I wish they'd include me in their investigation, but that's about as likely as snow in August."

"I didn't mean are you mad at Mike and Bill. I meant, are you mad at me."

"Oh." Hannah took a second to regroup. "You mean, be-cause you're spending your vacation with Michelle?"

Lonnie gulped again. "Um . . . yeah. That's exactly what I mean."

"No, I'm not mad." Hannah smiled, remembering her own college days. It had been a time of testing her wings and it was fairly obvious that Michelle was doing the same. "I just hope you didn't keep her from her classes. Good grades are very important to Michelle."

"I didn't keep her from anything. I went along to every class and sat in the back. Nobody seemed to mind and I even took notes in case Shelly missed something."

Hannah gave it up. It certainly didn't sound as if Lonnie had hurt Michelle in any way. "I need to talk to you about that stolen car report you wrote right before you left on vacation. Did you know that Sheriff Grant took it home with him?"

"I didn't know that, but it doesn't surprise me. He was really interested in that car thief. He told me he was going to handle the case personally and that was when he gave me two weeks of comp time for all the extra hours I'd put in working on it, effective anytime I wanted."

"And that was unusual?" Hannah asked.

"I don't know, for sure. But Sheriff Grant isn't . . ." Lonnie stopped and Hannah heard him swallow. "Sheriff Grant *wasn't* known for being really generous about time off, and vacations, and things like that. I figured I'd better grab it before he changed his mind, so I said I'd take the comp time right away and I left."

"That was probably smart. Let's get back to the car thief. What can you tell me about him?"

"I put everything I knew into the report. The guy wouldn't give me his name and he didn't have any I.D. on him. He just clammed up and I figured he was bound to lawyer up when I got him to the station, but he didn't. Sheriff Grant told me not to worry about it. He said he'd interrogate the guy himself and find out who he was. I'm assuming that's what he did. The guy was still in the holding tank when I left the station."

Hannah asked several other questions, but when it became clear that Lonnie couldn't give her any more information, she asked to talk to her sister again. After assuring Michelle that she wasn't about to tell anyone the identity of her houseguest, Hannah hung up and flipped through her notebook.

Car parts in Sheriff Grant's home office that belonged to him, not Jamie. A car thief Lonnie had apprehended. Sheriff Grant's interest in pulling Lonnie off the case so that he could interview the suspect himself. The fact that Sheriff Grant took Lonnie's report home in his special briefcase. Hannah was beginning to see how all these things might fit together. Could they be part of the big case that Sheriff Grant had needed to win the election? And did something he discovered while he was working on this big case result in his murder?

Just when Hannah thought her head would burst with churning ideas, the phone rang. She reached out to answer it without thinking, and only then did she realize that she should have locked up the shop ten minutes ago.

"Hannah?" It was Andrea's voice and she sounded excited. "I'm so glad I caught you!"

"Why's that?" Hannah asked, pulling out the cash drawer and starting to count the money for their nightly deposit.

"I wanted to tell you that I'm almost done with the recipes."

"Almost *done?*" Hannah was so surprised, she almost put a five-dollar bill in her stack of twenties. "But you just started!"

Andrea laughed, obviously pleased at Hannah's shocked reaction. "I've been at it for two days. I told you before that I'm a fast typist."

"I know, but I never expected you to finish this soon. What time do you want me to pick up Tracey tonight?"

"That's the other reason I called. Can you be here at seven-thirty? Lucy Dunwright just left and she took Tracey out for hamburgers with Karen. Then they're going trick 'n treating and they'll be back here at seven-thirty."

Hannah knew Lucy's daughter, Karen. She was a classmate of Tracey's and Hannah liked her. "If it's okay with Lucy, I can take both girls down to the Haunted Basement. Then Lucy can stay and visit with you until we come back."

"That's really nice of you, Hannah." Andrea sounded grateful. "I'd love to have company tonight. But I was calling to ask you for another favor and now I feel funny about it."

"What is it? I owe you more than one favor for typing all those recipes."

"No, you don't. I was happy to have something to do. But this is really important, Hannah."

Hannah frowned as she recognized a slightly panicked tone in Andrea's voice. "What is it?"

"It's Bill. He got so excited about going back to work, he forgot to replace his taillight."

"Uh-oh," Hannah groaned guessing the rest. "And they caught him out at the checkpoint again?"

"That's exactly what happened. He got another fixit ticket this morning and the next time it'll be a real ticket. He can't let that happen, Hannah. It would look awful for someone who's running for sheriff."

"That's true," Hannah said, waiting for her sister to get to the point.

"The problem is, Bill's bound to get that ticket tonight."

"Why tonight?"

"Because the checkout at the sheriff's station is staying open late. And there's no way Bill can drive home and not get one."

"So you want me to drive out there and give him a ride home?"

"Not exactly," Andrea sighed deeply. "Bill says it's really easy to replace a taillight on his car and if he had the part, he could do it in less than ten minutes. The only thing is, he doesn't have the part and if he drives out to get it, he'll get ticketed."

"Catch twenty-two," Hannah mused.

"That's exactly what it is. I just loved that movie, didn't you? I saw it on the old movie channel last year and I thought Alan Arkin was just perfect. But then there was Buck Henry's performance. It was marvelous. And Anthony Perkins, well . . ."

"So you want me to get the taillight and take it out to Bill at the sheriff's station?" Hannah interrupted her sister's rave movie review.

"If you don't mind, that would be really great."

"I don't mind at all. As a matter of fact, I was planning to go out there to have Ted taste the cupcakes I made from his mother's recipe. I'll get the taillight and stop by the sheriff's station on my way home to cook Moishe's dinner."

"You're *cooking* for Moishe now?"

"That's right. I've got a veterinarian-approved diet sheet for him."

"What are you cooking?"

Hannah thought about the boiled liver and the eggshells. "I don't think you want to know."

"Okay. I'll take your word for it. But don't forget to allow time to change into your costume. Tracey can hardly wait to see it. What are you going as?"

"It's a surprise," Hannah said, bemoaning her sister's grammar with half of her mind and wondering if she'd have time to wash and dry her ghost sheet with the other half.

Fifteen minutes later, Hannah had everything under control. She'd stuck the cornflakes and the plastic knife in the back of her truck for contingencies, locked up The Cookie Jar, packed the cupcakes for transit, and she was on the road to Ted Koester's salvage yard to get the taillight for Bill.

As she drove through town, the sky began to darken and Hannah smiled as she saw little trick 'n treaters skipping along the sidewalks, holding the hands of older siblings or parents. On her way to the highway, Hannah passed two boys in Elvis costumes, one King Kong, three fairy princesses, one Superman, two skeletons with day-glo bones, a hulking monster with green fangs, and nine ghosts. Perhaps it was a good thing she'd gotten her ghost costume dirty. It seemed that Lake Eden was swarming with ghosts tonight.

The spirit of Halloween infused even the traffic on the highway. Hannah spotted two cars with fluttering ghosts in the back windows and another with a fake arm hanging out of a truck. Several drivers wore Halloween masks and one trucker had decked his eighteen-wheeler out for the occasion by wiring a battery-operated jack o' lantern to his grill. The night was festive and Hannah was starting to get into the spirit as she pulled into Ted's salvage yard. She drove past the trailer that served as an office, headed for a parking spot, and smiled as she spotted Beatrice manning the counter. This was just perfect. Now she could have both Beatrice and Ted taste the cupcakes.

Hannah parked the truck, got out, and grabbed the bag of cupcakes. The wind practically knocked her off her feet as she dashed to the office and opened the door.

"Hi, Hannah," Beatrice greeted her warmly. "What's in the bag?"

"Cupcakes. I think I got it, Beatrice."

"Really?" Beatrice's lips turned up in a delighted smile. "That's wonderful, Hannah. Ted will be so pleased."

"Go ahead. Try one." Hannah handed her the bag. "I really think that this has got to be it."

"I hope so. I'm going to gain twenty pounds if I keep on tasting your test batches." Beatrice grinned to show she was joking as she opened the bag and took out a cupcake. She peeled back the paper, took a small bite, and then she took a larger one.

Hannah didn't realize that she was holding her breath until Beatrice had eaten half the cupcake. She let it out again in a relieved sigh. "It's Alma's recipe?"

"This is it, Hannah! It's just like Alma used to bake. What's the secret ingredient?"

"Raspberry syrup. And that's what came in all those bottles you found in her basement."

"Well, I'll be!" Beatrice said, polishing off the cupcake and wiping her fingers on one of the napkins Hannah had tucked into the bag. "Just wait until Ted tastes these!"

"Speaking of Ted, where is he? I need to buy a taillight for Bill's car."

"He's out with the tow truck. That's why I'm here filling in for him. He should be back any minute, but I can probably help you if you've got the make, model, and year."

"I do," Hannah said, handing over the note she'd written with the information Andrea had given her.

Beatrice opened a thick parts book. "I'm sure Ted's got it.

Once I get the part number, I'll type it into the computer inventory and it should tell us exactly where it is."

Hannah watched as Beatrice looked up the part and typed in the number. In just a moment, the answer appeared on the screen. "Here we go. Bill's taillight is in section seventeen, bin thirty-eight."

"Where's that?"

"Right here," Beatrice pointed to the section on the large map that hung on the wall in back of the counter. "Come with me. I'll take you over to the parts shed."

Hannah followed Beatrice to a large metal shed that took up almost a quarter of the salvage yard. Beatrice opened the door, flicked on the lights, and led Hannah down an aisle in the center. Each section was filled from floor to ceiling with metal shelving and Beatrice stopped when she came to section seventeen. "Bin thirty-eight should be right about . . . here."

"I see it," Hannah said, pointing up at the third tier of shelves. "But how do we get it? Do you have a ladder?"

Beatrice nodded and walked to the center aisle. A moment later, she came back pushing a rolling ladder, the kind Hannah had seen stock clerks use in home building stores. "Just watch. This is so easy with a ladder like this."

Before Hannah could offer to do it for her, Beatrice pulled on gloves, climbed up the ladder, reached into the bin, and came down with a taillight. "This is the one that'll fit Bill's car."

"Great," Hannah said, taking the part while Beatrice rolled back the ladder. "You don't happen to know where the cigarette lighters are, do you? I need one for my truck. It was missing when I bought it."

"They're in section twelve. But I didn't know you smoked, Hannah."

"I don't. It's just that you never know when you're going to need to light a candle."

"That's profound, Hannah. It's a metaphor, right?"

"I suppose it is, but I was just being practical. You never know when you'll have to light a candle to keep you warm when you're stranded in a snow bank. And, I really don't like that empty hole in the dash. It looks so unfinished."

Beatrice gestured for Hannah to follow her and headed toward the front of the shed. "Here they are," she said, pointing to a bin on the second tier and handing Hannah a pair of gloves. "Just reach in and get one. Almost all cigarette lighters are a standard size. Put on the gloves first, though. Ted got a nasty scratch on his arm when he forgot to wear his gloves last week. His shirt had so much blood on it, I had to throw it out."

"Jon Walker mentioned it. Ted and I are taking the same kind of antibiotics," Hannah slipped on the gloves and reached into the bin, "the really expensive ones."

Once Hannah had retrieved the cigarette lighter she wanted, Beatrice led the way back to the office. On the way, she pointed out a box-like structure about the size of a home garage. "That's our new crusher. Isn't it wonderful?"

"Yes," Hannah said, even though she didn't exactly know how a crusher could be wonderful. "How does it work?"

"It's open on top and Ted just hoists the car he wants to crush and drops it right in. The sides move in to crush the car and it ends up about the size of a breadbox."

A few moments later, they were back in the office. Beatrice was adding up Hannah's purchases when the phone rang. "Hold on just a second, Hannah. That might be Ted and I want to tell him you figured out the cupcakes."

"Ted's Salvage," Beatrice greeted her caller. "Oh, hello, honey! Are you and Krista all ready for your big performance tonight?"

Hannah smiled. It was obvious that Beatrice was talking to her granddaughter, Leah.

"Oh, dear! Is there anything I can do to help?" Beatrice

listened for a moment. "Of course I can, honey. I'll be there just as soon as your grandpa comes back."

"What's the matter?" Hannah asked, as Beatrice hung up the phone.

"It's Leah. She tore the wing on her bat costume and she can't seem to sew it back on right. And her mother's not home."

"So you're going to go over and help her?"

"Just as soon as Ted gets back. I'd close up right now, but he's waiting for an important shipment of scrap cars. He needs to dismantle them to get the parts he needs for his big customer in Minneapolis. There's no way we want to disappoint him!"

"He's an important customer?"

"He accounts for over half of our business. There's no way we could turn a profit if he ordered from someone else."

"He must buy a lot of car parts."

"I'll say! He faxes every Monday morning with a long list of car parts for Ted to locate and ship to him."

"Locate?" Hannah was curious. She knew nothing about the auto salvage business.

"That's right. I'm not exactly sure how Ted does it, but he must call around to the other auto salvage places to find the things he doesn't have here. I know he always gets all the parts by the end of the week and ships them off on Saturday morning."

Something niggled at the back of Hannah's mind, but she couldn't quite put her finger on what it was. There was something she had to ask Beatrice, or Ted. Perhaps she should offer to stay until Ted got back. She might think of it by then.

"Go and help Leah," Hannah said, acting on her impulse. "I'll stay here and wait for Ted. I want to see his face when he tastes those cupcakes."

"Are you sure?"

"I'm positive. Just tell me what to do when the transport comes in."

"There's nothing to it," Beatrice said, grabbing a clip-board and setting it on the counter next to the cash register. "The driver knows where to unload, so that's no problem. It'll be that area right in front of the big metal shed. That's where Ted does the dismantling."

"Got it," Hannah said.

"All you have to do is sign the receipt, give it back to the driver, and keep the bill of lading for Ted. Just put it on this clipboard on the counter."

"How about customers? Do you want me to try to find the parts they need?"

Beatrice shook her head. "That's too much trouble. I don't think you'll have any customers this late, but if you do, just tell them to wait until Ted gets back, or to come back tomor-row."

"Will do. Anything else?"

"One thing. When Ted gets back, tell him what happened with Leah's costume. And then give him a cupcake right away, so he won't be mad at me for leaving. Do you want me to plug in the heater before I go?"

"No, I don't think I'll need it. I'll just run out to the truck to get my jacket."

Hannah glanced at the clock as Beatrice hurried to her car and drove away. It was already after six and she'd promised to pick up Tracey and Karen at seven-thirty. If Ted didn't get back soon, she wouldn't have time to run home to feed Moishe. Of course, a late dinner wouldn't exactly kill him, especially when he'd had such a nice omelet this morning. If he got hungry enough waiting for his personal gourmet chef, he might just eat some of the senior nuggets in his bowl to tide him over.

Fudge Cupcakes

Preheat oven to 350 degrees F.,
rack in the middle position

4 squares unsweetened baking chocolate *(1 ounce each)*
¼ cup white sugar
½ cup raspberry syrup *(for pancakes—I used Knott's red raspberry)*
1 ⅔ cups flour
1 ½ teaspoon baking powder
½ teaspoon salt
½ cup butter, room temperature *(one stick, ¼ pound)*
1 ½ cups white sugar *(not a misprint—you'll use 1 ¾ cups sugar in all)*
3 eggs
⅓ cup milk

Line a 12-cup muffin pan with double cupcake papers. Since this recipe makes 18 cupcakes, you can use an additional 6-cup muffin pan lined with double papers, or you can butter and flour an 8-inch square cake pan or the equivalent.

Microwave the chocolate, raspberry syrup and ¼ cup sugar in a microwave-safe bowl on high for 1 minute.

Stir. Microwave again for another minute. At this point, the chocolate will be almost melted, but it will maintain its shape. Stir the mixture until smooth and let cool to lukewarm. (*You can also do this in a double boiler on the stove.*)

Measure flour, mix in baking powder and salt, and set aside. In an electric mixer (*or with a VERY strong arm*), beat the butter and 1 ½ cups sugar until light and fluffy. (*About 3 minutes with a mixer—an additional 2 minutes if you're doing it by hand.*) Add eggs, one at a time, beating after each addition to make sure they're thoroughly incorporated. Add approximately a third of the flour mixture and a third of the milk. (*You don't have to be exact—adding the flour and milk in increments makes the batter smoother.*) When that's all mixed in, add another third of the flour and another third of the milk. When that's incorporated, add the remainder of the flour and the remainder of the milk. Mix thoroughly.

Test your chocolate mixture to make sure it's cool enough to add. (*You don't want to cook the eggs!*) If it's fairly warm to the touch but not so hot you have to pull your hand away, you can add it at this point. Stir thoroughly and you're done.

Let the batter rest for five minutes. Then stir it again by hand and fill each cupcake paper three-quarters full. If you decided to use the 8-inch cake pan instead of the 6-cup muffin tin, fill it with the remaining batter.

Bake the cupcakes in a 350 degree F. oven for 20 to 25 minutes. The 8-inch cake should bake an additional 5 minutes.

Fudge Frosting

18 cupcakes, or 12 cupcakes and 1 small cake, cooled to room temperature and ready to frost.

2 cups chocolate chips *(a 12-ounce package)*
1 14-ounce can sweetened condensed milk

If you use a double boiler for this frosting, it's fool-proof. You can also make it in a heavy saucepan over low to medium heat on the stovetop, but you'll have to stir it constantly with a spatula to keep it from scorching.

Fill the bottom part of the double boiler with water. Make sure it doesn't touch the underside of the top.

Put the chocolate chips in the top of the double boiler, set it over the bottom, and place the double boiler on the stovetop at medium heat. Stir occasionally until the chocolate chips are melted.

Stir in the can of sweetened condensed milk and cook approximately two minutes, stirring constantly, until the frosting is shiny and of spreading consistency.

Spread on cupcakes, making sure to fill in the "frosting pocket."

Give the frosting pan to your favorite person to scrape.

These cupcakes are even better if you cool them, cover them, and let them sit for several hours before frosting them.

Chapter
Twenty-Nine

Hannah stared out the window at the highway in the distance and tapped her fingers against the counter. It was almost six-thirty and Ted still wasn't here. There also hadn't been any sign of his transport and Hannah was beginning to wish she hadn't volunteered to take Beatrice's place.

It was cold in the trailer and Hannah pulled her bomber jacket a little closer around her shoulders. Perhaps she should have taken Beatrice up on her offer to plug in the heater. It was going to be a cold night. The moment the sun had gone down, the wind had picked up in velocity. By now it was just about as fierce as a fall wind could get.

Gusting winds rattled the metal walls of the trailer and sent dead leaves skittering under the hulks of wrecked cars like thousands of miniature mechanics, trying to fix the impossible. At least it was a lot warmer inside than it was outside. When Hannah had dashed out to her truck to get her jacket and try the cigarette lighter in the hole in her dash, she thought she'd smelled a hint of snow in the air.

Hannah's Grandma Ingrid always claimed she could smell snow coming, and attempted to teach Hannah how to do it. Hannah had memories of sitting in a porch swing on the Swensen family farm, wrapped up in a warm quilt with her grandmother, so they could smell the freezing air. There *had* been a barely detectible odor. Hannah had smelled it. When she'd asked what it was, Grandma Ingrid couldn't identify it by name, but she'd insisted that whenever Hannah smelled that scent on the wind, it was going to snow.

Bright lights flashed as a vehicle turned off the highway. Hannah watched, her expectations high, as it came down the access road toward the scrap yard. As it approached the gates, Hannah could see that it was the kind of truck used to haul cars. She zipped up her bomber jacket and headed out the door to greet the driver. The transport was here at last.

The driver gave her a wave and proceeded to unload the cars, exactly as Beatrice had said he would. Hannah stood at the window and watched him do it, smiling at the ease with which he backed the big truck down the narrow road that led to the dismantling shed. But when the driver began to unload the cars, her smile turned to a puzzled frown. She was certainly no expert, but they looked much too nice to be sold as scrap and dismantled. There must be something seriously wrong with each of them that wasn't immediately apparent to the casual observer.

Once he'd finished, the driver climbed back into his rig and drove up to the trailer again. Hannah walked out to the driver's window, signed her name to the receipt he had on his clipboard, and took the bill of lading he handed her.

"Gonna be a cold one tonight," the driver said.

"Sure seems like it," Hannah answered.

"New here?" the driver asked, staring at her hard, as if to memorize her features. "I talked to Ted this morning and he said he'd be here."

"He had to go out on a tow, and I'm just filling in for his wife. She had a family emergency."

"Okay," the driver said, giving her a half salute before he rolled up his window. Then he put his truck into gear and pulled forward, heading for the gates.

Hannah watched his taillights until he'd navigated the access road and turned back onto the highway. Then she carried the bill of lading into the trailer and found the clipboard Beatrice had placed on the counter. She was just about to clip it on when she happened to notice the list under it.

It had to be from the man in Minneapolis. Hannah ran her finger down the neat column of typing and counted the items. Ted's customer must own a chain of repair shops. There was no way one shop could use all these parts in a week.

Hannah glanced at the top of the fax and began to frown. It had been sent from *Words, Etc.*, a company that placed kiosks in malls so that customers could have faxes sent, copies made, and computer disks printed. But wouldn't a large chain of repair shops have at least one with a fax machine? Hannah stared down at the list of parts again and compared it to the receipt for the cars the transport driver had delivered. Every one of the items on the car parts order could be obtained by dismantling the cars that looked too good to be sold as salvage.

The pieces of Sheriff Grant's murder puzzle began to turn and jostle for position in Hannah's mind. It was possible that Ted had bought these cars from other junkyards, but she was still disturbed by their like-new condition. What if there was nothing wrong with them? What if the cars had been stolen to fill the order from the man in Minneapolis? And what if Ted and Beatrice's newfound prosperity came from running a chop shop for stolen cars?

Hannah glanced at the receipt again. It listed the cars as salvage, but didn't you need a pink slip to sell a junk car? The driver hadn't handed her any of those. She zipped up her bomber jacket again and ran out to check, but the glove compartments in all four cars were as empty as the interiors. Was she right about the pink slips? Hannah wasn't a hundred percent sure, but it was too late to call the D.M.V. today and she didn't want to wait until Monday morning.

The moment Hannah thought of it, she picked up the

phone and dialed Eleanor Cox's number. Eleanor had been
the head clerk at the D.M.V. for almost twenty years before
she retired, and she was bound to know the answer.

"Hi, Eleanor," Hannah said when her call was answered,
thanking her lucky stars that Eleanor was home.

"Hi, Hannah. What's on your mind?"

"I need to ask you a D.M.V. question. Does a person need
a pink slip to sell a car for junk?"

"Is something wrong with your cookie truck that you're
thinking of selling it for junk?"

"No, nothing's wrong. The question just came up, that's
all. Do you know?"

"Of course I know. I didn't sit behind that counter at the
D.M.V. for twenty years for nothing. Yes, you need a valid
pink slip to prove ownership. The slip must be signed over to
whoever takes possession of the vehicle, whether it's a used
car lot, a private party, a donation to charity, or a salvage
yard."

"How about if one salvage yard sells the car to another
salvage yard?"

"The pink slip stipulations still apply," Eleanor said,
sounding very official. "The vehicle cannot legally change
hands without the pink slip."

"Thanks, Eleanor. You've been really . . ."

"It's not really pink, you know," Eleanor interrupted
Hannah's comment. "Everybody always says that, but pink
slips haven't been pink for years. But that's neither here nor
there. It's downright creepy, Hannah."

"What's creepy?"

"It's just that Sheriff Grant called me on the day he was
killed and asked me the very same questions."

Somehow Hannah managed to say goodbye and get off
the phone. The pieces of the puzzle surrounding Sheriff
Grant's death were spinning around a lot faster now. Car
parts in Sheriff Grant's home office. The fact the sheriff hid
Lonnie's stolen car report in his briefcase. Sheriff Grant's call

to Eleanor to ask about the pink slips. All this made Hannah certain that the sheriff had been down the road she was traveling, the very same road that had led to his death. But who had killed him? The driver of the stolen car transport? The man in Minneapolis? Ted?!

Hannah gasped as another piece of the puzzle clicked into place. Barbara Donnelly had told her that Ted had been wearing coveralls when he picked up Leah and Krista from dance class. What if Ted had used his coveralls to hide clothing splattered with Sheriff Grant's blood? And what about that scratch on his arm? Had he done it here at the salvage yard, or had he injured it on the lid of the Dumpster as he'd tumbled Sheriff Grant inside?

With her heart beating much faster than its normal rate, Hannah let the sheriff's murder play out in her mind. Sheriff Grant had spotted Ted as he pulled into the school parking lot in his work truck. Before Ted could switch to Beatrice's sedan and leave to pick up the girls, Sheriff Grant had asked him some tough questions. Ted put two and two together and realized that Sheriff Grant had discovered his stolen car ring. Ted knew that he was about to be arrested and he refused to go down without a fight. He resisted, getting in a lucky swing with something hard enough to break Sheriff Grant's skull, something he had with him in his truck like . . . a tire iron.

Hannah glanced out at Ted's work truck, which was parked right next to the trailer. Perhaps the murder weapon was still in there. It wouldn't take long to get his tire iron. Even if Ted had washed it off, it could still have trace amounts of Sheriff Grant's blood. She could take it out to the sheriff's office when she delivered Bill's taillight and they could test it.

In less than a minute, Hannah was back with the tire iron in hand. She supposed she should take it out and hide it in her truck, but the wind was gusting with a vengeance now and she was freezing. There was no reason why she couldn't hide it in plain sight. When Ted came back, she'd just buy it and he'd never suspect that it hadn't come from the big bin of tire irons in his parts shed.

Hannah put the tire iron on the counter, slid onto the stool she'd so recently vacated, and thought about the murder again. If Ted had scratched his hand while he was tumbling Sheriff Grant's body in the Dumpster, all Mike and Bill needed was a blood sample and they could match it to the blood they'd found.

Feeling much better now that she had two possible pieces of evidence, Hannah went back to her scenario. It all made sense, but something was missing. She thought about the information that everyone had given her and remembered the stain on Krista's dress. What if the stain wasn't rust? What if it was Sheriff Grant's blood, smeared inside the truck by Ted when he was in the process of slipping on his coveralls?

Suddenly Hannah had a frightening thought. If Clara and Marguerite Hollenbeck came back early, they might remove the stain from Krista's dress. She had to call and tell them not to touch what could be important evidence. Hannah picked up the phone, dialed their number, and breathed a sigh of relief when their answer machine kicked in. They weren't back yet. She'd leave a message telling them not to touch Krista's dress.

The two sisters had recorded a lengthy outgoing message and Hannah listened to more about Clara and Marguerite's schedules than she needed or wanted to know. She was just waiting for the beep to record her message when she heard a roar outside the window and looked up to see Ted Koester's tow truck pulling up in front of the trailer.

Hannah hung up the phone, waved at Ted, and plastered a smile on her face. It was a good thing he couldn't read her mind! All she had to do was explain where Beatrice was, tell him she'd taken his delivery, offer him a cupcake, pay for the tire iron, and get out.

"Hi, Hannah." Ted stepped inside the trailer, looking puzzled. "Where's Beatrice?"

"She had to go repair Leah's dance costume. I said I'd stay until you got here. Your delivery came. I signed for it and put the paper on the clipboard the way Beatrice told me to do."

"Thanks." Ted eyed the white bag on the counter. "What's that?"

"Cupcakes. I think I've got your mother's recipe figured out. Taste one and see."

Ted took a cupcake out of the bag and tasted it. He took another bite and then another. "You got it. What was the secret ingredient that Beatrice was grousing about the other night?"

"Raspberry syrup."

"I'll be!" Ted looked utterly amazed. "I never would have guessed that. So now the recipe will go in the cookbook?"

"Definitely."

"Glad to hear it. It serves my mother right for refusing to give anybody else the recipe. Did Beatrice tell you about that?"

Hannah nodded, wondering about the best way to excuse herself and get out with the evidence.

"Every time she came to visit, she said she forgot it. And then she promised to mail it to Beatrice, but she never did. Now everybody that reads the cookbook can have it. It serves her right."

Hannah swallowed hard. She'd never heard Ted do anything but praise his mother before. He wasn't acting like himself tonight and she should leave. "I need to pay for this tire iron and get out of here, Ted. I promised to take Tracey to the Haunted Basement and I'm late already."

"Okay. Leave those cupcakes here and I won't charge you for the tire iron."

"It's a deal," Hannah said, reaching for the tire iron at the same time Ted did.

"Hold on a second." Ted grabbed it first and reached for a bag. "It might be dirty."

Hannah watched as Ted flipped open a bag. He started to slide the tire iron inside, but he stopped and began to frown. "Where did you get this?"

"Uh . . . Beatrice found it for me. I got a taillight and a cigarette lighter too, but I already paid for those."

"Where did *she* get it?"

Hannah shrugged and did her best to look completely clueless. "From the parts building, I guess. I was busy picking out the cigarette lighter."

"No, she didn't. She got it from my work truck."

"How can you tell?" Hannah asked, trying to appear genuinely puzzled. "Don't all tire irons look alike?"

"This one's longer and heavier. It came from an old motor home and they knew how to make them back then. I need it because it's got better leverage and it's easier on my back. I just don't understand why Beatrice would sell it to . . ."

Hannah blanched as Ted stopped speaking and stared at her, his eyes narrowing in suspicion. Then he picked up the tire iron and began to whack the end of it against his palm. This wasn't good. Ted knew she'd been in his work truck and he also knew why she'd taken his tire iron. Trying to talk her way out of trouble hadn't worked and she'd run out of both time and options.

"Beatrice didn't get this for you. You got it yourself." Ted's voice was filled with menace. "And there's only one reason you'd want . . ."

Hannah didn't stick around to hear the rest of Ted's reasoning. She just whirled around, pulled open the door, and ran for her life.

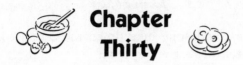

Chapter Thirty

The darkness folded around her like a welcoming blanket as Hannah raced across the uneven ground, heading straight toward her cookie truck. The advantage of surprise worked in her favor and she made it all the way there before she realized that she'd grabbed the bag of cupcakes, but she'd left her keys on the counter.

Her cookie truck sat adjacent to an area filled with disabled vehicles. Hannah whirled and ran with the wind at her back, across the dirt road that divided the salvage yard in half and straight into the darker area where the disabled vehicles were parked. Since there weren't as many lights in this area, there was less chance that Ted would spot her. Hannah ducked down and zigzagged past the hulking wrecks, heading toward the car at the very end, an old Cadillac with peeling paint and a cracked windshield. The door was a bit rusted, but Hannah's frantic jerk on the handle did the trick. In a flash, Hannah was inside the back seat, huddled on the floorboards, with the door shut tightly behind her.

For long moments Hannah didn't breathe, but all she could hear was the howling wind outside the car and the thudding of her own panicked heart. If Ted hadn't spotted her, she might be safe. He'd have to search every vehicle on his lot if he wanted to find her and while he was searching, she'd take a clandestine hike down the access road in the dark and catch a ride back to town.

Cautiously, Hannah took a peek out the back window, but she didn't see Ted. Should she attempt to run for freedom now? Or was he out there somewhere, his eyes scanning the rows of junked cars, hoping that was what she'd do? If only she had a cell phone! Her former objections seemed petty compared to the advantages in a situation like hers! They ought to issue them like pillows on an overseas flight. Anyone who jumped on-board a murder investigation would get one.

Even though the suspense was killing her and her muscles were screaming for action, Hannah decided to wait and listen. Since the cars were parked on gravel, she'd hear Ted's footsteps long before he arrived at her hiding place. She hunkered down on the floorboards, barely daring to breathe, listening for Ted over the sound of the wind and the occasional far-away honk of a car on the highway.

Was Ted still out there looking for her? Or was this an exercise in futility? Perhaps he had realized that it would take hours to find her and given it up as a bad job. His first priority would be to avoid arrest. It was possible that he was miles away by now, fleeing Winnetka County and the State of Minnesota in the fastest car he had on his lot.

Hannah reached for the door handle, but she pulled her hand back before she touched it. It was smart to be cautious. She'd count to a thousand and if she hadn't heard anything by then, she'd inch open the door and make a run for it.

Counting in the dark, her face pressed to a dusty floor mat, was a trial of the patience Hannah didn't possess. She got to a hundred quite easily, and to two hundred with a bit more effort. Three hundred was a struggle and four hundred a real battle. Five hundred was iffy, but she made it. And six hundred was even iffier. Seven hundred was achieved through sheer force of will, the eight hundred mark bespoke endurance she'd only dreamed of in the past, and nine hundred was a milestone of both determination and fortitude. Hannah

had reached nine hundred and thirty-two and she was beginning to think she'd make it all the way to the goal that had
seemed so unreachable only minutes ago, when she heard a
loud roar. And then something hit the Cadillac so hard, her
whole body bounced up from the floorboards and smacked
down again.

Hannah curled up in a ball, dizzy and disorientated. She
didn't seem to be injured, but it had felt exactly as if another
car had smacked into the Cadillac at highway speeds. When
she recovered her equilibrium, she realized that something
else was wrong. The Cadillac was rocking back and forth.
When at least thirty seconds had passed and the rocking had
failed to stop, Hannah risked a quick peek out the back window.

"Ohhh!" Hannah moaned, her mouth dropping open in
total shock. The Cadillac was no longer sitting on terra
firma!

Her mind refused to accept what her eyes were seeing.
Hannah blinked but the ground was still dropping down
below the Cadillac's tires. It took a moment for Hannah to
make sense out of what was happening. The ground wasn't
dropping; the Cadillac was rising. Ted was lifting it with the
claw, a giant crane he used to move disabled cars and trucks.

Hannah glanced down again and wished she hadn't. The
car was swaying sickeningly and the ground was receding
fast. She shut her eyes and moaned softly in fear. She was terrified. It wasn't the height that frightened her. She could
climb a ladder or an open staircase. She could even descend a
fire escape, as she'd had to do in college. But when it came to
swaying high in the air with nothing beneath her, she would
much rather take a pass. It was the reason she'd never ridden
in a hot air balloon, and why she'd refused to take Tracey on
the Ferris wheel at the Winnetka County Fair last summer.
Call it crazy, or phobic, or whatever, she really couldn't cope.

It was better if she didn't watch. The sight of the world
swaying beneath her was enough to paralyze her mind.

Hannah sank down with a groan and hugged the floorboards again. She had the sickening feeling that she knew what Ted was doing and it didn't bode well for her. Beatrice had told her about the new car crusher and how Ted used the crane to hoist the cars he wanted to crush and drop them inside. Beatrice had also mentioned that their efficient new piece of heavy machinery could reduce a luxury car into something approaching the size of a breadbox. Hannah wasn't sure exactly how big a breadbox was since no one had used them in years, but it was certainly smaller than she was and that brought up something she didn't really want to think about.

Cringing on the floorboards of the Cadillac wouldn't save her. Hannah took a deep breath and forced herself to look out the back window again. She was up really high, almost as high as the top of the trees, but she wouldn't think about that either. She took another deep breath and held it as she looked down at the ground.

Help had arrived! Mike was here in his squad car and he was talking to Ted!

Hannah stuck her head out the window and shouted, but her loudest yell was no match for the roar of the heavy machinery and the howling of the wind. The Cadillac was swaying right over Mike's head, but he didn't hear her. It was too far to jump, even if she were a daredevil, but there might be a way she could get Mike's attention.

Hannah scooted up between the front bucket seats. She grabbed the steering wheel and leaned on the horn. That should do it. But nothing happened and Hannah realized that there was no battery in the Cadillac. Ted must have removed it to sell it for parts before he scheduled this car for the crusher.

Not to be defeated by the absence of an easy way to get Mike's attention, Hannah stuck her head out of the hole where the passenger window used to be. Mike had gotten out of his cruiser and he was standing right below her. It was a case of so near and yet so far. Hannah knew she had to get his attention before he finished talking to Ted and left.

Quickly, Hannah wiggled out of her bomber jacket. She'd drop it right on Mike. Then, when he looked up to find out where it had come from, he'd see her leaning out the window. Hannah poked the jacket through the window, gave a little prayer for gravity to do its thing, and dropped it. It was perfect. It was going to fall right . . . uh-oh!

The wind gusted at the critical moment and the jacket sailed behind Mike, where he didn't notice. What else did she have to drop? Hannah glanced down at the bag of cupcakes. They'd have to do. She held one out the window and dropped it, but it fell short of the mark. She corrected her drop with the next one and she came a lot closer. One more and she should have it.

Hannah let out a whoop as the cupcake bonked Mike on the top of his head and bounced away. Ted said something and Hannah could see Mike smile and nod. Even though she was too far away to hear, Hannah could imagine the conversation. Ted had said, *Really windy tonight, huh?* And Mike had replied, *That's a fact. For a second there, I thought someone was throwing things at me.*

There was one thing Hannah knew for sure. If Mike left without looking up, her goose was cooked . . . or rather, pressed. She dropped the final cupcake and it hit Mike hard. Then she yelled for all she was worth and Mike looked up. But just as he figured it out, Ted jumped him.

Hannah's anguished cry reached no one's ears except her own. The man who was trying to save her was now in trouble. But what could she do to help him from a car that was suspended in the air?

Hannah thought fast. The Cadillac was stripped. There was nothing loose inside that she could throw. But she still had her boots and they might do some damage if she dropped them from this height. Hannah quickly removed them and dangled one out the window. Then she looked down to aim.

Ted was on top of Mike, fighting for the upper hand, when Hannah dropped her boot. It landed on Ted's shoulder and he shrugged it off, but that minor distraction gave Mike just enough time to gain the advantage and roll over on top. Hannah was watching with her heart in her throat when she caught movement out of the corner of her eye. Bill and Norman were here and they were rushing to Mike's aid.

Hannah gave a huge sigh of relief. That had been close. As Bill helped Mike subdue Ted and cuff him, Hannah raised both hands and clasped them in a victory salute. And then the Cadillac began to lower, inch by inch, foot by foot, with a squeal of steel cables. Since Bill and Mike were still busy taking Ted into custody, Hannah knew that Norman had found the proper lever to lower the car.

When the wheels of the Cadillac touched the ground, Hannah didn't waste any time climbing out of the car. Her knees were shaking, she was missing a boot, and her jacket was long gone. Her hands were smeared with chocolate, but when she saw Ted sitting in the back of the cruiser, a huge smile spread over her face. The good guys had won again.

Once her boot was back on her foot and Norman had found her jacket, Hannah was full of questions for Mike. "How did you know I was out here?"

"You'll answer my questions first," Mike ordered, grabbing her by the arm. "Did you know that car was headed for the crusher?"

Hannah was about to say something nasty about his high-handed attitude when she realized that his hand was shaking. Mike had been so terrified for her that he was still trembling. That fact that Mike was shaking made her start to tremble a bit, too. "I knew it where it was headed," she admitted in a small voice, "and I would have ended up there if you hadn't shown up."

"Attempted murder?" Mike asked, still hanging onto her arm as if he never wanted to let her go.

"That's right."

"Because you figured out that Ted killed Sheriff Grant?"

Hannah hesitated. This was her chance to let Mike save face. "I wasn't really sure he'd done it until he took off after me."

"And that was when you put the pieces together?"

Hannah nodded. In a way it was true. She hadn't known, for certain, until Ted had started whacking that tire iron against his palm. "My turn. Why did *you* come out here?"

"Lonnie called to tell me about the stolen car report and I came out here to ask Ted some questions about the cars he used for salvage. I had no idea that you were here or that you were in danger."

Hannah turned to Norman, who was standing next to Bill. "Why are you here?"

"I drove out to the sheriff's station to get some dental claim forms. I was just talking to Bill when Andrea called to ask if you were there and to say that you were late to pick up Tracey."

Hannah gave Norman a warm smile for catching on and not mentioning their investigation, and then she turned to Bill. "And Andrea told you she'd sent me out here to pick up the taillight for you?"

"That's right. When I couldn't get Ted on the phone, Norman and I drove out here."

"Good thing you did," Hannah said, glancing over at Mike. "Right, Mike?"

"That's right. I would have gotten him cuffed by myself eventually, but it was a lot easier this way. What evidence do you have for me, Hannah?"

"There's a tire iron on the counter in the office. It might be the murder weapon and you'll probably want to test it for traces of blood. And you'd better call Clara and Marguerite

Hollenbeck right away and tell them not to remove that stain on Krista's party dress. It could be Sheriff Grant's blood."

"Anything else?" Mike fought to keep the pleasant expression on his face and Hannah knew he hated to ask her for advice.

"Just one thing. I think Ted was running a stolen car ring and a chop shop, but I wasn't able to find anything to confirm that."

"We'll find it," Mike said. He looked less aggravated and Hannah knew she'd scored some points. Of course she could tell him exactly where to find the parts list for the man in Minneapolis and the bill of lading for the stolen cars, but she'd let him do it on his own. As Mike was so fond of saying, he was the law enforcement specialist, not her.

"It's after eight," Norman said after a quick glance at his watch. "If Mike and Bill don't need us, let's go get Tracey and take her to the Haunted Basement."

"I'll call Andrea and tell her you're on the way," Bill said, and then he turned to glance at Mike. "That's okay, isn't it?"

Mike nodded. He was obviously in the mood to be magnanimous, now that Sheriff Grant's killer was in custody. "Sure. Go ahead and do the Halloween thing with the kids. You can drop by the station when you're through and give us your statements."

"Your car, or mine?" Norman asked, walking with Hannah toward the office.

"Both. You go pick up Tracey and Karen and take them to the Haunted Basement. I'll run home to feed Moishe and join you there with the Corn Cookies for the party."

"Okay," Norman said, stepping forward to open the door of Hannah's truck. "Too bad I didn't bring a costume."

Hannah climbed in the driver's seat and reached in the back for her minimal costume. "I've got one you can use. I'll pick up another old sheet at the condo and come as a ghost."

"Cornflakes?" Norman looked puzzled as he accepted the

box, but he started to laugh the moment she handed him the plastic knife. "This is just great, Hannah."

Hannah's eyes widened. If Norman had caught on to her visual pun, he'd be the first person in Lake Eden who had. And then Hannah remembered what Beatrice had said about Doctor Love and how romantic partners should share similar senses of humor. "Do you know what it is?"

"Sure," Norman said, grinning at her. "It's just brilliant, Hannah. I've worn a lot of Halloween costumes over the years, but I've never been a cereal killer before."

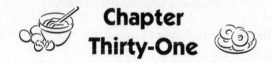

Chapter
Thirty-One

It was seven o'clock on election night when Hannah emerged from her bedroom. She was wearing the new outfit Delores had insisted on buying for her from Beau Monde Fashions, a blue silk dress that Claire had recommended. Hannah had found shoes to match at the mall, blue leather heels with a red, white, and blue braided strap that had been marked down to practically nothing. She was fairly sure the shoes were leftovers from the Fourth of July, but they worked beautifully for what would surely turn out to be Bill's victory party.

Hannah took one last look at the election coverage on KCOW television before she headed off to the kitchen. Bill had already won over eighty percent of the vote and the victory party at the Lake Eden Inn would be standing room only, except for Andrea. Doc Knight had given her permission to attend as long as there was a place for her to recline and elevate her feet. Since a simple chair wouldn't do, Delores had contributed a fancy antique lounge chair for Andrea to use.

There was a smile on Hannah's face as she dished up Moishe's yogurt. Doctor Bob and Sue had come up with a solution that suited both human and feline. The moment that Hannah placed the dish on the coffee table, Moishe jumped up and stood there expectantly.

"Hold on a second," Hannah said, loosening the cap on

the vitamin bottle. But the cat who'd hidden under the bed when threatened by the very same bottle just sat there and purred. Hannah squelched her desire to say *I told you so* to her cat and squirted a stream of vitamins over the top. A scant second later, Moishe was eagerly lapping it up.

Hannah was just about to pick up the new purse her mother and Andrea had insisted she buy when there was a knock at the door. Andrea had called earlier to say that she was sending a car for Hannah and even though Hannah had told her it wasn't necessary, her sister had insisted.

A box from The Cookie Jar sat on the counter and Hannah picked it up. It was a special present for Bill, a pan of his favorite Apple Orchard Cookie Bars. Hannah figured the treat was appropriate since Ted Koester had confessed to killing Sheriff Grant and was behind bars awaiting his trial.

Hannah opened the door with a smile on her face, but that smile quickly changed to an expression of surprise. Instead of the hired driver that Andrea had led her to expect, both Norman and Mike were standing there.

"Hi, Hannah," Norman said, giving her a grin and then turning to Mike.

"We're your drivers tonight." Mike reached out to take her arm. "Andrea asked both of us to escort you."

"That's nice," Hannah said, making a mental note to have a long talk with her sister. If Andrea had hoped to promote jealousy between the two, it had backfired. Both Norman and Mike looked as happy as clams.

Mike held the bakery box while Norman helped Hannah into her coat. Then Mike locked the door behind them and both men escorted her down the stairs.

"Look! It's snowing!" Hannah lifted her face to the night sky as a few gentle flakes started to fall. They swirled lazily under the old-fashioned streetlights the builder had installed in the condo complex and fell to the walkway, keeping their form for a moment or two and then melting.

"Do you want to go back for your boots?" Norman asked. "There could be snow on the ground before the party's over."

"Not really," Hannah said, glancing down at her shoes. Even if she'd owned a pair of dress boots, they wouldn't have looked good with her dress.

"She doesn't need boots," Mike declared, motioning to Norman. "Excuse us for a second, Hannah. We have to work out some logistics."

Hannah stared after Mike in some confusion as he pulled Norman a few feet away and spoke to him in a low voice. But the night was too beautiful to spend staring at two men discussing something or other, and she watched the snowflakes instead.

Even though there had been the predictable uproar at Ted Koester's arrest, things had calmed down quite rapidly. Beatrice was cleared of any wrongdoing regarding the chop shop and stolen car ring, and one of her grown sons was coming back home to help her run the salvage yard. She'd told Hannah that she'd suspected something was wrong, but she'd never dreamed that her husband had killed Sheriff Grant.

The jury was still out on Winthrop Harrington the Second. Norman was attempting to check several British databanks, but so far he'd learned nothing. Unfortunately, Winthrop was out of town and wouldn't be attending Bill's victory party. Hannah figured that she'd meet him eventually and then she'd make up her own mind.

Now that Barbara Donnelly had returned to work, Shawna Lee Quinn was back in the typing pool. That distance wasn't far enough to suit Andrea and she'd told Hannah that she planned to deal with that problem just as soon as little Billy was born and she was back on her feet.

"Your chair awaits you," Norman said, and Hannah whirled around to find both men standing behind her with crossed and clasped hands.

"You're going to carry me?" Hannah asked, not quite believing it.

"That's right." Mike moved forward and so did Norman. "Sit down, Hannah. And put your arms around our shoulders. We'll carry you to the car."

Feeling just a bit like a damsel in distress and enjoying it immensely, Hannah took a seat on their crossed arms and steadied herself. And then her two escorts began to walk, carrying her down the path toward the waiting car in the first powdery snow of the winter.

"Lovely," Hannah breathed, not sure of the etiquette in such a situation, but loving every moment of it.

Apple Orchard Bars

Preheat oven to 375 degrees F.,
rack in the middle position.

½ cup melted butter *(1 stick)*
½ cup white sugar
1 cup brown sugar firmly packed
½ teaspoon baking soda
½ teaspoon salt
½ teaspoon baking powder
2 teaspoons vanilla
1 teaspoon cinnamon
2 beaten eggs *(you can beat them up with a fork)*
½ cup rolled oats *(uncooked oatmeal)*
1 cup peeled chopped apple *(I used 2 medium
Gala apples)*
2 cups flaked coconut
1 ½ cups flour *(not sifted)*

Melt butter, add the sugars, and stir. Add baking soda, salt, baking powder, vanilla, cinnamon, and beaten eggs. Mix well. Then add chopped apple and 1 ½ cups flaked coconut. *(Reserve ½ cup for on top.)* Add the flour and mix it all thoroughly.

Grease a 9-inch by 13-inch cake pan. Spoon the dough in and smooth it with a rubber spatula. Sprinkle the ½ cup coconut you reserved evenly on top.

Bake at 375 degrees F. for 25 to 30 minutes, or until slightly browned on top.

Let cool and cut into bars like brownies.

(Bill likes these with hot chocolate—he says it brings out the taste of the apples.)

(Tracey's still trying to convince Andrea that they're health food and she should have them for breakfast.)

Baking Conversion Chart

These conversions are approximate, but they'll work just fine for Hannah Swensen's recipes.

VOLUME:

U.S.	Metric
½ teaspoon	2 milliliters
1 teaspoon	5 milliliters
1 Tablespoon	15 milliliters
¼ cup	50 milliliters
⅓ cup	75 milliliters
½ cup	125 milliliters
¾ cup	175 milliliters
1 cup	¼ liter

WEIGHT:

U.S.	Metric
1 ounce	28 grams
1 pound	454 grams

OVEN TEMPERATURE:

Degrees Fahrenheit	Degrees Centigrade	British (Regulo) Gas Mark
325 degrees F.	165 degrees C.	3
350 degrees F.	175 degrees C.	4
375 degrees F.	190 degrees C.	5

Note: Hannah's rectangular sheet cake pan, 9 inches by 13 inches, is approximately 23 centimeters by 32.5 centimeters.

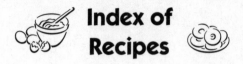

Index of Recipes

The holidays are the icing on the cake for bakery owner Hannah Swensen. Surrounded by her loved ones, she has all the ingredients for a perfect Christmas—until murder is added to the mix. . . .

When it comes to holidays, Minnesotans rise to the occasion—and the little town of Lake Eden is baking up a storm with Hannah leading the way. The annual Christmas Buffet is the final test of the recipes Hannah has collected for the *Lake Eden Holiday Buffet Cookbook.*

While Hannah is baking the day's goodies at The Cookie Jar, the evening's plans begin to jell. Start with the best Lake Eden culinary creations, add two of Hannah's "sometime" boyfriends, a pinch of her ready-to-pop pregnant sister, and a dash of her mother and new significant other, an actual British lord, and what do you get? A recipe for disaster, but the juiciest ingredient is yet to come. . . .

The recently divorced Martin Dubinski arrives at the buffet with his new Vegas showgirl wife—all wrapped up in glitter and fur. His ex-wife, however, seems as cool as chilled eggnog. And when Hannah's mother's antique Christmas cake knife disappears, its discovery in the décolletage of the new—and now late—Mrs. Dubinski puts the festivities on ice.

With everyone stranded at the community center by a blizzard, Hannah puts her investigative skills to the test, using the ingredients at hand: half the town of Lake Eden—and a killer. Now, as the snowdrifts get higher, it's up to Hannah to dig out all the clues—and make sure that this white Christmas doesn't bring any more deadly tidings. . . .

**Please turn the page for an exciting sneak peek of
SUGAR COOKIE MURDER
now available!**

Hannah groaned as Edna's words sank in. "Mother's cake knife is missing?"

"That's what I said."

"And you looked on the dessert table?"

"That's what I said, too!"

"All right. Don't panic. It's got to be here somewhere."

"Where? I looked everywhere!"

"Take a deep breath and let it out slowly," Hannah advised, taking a moment to do exactly that. "When is the last time you saw it?"

Edna did exactly what Hannah said, inhaling and exhaling slowly. It was proof of how upset she was, since Edna rarely took anyone's advice about anything. "It was on the dessert table when I carried out the second crock of meatballs. I remember thinking how pretty it looked under the lights."

Hannah glanced at the elaborately carved wooden container on the kitchen counter. "Maybe someone put it back in the chest?"

"Nope. I checked that right off. That box is as empty as Redeemer Lutheran on the Sunday after Jordan High's homecoming game."

Hannah bit back a laugh at Edna's description. It was true that most people celebrated a bit too much on homecoming weekend and not that many had the urge to get up early on Sunday morning and make it to church.

"I'm sure you're right, but . . . I just have to check for myself." Hannah walked over to the box and raised the lid. It was empty, just as Edna had said. "Sorry, Edna."

"That's all right. I checked it twice myself."

Both women leaned up against the counter to think about the seemingly insurmountable problem at hand. They were so quiet Hannah could hear the kitchen clock ticking as the minute hand moved up a notch.

"Do you think someone could have used it for something else?" Hannah finally asked, after another notch had clicked off. "I mean, picture this . . . someone in the buffet line needs another knife for the turkey, or whatever. They're about to go back to the kitchen to get one when they notice Mother's knife on the dessert table. So they take it and use it and . . ."

"And they leave it on the entrée table!" Edna interrupted, somehow managing to look doubtful and hopeful at the same time.

"Exactly right. It could have happened that way."

"That means we'd better check the other buffet tables. I don't want your mother to know it's missing until we know for sure. Will you do it . . . um . . . you know . . ."

"Surreptitiously?" Hannah supplied the word she thought Edna was trying to say.

"That's exactly what I mean. I'm so upset, I couldn't think of the polite word for sneaky."

A cake knife the size and commanding presence of her mother's antique silver heirloom couldn't hide for long on any of the other tables. Just to be sure, Hannah lifted platters and checked under bowls and centerpieces, but she really hadn't expected to find it, and she wasn't surprised when it didn't turn up.

"You didn't find it," Edna said, reading Hannah's expression when she returned to the kitchen.

"I'm afraid I didn't."

"Your mother's going to kill me. You know that, don't you? We've just got to find it before she realizes that it's missing." Edna sat down on a kitchen stool, thought for a moment, and raised her head to look at Hannah. "Do you think someone stole it?"

"In Lake Eden?"

"You're right. Nobody here would do something like that."

"Chances are it's just misplaced, and that means it has to be around here somewhere. Why don't you take a look to see if anything on the tables need replenishing? I'll stay in here and go through every cupboard and drawer in this kitchen."

"Good idea," Edna said, taking the top from a huge Tupperware container shaped like a dress box. "While I was out there looking for the cake knife, I noticed that some of your Christmas cookies were gone. Can't say as I blame the folks that took 'em early. Your cookies are prettier than the ones they show in the magazines."

"The pretty part is Lisa's doing. She decorated them. All I did was bake them."

"They're tasty, too. Sweet and crunchy, with the taste of butter in every bite."

"You ate one?" Hannah was surprised. When Edna managed a potluck dinner, she waited to eat until they'd carried the food back into the kitchen. And unlike Hannah, who sometimes couldn't resist sampling something yummy, Edna wasn't the type of person to eat dessert first.

"It was a Santa with one leg broken off. If I'd put it on the platter that way, sure and shootin' some child would have had nightmares about it." Edna headed for the door, but she turned back for a final comment. "I've got a bad feeling about this, but I'm going to keep my fingers crossed."

Once Edna had left to restock the cookie platter, Hannah searched systematically, determined to go through every cupboard and drawer. Edna buzzed in and out, putting out more food where it was needed. Then she began to get out the rest of the desserts and prepare them for presentation.

Hannah met Edna's eyes several times while the older woman was cutting cakes and pies in even slices and arranging platters of cookies and cookie bars. Each time Edna's eyebrows elevated in a question, Hannah shook her head. The missing cake knife was still missing, and Hannah's hope that she'd find it stuck away in a drawer or mixed in with other serving implements was dwindling faster than an ice cube in a mug of steaming hot coffee.

It took awhile, but at last Hannah knew she'd left no metaphorical stone unturned. She'd been so thorough, she would have sworn on a stack of Bibles that her mother's cake knife was not in the Lake Eden Community Center kitchen. Hannah headed for a stool at one of the center work islands. She had to tell Delores the bad news before she discovered it for herself. There was no way Hannah would shirk that duty, but she did need time to think of a way to phrase the message that wouldn't immediately result in the death of the messenger.

Delivering bad news had never been one of her skills. Hannah tended to blurt things out, a bit like jerking a bandage from a wound rather than inching the tape off. She didn't think she was quite as outspoken as Edna, but people weren't that far wrong when they accused her of having no tact.

The pantry door was open slightly and Hannah noticed that the light was on. She hadn't bothered to check the pantry, because she'd assumed that no one had used it. Since it was a potluck dinner, everyone had brought in fully cooked dishes. Edna and her helpers had simply kept things warm or chilled, depending on the dish, until it was time to serve.

Hannah's mind spun, imagining a possible scenario. Someone who'd brought in a dessert suddenly realized they'd forgotten powdered sugar to sprinkle over the top. Rather than rush home to get it, the frantic cook stepped into the community center pantry hoping to borrow some. Had that person also picked up the antique cake knife, intending to use it to slice her dessert? It was certainly possible . . . perhaps unlikely, but still possible.

Rising quickly, Hannah hurried to the pantry and opened the door. A quick scan of the neatly stocked shelves disproved the theory that had seemed plausible only moments ago. The cake knife was nowhere in sight. Hannah was about to turn off the light and step back out into the kitchen when she noticed that the dead bolt on the door to the parking lot wasn't locked.

Hannah opened the door and took a step outside. Through the blowing snow, she could see the icy hulks of parked cars. This was the delivery entrance and since it opened onto the parking lot, it would be a perfect escape route for a thief. If someone really had stolen her mother's antique knife and ducked out to the parking lot through this door, they'd be long gone by now.

A blast of cold wind carrying icy needles of snow made her shiver. Hannah was about to step back into the warmth of the pantry when she noticed something bulky on the ground between two of the parked cars. It looked furry, like some sort of animal, but it was too small for a bear, and too large for a dog.

Curiosity trickled, gathered force, and grew into a mighty waterfall. There was no way Hannah could turn around and go back inside without finding out what kind of animal was in the parking lot. She headed out at a trot, glad that she was wearing her all-purpose footwear, the moosehide moccasin boots that were so politically incorrect with people who'd never even seen a moose . . . or smelled one, for that matter.

Hannah's sweater was dusted with flakes of snow by the time she got close enough to see. She bent over to examine the large lump of fur, and reached out to steady herself on the nearest car. The animal she thought she'd seen had been made into an expensive fur coat that Martin's new wife was wearing. The only other animal in sight was the reindeer sugar cookie that was broken near Brandi's feet, along with the pieces of a Christmas tree cookie, and a bell decorated in red and green icing. Brandi must have taken several cookies from the dessert table and come out here to eat them. The big question was, did she also take the antique cake knife?

Hoping that she'd just slipped and fallen, Hannah reached down to tap Brandi on the shoulder. "Brandi? Do you need help getting up?"

There was no answer and Hannah began to frown. This didn't look good. "Brandi?" she called out again, shaking her a little harder and wondering if she should go for help. The former dancer wasn't moving, but she could be faking it. If Hannah left her alone and Brandi had the cake knife, she might make a run for it with the valuable antique.

Hannah knew that it was dangerous to move someone who had undetermined injuries. Accident victims had died from the ministrations of well-meaning bystanders who had tried to move them without backboards and stabilizing collars. Hannah certainly wouldn't risk moving Brandi, but she'd taken a first aid class in college and she knew there was a pulse point just under the jawbone on the side of a person's neck.

The collar of Brandi's coat was in the way and Hannah pushed it back. This caused the coat to fall open and Hannah gave a strangled gulp as she caught sight of Brandi's chest.

Hannah felt for a pulse, even though her rational mind told her it was useless. No one could live with a wound that deep. She'd just straightened up, dizzy and slightly sick to her stomach at the sight of the blood that had been soaked up by the expensive fur, when the pantry door banged open and she heard Edna's voice.

"Hannah? Are you out there?"

"I'm here."

"Did you find the knife?"

Hannah glanced down at her mother's valuable antique knife, buried to the hilt in Brand's too-perfectly-proportioned-to-be-natural chest. "I found it."

"Thank the Lord," Edna shouted out gratefully. "Bring it here before your mother realizes it's missing."

Hannah considered that for a moment. The urge to jerk the knife out of Brandi's chest and head for the kitchen at a run was strong. But equally strong was the awareness of her civic duty. Brandi didn't stab herself, and that meant murder. And disturbing a crime scene by removing the murder weapon was a big no-no. "Sorry, Edna . . . I can't bring it in."

"Why not?"

"Because Brandi's got it." And with that said, Hannah turned and headed back to the kitchen to explain.

With the Cookie Jar, Hannah Swensen has a mouthwatering monopoly on the bakery business of Lake Eden, Minnesota. But when a rival store opens, tensions begin to bubble....

As she sits in her nearly empty store on Groundhog Day, Hannah can only hope that spring is just around the corner—and that the popularity of the new Magnolia Blossom Bakery is just a passing fad. The southern hospitality of Lake Eden's two Georgia transplants, Shawna Lee and Vanessa Quinn, is grating on Hannah's nerves—and cutting into her profits.

At least Hannah has her business partner Lisa's wedding to look forward to. She's turned one of Lisa's favorite childhood treats into a spectacular Wedding Cookie Cake. But Hannah starts to steam when she finds out that Shawn Lee has finagled an invitation to the reception—and is bringing the Magnolia Blossom Bakery's Southern Peach Cobbler for the dessert table.

Hannah doesn't like having the Georgia Peach in the mix, especially when both Shawna Lee and Hannah's sometime-boyfriend, Detective Mike Kingston, are no-shows to the wedding. Hannah has suspected that Mike is interested in more than Shawna Lee's baking abilities. So when she sees lights on at the Magnolia Blossom Bakery after the reception, she investigates—and finds Shawna Lee shot to death.

Everyone in town knew The Cookie Jar was losing business to the Magnolia Bakery—a fact that puts Hannah at the top of the initial list of suspects. But with a little help from her friends, Hannah's determined to prove that she wasn't the only one who had an axe to grind with the Quinn sisters. Somebody wasn't fooled by the Georgia Peaches and their sweet-as-pie act—and now it's up to Hannah to track down whoever had the right ingredients to whip up a murder....

**Please turn the page for an exciting sneak peek at
PEACH COBBLER MURDER
now available!**

Hannah glanced at the clock. She'd unloaded her cookie truck in only ten minutes. The earliest that Norman could arrive was five minutes from now and that was probably optimistic. She went back to her favorite table, but she couldn't seem to relax. There was something about the bright lights glaring in the interior of the Magnolia Blossom Bakery that made her nervous.

Perhaps there'd been a robbery. The moment the idea occurred to Hannah, her imagination was off and running. If the robbery had happened during the day, the robber might not have realized that all the lights were on. At this very moment, the cash drawer could be open and the Magnolia Blossom Bakery could be minus the day's receipts. A good citizen of Lake Eden, one who could put aside petty jealousy and hold the welfare of a neighboring business paramount, would check to make sure the cash register at the Magnolia Blossom Bakery was intact.

Hannah groaned. The last thing she wanted to do was put on her boots and her coat, and walk across the street to make sure no burglar had invaded her competitor's bakery. But basic decency demanded she do so, and she liked to think of herself as a basically decent person. Hannah stuffed her still-aching feet into her boots and slipped into her parka coat, zipping it up all the way. She scrawled a note to Norman: *Across the street at Shawna Lee's—maybe a burglary?* and taped it to the outside of the back door. And then she hurried around the side of her building to see if there was a problem with the Magnolia Blossom Bakery.

The wind had teeth and shards of ice pelted Hannah's face as she left the protection of her building. She turned up the collar of her parka coat and held her hand up to shield her eyes as she dashed across Main Street. She ducked under the pseudo-Jeffersonian portico of Lake Eden Realty and peered in the plate glass window of her cobbler challenger.

Andrea's description hadn't done the Magnolia Blossom Bakery justice. It was gorgeous and Hannah would be the first to admit tit. The magnolia tree mural the Minneapolis artist had painted was spectacular, all the tables and chairs matched, and everything was new and shiny. The color scheme was incredibly appealing and everything Hannah saw fit in perfectly. The homemade decorations at The Cookie Jar couldn't hold a candle to the decorator embellishments at Shawna Lee and Vanessa's Bakery.

Hannah sighed. She didn't like feeling second-rate, even in the category of decorations. Comforting herself with knowledge that at least her baked goods were better, she took another, less envious and more appraising look, and came to the conclusion that absolutely nothing was out of place. The cash register drawer was pushed in, there were no signs of vandalism, and everything looked ready and set to go for business in the morning. But something about the bright lights really bothered her, and she felt she should check further. Even though there wasn't much petty crime in Lake Eden, it was possible that a group of teenagers had waited until Shawna Lee had left and then broke in to steal whatever pastry they could find in the kitchen. The lights were on in there, too. She could see them blazing through the diamond-shaped window in the swinging door.

Hannah wished that Norman were with her, but no cars had driven past and he was probably still doing what they not so jokingly called "mother duty." She didn't relish going inside to check out someone else's kitchen, but she couldn't just stand here and do nothing. She tried the front door, hoping it would save her a trip around to the back, but it was locked securely. If pastry bandits were to blame for turning on the lights, they must have entered and left by the back door.

"Shawna Lee?" Hannah called out, knocking loudly on the front door. When that didn't work, she balled up her fists and hammered loudly, doing her best to wake anyone who might be sleeping upstairs. No one was home. She was certain of it. Only the dead could sleep through the racket she'd made. Hannah pushed that very unwelcome thought aside and decided she'd have to go around to the back.

Keeping a sharp eye out for broken or pried windows, or any other signs of unauthorized access, Hannah walked around the side of the building. Everything looked secure, but a glance in the kitchen window made her frown. There was a colorful pink and green box on the counter and the label read, *Betty Jo's Frozen Peach Cobbler, a division of Macon Foods.* Shawna Lee had claimed that her Southern Peach Cobbler was made from an old family recipe. Maybe that was true, but it was Betty Jo's family recipe, not Shawna Lee's.

Hannah's gaze moved toward the ovens and what she saw made her frown deepen. A pan of peach cobbler was on the floor next to the open oven door. It was a mess, a jumble of sliced peaches and biscuit topping strewn over a puddle of sticky juice on the white tile floor. Had Shawna Lee simply dropped the pan as she was taking it from the oven? Or was there a more sinister reason for the baking disaster?

A glance at the other kitchen window gave Hannah an unwelcome answer to her question. There were two round holes in the glass, and each hole was surrounded by a spider web of cracks. She was no expert, but they looked like a couple of bullet holes to her!

Hannah swallowed hard as she pressed her nose against the glass and held her breath so it wouldn't fog up. Was that a shoe she saw peeking out from behind the work counter?

There was the wise thing to do and the foolish thing to do. Hannah knew the wise thing would be to call for help, or wait for Norman, or do anything other than go into the kitchen to check it out by herself. But the time it took to do the wise thing could spell the difference between life and death for whoever was wearing that shoe.

Maybe the best thing to do is nothing at all, the not-so-nice side of Hannah's psyche whispered in her ear. *What difference would it make if you just went back to The Cookie Jar and pretended you hadn't seen that shoe? Who would know?*

"I'd know," Hannah answered out loud, accepting the burden of her own good character. It didn't matter what she thought of Shawna Lee personally. If her cookie competitor was hurt or in trouble. Hannah had a responsibility to do what she could to help.

Once she'd made up her mind, Hannah moved quickly. She raced to the back door, fully prepared to kick it in if that's what it took, but when she turned the knob she found it unlocked. She pushed the door open, praying that the two holes she'd seen weren't bullet holes, the shoe behind the counter had no foot in it, and the peach cobbler on the floor meant nothing more than a slip of an oven glove. But where was Shawna Lee? And why hadn't she shut the oven door and cleaned up the mess?

"Uh-oh," Hannah gasped, skidding to a stop as she rounded the corner of the kitchen counter. Shawna Lee was down on her back on the tile floor and there was a huge blossom of what looked like dried strawberry syrup on the bib of her white chef's apron. There was also a neat hole in the middle of the blossom and Hannah knew that there was no point in continuing to contaminate what was surely a crime scene. Shawna Lee had been shot in the chest and anyone with an ounce of brains could see that she was dead.

Thanksgiving has a way of thawing the frostiest hearts in Lake Eden. But that won't be happening for newlywed Hannah Swensen Barton—not after her husband suddenly disappears . . .

Hannah has felt as bitter as November in Minnesota since Ross vanished without a trace and left their marriage in limbo. Still, she throws herself into a baking frenzy for the sake of pumpkin pie and Thanksgiving-themed treats while endless holiday orders pour into The Cookie Jar. Hannah even introduces a raspberry Danish pastry to the menu, and P.K., her husband's assistant at KCOW-TV, will be one of the first to sample it. But instead of taking a bite, P.K., who is driving Ross's car and using his desk at work, is murdered. Was someone plotting against P.K. all along or did Ross dodge a deadly dose of sweet revenge? Hannah will have to quickly sift through a cornucopia of clues and suspects to stop a killer from bringing another murder to the table . . .

Please turn the page for an exciting sneak peek of Joanne Fluke's next Hannah Swensen mystery RASPBERRY DANISH MURDER now on sale wherever print and e-books are sold!

Michelle was smiling as she turned to Hannah. They were sitting in front of the giant-screen television, and they'd just watched the commercial that P.K. had made for the Thanksgiving play. "I loved it! How about you?"

"P.K. did a super job. Everyone who saw it is going to come to the play."

"Irma's keeping track of advance ticket sales. I'll check in with her to see if there's a jump in sales tomorrow. The cast really looked good, didn't they?"

"The cast looked really great," Hannah agreed. "I loved those costumes."

"I'm really glad we took the time to do makeup and get into our costumes." Michelle gave a little smile. "At first, I was upset when P.K. suggested it because it takes so much time, but he was right. It looks so much better than seeing the characters in their everyday clothes."

Hannah was about to go to the kitchen to get more coffee when Michelle's cell phone rang. "That's probably P.K. to see if you liked his commercial," she speculated.

"I bet you're right," Michelle said, reaching out for her cell phone. "I'm going to record it to see if he liked his commercial." She answered the call, and almost immediately began to frown.

"What is it?" Hannah asked quickly as a distressed expression crossed Michelle's face.

"It's P.K. There's something wrong, Hannah! Look!"

Hannah glanced at the display and realized that she was watching a video of P.K. driving Ross's car.

"It's real time," Michelle said quickly. "He's got his phone in the dashboard holder Ross has in his car."

"Mic . . . kie," P.K. said, giving a lopsided smile. "How . . . you, girl?"

"He sounds drunk!" Michelle exclaimed.

"Or drugged. Can you ask him if he's okay?"

"Are you okay, P.K.?" Michelle asked.

"Mic . . . kie." P.K. reached up to rub his face. "Pret . . . ty Mic . . . kie. Doan feel goooood."

P.K.'s phone was positioned so that they could see his face and also the driver's side window. As the two sisters watched, the edge of the road appeared to move forward and then recede.

"Tell him to pull over!" Hannah said, grabbing Michelle's arm. "Hurry! He almost went in the ditch!"

"Pull over, P.K.!" Michelle said loudly. "You shouldn't be driving. Pull over right now!"

Hannah moved closer so that she could listen for his response, but there was no response at all. "Please, P.K.," she shouted. "Pull over!"

"It's no use," Michelle told her. "Either he's got our audio off or he's too drunk or stoned to listen to us."

"Noooo," P.K. said, and both sisters could see that his eyes looked vague and unfocused. "Thought I . . . juss hung . . . gry. Ate Rossss . . . hiz . . . desk. Can . . . dees . . . sickkk."

"Pull over!" Hannah shouted again as the car veered toward the center of the road and then lurched back toward the ditch again. "Pull over, P.K.!"

"Please pull over!" Michelle added, the panic clear in her voice.

There was no response to their pleas and Michelle shook her head. "He can't hear us, Hannah."

"You're probably right, but at least he's back on his side of the road again."

"No . . . more . . . can . . . dees," P.K. mumbled, and then his eyelids began to lower. "Got . . . ta get . . . Doc . . . hospit . . . uh . . ."

Both Hannah and Michelle watched in horror as the car weaved from one side of the road to the other, barely missing a county road sign. They had just given sighs of relief when the car began to drift toward the wrong side of the road again.

"Wake up, P.K.!" Michelle called out, leaning close to the phone. "Listen to me! You've got to stay awake!"

Again, there was no response from P.K. The only thing they heard was the sound of the engine growing louder and louder.

"He's stepping on the gas!" Hannah said in horror.

"I know! I can hear it! And he's . . . oh no!"

Michelle's last word was an anguished cry, and Hannah felt as if it had come from her own throat. P.K.'s eyes were closed now, but the car was going faster and faster.

The scene outside the driver's side window appeared to bounce up and down as the pine trees rushed past at breakneck speed. Then there was a loud blaring sound.

"The horn's on!" Michelle identified it. "P.K. must be blowing it for help."

Or he's wedged on the steering wheel, Hannah thought, but of course she didn't say what she was thinking.

"Look!" They watched as the bakery box with the Raspberry Danish that they'd given P.K. that morning flew past the screen as if it had suddenly grown wings.

"He's in the ditch!" Michelle gasped. "And the car's still going!"

Her horrified words were no sooner spoken than the screen on Michelle's cell phone went black.

"His phone shut off, or broke, or something!" Michelle gasped. "We have to do something, Hannah!"

Hannah thought fast. "You said you were going to record the call."

"I did!"

"Can you send that video to Mike's cell phone?"

"I . . . yes, I think so."

"Do it right now. I'll call Mike and tell him it's coming."

While Michelle figured out how to retrieve the video and send it, Hannah placed a call to Mike. Then she ducked into the kitchen to speak to him in private. Michelle was upset enough already. There was no way Hannah wanted her to overhear the conversation she was about to have with Mike.

Luckily, Mike answered on the second ring, and Hannah told him the video was coming. "It looked really bad, Mike, and I recognized a couple of landmarks. I think P.K. went off the road right before Abe Schilling's back pasture, the one where he keeps his bull in the summer. Do you know where that is?"

When Mike had assured her he knew the particular pasture she'd described, Hannah added her final sentences, the ones she hadn't wanted Michelle to overhear. "Hurry out there, Mike. There may be a chance that P.K. is still alive, but . . . I really doubt it."